# JANET DAILEY

# THE GLORY GAME

## POCKET BOOKS

New York    London    Toronto    Sydney    Tokyo    Singapore

This book is a work of fiction. Names, characters, places and incidents are either the product of the author's imagination or are used fictitiously. Any resemblance to actual events or locales or persons, living or dead, is entirely coincidental.

POCKET BOOKS, a division of Simon & Schuster Inc.
1230 Avenue of the Americas, New York, NY 10020

Copyright © 1985 by Janbill, Ltd.
Cover art copyright © 1986 Roger Kastel

ISBN: 0-671-87503-5

First Pocket Books printing April 1986

15  14  13  12  11  10  9

POCKET and colophon are registered trademarks of Simon & Schuster Inc.

Printed in the U.S.A.

# Part I

# CHAPTER I

"Ladies and gentlemen," the announcer's voice boomed over the loudspeaker, resonating beyond the sparse crowd in the stands to the players and their ponies on the turf. "I want to welcome you to the final match of the Jacob L. Kincaid Memorial Cup here at the Palm Beach Polo Club. Most of you knew Jake Kincaid, a seven-goal player in his prime and a loyal supporter of polo throughout his life. He was a worthy competitor and a true ambassador of the sport. His presence will be missed." The announcer paused before continuing, the tone of his voice lifting from its serious level. "I'd like to direct your attention to the front box seats, where the Kincaid clan has gathered."

"Not the whole clan, George!" The shouted correction came from a stylishly slim woman seated in the Kincaid box, her ash-blond hair protected from the Florida sun by a white straw hat. Even shouting to carry to the announcer's roofed stand atop the stadium, her voice had a cultured sound, smooth and dry, like an excellent Bordeaux. "If all of us were here, we'd fill half the stands."

Smiling spectators who knew the family chuckled. By anyone's standards, the Kincaids were a large family, six children in all, three boys and three girls. They'd always been a boisterous, energetic group, obviously spoiled yet possessing an engaging charm that maturity enhanced. Time had thinned the ranks of that generation; Andrew, the oldest, had died tragically in Vietnam when his helicopter landed in a minefield; and Helen had been killed two years ago in a drunk-driving accident. Of course, Andrew and Helen had left their parents a brood of grandchildren to raise, and the rest had added to the number.

Informality was part of the essence of a big family, so it seemed right that the formality of this occasion should be broken by a Kincaid. And polo, for all its prestigious facade, was an informal sport, enjoyed by an elite few who considered themselves to be part of one big polo-loving family.

"You should have brought them, Luz. We could have had a full house today," the announcer responded.

"Next time," the elegant woman responded. Luz Kincaid Thomas had been christened Leslie, but no one called her that anymore, and hadn't for years. She looked thirty; an unkind eye might guess thirty-seven, but people were always surprised when she admitted she was forty-two. Her skin had a fresh and youthful glow, lightly tanned by the Florida sunshine, never overexposed to be browned into leather. Many discreetly looked, but there were no scars near the hairline to betray nips and tucks taken to correct sagging flesh.

When she was a debutante, her features had been too strikingly defined, but she had matured into a beautiful woman. Age had softened the distinctive Kincaid jaw while time brought her natural brows into style to draw flattering attention to lively brown eyes, her most attractive asset.

Her shoulder-length hair, presently tied at the nape of her neck with an Italian designer silk scarf, was that indefinable natural shade between pale blond and light brown. If her hair stylist used a rinse to enhance the lighter streaks or mask the odd strands of gray, few were the wiser.

Over the years, Luz Kincaid Thomas had acquired her own sense of style and the confidence that went with it. She had everything, not just beauty and poise, but financial security, a close family, a stable marriage, and two grown children. There were minor annoyances and vague yearnings from time to time, but basically her life had an order and meaning that she found satisfying.

"Audra Kincaid is with us today—Jake's widow," the announcer continued, reading from his prepared notes on the proceedings. "At the conclusion of the finals match, she will be presenting the trophy, named in her husband's memory, to the winning team. I'm glad you could be with us today, Audra."

Out of the corner of her eye, Luz caught the motion of her

mother's hand lifting in a casually regal acknowledgment. A scattering of applause from the small crowd followed the gesture. Audra Kincaid was very much the respected and admired matriarch, and a very handsome woman even at sixty-nine. She carried her age well; Luz supposed she had inherited her own youthful appearance from her mother.

Luz turned slightly to study her mother, seated in the canvas-slung lawn chair beside her. Always so impeccably dressed for the occasion, never over- or underdoing it, this time Audra Kincaid had on a short-sleeved green sundress trimmed with white piping, with a matching jacket. It was suitable for the occasion as well as for her age, yet sufficiently sporty so that others in slacks or bermuda shorts would feel comfortable around her. And the green was the color of growing things that says life goes on—even for a woman mourning a husband dead these last three months.

Did Audra mourn him? Luz felt a twinge of guilt for even wondering. No one could ever accuse Audra of not being a devoted wife and mother. But Luz couldn't remember the last time she'd called Audra Mother. She remembered Audra had cried in her arms when the heart specialist informed them Jake Kincaid hadn't survived the second stroke, but had it been with relief? Some said it was a blessing that he had died and not lingered, constantly needing care, but Luz wasn't thinking of it in those terms. Had Audra been glad he died, glad she was at last free of all pretense? It seemed impossible that she still could have loved him.

Jake Kincaid had been the best father any girl could have; she'd been father-spoiled and mother-disciplined. He loved as he lived, generously. He loved power, polo, and women—not necessarily in that order. His various affairs with other women were never a secret for long. The Kincaid name was too well known, too socially prominent. What was hinted at in society columns was elaborated on by gossips.

Luz had learned what assignation meant when she was eleven years old, and not long afterward, she had understood the hurt and humiliation her mother suffered. Through most of her teen years, she had hated her father for what he was doing to her mother, then she had hated Audra for letting him do it, and maybe for being to blame.

She remembered the advice Audra had offered before her

marriage to Drew Thomas: "Marriages are based on trust. A man will have his peccadilloes, even Drew, but you must trust he will always come back to you—his wife."

Even though she had come to understand Audra's reasoning, Luz still wondered how her mother truly felt, especially now that he was gone. She couldn't ask. Any mention of Jake Kincaid's indiscretions was forbidden, and his death hadn't changed that. It was not discussed then, and certainly not now.

". . . and now, I'd like to introduce the players who will be riding for the Black Oak team in the championship game." The announcer's voice intruded on Luz's thoughts, and she shifted her attention to the huge, thickly turfed polo field, four times the size of a football field. Her glance skipped past the four helmeted riders in black jerseys and white breeches and scanned their four opponents in blue jerseys. Her pride swelled when she found the lanky rider wearing the numeral 1 on the back of his jersey: long hair, the same shade as her own, curled well over his collar, and his mallet held upright in a position of readiness.

"Where is Drew?" The question from Audra briefly distracted Luz's attention. "He's going to miss the start of the game."

"He's waiting outside for Phil Eberly and someone else from his office. They must be late." Luz glanced in the general direction of the stadium entrance, but the familiar silvered head of her husband wasn't in sight. "If they don't show up soon, I'm sure he'll come to watch the opening toss."

"Bill Thorndyke, probably. He enjoys watching polo."

"What?" Her concentration had returned to the field for the introduction of the next four players, lined up facing the stands in numerical order, so Luz was slow to follow Audra's meaning. "No. Bill Thorndyke isn't coming. It's some new attorney who's just joined the law firm. A woman. You remember how much hassle Drew had with the Equal Opportunity Office, so he's giving her the royal treatment."

She passed on the information with the degree of vagueness with which she usually regarded the inner workings of the law firm Thomas, Thorndyke & Wall—except when she was expected to entertain a client. If clients were that important, she usually knew them or their family. She was intelligent, but she was by no means a "brain." She had her bachelor's degree in liberal arts from the University of Virginia, but she knew she had passed by the skin of her teeth. One of the requisites she had sought in a husband was that he had to be smarter than she was. Drew was.

". . . and now for the opposing team, it seems fitting somehow that one of the teams competing for the Jacob Kincaid Memorial Cup in this finals match should be Jake's old team, the Blue Chips. And keeping the Kincaid polo-playing tradition alive is his grandson, Rob Kincaid Thomas, playing the Number One position."

Applause sounded through the stands, but the cheering came from the Kincaid box, and Luz was loudest of them all as he cantered the steel-gray forward when his name was called. The crowd's reaction nearly drowned out the rest of the announcer's words.

". . . riding the gray gelding that's familiar to a lot of you, Jake Kincaid's top mount, Stonewall. Watch this boy. He's only nineteen and already has a two-goal handicap."

Audra pursed her lips in a subtle gesture of disapproval that Luz remembered well from childhood. "He should have saved the gray for the last chukkar. Jake always did."

"I suggested the gray to lead off the match," Luz stated, the smile freezing on her lips while she continued to applaud for her son. "That gray horse is as steady as his name. He'll settle Rob's nerves and get him into the rhythm of the game."

"We'll see." Which meant "I know better."

"Besides, by the time they start the sixth chukkar, the gray will be rested enough for Rob to ride him again if he has to." Even though confident of her own judgment, Luz was annoyed by this need to convince Audra she was right, an obvious remnant of their former parent/child relationship.

Her sister, Mary Kincaid Carpenter, older than Luz by two years, leaned forward to remark to both, "You can sure tell which team is the favorite. Listen to the way they're clapping for our side."

Luz nodded, then turned her head slightly without taking her eyes off the field, where the riders were squaring off. "If you'd ever get all your children together in one place and on horseback, we could have a whole league of our own."

It was a family joke; she and her stockbroker husband had twelve children. An even dozen and no more, Mary had often said after the birth of the last, quick to add she had married a Carpenter, not a baker. Only three were still living at home; the rest were at prep school, college, married, or on their own.

Just keeping track of where they all were was a feat in itself, and a family gathering could turn into a logistical nightmare. Luz often marveled at her older sister's ability to juggle everything and still find time to attend functions like this and cheer her nephews or nieces. Of course this was a special occasion, a tribute to their father as well.

Mary had inherited his larger bone structure. Never pretty, she was a handsome woman, like their mother, and the pace of a big family kept her slender, in spite of birthing twelve children. Without a doubt, Luz was closer to Mary than she was to their oldest brother, Frank, or the baby of the family, Michael. Happiness radiated from within Mary; that's where her beauty lay. Sometimes Luz envied her that.

"Don't wish polo ponies on me, Luz. We already have three horses, two Shetlands, four dogs, and I don't know how many cats. I don't mind the children's leaving home, but I wish they'd take their pets with them instead of letting me look after them," Mary stated with little genuine complaint. She leaned back as a mounted umpire, one of two on the field, rode to his position for the throw-in to start the game.

Viewed from the sidelines, the beginning of a polo match always seemed a scene of confusion. The eight players, four riders on each team, were clustered on their respective sides of midfield, more or less angled to face the umpire, depending on the nervous prancing of their horses and the individual jockeying for no apparent advantage over another. Into this narrow gauntlet between opposing teams of horses and riders, the umpire tossed a white ball measuring the regulation three and one-quarter inches in diameter. Luz lost sight of it almost immediately amid the legs of horses with their colorful protective sandowns bandages and the hooking sticks going for the ball. She didn't see the actual hit that knocked it free of the tangle, just the white ball bouncing down the center of the field toward the opponent's goal.

Horses and riders shot after it. A black-shirted player had the angle on the ball, and his forward teammate spurred his horse toward the posts, breaking away from the slower-reacting blue defensive back. Racing hooves drummed the ground as

Luz watched the near-perfect form of the black rider's swing and silently hoped the mallet would miss the ball. It didn't.

The ball sailed in a long, lobbing pass, landing sixty yards downfield in perfect position for the free-running Black Oak forward to knock it between the goalposts. The first chukkar was less than a minute old and already the score was Black Oak one, Blue Chips zero.

Mary gave Luz a consoling pat on the shoulder. "That was just luck. Wait until our guys get going."

But the announcer had a different opinion. "Martin gets the score for Black Oak after a brilliant pass by Raul Buchanan. Plays like that are what earned that Argentine his nine-goal handicap. Looks like the Blue Chip players are going to have their hands full this afternoon."

Her glance picked out the black-shirted professional, riding his horse back to midfield for the throw-in that followed a score. The white numeral 3 on his back referred to the position he played on the team, a defensive back and playmaker, usually given to the team captain and most skilled member of the group.

Polo teams were almost always a mixture of amateur and professional riders, with certain exceptions, but the enlistment of this Argentine star's services indicated how badly Chester Martin, sponsor of and player on the Black Oak team, wanted to win.

A high-goal polo player had to be an expert horseman, and from Luz's own riding experience she knew this man was one. At any given moment, he knew without looking which hoof was on the ground and which was lifting, where the horse's center of balance was, and what its attitude was. He could sense it and feel it through his legs and the reins.

At this distance, there was little Luz could discern about the man himself except that he had a rider's trimly muscled build, narrow-hipped and wide-shouldered. The white polo helmet and faceguard increased the difficulty in distinguishing any features, but now that Luz had sized up the main opposition, her attention shifted to her son as he rode up to the midline bisecting the three-hundred-yard-long field.

The quick score against his team appeared to have eliminated the anxious jitters Rob usually suffered in the early minutes of a game; he looked settled and calm, ready for serious play. Luz smiled faintly, pleased with his developing maturity. He was outgrowing those abrupt mood swings from high to low and back again that had marked his early teens.

"There's Drew coming now." At her mother's announcement Luz turned, hearing an unspoken reminder that Audra had warned he would miss the start of the game.

As far as Audra Kincaid was concerned, good manners dictated punctuality, and there was no excuse for tardiness. Luz could remember the raging argument she'd had with her mother when she was seventeen and wanted to arrive fashionably late to a party. On reflection, Luz realized that it hadn't quite been a raging argument; she had raged, but her mother had never raised her voice, and the argument had been lost. The lesson had been learned well, Luz realized, because she was rarely late for any appointment now.

And Drew was rarely on time, which was a constant source of annoyance to her. As he approached the box, she could see there wasn't a glimmer of regret that he had missed the opening play of the match even though he knew how important this game was to Rob.

Smothering that flash of resentment, Luz reminded herself of his good qualities as a provider, father, and husband. He was still an attractive man, distinguished with those silver tufts in his dark hair, proud of the way he'd kept his shape by playing a lot of tennis and golf instead of turning into the round butterball Mary's husband had become.

His thriving law career took a lot of his time, and even when they did spend time together, they didn't talk much, but after being married for nearly twenty-one years, they knew just about everything there was to know about each other, so what was there to discuss? Politics? The weather? The children? A recap of the day's happenings? Luz didn't mind the silences. She supposed they were what writers described as "comfortable" ones.

"I see his guests finally arrived." Audra's observation prompted Luz to glance at the couple following Drew to the box. Her first glimpse of the woman startled Luz. This strikingly lovely brunette with her curious eyes and laughing smile did not fit the mental picture Luz had of a female lawyer, with a prim mouth and black-rimmed glasses. Drew had failed to mention how beautiful she was. Surely in the month she'd been with the firm he had noticed that little detail.

Immediately, Luz detected the catty tone of her thoughts and suppressed it. She wasn't going to play the role of a jealous wife just because her husband had hired some pretty young thing to work in his office. She had her suspicions that Drew had stepped out on her in the past. They'd only been one-night stands. Every man she knew indulged in those, given the opportunity. But Drew had never kept a mistress, she was sure of that.

"I remember that Eberly boy now," Audra murmured to Luz. "He's the bachelor that gave Mary's Barbara such a rush last fall."

"Yes." Luz couldn't ignore the relief she felt when she finally noticed the handsome junior partner in the law firm. Tall and dark, definitely Harvard, he could have been a Madison Avenue model for a rising young attorney.

As the three late arrivals entered the ringed enclosure, the polo match resumed play. Courtesy dictated that Luz ignore the action on the field in order to meet Drew's guests. Drew offered an excuse about traffic for their tardiness, for Audra's benefit.

"I hope we didn't miss much," the brunette said, smiling. She was very poised yet disarmingly open and friendly.

"The game has barely started," Luz assured her graciously.

Drew took over the formal introductions. "Audra, I'd like you to meet the newest member of my staff, Miss Claudia Baines. This is Audra Kincaid."

"It is a privilege to meet you, Mrs. Kincaid." Claudia Baines extended a hand in greeting, not showing any awe of the Kincaid dowager. Luz wondered if she knew how closely she was being inspected, her scarlet-and-white slack suit judged as to line and fit, the soft cut of her dark hair examined for faddish extreme. The appraisal points were numerous, but all reviewed in the sweep of an eye.

"And, of course, you remember Phil Eberly from the firm." Drew stepped aside to allow room for the young lawyer to present himself to Audra Kincaid.

"Yes, we've met before." And her comment to Luz had been that the young man was "too full of himself."

That had been her opinion of Drew twenty-two years ago. At the time, the Bridgeport Thomases were an old and socially acceptable family with little money and a lot of hubris. Determined to make it on his own, he had refused Jake Kincaid's offer to work in the legal department of his investment banking company. Over the years, Luz had often wondered if Drew ever guessed how many of his high-paying clients in those earlier years had been referred to him by Jake Kincaid. Not that they had ever struggled, since she had her own money, her own inheritance from her grandfather—and even more now that Jake was gone.

Then it was her turn to meet Claudia Baines. The sparkling zest in those wide hazel eyes made it easy for Luz to smile back at her. She reminded Luz of her daughter; that youthful optimism was contagious. After the usual exchange of pleasantries, with the rumble of pounding hoofbeats and the crack of locking mallets in the background, Drew started to extend the introductions to the back row of the boxed area, where Mary, her husband, and three of their children were seated. She waved aside the attempt with a good natured "Down in front. It can wait until this first chukkar is over."

"Sit in the front row." Luz motioned to the empty chairs one level down from the ones she and her mother occupied. "You'll be able to see better."

The chair on her immediate right was vacant. Drew paused beside it, bending toward her and nodding his head in the direction of his two guests taking their seats in front of her. "I'd better sit with them so I can explain the rudiments of the game."

"Of course." Her attention was already attempting to shift to the action on the field, but Drew was blocking her line of sight and Rob's team appeared to be near the goal. Behind her, Mary groaned in disappointment. "What happened?"

"Rob's shot went wide of the goal. That Argie forced him to take a bad angle." The ball had gone out of bounds along the backline, and the riders were pulling in their ponies to regroup. "Black Oak will have the knock-in."

"Where's Trisha?" Drew turned in his chair to ask about their daughter.

"At the picket line, where else?" Luz glanced toward the end of the field, where the additional polo ponies waited for their chukkar of play. "As Rob says, who needs a groom when you have a sister?"

"Our seventeen-year-old is horse-crazy," Drew explained to

his guests, and Luz noticed that the brunette occupied the middle chair, between the two men. "I suppose I shouldn't complain. The time to start worrying is when she discovers boys."

"She knows about them." Luz didn't doubt that for a minute, although she refrained from reminding Drew that Trisha would be eighteen in a short two months. And Trisha wasn't horse-crazy. It was the action on the sideline she preferred to the inaction of the grandstand seats. "If you're going to worry, worry about when she discovers men."

"That's not fair, Luz," Phil Eberly protested, then leaned a shoulder closer to Claudia Baines's chair. "She makes us sound evil, and we're not, are we?"

But she appeared not to hear him, directing all her attention to the field. "Which one is your son, Mr. Thomas?"

"Let's see, he's . . ."

When Luz heard the uncertainty in her husband's voice, she pointed him out. "He's on the blue team, riding a gray horse."

"The gray horse, that's easy to spot," Drew said and smiled. "Usually she tells me something like 'He's riding the bay horse with the white snip on its nose.' Out of the eight horses on the field, ten counting the two umpires, half of them will be a bay or brown color. And who can see its nose?" The obvious dilemma such a description created drew a warm, infectious laugh from Claudia. A part of Luz listened to the conversation going on in front of her while she focused on the game. The black team controlled the knock-in and moved it toward midfield. "Of course, Luz is more familiar with the horses than I am. She exercises them and helps our son keep them in condition."

"Do you ride?"

"No, I'm no horseman." On the field, shouts and absent curses mingled with the grunts of straining horses, the clank of bridle chain, and the groan of leather. Digging hooves threw divots of turf into the air as the horses were directed by their riders into tight reverses, sharp turns, and hard gallops after a backhanded ball. "Now, Luz comes by it naturally. She was born and raised in Virginia, rode in the hunt clubs while she was growing up. Do you follow horseracing, Miss Baines?"

"No, it isn't one of my vices." She sounded playful, but Luz couldn't tell whether she was being deliberately provocative.

"Then you probably have never heard of Hopeworth Farm.

It's a large Thoroughbred breeding farm in Virginia, owned by the Kincaid family."

"Really? I knew he controlled several financial institutions and insurance companies, but—"

"—and a large brokerage firm and a lot of real estate along the East and West Coasts plus a few points in between." Drew had lowered his voice and Luz could barely catch his words. "And Hopeworth Farm was the start of the family fortune. The first Kincaid to come to Virginia arrived shortly after the Civil War and bought the former plantation for back taxes. In those days, I believe they called such people 'carpetbaggers.' He bought more land, started a bank, and ended up making a lot of money from the South's misery."

Everything Drew said was public knowledge. No dark family secrets had been related. Yet Luz was surprised that he told the story so freely, with no prompting for information. He spoke as if he were an outsider repeating gossip instead of a member of the family, albeit through marriage.

A whistle sounded across the arena. "What does that mean?" Claudia Baines asked when the play continued without a break in action.

"It's a warning to the players that only thirty seconds are left to be played in the chukkar," Drew replied just ahead of the announcer's explanation.

"I might as well ask: What's a chukkar?" The admission of ignorance carried refreshing candor and a trace of self-mockery.

"A polo game is divided usually into six periods—or chukkars—each seven minutes long. Like quarters in football and basketball." The whistle was blown again, signaling the end of the first period of play.

"Now what happens?" She watched the riders trotting their blowing horses off the field toward their respective picket lines, where the fresh mounts were tied.

"The players change ponies and tack, if they don't have an extra saddle and bridle. There's usually time for a quick conference and something to drink before the next chukkar starts. There's a longer rest break between the third and fourth chukkar—halftime, I guess."

The scoreboard indicated Black Oak had the lead over the blue team by four to one. Luz removed the binoculars from the case by her feet and held them up to her eyes. After locating Rob's picket, she adjusted the focus to zero in on her son.

With methodical and meticulous care, he checked the tack on the sorrel horse, all saddled and waiting for him. Then he went over his equipment with the same deliberation, ignoring the chestnut-haired girl impatiently waiting for him to drink the Gatorade from the cup in her hand.

It wasn't fair to call Trisha a girl anymore. She had outgrown the coltish angles of her early teens, her slim figure rounding out nicely. She was fun-loving, outgoing, outspoken—too outspoken, Luz thought sometimes, venturing opinions without being asked, which didn't rank her too favorably in Audra's book. But Jake had loved that about her, calling her spirited instead of sassy. Luz often said Trisha had been born knowing her own mind and speaking it.

She wasn't like Rob, who was so moody, sensitive, and indrawn, a fierce competitor with himself, yet so well-mannered. Her son had the long hair, but her daughter was the rebel. Through the magnifying lenses of the binoculars, she watched him take a swig of the thirst-quenching liquid, then swing into the saddle. Trisha handed him the polo stick, shaped like a croquet mallet with a long handle.

"Why do they call them ponies? They look like horses to me," Claudia Baines commented, and Luz laid the binoculars in her lap, observing that the woman had a never-ending supply of questions for Drew, and he didn't seem to mind.

"It's a holdover from the early days of polo, the turn of the century. Back then, the rules stated the players had to ride horses fourteen hands high or smaller—pony-size, in other words. Times changed, the rules changed, the horses got bigger, but the name stuck—they still refer to them as polo ponies."

The players took the field while a sea breeze stirred the tops of the palm trees that formed a tropical backdrop for the turfed playing area. The second chukkar began without fanfare, but the Black Oak team immediately set a swift pace. Time and time again, the blue players were caught flat-footed or out of position under the merciless drive of their opponents. Three goals were scored to their one, and that one came on a fluke when Tex Renecke's horse accidentally ran over the ball and knocked it between the goalposts. They fared little better in

the third chukkar. At the midway point in the game, the score
stood at eight to three in favor of the opponents.

During the lull in the action, Drew finished the introductions. Then Ross suggested that he and the children fetch drinks
for everyone from the lounge concession. Luz noticed the look
Drew directed at Phil Eberly just before the junior partner
volunteered to go with Carpenter.

After they left the private box, Audra Kincaid turned her
attention on the dark-haired guest and smiled warmly. "Tell me
what your impressions are of your first polo match, Miss Baines.
Is it what you expected?" Her interest was genuine. She never
asked a question if she didn't want to hear the answer.

"It's confusing," Claudia admitted ruefully. "I know the
objective is to hit the ball between the goalposts to score—as
in hockey or soccer—but it all happens so fast that half the
time I don't know where to look or why."

"Part of the confusion lies in the fact that every time a team
scores, they change goals. A novice to the game sometimes
has the impression goals can be scored at either end by the
teams, which isn't true," Audra explained.

"It is a fast game, though," Drew agreed with Claudia's
previous assessment. "I sometimes have the feeling that I'm
watching a cavalry charge from one end of the field to the
other. It's a game that requires highly skilled players—and
horses. When you put it in simple terms, it sounds impossible.
A man astride a galloping horse is expected to accurately hit
a ball only three and a quarter inches in diameter roughly seven
feet away from his shoulder with a stick somewhere around
fifty inches long that has a mallet head maybe nine inches long.
Now when you add that the player has to hit a moving target
from a moving horse, and control both at the same time, you
see that a player has to be a combination daredevil, stunt rider,
billiard player, and juggler. And there's generally two or three
other players close by with the same idea who will try to get
in your way or beat you to it."

"Don't forget the horse," Luz spoke up. "Some professionals claim a horse is seventy-five percent of the game. You see,
Miss Baines, a polo pony is asked to do things that go totally
against its instincts. It is trained to not swerve away from an
oncoming horse. A pony is expected to stop suddenly out of
a dead run, turn sharply, and within two strides, be in a hard

gallop or maneuver in close quarters with another horse while mallets swing all around its legs for the ball. But more than that, the pony is expected to do that nonstop for seven minutes. And, as you said, it all happens so fast."

A small frown creased her forehead as she thoughtfully considered their collective assessment. "It sounds dangerous."

"It is." Drew chuckled, the sound coming from low in his throat, while he studied the young woman with an indulgent look. "Those horses weigh anywhere from twelve to fifteen hundred pounds, close to a ton adding the rider. They travel at speeds of twenty-five to thirty miles an hour. When they collide, even in a legal bump, the impact has brought more than one horse down."

With a mild shake of her head, Claudia glanced at the distant players resting by the picket lines. Most were either lounging wearily in lawn chairs or sprawling on the lush carpet of thick green grass. "Why do they do it?"

"That's easy." Luz laughed, and her ear caught the differences in sound between the low, cultured ring of her own and Claudia's light, melodious laughter. Hers had been like that before she learned to temper her bold feelings, to develop that indefinable aura her mother called "class." And class was never dull. "People play polo because it is fast, dangerous, and exciting, always testing one's skill to discover the limits—then go one step beyond them. It's addictive. It challenges a player's nerve, his courage. More basic than that, I think it brings out the competitive drive in a person. It's a game with winners and losers, and a rider plays to win—for the sheer glory of winning."

"Don't they get anything for it? A prize or something?" Claudia sounded puzzled and vaguely surprised by the possibility as she turned to direct her question to Drew.

"Usually just a trophy. There are a few high-goal tournaments now that offer a cash prize, but very few." His attention was naturally centered on the brunette as he answered. Luz noticed the animation in his expression and knew it wasn't polo that had generated the lively interest in his dark eyes. He didn't care about the sport unless Rob was playing. "It's strictly a hobby—and an expensive one when you consider how much it costs to stable, feed, and maintain a string of polo ponies.

Rob has—what? Fifteen horses now?" He glanced to Luz to confirm the number, and she nodded affirmatively.

"I suppose it's another case of if you have to ask how much, you can't afford it," Claudia responded with a smiling grimace. Drew laughed, and he wasn't a man who laughed often.

"What did I miss?" Phil Eberly led the returning, drink-laden entourage into the private box. He flashed a dazzling smile at Claudia, but she didn't appear bowled over by his flattering attention or virile looks.

"Nothing. Just small talk—polo talk." She took her iced drink from his hand and turned away. Luz noticed his mouth tighten to suppress a ripple of irritation before he forced it into a stiff smile. She had the impression he was getting nowhere fast with Claudia, and Phil Eberly wasn't accustomed to rejection. "I suppose I sound like a curious child always asking questions, but . . ." She paused as the other drinks were passed around and Drew received his glass.

"Go ahead," Drew prompted the question he guessed was coming.

"I don't understand this business about goals and how many a player has. The announcer has said that some have six or three, but the score isn't that high."

"I'm sure the announcer was referring to a player's rating. Our son, for instance, is rated as a two-goal player. It's a handicap system, similar to golf, based on a player's skills. Except in golf, the better the player, the lower his handicap, whereas in polo, the opposite is true. The better players are given higher ratings, with the top being a perfect ten."

"There's only a handful of ten-goal players in the entire world," Luz added. "Until recently, there weren't any U.S. players with a ten-goal rating. That elite group has been predominantly from Britain, Argentina, and Mexico, although India and Europe have been represented, too."

"Do women play polo?"

"Yes. As a matter of fact, there are several women's leagues in the United States, but you don't often find mixed teams . . . unless it's a family tournament." Luz sipped at her drink, using the plastic straw. The wide straw brim of her hat briefly blocked the woman's face from her view.

"Have you ever played polo, Mrs. Thomas?"

"Yes. In college." As she lifted her head, she wondered at

her failure to insist on being called Luz. Usually she felt the stodgy "Mrs. Thomas" had always belonged to Drew's mother, not to her. She thought of herself as Luz Kincaid Thomas, distinct and separate, even though his mother had passed away ten years ago. "Then I married Drew, and the children came along. After that, I played only occasionally . . . in family tournaments with my father or with Rob and Trisha when they were younger. Now I mainly help Rob practice by hitting balls to him."

"It all sounds exciting," Claudia conceded while reserving a measure of doubt. "But I think I'll stick to tennis."

"I'll go along with that," Drew agreed warmly.

For an instant, Luz saw her husband through Claudia's eyes. Things she hadn't noticed in years were suddenly clear—the wide, square jaw, the deep cleft in his chin, the slight hook in his long nose, the rich tanned skin, and the dark eyes that could make you believe you were the only person in the room when he looked at you . . . the way he was looking at Claudia now.

Luz had never considered him to be handsome. That was a word she reserved for men like Phil Eberly, but she suddenly realized Phil's looks were too smooth and superficial. He lacked the character lines that gave depth and interest to Drew's face. Her husband was a very attractive man, and she felt a surge of pride that he belonged to her.

Behind her, Mary summoned her twelve-year-old daughter. "Anne, come sit down. They're getting ready to start the game."

As the blond adolescent hopped off her perch atop the iron rail surrounding the private box, Luz shifted in her chair to redirect her attention toward the polo field. The rest followed suit to watch the resumption of play.

The strategy of the Blue Chips team was apparent to Luz the minute they gained possession of the ball and she saw the Number Four player join the attack, instead of cautiously lagging behind his teammates in case their opponents stole the ball. The role of the Number Four player was defensive. If he made an offensive play, then another rider temporarily assumed his defensive position. But not this time. Her son's team was going all out, taking risks in a desperate attempt to even up the score.

The pace was fast and furious, and the Black Oak team appeared rattled, committing three fouls during the chukkar, which gave the blue team two penalty shots from the forty-yard line and the third from the sixty.

By the end of the fourth period, the Kincaid team had closed the gap until only two points separated them. Luz thought Rob and his teammates had a good chance.

But the rally was broken in the fifth. Luz gave most of the credit for the Black Oak team's resurgence to the blood bay horse the Argentine player rode. Its reflexes were lightning-quick, and its speed left the other horses far behind. More than once during that next-to-last period, Luz saw the gleaming bay come streaking out of nowhere and overtake a blue rider to spoil a goal shot or a pass.

The final chukkar was anticlimactic. Black Oak had won the game in the fifth, but they wound up with a score of fourteen to nine. Luz could taste Rob's bitter disappointment as he congratulated the winners, then rode off the field. He had wanted to win the Kincaid Trophy. She knew he'd blame himself for his own inadequacies in the game and not make any allowances for his youth. To him, a Kincaid should win the Kincaid Trophy. Losing it was like losing the family honor.

"Poor Rob." Her sister laid a consoling hand on Luz's shoulder.

"I know. He'll be practicing his swing and hitting balls every spare minute for the next two weeks." Luz knew the way he punished himself when he failed at whatever he set out to do.

"Be sure to tell Rob for me that he played very well, Luz." Audra Kincaid stood up, her action prompting the others to do the same. "He didn't let us down at all. Now it's my dubious privilege to present the trophy to the winners. Ross, would you escort me to the circle?" It was a command, not a request, as they all knew, and Mary's husband moved forward to take her arm and guide her out of the box.

Luz wasn't interested in watching the presentation ceremony, so she turned her back on it to gather her purse, binoculars, and camera. She knew Chester Martin would be gloating over the victory. The polo rivalry between Martin and Jake Kincaid had bordered on a feud these last years before her father's stroke. Now Martin had won.

A hand touched her arm. "Excuse me, Mrs. Thomas." The voice belonged to Claudia Baines. Luz swung around, adjusting the knotted sleeves of the teal-blue sweater tied around her neck. "I know your mother will be tied up for a while with the presentation and pictures. Please tell her how honored I was to have met her. Phil and I must be going. I wanted you to know how much I enjoyed this afternoon, and I'm sorry your son's team didn't win."

"Why don't you and Phil have drinks with us at the club, then dinner later?" Drew suggested as he moved to Luz's side.

A playful mockery glittered in the look Claudia directed at Luz. "He asks, knowing that tomorrow morning he's going to want to review the final draft of a complicated merger contract." She smiled at him. "I'd like to join you, but I have a lot of work waiting for me. I promise I will attend your party next Saturday night, though. Thank you for the invitation, Mrs. Thomas."

"Not at all." Luz had no recollection of Claudia Baines's name on the invitation list, but she concealed her surprise.

"Goodbye, then."

"Wait just a minute and I'll walk you to your car," Drew told the pair, then turned to Luz. "Will you be going to see Rob?"

"Yes." Luz nodded, frowning slightly. They usually went together after a game.

"When you're through, come back to the lounge. I'll meet you there for drinks," he said as he moved away from her.

"Okay." She returned his smile, but it faded when he turned away and walked with his guests toward the parking lot. She watched them leave, noting that Drew's arm rested lightly on the brunette's shoulders. It had been draped behind her chair through most of the game. Determinedly, Luz shrugged away the vague sense of unease.

"I understand she's been with the firm only a month." Mary was standing next to her.

"Yes." Luz hastily picked up her things, thinking that sisters could sometimes be too close. "She's new to the area, so Drew is introducing her around, trying to make her feel welcome."

"Men always make you wonder whether they'd go to so much trouble if she wasn't pretty."

"Probably not."

"That Argentine's bay horse was named Best-Playing Pony," Mary said, and Luz appreciated the change of subject.

"I'm not surprised." She had missed the announcement. Her

glance strayed to the cluster of people crowded around the presentation area. The ceremony itself was over, and all but one black-shirted rider were walking their sweat-glistening horses back to the picket lines. Chester Martin remained behind to have several photographs preserve the moment when Audra Kincaid had given him the large brass trophy cup. "Are you coming with me to the stables?" Luz asked her sister.

"I'll wait for them," she said, indicating her mother and husband. "We'll see you at the lounge."

After slipping her purse and the leather cases containing her camera and field glasses into her straw tote bag for easy carrying, Luz left the stands and skirted the presentation area crowded with its celebrants, photographers, and club officials. Groundsmen were busy replacing the divots to put the polo field back in playing condition, restoring the uniform thickness of grass as if a tense contest had never taken place there.

# CHAPTER II

Since Rob had dismounted at the picket line at the end of the game, he hadn't said one word. Trisha was getting tired of her brother's grim silence. She sponged out the pony's mouth while Rob unfastened the safety girth over the saddle.

"Rob, will you stop acting like the whole world is on your shoulders?" She resisted the impulse to throw the wet sponge at him and dropped it in the water bucket instead. "It was only a game, for heaven's sake!"

His teal-blue polo shirt was plastered to his back by perspiration. It made ringlets of his long, sandy hair. He lifted the saddle and pad off the horse's back and turned to glare at her. "Who the hell asked you?"

"He speaks," she murmured sarcastically and rested her hands on her hips, a stance that held a challenge. But Rob simply walked around her, carrying his saddle and pad, and depositing them on the ground beside the damp martingale, polo helmet, mallets, and whip.

"Take the bandage off his tail."

"Do it yourself!" She hated it when he bossed her around in that tone she called his Kincaid voice. "You're a royal bastard, you know that?"

He crossed to the sorrel's hindquarters and began removing the bandage that bound its tail to prevent it from interfering with a swinging mallet. His glance skimmed her from the twisted sweatband around her rust-brown hair down the front of her horse-stained T-shirt to the faded denim of her tight jeans and the scuffed, manure-dirty, but expensive leather boots.

"You look like a Texas shitkicker," he retorted contempt-uously.

"What do you expect me to wear around these horses of yours?" Trisha demanded angrily. "They're always butting their heads up against me or slobbering all over me. I'm not about to let them ruin my good clothes! It isn't my fault you gave Jimmy Ray the day off," she said, referring to the regular groom.

"Hey, I never asked you to help with the horses. That was your idea!" He jabbed a finger in her direction. "I can always find a groom!"

"Sure you can. You're a Kincaid. You can get anything you want!" She mocked his arrogance.

"That isn't what I meant at all," Rob muttered under his breath. He balled up the unrolled bandage in his hand and hurled it at the rest of his equipment on the ground. "When Grandmother Kincaid sees you like that, she'll have a fit."

"So? I won't let her see me." The solution was simple.

"Yeah, but she'll hear about it. You could wear something nicer, Trish. Other people around here know you. Don't you care what they think when they see a—"

"I know," she interrupted. "A Kincaid. Everybody seems to have conveniently forgotten that I'm a Thomas, too. Why are you so hung-up on this?"

"I don't know." He combed his fingers through his hair in a defeated gesture. "I guess it's the game. I wanted to win that cup."

"All of us wanted you to," Trisha reminded him.

Anger and impatience returned to his expression as he dis-missed her answer. "I can't expect you to understand," he muttered thickly.

"Why?" She hated it when he adopted this intellectually superior attitude.

"I'm a Kincaid!" His angry declaration indicated that was a sufficient explanation.

"So what? You aren't the only one on this earth—we have relations by the score!"

He turned and leaned against the horse's hot flanks, draping his arms over its sweaty back. "But I'm the one who was playing today." His voice was low, almost muffled, and cutting in its self-condemnation.

Her anger faded. Fights between them were frequent, sometimes initiated by a lot of goading on Trisha's part usually when she was fed up with the damned noble ideas he'd get in his head. But she could rarely stay mad at him for long. She crossed to the horse and stood beside it, leaning a shoulder against the sorrel's withers and folding her arms in front of her. At five inches over five feet she was nearly six inches shorter than her brother, but she was never conscious of it. The air she breathed was strong with the earthy smell of horse, an aroma she'd always liked.

"Rob, there were three other players on your team today. Two of them had five- and six-goal handicaps. They made mistakes out there. You weren't the only one."

"I should have played better." He dug the toe of his boot into the grass as he made the critical assessment.

"Rob, loosen up!" Trisha declared in exasperation.

He turned his head to look at her. The expression on his raw-boned features was so earnest and intense it was almost frightening. "You don't know what it's like to play serious polo, do you? It's just a game on horseback to you, isn't it? It's position, always position."

Trisha stopped him before he could go further in his lecture on polo tactics. "Don't get serious on me. I can only take so much of your heavy thinking."

Rob pushed away from the sorrel pony and reached for the sweat scraper. "I have to practice more."

She mussed his hair, flattened by the helmet, as he swiped the scraper over the horse's wet back, then dodged his upraised arm when it attempted to knock her hand aside. "All work and no play makes Rob a very dull boy."

"Now, that's original, Trish," he mocked. "I guess that platitude makes you the life of the party." His mouth quirked in a rare smile that assured her he wasn't angry.

"I'm certainly not going to tell you!" She laughed. "You'd feel honor-bound to tell Luz."

Rob shook his head in mild amazement. "How'd I get such a hellion for a sister?"

"Retribution, dear brother, for being so perfect." She jabbed at his ribs in a playful poke. "You're not perfect, you know. What you need is a hot shower and some good sex. They're guaranteed to take your mind off whatever troubles you think you have." Trisha laughed at his startled expression and slapped him on the rump as she walked away. "While you think about that, I'll take Clover, Stony, and Hank back to the trailer, then come back for the others."

Rob watched her untie the three horses and back them away from the picket line. As brother and sister they didn't really get along together very well. Even though Rob was a year and a half older than Trisha, she had never deferred to him as an older brother. Because Rob had been held back a year in grammar school, they were at the same grade level, and Trisha thought of herself as more mature than Rob. Vinegar and oil was the comparison Trisha used; you can shake them together, but they always separate.

Feeling the fatigue and strain of exertion, he stretched the tight muscles in his shoulders with a flexing shrug, still knotted from the game's tension. The hot shower part of Trisha's advice sounded good. He reddened slightly under his tan, acknowledging to himself that the second part did as well. Still, it bothered him to hear her talk about sex—maybe because he knew how guys were with girls. And maybe because it was all right for him to make it with somebody else's sister, but nobody'd better do it with his.

He frowned, vaguely disturbed. About the only time he felt right about anything was on the polo field—with a horse under him and the juices pumping. He loved that tight, high feeling when all his senses were sharpened and his heart was somewhere in his throat. Maybe that was the problem. He got so up before the game, and high during it, that when he came crashing down it was a long way to the bottom. He stared trancelike at the scraper as he dragged it across the horse's sweat-wet back. He was good at polo—not as good as he could be, but he had potential. And he was determined to realize it fully.

That's where the contradiction within him began. He was proud of being a Kincaid; all his life it had made him "somebody." Yet he wanted to be more than somebody's son or grandson. He'd grown up surrounded by the sons and daughters of rich and influential families and had gone to prep school with them. Their lineage gained them acceptance in society and the business world. Being someone's son was sufficient qualification for becoming an executive in a family corporation, usually in a manufactured position with little, if any, responsibility—and everyone knew it.

But on the polo field, it was different. No one cared about who he was, only about his ability to play the game. He received no special favors from his teammates, and certainly not from his opponents. The only way to reach the elite circle of high-goal riders was to excel at the game. The family name and money couldn't buy his entrance into it. Polo was like any other sport—the top players had an identity of their own, regardless of family background. They were not just "somebody"; they were somebody "special."

A building pressure pounded inside his head. Rob spread a hand across his brow and squeezed at the temples in an effort to check the hammering pain. The problem with always getting whatever he wanted was that it made him want more. Being a Kincaid wasn't enough. Trisha was right when she said there were Kincaids by the score. He wanted to be special. He wanted it all.

But that wasn't something he could put into words; it would sound too greedy. He glanced in the direction his sister had taken, wondering if she ever felt the way he did, and doubting it. All he could see was the muscled rumps of the horses gleaming in the afternoon sunlight as the girl leading them walked at a leisurely pace toward the barns.

A horse and rider entered his side vision, traveling at an angle that would intersect his sister's path. Rob immediately recognized the black-shirted rider who had been his nemesis during the game, the Argentine Raul Buchanan. The bitter taste of defeat filled his mouth. Angrily, Rob turned away from the sight, cast aside the scraper, and picked up a chamois to wipe the sorrel dry.

So much had been riding on today's game. If he'd won, he could have used the victory to persuade his father to let him postpone college for a year and concentrate on improving his polo skills. He wasn't worried about persuading Luz. His mother had always been on his side, always willing to listen, and always ready to help even when she didn't understand.

His father was another matter. Rob knew he could never please him. A good education, college, that's all he talked about. He couldn't see that Trisha was the one with the brains. She breezed through school while Rob had to struggle to keep his grades high enough to play polo on the school team. He loathed the idea of four more years of classrooms. Let Trisha become the lawyer.

A few spectators who had watched the polo match from the comfort of their cars, some enjoying champagne-and-caviar tailgate parties along the sidelines, were departing. One of the cars blocked Trisha's path while the driver waited for an opening in the traffic on the club road. She halted the ponies on the shoulder and absently rubbed the forehead of the nudging gray horse.

There was a pull on the nearside lead rope she was holding as the blaze-faced Thoroughbred turned its head outward. Trisha glanced idly in the same direction to confirm there wasn't an oncoming vehicle to be concerned about, and saw another horse and rider approaching. She started to look away, then recognized the black-shirted player from the game.

His horse slow-trotted the last few yards to her position before the rider pulled up on the double reins. The blood-red bay horse halted close to Trisha, its front shoulders slightly ahead of her and the saddle even with her. All she could see of the rider was the polished brown boot in the stirrup ring and a white-breeched thigh and hip. To see the rest of him, she had to tilt her head back.

Trisha had forgotten how intimidating a man on horseback could appear to someone on foot. She stood barely at eye level with his hip. When the bay horse stirred restively, shifting its weight and chewing on the iron bits, Trisha had an immediate sense of immense power, yet the brute strength of the animal, an animal six times heavier than the man on its back, was under the control of the rider. Its shiny sides heaved, straining the girth as the horse blew loudly, punctuating the creaking sounds of leather.

Her glance flicked upward, pausing on the polo helmet the right hand held propped against his hip, then traveling up the sun-bronzed arm sinewed with hard muscle. The thin material of his short-sleeved jersey was cut to fit his flatly muscled torso snugly and allow complete freedom of movement. What began as an idle inspection of a man she had watched ride all afternoon shifted to feminine interest when Trisha saw his face.

Deeply tanned by the sun, it was angular and broad, masculine and strong in its composition of jaw and chin. Dark brows and blunt lashes framed a pair of piercing blue eyes that glanced restlessly about him. Fatigue deepened the grooves around his mouth and the creases near his eyes, but an impression of latent vitality remained. His hair was a dark shade of brown. Its damp thickness showed the furrows made by careless raking fingers. The blue eyes surprised Trisha. She tended to think of Argentines as being of Spanish or Indian descent, although the Buchanan surname should have given her a clue. As if sensing her study, he glanced down at her.

"Good game," she said.

"Thank you." His reply was distantly polite, with little trace of an accent in the low-pitched voice. A second later, he was looking away, preoccupied and aloof. His apparent lack of interest didn't discourage her.

Trisha switched her attention to his horse, the one that had performed so brilliantly in the fifth chukkar. "Your horse is a beauty," she remarked. "He won Best-Playing Pony, didn't he?"

His glance came back to her. "Yes."

"He deserved it." The corners of his mouth lifted in a tired semblance of a smile, acknowledging her praise. The driver in the waiting car gunned the motor, attracting their attention, but the steady trail of slow-moving vehicles gave him no entrance to the road. "It looks like we're going to be here all afternoon." Picket lines and a parked horse trailer made it impossible to go around the car. "You'd think someone would let him in."

"Someone will." He dismounted. The bay moved back a step as he bent to run a hand down its near foreleg, checking for any abnormal heat or swelling.

The horse stood quietly until he had finished the examination, then it turned its head to look at Trisha's three charges and lifted its nose, blowing softly at their scent. A narrow white streak ran down its face, contrasting with the dark red of its coat. The animal had an intelligent head, Trisha noticed, and large velvet brown eyes with none of the white showing.

"Your horse has kind eyes." It was a quality a player looked for in a polo pony, Trisha knew. A nervous, high-strung horse rarely made a good game mount. She held out her palm to the animal so it could smell her, mindful of the man walking to its head. "What's his name?"

Her persistent effort at conversation finally commanded more than a passing look from him. Raul Buchanan preferred to spend these few minutes alone to replay the game in his mind and isolate his mistakes, but the girl's chattering kept distracting him. He wondered why all female grooms seemed to be horse-crazy.

"I call him Criollo." Stable girls came in all ages, shapes, sizes, and backgrounds, so Raul wasn't surprised to detect an air of cultured breeding about the girl. But he hadn't expected to find her looking at him instead of the horse.

"That's Spanish for 'native-born,' isn't it? The translation is Creole." She reached out to stroke its forehead, but her interested glance was slow to leave him.

Although it was a different twist, he'd seen it before. During his years on the polo circuit, Raul had run across women who transferred whatever sexuality they saw in a horse to the man on its back. This one was young, which wasn't to say he didn't appreciate his view of the firm young breasts outlined under the T-shirt, the nipples clearly discernible. Few women wore bras anymore, he'd noticed, especially the *chicas* who didn't have to worry about sagging breasts.

"Do you speak Spanish?" He lifted his glance, taking note of the blue-and-gold sweatband. Her chestnut hair was cut in layers, creating a shaggy mop of loose curls.

"I only know some words and phrases, mostly from helping one of my girlfriends study for a language test. I took French." The lack of embellishment or claim to worldly experience indicated a high degree of self-confidence to Raul.

There was a gap in the traffic, and the waiting car slipped into it. With the way clear, they both started forward, leading their horses. The swish of horses striding through the grass was accompanied by the muffled thud of hooves and the odd rattle of a curb chain or lead shank. They were faint echoes of the game, played at a slower speed, and his thoughts started to wander back.

"What did you think of the game?" Again her voice intruded on his thoughts.

He'd already recognized the horses she was leading, especially the gray from Jake Kincaid's old string. Raul had played against Kincaid many times, but never for him. Kincaid had approached him in the past when he was putting together a team for a particular tournament, but there had always been a conflict of schedules. The old man had been a tough competitor, playing the game well into his sixties, and had continued to sponsor teams after he could no longer play. The string of ponies was testament to the quality of teams he put together, and the grandson had ridden the best of them today, playing the Number One position.

"It was a good contest." Politically, there was little else he could say to someone on the losing side.

"It would have been a good contest if you throw out the fifth chukkar," she mocked good-naturedly. "You spoiled an awful lot of Rob's shots. Of course, your horses were better than his."

"He has an excellent string of ponies, especially that gray." The best money could buy or train.

"I'm afraid the old gray ain't what he used to be." She shook her head to reinforce her opinion. "He's seventeen years old."

"Is that why he was afraid to ride him?" Raul wondered absently.

"Rob? Afraid?" The young girl came to an abrupt stop, a sudden anger flashing in her dark eyes. "What do you mean by that? My brother isn't afraid to ride anything."

Pausing, he arched a brow in surprise. "Your brother? Then you are—"

"A Kincaid, yes." There was something more than indignant anger in the decisive snap of her answer, as if she resented the name. "Who did you think I was?"

"The groom." Raul smiled dryly at his own mistake.

She appeared frozen for an instant, then the temper that had flared so quickly dissolved into a laugh as she looked down at her stable clothes. "I guess I do look like a stablehand. I promised Rob I'd help with the horses today. It sounded like more fun than sitting with the family." She started forward, resuming the walk. "By the way, my name's Trisha. Trisha Thomas. And yours is Raul Buchanan." With a half-turn of her head, she eyed him. "Why did you say Rob was afraid?" This time there was more curiosity than demand in her voice.

Since he had made the critical observation, Raul felt compelled to support it. "Toward the end of every chukkar, I noticed that he let his mount go wide on the turns, and he did not use his spurs or go to the whip. He saved the pony."

"Some of them aren't young horses anymore. They were

tired." She was quick to come to her brother's defense. "I don't see that what he did was so wrong."

"Games are not won by sparing your pony. It is an athlete. A rider cannot be concerned whether his mount is tired. Whatever the command, the horse must obey, and if he protests, the rider must make him obey. The horse has to push itself the same way a man pushes himself to do more than he thinks he can. At no point should your brother have cared whether his horse was too tired to make a hard run. And if they were too tired to play competently, he should have switched to a fresh horse during that chukkar of play instead of waiting until it was over." When he'd finished, Raul looked at her. "I am sure I sound very harsh to you."

"Yes," she answered frankly. "But it fits. You were relentless out there this afternoon." And he sensed she wasn't sure whether she approved of that. As they neared the barns, there was an increase in activity. Horses were being walked to cool them down; others were being loaded in trailers; some were being rubbed down by their grooms. Trisha seemed to throw off their previous conversation. "What are you doing tonight?"

At six o'clock, he had an appointment at the health club with the masseuse, but he knew that wasn't what she meant. "Chet Martin is having a party tonight to celebrate winning the cup."

"You mean, to gloat over winning the cup," she corrected, then warned, "You won't like it. The Martins give dreadful parties. Why don't you slip away earlier and I'll meet you somewhere?"

"How old are you?" It was impossible for him to tell. He'd met some girls that he'd thought were eighteen or older and had learned later they were only fourteen, mere children. And children were not enticement for him.

After a small hesitation, she shrugged. "Seventeen. I suppose you think I'm too forward."

"No. Too young." And Raul had twenty years on her. There was a degree of flattery in the fact that she found him attractive, but long ago he had learned wisely and well not to get mixed up with pretty young daughters from wealthy families.

Her steps slowed as they reached the stables and the horses bunched close to her. "Our trailer is parked over there," she said, indicating that here they parted company. "Would it have made a difference if I'd told you I was eighteen? I will be in two months. I'm attracted to you, and I'd like to see you again." It was an outright challenge of his decision, not a plea to reconsider.

"Nothing is wrong with that."

"In that case, my parents are having a party next Saturday night. Will you come?" Her head was tipped to the side at a provocative angle, her dark eyes gleaming.

"I am a professional," Raul reminded her. "Next week, I will be playing with a team at Boca Raton. I may not be here."

"*If* you are, will you come?"

"We'll see."

"I'll expect you." One of the horses nudged her from behind, urging her to continue to the barns.

"You could be disappointed," he warned.

"No, I won't. You'll be there." After that confident statement, she turned and led the horses toward the parked trailers.

For the last fifteen years, Raul had lived among the rich, and during the last ten, the scope had been international. He had dined at their tables, slept in their houses, played polo with or for them, ridden to hunts with them, driven cattle and sat in bars with them. He'd held clinics to teach them the finer points of polo and sold ponies to them. He'd met their friends, children, grandparents, and hired help. And he had learned they were no different from other people. They had their braggarts and misers, spoiled brats and painfully shy children; some were good and decent and fair, and there were others you didn't dare trust. So he avoided putting a label on Trisha, not classifying her as spoiled or wild or headstrong. At the moment, he didn't know if he even wanted to see her again.

That was the advantage of being among the best polo players in the world. People came to him for the privilege of having him play with them. He didn't have to be nice to their daughters or sleep with their wives—or the men either. Polo had given him independence and freedom from want. He rode his own horses now and came and went as he pleased.

It was a far cry from those hungry days on the Pampa when he'd been a scrawny kid too short to climb on the horses he watered at the *estancia*. From that he'd graduated to mucking out stalls and grooming horses. Later he'd worked as a groom and exercise boy at the Palermo Race Track in Buenos Aires.

Then a horsebreeder had hired him—a horsebreeder and weekend polo player. He'd had his first taste of the game as a last-minute substitute for one of the players. He had filled in for others on several occasions after that, practicing in the meantime while he exercised the owner's horses.

It had been a long way, Raul realized. Yet the dream was still before him—the ten-goal rating that would make him a master of the game. That had thus far eluded him. He tapped the padded helmet against the side of his leg and headed toward the section where his horses were stabled, the blood-red bay pony in tow.

Cars and trucks towing horse trailers hummed steadily along the road that bordered one side of the polo field. Some players remained at the picket line, their voices punctuating the drone of vehicles as they talked with family and friends. Here and there a groom led a group of horses to the stables while their snortings and whickerings mingled with the other sounds. All of it combined to prevent Rob from hearing Luz approach.

She paused a minute to study him as he wiped down the sweat-damp sorrel pony. He appeared absorbed in the task, but Luz noted the forceful pressure in his strokes. His thoughts were far from what he was doing. She wished that she knew what she could say to console him that wouldn't sound banal or preaching. When he'd been a youngster with troubles, she could hold him on her lap and assure him it would all work out all right, and he'd believe her. But not anymore. He had reached the age of reason, and she was no longer the final authority. Being the mother of an adult—or near adult—was so frustrating, because they no longer listened.

The sorrel Thoroughbred turned its head, pricking its ears in her direction, and whinnied in recognition. Luz saw Rob look up and fixed a quick smile in place as she strode forward.

"Hi," she offered warmly and watched his head dip in a mute rejection of any sympathy. Hurt by the unintentional rebuff, Luz lowered her chin slightly so the wide brim of her straw sunhat shaded more of her face. She walked to the front of the horse, transferring her attention to it. "How's my baby?" she crooned and rubbed its poll. It nuzzled the knotted sleeves of her sweater in front, responding to the caress of her voice and hand. "Sorry, but I don't have any sugar for you this time,

Copper." Gently, she scratched the top of its satin nose and glanced sideways at Rob. "He played well today."

"Yeah." He didn't look at her, his face smooth of any expression.

"It was a tough game." Luz eyed him. "Do you want to talk about it?"

"No. It's over and we lost."

But she knew it wasn't that cut and dried emotionally. "Where's Trisha?"

"At the horse trailer. She should be back soon for the rest of the horses." He cast an absent glance over his shoulder as if expecting to see her.

Luz gave the sorrel one last pat and moved away to saunter closer to Rob. She thrust her hands in the side pockets of her slacks, assuming a casual stance. "I suppose right now you're wishing we had accepted your Uncle Mike's invitation to spend the midterm break at their chalet in Gstaad. You could be skiing in Switzerland instead."

"No, I'm not," he denied in a voice flattened of feeling. He made one last swipe over a sleek flank before folding the chamois in half.

"Why not? If we'd gone, you wouldn't have played in the tournament, and you would have missed feeling as miserable and rotten as you do now. Why would you want to go through all this when you could be having a good time on the slopes?" Luz reasoned.

"Because I wanted to play!" Rob flashed her an impatient look at what he saw as a lack of understanding on her part.

Luz smiled faintly. "Remember that. Regardless of the outcome, you wanted to play."

His head came back sharply as a deep furrow pulled his light brows together. "Yeah," he realized. "Yeah, I guess I did."

"I'm glad." Her smile deepened in compassion. "Although I know it doesn't make you feel any better."

"No." He admitted that, too, as he glumly tipped his head down.

A horse cantered toward them. Luz recognized the fat pinto on which both Rob and Trisha had learned to ride. It was now a family pet relegated to the easy life of stable pony. Trisha reined it to a halt beside them and slid off its bare back. Her glance skimmed Rob before it swung to Luz.

"I see you had the same success I did, Luz, trying to cheer up laughing boy," Trisha remarked dryly.

"It hurts to lose something you want very much." Luz was tactfully appealing for a little display of understanding.

Trisha cocked her head to the side, frowning curiously. "What have you ever lost, Luz?"

Her mind went blank. "Nothing that seems very important now." In truth she couldn't think of anything. She'd always had whatever she wanted. She couldn't very well include deaths in the family. And she hadn't known any heartbreaks or un-requited love.

The answer gave Trisha nothing to pursue, and she shrugged aside the topic to move on to something else. "I met Raul Buchanan. He had his own opinion on why you lost the game, Rob."

"What was that?" His interest in the answer was wary and skeptical.

"He claimed you spared your ponies the minute they showed signs of tiring, and said you should have switched to a fresh mount if your horse couldn't go the distance."

"He's probably right," Rob admitted grudgingly. "I thought about it a few times, but I was afraid I'd find myself going into the last chukkar without a fully rested horse."

"At least you've learned something, Rob," Luz said.

"Yeah, I'll know better next time."

"Maybe Raul can give you some more pointers," Trisha suggested. "I've invited him to the party Saturday night." Be-latedly, she turned to Luz. "I didn't think you'd mind if I asked him."

First Drew had extended an invitation without her knowl-edge, now Trisha. She felt a stir of irritation. "What about you, Rob? Have you asked someone that I don't know about, too?"

"No." He appeared taken aback by her tautness.

Luz sighed heavily. "It doesn't matter. You know you're both welcome to invite people to the house anytime." She made a determined effort to put aside her annoyance. "Do you need any help with the horses?"

"No," Trisha answered. "Jimmy Ray is at the trailer looking after them."

"He is?" Rob stiffened, tension knotting the pit of his stomach.

"Yes." Suspicion gleamed in the narrowed look Trisha gave him. "I thought you said he was going to be out of town this weekend."

"He was," Rob said. "I guess he got back early."

"I don't like him," Trisha announced flatly.

"Trisha." Their mother's voice was reproving. "Jimmy Ray Turnbull is the best handler and groom we've ever had. I don't think you could find anyone more knowledgeable or conscientious in the care of the horses."

"I don't care. There's something about him I don't like," Trisha insisted while Rob carefully kept silent. "Every time I see him, he's wearing those same khaki workclothes. And I'll bet he wears that slouch hat all the time because he doesn't have any hair on the top of his head. What really gets me is the way he goes around all the time with that weak smile and that pipe drooping out of the corner of his mouth. He never lights it."

"I'd fire him if he did," Luz stated. "Smoking around the stable is dangerous." She shook her head in a gesture of mild confusion. "I don't see how you could dislike such a kind, gentle man."

"I don't know. He's just too quiet." Trisha placed condemning stress on the final word.

"Maybe people like you have talked him to death," Rob suggested, some of his apprehension fading.

"I guess he reminds me of Ashley Wilkes," Trisha decided. "I always thought he was such an insipid character."

"You have made your opinion of the man very clear, Trisha, so I suggest you drop the subject," Luz warned. "Now, since Jimmy Ray is here to take care of the horses, why don't you two shower and change and have dinner with the rest of the family at the restaurant?"

"Count me out," Trisha said. "A bunch of us are thinking of trying out that new health-food restaurant."

"A bunch of us. A bunch of what? Bananas?" Luz demanded icily.

"The usual crowd—Jenny Fields, Carol Wentworth, and the rest." She was irritated at being questioned, and she didn't try to hide it.

"And where are you going afterward?"

"I don't know." A smile unexpectedly widened her lips, the kind Rob never trusted. "I was thinking it might be fun to crash Chet Martin's party tonight, but don't worry, Luz. I wouldn't want the Martins to acquire a reputation for giving fun parties. We'll probably come back to the club and dance or play tennis."

"What time will you be home?"

"Ten or eleven." Trisha shrugged.

"You be home by eleven o'clock," Luz ordered, then turned to him. "What about you, Rob? Shall we expect you for dinner?"

"I'd rather not. I couldn't stand the thought of people coming up to me all evening to say how sorry they are that we lost the game."

She contained her disappointment that neither would be joining the family for dinner. "All right. See you two later."

"Come on." Rob urged his sister into action as their mother walked away. "Let's get the rest of the horses and this equipment back to the trailer."

"I'll bring the horses." Trisha looped the reins over the neck of the spotted horse and moved to its side. "Give me a leg up, Rob."

Stirred by agitation, Rob crossed to the horse and cupped a hand for her foot to step in, then boosted her onto the animal's wide back. After she had settled into position, she looked down at him with troubled eyes. "Be honest, Rob. Do you like Jimmy Ray?"

He couldn't hold her look. "As long as he does the job he's paid to do, it isn't essential that I like him."

"I suppose not." But she didn't appear satisfied, and Rob wondered if she had any concrete reasons for her dislike.

# CHAPTER III

Outside the roomy stall, the winter sky darkened early. All was quiet in the stable. The only sounds were the odd stamp of a horse and the rustle of hay. Rob stood at the head of the steel-gray horse, tied by two lead ropes fastened to opposite sides of the lighted stall. His hand absently rubbed its forelock while he watched the tan figure crouched beside the horse's front legs. The faded brown hat blocked the man's face from his view, so Rob couldn't watch his expression while he conducted the tactile examination of the swelling in the pony's leg.

After interminable minutes had passed, Rob could stand the waiting no longer. "Does it look serious?"

The man rocked back on his heels. "No." Teeth clenched to hold the pipestem muffled the answer. Unhurried, Jimmy Ray pushed himself upright and took the dead pipe out of his mouth to offer a more complete answer. "The legs are filled up some from running on the hard ground. I've got a paste I can smear on them. Stony'll be fine." His voice had a low and soothing pitch to it, almost hypnotic in its softness. The loose-fitting clothes gave the impression of a tall, spare man, but Jimmy Ray Turnbull was shorter than Rob and wider in the shoulders.

"Good." Rob concentrated on the dark, gunmetal-gray forehead with its wide set eyes and tried to ignore the fine tension that wired his nerves when the handler glanced at him. He knew what was in those soft, knowing eyes.

"You're feelin' bad about losin' that game, aren't ya?" Jimmy Ray held the pipe close to his mouth, ready to clamp it between his teeth the minute he finished talking. "It's got you down pretty low, hasn't it?"

Something snapped inside. "I don't want anything!" Rob lashed out, and the gray horse reacted to the sudden anger and fear in the atmosphere, snorting and pulling back on the ropes.

"Never said you did," Jimmy Ray replied calmly and laid a soothing hand on the horse's neck, transferring his attention to the animal to settle it down.

Rob swung away from the horse and leaned on the manger, tightly gripping the board. He struggled with his own weaknesses, the rawness of want and the conflict with his conscience. Yet he'd known all along this would happen, expected it . . . wanted it. He scraped a hand through his hair and turned slowly back to the man.

"How much?" The starkness in his voice matched his expression.

"How much you want?" Jimmy Ray placidly chewed on his pipestem.

Agitated, Rob dropped his glance to the straw-covered stable floor. "Just one. That's all."

Jimmy Ray gave the horse one last pat on its sleek neck. "You just wait here. I'll be back with somethin' to fix you up." The lazily drawled words seemed to be directed to both the gray Thoroughbred and Rob.

At a pace neither hurried nor slow, Jimmy Ray left the stall and turned in the direction of the equipment room. More on edge than before, Rob waited, listening for returning footsteps and resisting the urge to pace. He wished a thousand times he hadn't asked for the stuff, but when he heard Jimmy Ray coming back, he turned eagerly.

As he entered the stall, the overhead bulb threw its light on the container filled with some pasty substance he carried in one hand. Rob's glance immediately darted to the other one.

"Here." The hand lifted, and Rob quickly reached to take the sealed packet of white powder.

"How much?" He fingered the plastic-wrapped cocaine, reminding himself that he didn't *have* to have the drug. It wasn't a habit with him. In his whole life, he'd taken it only maybe a half-dozen times. He wasn't like some of the guys at school who were tooting the stuff nearly all the time.

"On the house." Jimmy Ray crouched down beside the horse

and dipped his long fingers into the white goo in the metal container.

"I'll pay." Rob wasn't sure whether he insisted out of pride or a need to assert his independence.

"Suit yourself," he said through teeth biting down on the pipe's mouthpiece. "Be twenty."

Rob dug into his pocket and pulled out a bill, then let the folded money fall to the floor. Jimmy Ray never physically took the cash. Rob paused uncertainly, waiting for the handler to pick it up, but he ignored it. Clutching the packet more tightly in his hand, Rob hesitated, then bolted from the stall.

On either side of the road, separate driveways led to ranch-style estates ranging from five to twenty acres in size, most of them complete with barns, paddocks, swimming pools, and tennis courts to complement the mansion-sized homes. Here in the exclusive community of West Palm Beach, located a comfortable distance north of Miami and Fort Lauderdale on the Atlantic, such spacious and luxurious estates were standard for the international set.

As Drew turned the car onto the cobblestoned lane, the Mercedes's headlamps swept the long circular drive, illuminating the lush tropical plantings around it. The foliage of palms, tamarind, and flowering shrubs partially concealed the white-stuccoed walls and red-tiled roofs of the two-story Spanish-style home. Beyond were the stables, pasture, and a stick-and-ball practice field on the fifteen-acre tract. Drew stopped the car in front of the two long steps that led to the impressively carved entrance door.

"I'll put the car in the garage and join you inside," he said to Luz. When she stepped out of the brown car he drove away.

The outside light for the recessed entry came on as Luz approached the door, passing the tall clay urns that flanked the low steps. Emma Sanderson opened the door to admit her. The plump fifty-year-old woman managed the Thomas home, supervising the household help and the groundskeepers, and serving as a social secretary for Luz as well. With her ready smile and pleasant ways, she was hardly a martinet, but neither did she tolerate any nonsense. Widowed, she lived in the house, occupying the maid's quarters at the end of the broad galleria on the main floor.

"Good evening, Emma." Luz paused inside the entrance hall, which was dominated by the heavy oak stairs leading to the second floor. The upstairs was devoted entirely to the master suite. The other three family bedrooms were located at either end of the first-floor galleria. "Have Rob and Trisha come home yet?" She glanced in the direction of their rooms.

"Rob is here, but Trisha isn't in yet."

Her watch showed her daughter still had an hour before her appointed curfew. "Thanks, Emma." She moved toward the stairs. "Good night."

"Good night."

The master suite included two bedrooms, connected by a common sitting room with French doors that opened onto a private deck. Luz went directly to her capacious room, done in cream and muted greens and furnished in French Provincial. An artfully designed window of antique stained glass adorned the wall above the large bed, but the black night outside obscured its brilliant color. As she entered the dressing room to change into a lounging robe, Luz heard Drew coming up the stairs. Absently, she listened to his footsteps while she waited for the sound of Trisha's car pulling into the driveway. She was conscious that Drew entered his own room.

They had slept separately for years now, their sleeping habits incompatible. Drew was a light sleeper and Luz was a restless, fitful one, often up at the crack of dawn. During the early years of their marriage, they had put up with the disharmony, but gradually the need for rest took precedence over sex, or more precisely, the quick availability of it. After more than twenty years, it was to be expected that urgent passion would fade, but that didn't signal the end of love, as far as Luz was concerned. So now, they each had their own bedroom with separate bath and dressing room tailored to their own individual wants; Drew's contained exercise equipment and sauna, while her delicate ivory-and-amber bath had Sherle Wagner fixtures and a spa tub.

Luz tied the belt on her red satin Givenchy kimono trimmed in black piping and a zigzag pattern of black lace insets around the full sleeves. Then she sat down at the vanity in the dressing room, its mirror outlined with bare light bulbs. After she had pulled her hair back, she secured it with a clip and began creaming the makeup from her face.

From the sitting room, Drew's voice called, "What about a drink?"

"Please," she answered somewhat absently, not bothering to request a brandy, since that was what she usually had if she drank this late in the evening. The methodical action of wiping the cream from her face seemed to encourage a pensive mood.

Drew walked into the room as she removed the last of the cleanser. "What are you thinking about?" He set a snifter of brandy on the table beside her and glanced at her reflection in the mirror. "You look far away."

"The children." She smiled ruefully. "Although I guess it isn't fair to call them children anymore. They are almost adults."

"That's true." He sipped at his Scotch, one hand tucked in the pocket of his blue smoking jacket. "Where are they, by the way?"

"Rob's home, in his room, I expect. Trisha's still out—who knows where." Luz shrugged and idly picked up the brandy glass, gently swirling it in her hands. "Do you remember when they were always running into our rooms, so anxious to tell us everything they'd done they couldn't wait? When did they stop doing that?"

"About the time they started doing things they didn't think we should know about," he answered wryly.

"They don't really need us anymore, Drew," Luz realized. "They have their own friends, their own lives that have nothing to do with us. I'm beginning to feel superfluous. Like today, when neither of them wanted to have dinner with the family because they had made their own plans. Or Trisha. She *informed* me that she invited someone to the party on Saturday. She didn't even have the courtesy to ask if it was all right."

"I'm afraid I was guilty of that, too," Drew reminded her. "I intended to mention to you that I'd taken one of the party invitations from your desk so I could give it to Miss Baines, but it slipped my mind until she said something about it this afternoon. I thought it would be a good way for her to get acquainted socially with some friends who are also clients. Thanks for not letting on that you didn't know about the invitation. I hope you didn't mind."

"Not at all." She didn't fully understand his reasoning, since the young woman had just recently joined his staff and therefore occupied a very junior position. She couldn't recall Drew's doing this with others, but she accepted his judgment.

"What did you think of her?"

"She is a young and beautiful woman." Luz felt oddly reluctant to voice her impression, and searched for the right noncommittal words. "She seemed friendly and warm. Obviously she's intelligent or she would never have passed the bar."

"Poor Phil certainly hasn't gotten anywhere with her," Drew chuckled, looking pleased. "And it isn't for the lack of trying."

"I noticed she was paying a lot of attention to you." Almost exclusively so, she remembered.

"I am the boss," he reminded her modestly, but he preened slightly. Luz supposed it was flattering to have a young, beautiful woman pay attention to him.

"I don't think that was the only reason. You are a very good-looking man, Drew." She played to his vanity, not unkindly.

He glanced admiringly at his reflection in the lighted mirror. "Not bad for fifty."

"Not bad at all." Smiling, Luz stood up and kissed him on the cheek, but he seemed unmoved by the display of affection as he continued to look at his image.

"Of course, that also makes me old enough to be her father." The regret in his voice made Luz uneasy, especially when he turned away from her. "She's like a breath of fresh air in the office. You wouldn't believe what a change she's made in the short time she's been with us. People are smiling and laughing. The entire atmosphere has improved."

"That's wonderful," she murmured, watching the animation in his expression as he talked about the Baines woman.

"And she absorbs things like a sponge. You saw the way she was at the polo match today, asking endless questions like a curious child. Now I know how a teacher feels when he has an apt pupil in his class, eager to learn everything." He warmed to the subject, carried by his own enthusiasm. "Here's a young mind ready to mold. The challenge, the responsibility of it is incredibly stimulating. She keeps me on my toes all the time, arguing points of law and questioning contract clauses. It reminds me of my law-school days when it was all so exciting and new. I can hardly wait to go to the office in the mornings."

"That's wonderful." Luz wasn't conscious of repeating herself, and Drew didn't appear to notice either.

"I can't believe how reluctant I was to have a female attorney in the firm until I met her." A half-smile lifted one corner of his mouth as he stared into his drink glass. He seemed to catch himself in a musing reverie and briskly lifted his head, taking a deep breath. "Well . . ." He exhaled in a long sigh. "I guess I'll turn in. I've got a heavy schedule at the office tomorrow."

As he turned in the direction of his own rooms, Luz frowned. "Drew?"

"What?" He paused.

"Aren't you going to kiss me good night?" she chided him with a weak laugh.

"Sorry." He stepped back to plant a short kiss on her upturned lips. "I guess my mind was elsewhere. Good night, dear."

"Good night." She knew precisely where his mind had been— on Claudia Baines.

After he'd gone, she sat back down on the cushioned bench, facing the mirror. She was jealous. It was such a new feeling, she didn't know how to cope. It was ridiculous. She had no cause. Granted, Drew was plainly captivated by the brunette, singing her praises and exclaiming over her like a little boy with a new toy, but it was a working relationship. She shouldn't feel that she had to compete with Claudia Baines for Drew's attention.

Luz studied her image in the mirror, remembering the brunette's smooth, youthful skin. She stretched her neck and ran her fingers down its long curve, wondering why she hadn't noticed those faint wrinkle lines before. When she leaned closer to the mirror, her gaze was caught by the creases fanning around her eyes, lines that deepened when she smiled. She opened the jar of moisturizing cream and dabbed some around her eyes, carefully pressing it in with her fingertips. She had never worried about growing old and silently pitied women who endured the excruciating pain of a facelift and the months of numbness afterward, all for the sake of looking younger. She was a mature, attractive woman, poised and confident—or so she'd always thought.

It wasn't fair. Inside, she didn't feel any older than Claudia Baines. And no one ever guessed her true age. Yet tonight, the children, Drew, and the lines in her neck had all combined to remind her she wasn't young anymore. When she hadn't been looking, time had caught up with her. Once she had said forty-two as blithely as she'd said twenty-four. But when she was twenty-four, she had thought forty-two was middle-aged. What a cruel word.

A predawn shower had washed the air clean. It gave a sparkling clarity to the practice field and sharpened the contrast between the high blue sky and rich green of the grass. Despite the rain, the footing was good, in large part because of the perforated pipes underground that drained off excess water or irrigated the field depending on the need.

Luz slow-cantered the dull-brown Thoroughbred toward the white ball sitting near midfield. Dressed in a bisque-colored turtleneck and tan riding slacks, she wore a polo helmet to protect her from a wild-hit ball. As she approached the plastic practice ball, she held her ready position until she was almost on it, then swung the cane mallet. She heard the clunk of contact and felt the vibration from the impact travel through her arm as she completed her follow-through. The white sphere arced through the air. Luz didn't give chase. Rob was coming from the opposite direction to practice a head-on shot. The brown horse snorted its boredom with this stick-and-ball work, preferring the hell-bent-for-leather excitement of a game. She reined the horse in to watch her son position his galloping mount for the shot.

With the ball running toward him, the correct timing of his swing was essential. His arm came down in an arc, his stick an extension of it. The mallet head made contact with the ball and Rob pushed it sideways, the abrupt reversal of direction giving the ball a topspin. He turned his horse to go after the ball. Luz grimly shook her head when she noticed his pony was on the wrong lead, the stride of the outside leg overreaching the inside leg of the turn. Rob made no attempt to correct it. He knocked the ball to the middle of the field where she waited, then rode up to meet her.

"I think that's enough for one morning, Rob," she said as he swung his blowing horse alongside hers.

"Another hour," he stated.

"It's time to call it quits," Luz insisted. "You're making

mental errors. That last cut up the field, your pony was on the wrong lead. That's an amateur's mistake, Rob."

He shifted in the saddle, putting his weight onto the stirrup irons. Leather groaned as he settled back onto the seat. "I must have been concentrating on the ball." He avoided her eyes.

"You've been pushing yourself hard all week. It's time to let up."

"Maybe you're right," he sighed.

"I know I am." She collected the Thoroughbred, making contact with its mouth, and squeezed her legs to urge it forward.

While she loped her mount to the sideline where their soft-spoken handler stood, Rob followed, propelling the ball along with his polo stick. She slowed the horse to a halt near Jimmy Ray and, slipping her wrist free of the strap, passed him the mallet, then dismounted. He took the reins and led the horse out of the way as Rob rode up. Luz pulled off the helmet and shook her hair free. Her cream-white Mercedes convertible was parked on the grass not far away.

"I have to get back to the house and help Emma with the party arrangements." She peeled off her gloves and tucked them inside the helmet under her arm, glancing at Rob as he swung off his horse.

"Can you wait a minute, Luz? I need to talk to you about something." He turned and held out the horse's reins to Jimmy Ray. "Take them to the stable and cool them out."

Luz waited until the handler had led both horses away. "What about?" She studied Rob's expression, guessing the subject must be serious.

"Dad's been pressuring me to make a decision about which college I want to attend."

"I know graduation seems months away right now, but you really don't have much time to make up your mind," Luz said in her husband's support.

"But that's just it. I've already made up my mind. I don't want to start college this fall." He spoke quickly, before she could voice the protest forming on her lips. "I want to sit out a year."

"Rob, I don't know." She doubted that Drew would agree to it. "What would you do?"

"I want to concentrate on polo—not just play in a tournament here and there, but do it full-time. I want to find out how good I can be," he argued earnestly.

"He has his heart set on your attending college." Luz could hear the arguments in her head. "There are any number of universities with fine polo programs—Virginia, where I went, or USC, Cornell. You could do both."

"No." He stared at the whip he twisted in his hands. "You know what it's like for me in school now. I have to study all the time just to get passing grades. If I have to attend college and play polo at the same time, I won't do well at either of them. It's one or the other. It can't be both. You know that."

"Yes." She sympathized with him. School had never been easy for her either. But he needed the education, certainly more than she had. Her heart went out to her grave young son, and the sharply poignant plea of his eyes moved her.

"Talk to him, Luz. Make him understand," he urged.

"I don't know how much good I can do." She had an urge to suggest that he'd have a better chance if he enlisted Claudia Baines to plead his case with Drew. A half-dozen times this week, Drew had made some glowing comment about the young woman, and Luz had become highly sensitive to the mere mention of her name.

"All I'm asking is to sit out college for a year. A lot of guys do that," Rob argued.

"I can't promise anything, but I'll talk to him," Luz agreed.

"When?"

"After the party tomorrow night. There's too much going on right now." She didn't know when she could fit in the time for the long discussion this would entail.

"After?" Rob looked disappointed.

"Yes. Why?"

"I was thinking that I'd leave Saturday to head back to school," he told her.

"But I thought you were going back on Sunday?"

"I was, but why wait? What difference does it make if I leave a day early?" His shoulders lifted in a resigned shrug.

The difference was having him home one more day. "I wish you'd wait, but if you've decided, I suppose it's all right."

"What about Dad and college this fall?"

"Maybe it's just as well that you aren't here when I talk to him about that." It wasn't that she feared an explosion. Drew never lost his temper in an argument, but he could destroy a person with his logic. Rob didn't face up to his father well, always withdrawing into those silences that invariably lost him whatever points he'd made. Luz examined his soberly drawn face, wishing he didn't take everything to heart so. Nothing was the end of the world. "Do you have any more surprises to lay on me?"

"No. That's all for now." A troubled agitation seemed to stir him as he glanced over his shoulder. "I gotta go to the stable. I need to see Jimmy Ray about something."

"Want a ride? My car's right here."

"No thanks. I want to be by myself for a while." His glance skipped off her in a mute apology for rejecting her company.

"Well, I have an appointment with the caterers at eleven, so I'd better run. I'll see you later at the house."

"Sure." He was already turning away from her.

Frowning slightly, Luz watched him walk toward the barns, his polo helmet dangling from his hand by its chinstrap. He was such a brooding figure. Yet a couple of times this past week he'd come to the house in such high spirits, laughing and cutting up with Trisha. Rob was so mercurial in his moods— high and low, and very little in between. After a troubled shake of her head, Luz walked to the car and tossed her helmet and gloves in the rear seat of the convertible.

The French doors in the dining and living rooms were thrown open to the spacious rear patio, surrounded by hanging greenery and potted plants and lighted by blazing torches set at intervals. A small band occupied the far corner of the patio, where an area had been cleared of the colorfully cushioned white wicker patio furniture so that couples could dance. An up-tempo song drifted above the hum of the laughing, talking voices, with more guests arriving all the time. While the torch flames danced in the tropically mild winter night, Luz wandered inside the house to circulate and greet the latest arrivals.

The coffered, mirrored ceiling in the dining room reflected the sumptuous buffet set up for the party guests. Instead of the usual boring fare of dainty canapés, cheap caviar, and fruit and fondue dips, Luz had opted for a menu that included scandalously tasty finger ribs and crispy fried chicken. She loved the sight of diamond-bedecked women licking their sticky fingers.

It created a wonderfully informal atmosphere, breaking down barriers and letting people be themselves. Bound for so long by the constraints of family expectations and pressures herself, she enjoyed the informality as well.

The lively sway of her dangling earrings, each a large pearl suspended on a long black bead, seemed to match her personality, bold and outgoing. The crystal-pleated two-piece lounger was comfortable yet dramatic in its use of black and white, slightly puffed shoulders, and wide, full sleeves. She wore her hair in a sleek uplifted wave away from her face, its length secured atop her head in a smooth coil. The simplicity of style and color exuded elegance.

She paused in the doorway to the living room and skimmed the crowd with a glance. There was a constant ebb and flow of guests around the fully equipped wet bar, strategically positioned near the French doors to the patio. Luz noticed Trisha hovering near the front entrance hall, obviously still waiting for her guest to arrive.

"There you are, Luz." The woman's voice came from behind her, and she turned.

"Connie!" she declared in delighted recognition of her chubby friend, who was delicately sucking barbecue sauce from her fingers while holding a tray full of food in her other hand. "How long have you been here?"

"Long enough to know I'm going to fill some doggie bags before I go home." The dark-haired woman unabashedly admitted her love of food, and the proof of it was the way she was packed into her red dress. "Speaking of food . . ." She lowered her voice to a conspiratorial level. "Have you seen Veronica Hampton? She and George came only a few minutes ago."

"I was outside." Her glance searched the crowded room for the newcomers.

"Over by the bar." Connie Davenport directed her gaze to the tall, painfully thin woman in pink. "She's been on that new diet. Isn't she pathetic? She's nothing but a sack of bones."

"I believe that's called 'stylishly anorexic,'" Luz murmured.

"Whatever it is, I'll never know." Connie laughed.

"Neither will a lot of us," Luz agreed, although she had never had a weight problem. Between horseback riding and other outdoor activities, she had managed to keep a trim figure.

"Where's Rob? I haven't seen him yet."

"He left for school. Trisha goes back tomorrow. It's going to be very quiet around here with both of them gone. I probably won't know what to do with myself," she admitted ruefully.

"You should be used to that by now."

"What makes it worse this year is having Jake gone, too. Late winter's the time my father and I usually spent together in Virginia arguing bloodlines, and which mare to breed to which stallion, or checking out the crop of two-year-olds for polo prospects. I'll miss that."

"You could still go there. By yourself, I mean," Connie suggested. "I know it wouldn't be the same, but it would be better than doing nothing."

"Maybe." She shrugged a shoulder. "I know Audra has been talking about closing the house there. I think she has decided to live year-round here in Florida. If she does, maybe I could go back and supervise the closing for her—and have a last look around my childhood haunts." It was a possibility to consider, but hardly important now. "We'll see."

"Either way, with the kids gone, you'll have that much more time to spend with Drew without having them underfoot."

"Unfortunately his law practice keeps him very busy." He left early in the morning and she usually didn't see him until dinner that night, which was generally late.

"Isn't that always the case? Successful businessmen equals idle wives, filling their time with charity benefits and fund-raising bazaars. If you look around this room, every worthy cause is represented by someone here."

"Don't sound so cynical, Connie. It's the least we can do for the community. Besides, if we didn't, who would?" Luz chided, having chaired several such benefit committees herself.

"Don't mind me," Connie sighed. "I just get bored with it all from time to time." She picked up a chicken leg from her plate and nibbled on the crunchy coating, lifting the plate closer to her chin to catch the crumbs. "By the way, who's that brunette with Drew?"

"Claudia Baines." Luz had spoken briefly to her when she arrived, before Drew had taken charge of her to introduce her to their other guests. They were talking to another couple, blocked from her view, in the living room. She noticed that Drew had his arm around the woman's shoulders, drawing her close to his side. She glanced quickly away, fighting the coiling tightness in her stomach. "She's a new lawyer with the firm."

"He certainly is paying her a lot of attention." Connie raised an eyebrow in silent speculation.

"She's a protégée of Drew's."

"Is she the reason he's been so busy lately?"

Luz's fingernails curled into her palms as she made a good show of laughing off the question. "Don't be silly, Connie. She's young enough to be his daughter."

"That's the most dangerous kind, Luz." The knowing tone of her voice reminded Luz that Connie's husband was notoriously unfaithful.

She felt suddenly uncomfortable, slightly sick to her stomach and cold. She could understand why Connie would think that way. Her own experience would encourage her to see something sordid in the situation. But it was truly ridiculous. Drew wasn't that type. But, God, she wished he'd take his arm away from her shoulders, Luz thought frantically. The contact intimated something more personal. If Connie thought that, others might, too.

"I know Drew," she insisted to Connie. "I'm not worried." Someone walked into the living room from the entrance hall. Luz was grateful for any distraction that would extricate her, and relieved that it was her sister. "Excuse me, Connie. Mary just arrived."

With long, quick strides, Luz crossed the room, the voluminous pleated black material of her pants swinging about her legs. She intercepted Mary before she had gotten very far into the room.

"I see you finally made it." They exchanged sisterly pecks on the cheek.

"No lectures on punctuality, please. It was Murphy's Law— or the Carpenter version of the same. Everything that could go wrong, did. Anne cut herself on a broken glass as we were walking out the door; Ross forgot to put gas in the car; we had a flat tire and no spare; you name it, it happened."

"Where's Ross?" Luz glanced back to the entrance hall.

"He went to wash up. After we finally got the tire fixed, he wanted to go home and change clothes, but I said absolutely not!"

She laughed and hooked an arm around her sister's. "This way to the bar."

"I'll drink to that," Mary declared.

Their path took them past Drew. He hailed them as they walked by. "Mary! We'd just about given you up. You remember Claudia, don't you?" The affectionate squeeze of his arm pulled the brunette slightly off balance, and she leaned against him.

Unconsciously, Luz tightened her jaw, clamping her teeth together. Claudia, was it? Now they were on a first-name basis. Instantly, she justified it. After all, this was a party, hardly the place to stand on formality. Distantly, she heard the brief exchange between Mary and the Baines woman.

"I hope you're enjoying yourself . . . Claudia." The name momentarily stuck in her throat as Luz attempted to be more magnanimous.

"Yes. Drew is keeping me entertained," she answered, smiling at him.

"We've been swapping stories," he said. "Did I ever tell you about these two men who split up after living together for years? They each hired an attorney—one of them was me, naturally—to resolve the problem of dividing the possessions they had acquired . . . house, car, savings account. Well, they had this dog—"

"Excuse me." Luz backed away and pulled Mary with her. "But I've heard this one before."

Drew acknowledged her departure with a lift of his fingers and picked up the story with hardly a break. Luz and Mary proceeded toward the bar, winding their way through the thickening crowd. Behind them, they heard a burst of laughter.

"Drew must have reached the punchline of his story," Mary remarked dryly.

"It's strange. I must have heard him tell that a hundred times or more." Luz paused to look back at the pair, focusing on Claudia's laughing expression. "I don't ever remember it being that funny."

"She looks at him as if he makes the sun rise in the morning," her sister mused, then sighed. "I hope Ross doesn't go through the middle-aged crazies."

Luz didn't like the suggestion that Drew was suffering from the malady and wished people would stop planting these seeds of doubt. She had no cause to be jealous, but it was like an acid eating away at her.

"It looks like the party is in full swing on the patio." Mary gazed outside, observing that group's spirited exuberance. "Would you like to bet one of them brought his own sugar bowl?"

"No. Someone invariably brings coke to parties." It was impossible to prevent even if she tried. Luz turned away from the sight. Drugs didn't interest her, although she had friends—acquaintances, really—who sniffed cocaine on occasions. Supposedly, it wasn't physically addictive, but she'd seen the emotional dependence that developed and considered that just as destructive. As a young adult, she had smoked marijuana, more as an act of rebellion than any other reason. Once she had lit a joint in front of her father—that was during her father-hating days. When he had failed to be shocked or outraged, she had lost interest. But drugs were too easily attainable now, and she worried about the children, especially Trisha, who was just wild and adventurous enough to try anything. And there seemed so little she could do about it.

# CHAPTER IV

By nine o'clock, Trisha was forced to concede that Raul wasn't coming. A dozen times during this past week, she had considered seeking him out and confirming the invitation, even going so far as to find out where he was staying and where his horses were stabled, but she hadn't done it. She supposed it was some kind of test of her feminine powers to see if he'd come without further persuasion. He hadn't come, but neither had she given up.

She slipped away to her room, where she had her own private telephone line, and dialed the polo club's office on the off chance someone would still be there. His telephone number would be in the files. She listened to the ringing on the other end of the line, then—miracle of miracles—someone answered.

"I'm trying to locate Raul Buchanan. Can you tell me where he might be or how I can reach him?" Trisha attempted to sound very businesslike.

"As a matter of fact, I just saw him at the barns," the voice drawled thickly. "Got an injured mare."

"Thank you." Trisha didn't wait for any more information but quickly hung up the receiver. There wasn't time to waste.

No one noticed her pass through the living and dining rooms to the kitchen, and the caterers were too busy to pay any attention to her when she appropriated a bottle of cold champagne and two glasses, then left the house by the back door. The palm trees and shrubbery shielded her from the view of the guests outside as she made her way to the garage where her sports car was parked. Her only difficulty was negotiating the jam of vehicles parked in the driveway. After that, it was a quick drive to the polo grounds.

There were lights and two silhouetted figures moving near the middle of the long stable. Trisha parked her car in the area reserved for vehicles and gathered up the champagne and glasses from the seat. The moonlight glistened on the antique ivory satin of her dress as she picked her way across the uneven footing of crushed shells in her high-heeled sandals. Then she reached the firmly worn path leading down the stable row. A dog barked, far away. Closer, Trisha could hear the low murmur of voices speaking in some fluid tongue. Spanish, she thought, but she still couldn't tell if either of the two men was Raul. She was nearly upon them before she finally recognized him.

"Hello." Her heels had made little sound on the hard-packed ground.

He pivoted with a frown at her greeting. The frown deepened when he saw her standing there. "What are you doing here?"

Trisha raised her hands to show him the champagne bottle in one and the glasses in the other. "Since you didn't come to the party, I brought the party to you." But he was neither amused nor pleased by her announcement. He swung back to face the webbed gate stretched across the stall's doorway. Beyond him, she could see a black horse and an attending groom crouched near its front legs. Trisha moved closer. "What's wrong?" The right foreleg was packed in ice.

"The mare fell this afternoon," Raul said. "We thought it was a badly sprained knee, but the swelling has grown worse. The veterinarian is coming out to take another look. It is possible there is a small fracture."

"Poor lady." The bottle clunked against the glasses as Trisha switched it to her other hand so she could rub the horse's muzzle. The dullness of the dark eyes and the low-hanging head were evidence of the mare's pain.

"Careful. You will ruin your dress," Raul cautioned.

"How do you like it?" She posed slightly for him, aware the high neck and leg-of-mutton sleeves gave a touch of sophistication while the back exposed a large triangular area of bare skin. "Now, you have to admit that I hardly look like a schoolgirl in this. Tell me the truth, Raul—if I had been wearing this when we met, would you still have thought I was too young?"

A wide smile split his lips apart. "Perhaps not."

"You see? I had to come tonight to prove your first impression of me was wrong," Trisha stated.

He said something in Spanish to the groom, then cupped her elbow in his hand and guided her away from the stall. The stable roof extended into a wide galleried walk in front of the stalls, supported at intervals by upright posts. They moved several feet into the shadowed half-light of the overhang before Raul stopped near a hitch rail.

Trisha held out the bottle of champagne to him. "Aren't you going to open it before it gets warm?"

He glanced at her in a momentary hesitation, seeming to debate something, then he took the bottle and peeled away the seal. She watched him gently and expertly ease out the cork.

"If the mare hadn't been injured, would you have come to the party?" She held the glasses ready.

"No." A small pop punctuated his reply, but the cork didn't explode into the air. Trisha was quick to hold a glass under the mouth and catch the foaming wine when it bubbled out, never losing a drop.

"Honesty in a man. How rare." She held the second glass for Raul to fill, then handed it to him.

He inspected the tulip-shaped glass. "I see you know how to serve champagne properly." The wide, shallow glasses commonly called champagne glasses released the wine's effervescence too quickly, leaving it flat.

"I'm a Kincaid. My education in life's finer points is nonpareil," she mocked and sipped at the sparkling wine, fizzing so softly in the glass.

"Why did you use that tone?" He cocked his head to the side, the slant of the moonlight throwing his strongly cut features into sharp relief.

Trisha shrugged a shoulder, trying to pretend an indifference. "I think I'm a disappointment to the family. I'm afraid I'm more Thomas than I am Kincaid." But she hadn't come here to discuss family allegiance. "Couples always dance at parties. This is supposed to be a party. Aren't you going to ask me to dance?"

"We have no music."

"Then we'll have to make our own." She curved the hand with the wineglass on his shoulder and held up the other for him to take. There was that momentary hesitation again, that weighing of some decision, before he circled an arm around her waist and rested his hand against hers, the wineglass still in it. His feet moved, his legs brushing against her skirt as they moved to some slow, soundless rhythm. She liked the pressure of his hand on her back and the sensation of being so close to him. "Tell me about yourself, Raul. Where are you from? What do you do?"

"I play polo." The lightness of his blue eyes gave them an intensity, their black centers large in the dim light. Trisha was fascinated by them, and the firm line of his mouth. "And I teach others to play. I have some land outside Buenos Aires where I raise and train polo ponies. Polo is what I do."

"Are you married?" She sipped at the champagne, watching him through the tops of her lashes.

"No." A wry humor flickered briefly across his expression.

"Have you ever been married?"

"No."

"Why?" Trisha asked challengingly. "Haven't you ever found the right girl?"

"I suppose not."

"Would you like to marry someday?"

His mouth curved. "You would not like being married to me. I am Latin. I believe a woman's place is in the home. And I am seldom there."

"Always supposing I was interested."

"Always supposing," he agreed dryly.

"What about your family?" she wondered.

"My mother is dead. My father left when I was small. I have no other close relatives."

"Your name—Buchanan—are you half English?"

"No. I am Argentine." She heard the pride in his voice. "My country was a melting pot of nationalities, like the United States. You can open a Buenos Aires phone book and find any number of names like Buchanan, Gonzales, Zimmerman, or Caruso. The Spanish, the Italians, the English, the French, the Germans, and countless others, all came."

"I didn't realize that." She had always supposed it was predominantly Spanish, like Mexico.

"Then you have learned a valuable history lesson to file away with your schoolbooks." He halted the aimless shifting of their feet. "The music has stopped playing. The dance is over." He backed away from her, angling his body to the side. The abruptness of his action took Trisha by surprise. "I'll walk you to your car."

"But we've hardly drunk any of the champagne." The nearly full bottle was sitting on the ground by a post.

"I do not care for any more. You can take the rest home with you." He regarded her steadily, his manner polite but firm.

By then, it would be warm and flat—and so would the evening. "There's no need for me to leave yet."

"Yes, there is." Raul lightly took her arm and drew her abreast of him to start down the galleried walk. "Dr. Carlyle will be here any minute to examine the mare. I will be tied up with him for a considerable time."

"That doesn't matter. I can wait until you're finished."

"No."

It was impossible to protest any further without sounding childish, so Trisha walked with him in silence half the distance to the corner of the stable. "I'm leaving tomorrow," she finally said.

"And I am leaving the day after, so it is not likely we will meet again in the near future."

"Why are you so determined to get rid of me?" she blurted.

"I am trying to spare us both from a possibly awkward and embarrassing situation." He spoke patiently, as one would to a child. "It may surprise you to learn that I have been on the receiving end of teenage crushes before."

"What do I have to do to convince you I'm not a schoolgirl?" An exasperated sigh escaped her. "I'm attracted to you. What's so adolescent about that?"

"Nothing," he replied calmly. "Lolita was a schoolgirl."

"Damn you," she swore in frustration.

"Yes," he murmured and steadied her when she nearly turned an ankle on the crushed shells. As they approached the parking area, Raul glanced ahead and picked out her sports car, an easy choice since the few other vehicles were pickup trucks or older sedans. He walked her to the driver's side and stopped. "Your glass." He offered it to her stem up.

"Thank you." She took it, avoiding eye contact and thinking angrily that he probably thought she was a spoiled rich kid sulking because she didn't get her way. Which was very nearly the truth.

"Good night, Trisha."

It was the first time he'd used her name, the first time he'd indicated that she was a person, not a troublesome adolescent. Trisha suddenly had hope that something could be salvaged from this fiasco.

"Wait." Confidently she placed a hand on his arm to detain him. He paused expectantly. "Isn't it customary for a man to kiss a girl good night after he's walked her to her car?"

In the darkness and shadows, his hair appeared more black than umber brown. Trisha caught the small, impatient movement of his head.

A second later, he curved his hand along the side of her neck, fingers sliding into the edges of her chestnut hair, a thumb resting against her jaw. As he bent his head toward her, his face filled her vision. She anticipated the warm pressure of his mouth, her pulse increasing its tempo. When it came, Trisha leaned into him, but it was the gently sweet kiss a man gives a schoolgirl. Frustration sparked her temper, and she pulled away from him.

"Raul, I'm not a virgin!" She curled her hands around his neck to force his head down while she stood on tiptoe to reach it. Ignoring his resistant stiffening, she opened her mouth to devour his lips with demanding passion. She pressed her body against his solid length, stimulated by the feel of his strong thighs against her legs. The taste of him was stimulating, and he wasn't completely indifferent to her. There was an almost instinctive return of her mouth's hungry pressure.

Then his hands were gripping her forearms and forcing them down. When he set her away from him, her pulse was racing and her breath was coming shallow and fast. Aroused, she gazed at him with longing.

"I wish you had been the first," she said softly.

"That is enough. Spare me from your seduction." He glowered at her, no longer showing a bland tolerance for her behavior. This time Raul opened the car door and ushered her into the driver's seat.

"We'll meet again," Trisha told him as he closed the car door.

He paused, leaning on the doorframe. "Somehow I do not

doubt that," he admitted with a degree of resignation, then pushed away from the car.

"When we do, I'll be older," Trisha warned.

There was no response. He turned his back on her as he walked back toward the stable. For a long time she sat motionless in the car, watching his retreating figure as the darkness swallowed it up. Her flesh still tingled with the sensation of his hard, muscled body, and her lips with the feel of his mouth. She could taste him yet.

She had meant it when she said that she wished Raul had been the first man to make love to her. Maybe the experience wouldn't have been so humiliating and degrading. She remembered lying on that blanket in the woods, waiting for the boy to finish shedding his clothes. She'd been frightened—Trisha Kincaid Thomas, frightened—from the uncertainty of what to do and what to expect.

Max was supposed to know. He'd had sex plenty of times before—to hear him tell it. She remembered the kissing, the nuzzling, the touching, all the prelude to the moment when he wedged himself between her legs. Everything went wrong from there. He hadn't been able to get it in, and she hadn't known how to go about helping. All that hard jabbing and prodding.

"Push, dammit." That's what he had said to her.

Then she'd felt the first pain and had tried to pull away from it, but his hands had held her fast and the ground would not give. After that, it all became lost in the agony of searing pain and the slamming of his hips pounding into her and the disgusting sound of his groans.

That had been the last time she went out with Max. Since then, there had been two other boys who had managed to show her there was some pleasure to be derived from sex. Now Trisha found herself wondering what it would be like for Raul to hold her—for him to kiss her breasts and caress her body—the weight of him settling onto her. The thought aroused a quivering ache between her thighs.

Sighing, Trisha turned the key in the ignition, and the motor rumbled to life. As she reversed the small car out of the parking space, she saw the headlights of an approaching car. She supposed it was the veterinarian Raul was expecting. Once on the road, she floored the accelerator, sending the car shooting forward.

* * *

By two o'clock in the morning, the last of the guests had departed. The caterers had cleared away most of the debris. Luz supervised the replacement of the furniture with efficiency, but inside she was tight and angry.

Drew wandered into the living room as she directed two of the hired staff who were moving the striped companion chair. "Turn it more to the left."

"Where's Trisha? Has she gone to bed already? I've hardly seen her all evening."

Luz was surprised he'd noticed their daughter's absence at all. He'd hardly left Claudia Baines's side for more than two minutes all evening. She'd had to watch them laughing and talking together all night, dancing close together, or Drew's arm so familiarly draped around her shoulders. Then she'd had to stand silently by while he kissed her good night at the door. It all left her cold with rage.

"Her date stood her up, so she's been in her room most of the evening," she replied stiffly.

"She should be out here helping you."

"I believe she's finishing her packing."

"Oh." He tiredly rubbed the back of his neck. "I could use some coffee. Is there any left?"

"Check in the kitchen." Luz wasn't about to fetch it for him.

A faintly puzzled frown creased his forehead at her crisp response, but he said nothing. Out of the corner of her eye, she saw him walk toward the kitchen. With the placement of a lampstand, the living room was put back in order. A vacuum cleaner hummed in the dining room. To Luz's inspecting eye, there appeared little left for the catering staff to do, except finish loading their equipment into the van.

"I managed to save the last of the coffee before they poured it down the drain." Drew returned, carrying a cup and saucer in each hand. "I brought you a cup."

"I don't care for any." She crossed to the French doors and closed them, checking to make sure they were securely latched.

"Emma said to tell you the kitchen has been cleaned."

"Good." Her head was throbbing with tension. She didn't think she could take another minute of this without screaming.

"In that case, you can stay down here and lock up after the caterers leave. I'm tired. I'm going upstairs."

She left him standing in the middle of the room, staring after her. When she reached her dressing room, she stripped off the two-piece lounger. For once she didn't take the trouble to hang up her clothes but left the crushable pleated outfit in a pile on the floor, adding her black stockings and flesh-colored lingerie to the heap. Her necklace and earrings she dropped on the vanity table. She pulled a narrow-strapped nightgown of green silk over her head and paused long enough in front of the lighted mirror to pull the pins out of her hair, but she didn't bother to remove her makeup. The agitation that pulsed within her was too strong.

Before leaving the dressing room, Luz grabbed her hairbrush. She ran it through her hair as she walked into the bedroom to sit on the edge of the satin-quilted bed. With hard, brisk strokes, she raked the bristles through her hair until her scalp tingled with pain, as if she needed the physical discomfort to alleviate her inner torment.

She could hear the distant murmur of voices coming from downstairs. A door closed. Then she was able to distinguish Drew's voice when he wished Emma a good night. She held the hairbrush in her lap until she sensed Drew's presence in the sitting room. Her door stood open, and she knew he could see her sitting there.

"Everything's all locked up." He leaned a shoulder against the doorframe, bending one leg.

"Good." Luz continued brushing her hair.

He stirred, entering her room. It took all her control not to throw the brush at him. "It was an excellent party. You outdid yourself, as usual."

"I'm surprised you noticed." She tried to suppress the cattiness in her voice, but didn't succeed.

"What does that mean?" A confused laugh broke from him.

Unable to sit still, Luz stood up and paced restlessly away from the bed. "How can you ask?" The anger simmered just below the surface.

"Because I want to know what you're talking about."

"How can you stand there and say that after the way you behaved all evening?" She turned on him.

"What did I do?" He lifted his hands in a gesture of confusion.

She didn't want to put it into words, but she couldn't stand his innocent attitude. "You didn't take your eyes off that Baines woman all evening."

"What?" Drew laughed with incredulous amusement.

"Everyone noticed. It was so humiliating to have people watch me and whisper behind their hands, wondering whether I saw what was going on. You monopolized her the whole time and ignored all the rest of our guests."

"Luz, that simply isn't true. Yes, I was with her. What did you expect me to do? She didn't know a soul at the party. I couldn't very well let her stand around by herself. As the host, I felt it was my duty to take her around and meet the other guests, so I did circulate. As a matter of fact, I think we talked to everyone there."

"Your duty," she said icily. "And what arduous duty it was, I suppose. I'm sure you had to force yourself to laugh and smile all that time."

"I'm not going to deny that I enjoyed being with her." There was a slow, patient shake of his head, his smile warm and indulgent. His calmness only increased her frustration and anger. "She made me feel young."

"Then what do I make you feel? Old?" Luz stalked back to the bed and sat down again.

"Of course not. I was only trying to say that she was fun to be with."

"And was it *fun* kissing her good night?" She dragged the brush through her hair once, then clutched it between her hands to stare at the bristles.

"I don't believe this," Drew murmured. "Luz, I kissed practically every woman goodbye when she left." She bit at the inside of her lip, realizing that was true. He walked over to the bed and sat down beside her, bending his head to peer at her face. "I believe you're jealous."

"Wouldn't you be? Everyone was making sly remarks." She flashed him an accusing look. It had all been bottled up inside too long for her to get over the hurt so quickly—imaginary or not.

"I regret that. I'm sorry." He gazed at her with contrite

affection, yet it was his handsome looks Luz saw—that artful silvering at the temples and the deep cleft in his chin.

Again, the brush absorbed her attention. "Maybe you've had other women since we've been married. I don't know. Infidelity seems to be a male characteristic. But don't ever flaunt an affair in front of me, Drew. I won't stand for it." She felt she had to say that so that there would be no doubt in his mind.

His hand cupped the side of her jaw, the pressure of his thumb lifting her chin to force her to look at him. "How could there be another woman? After all this time, don't you know how much I love you?"

She softened under his intent regard, the corners of her mouth deepening in a whisper of a smile. "It might take some convincing."

He leaned toward her and covered her lips in a kiss that grew steadily stronger. Luz relaxed against him, tilting her head farther back to invite more ardent pressure. He obliged for several satisfying seconds before slowly ending the kiss. She opened her eyes to see his heavy-lidded glance follow the trail of his hand as it slid down her neck to finger the string straps of her gown.

"It's been a long time since I undressed you," he murmured, and he gently pushed the strap on one side, then the other, off her shoulder.

A tremor of excitement quivered through her. It deepened into a wonderful shudder when his hand slipped underneath the lace bodice, cupping her right breast in his palm. Her nipple hardened to a nub in its center. The invasion of his hand forced the material downward, and Luz pressed her arms close to her side to let the straps fall the rest of the way, then slipped free of them.

With the gown loose about her waist, Drew hooked an arm behind her to lift her back until she was lying crosswise on the king-sized bed. The action pulled the gown lower until it was resting on her hips. After that, a single movement of his hand drew it away from her body, the satin gown gliding over the satin quilt to land on the floor.

Drew stepped back to admire her naked figure, lingering over her high, rounded breasts, and her parted legs, while he unbuttoned his shirt and stripped off his clothes. His slow study of her body made Luz feel hot all over, and aroused. When he moved onto the bed to lie beside her, his muscled body so trim and tan, she watched him in anticipation. His hand stroked her, traveling over the tips of her breasts to the pale, curling hairs on her pubic bone.

"You're beautiful." He nuzzled her lips as she reached to hold him and feel his warm flesh.

With his hands, his lips, and his body, he worshiped her. It was a wild and heady sensation that made her body hum with need. This intensity of passion was almost a forgotten thing. Yet there was no haste about it. They spent time savoring and enjoying the delight they found in each other. When the coupling came, it was a sweet and fiery culmination that left them both happily drained.

Afterward, Luz lay stretched at full length on the bed, smiling in blissful contentment, the thin sheet drawn across her breasts and an arm flung above her head on the pillow. Drew was beside her, his head cradled on his own pillow. She knew he wasn't sleeping; he was just lying there, as she was, still warmed by the glow of their lovemaking. She turned her head to look at him, staring at the ceiling, his expression lazy and pleased.

"That was wonderful," she murmured, but it had been more than that. Leaning over, using her elbow for a pivot, Luz kissed the curved point of his shoulder. "It was the best sex we've had since our honeymoon."

He quirked an eyebrow. "That isn't saying much for all the years in between."

She laughed. "That isn't what I meant."

His arm circled her waist and pulled her across his body to lie on his other side. "Then you'd better explain yourself, woman," he ordered with mock menace.

This playing reinforced her feelings. "It all seems so new and exciting. It was like—discovering each other all over again." She could feel the light of reborn love inside her, glowing brightly. Her fingers threaded into his chest hairs as she snuggled closer to him. "I guess I feel like a bride."

"You'll always be my bride." He pressed a warm kiss on top of her head, now pillowed on his shoulder.

"What time do you think it is?" she wondered.

"Don't ask." His chest lifted with a warning chuckle that vibrated into her. "It was going on three when I came upstairs."

Luz craned her head around so that she could see the digital clock on her nightstand. "It's almost four." Drew groaned. "Let's stay up and watch the sunrise."

"Are you serious?"

"Yes, I am." She playfully pulled at the hairs on his chest. "I'll go make some fresh coffee and we can drink it outside on the deck."

"Luz, I don't think the sun comes up until sometime after six. Do you know how tired we're going to be?"

"Are you tired?" She sat up, looking back at him.

"Not right now," Drew conceded.

"Then get out of bed, lazybones." She pushed him toward the side. "Let's go." He caught at her hands, and they wrestled for a few minutes in fun until Luz escaped his clutches and scampered out of bed. Drew immediately settled back against the pillows, folding his hands under his head to watch her slip on the red kimono. "You'd better be out of there when I come back upstairs with the tray," she warned. "Or you're going to find yourself having coffee and orange juice in bed—and I don't mean in a cup." He smiled, unconcerned.

But when she returned with the tray laden with coffee, orange juice, and a basket of Danish rolls, the bed was empty. The French doors to their private balcony were ajar, and Luz found him outside, his hair damp from a shower and his face freshly shaven.

"Rolls." He spied them first. "How did you know I was hungry?"

"You always are after you exercise." She set the breakfast tray on the glass-topped wrought-iron table and tried to remember the last time she had engaged in such wordplay, infusing ordinary words with intimate meanings. Romance seemed to have reentered their marriage. The night air touched her. "It's cool." She shivered slightly as she poured their orange juice and coffee.

"Come here." When she brought the coffee, Drew wrapped an arm around her and cuddled her to the warmth of his body. It made drinking awkward, but the compensations more than made up for it.

An hour later, they lay crowded together, sharing the lounge chair. A double-knitted afghan was bunched high around their necks to keep out the predawn chill. The pearly horizon showed its first shadings of pink in the east.

"Are you awake?" Luz stirred, glancing upward to see if his eyes were still open.

"Mmm." She supposed that answer was affirmative.

"Before he left, Rob asked me to talk to you about something." Luz doubted if she'd find Drew in a more responsive mood.

"What?" It was a drowsily worded question.

"It's about college. He wants to wait a year."

"What? Why?" He was fully awake.

"He says he wants to concentrate on improving his polo game, but I don't think that's the whole reason."

"And what do you think is?"

Luz shifted onto her side to watch his face while she argued Rob's cause. With the tip of her finger, she traced the deep pit in his chin. "You know what a tough time Rob has with school. He's had to study hard the last four years to keep his grades high enough to meet college requirements. I think he just wants a break from the pressure."

"I don't like the idea at all."

"I didn't think you would."

"And you approve, I suppose."

"I understand." Luz emphasized the difference, tapping him lightly on the lips. "What he's asking isn't so unusual. There are any number who sit out a year on the pretext of touring Europe or some such thing."

"That's true."

"So? What should I tell Rob?" She ran her finger around the corner of his mouth.

"You don't want to insist that he start college this fall, do you?" Drew held her gaze.

"No."

"I can hardly argue against both of you, can I?" He smiled wryly.

"Drew." His easy capitulation after so little argument stunned her. She tunneled her fingers into the hair at the back of his neck and pulled his head down so she could kiss him. It turned into a long one, with a breath of the magic they'd shared in the bedroom. "I love you." She sighed when it was over.

"Guess what?"

"What?" Luz smiled, expecting him to return the phrase.

"You're missing your sunrise."

She turned to see the golden arc of light crowning the horizon. It was the birth of a new day—a new love, a new rapport. This is what they'd done on their honeymoon night, stayed up to watch the sunrise, a symbolic way to start their new life together. Luz wondered if Drew remembered. She hugged his arms more tightly around her middle and settled back to watch the sun climb into the sky.

# CHAPTER V

Sunlight glistened on the smooth surface of the swimming pool; the pool's blue bottom matched the sky. Luz adjusted the brace on the chaise longue to a more comfortable angle, then leaned back against the colorful plastic webbing. A wide-brimmed white hat protected her hair from the sun, but the strapless multicolored swimsuit exposed much of her oiled flesh to its tanning rays. Mary reclined in the chair flanking hers, close enough so talking wouldn't be an effort while they concentrated on soaking up the sun.

"I can't believe how angry I was that night." Luz had her eyes closed behind the dark sunglasses and she talked without turning her head. "I hated Claudia so much I could have cheerfully clawed her eyes out."

"I believe that."

"I had no reason. I felt so foolish afterward. I never should have doubted Drew, but I'm glad I did."

"That's a strange thing to say," Mary declared.

"Not really. If I hadn't told him all my nasty suspicions, none of the rest of this would have happened. These last two weeks have been like a honeymoon." She smiled. "Honestly, I think I'm falling in love with Drew all over again. After twenty years, a lot of the spark was gone. We'd taken each other for granted too long, dwelt more on the failings and faults, let the little things irritate us."

"I know what you mean. It drives me crazy to listen to Ross's jaw pop when he chews. And Lord knows, he does a lot of eating."

"I've noticed."

"So what about Claudia? Is she still around?"

"Of course. Drew still talks about her frequently, but it doesn't bother me anymore." When Luz attempted to shrug her shoulders, her skin stuck to the plastic webbing. "I'm starting to perspire. Maybe it's time we moved to the shade."

"Not yet." There was a pause before Mary added, "I'm glad you and Drew are spending more time together. For a while there, you hardly saw him at all."

"I still don't see that much of him. Things haven't slowed down any at the office."

"And you call it a honeymoon?"

"I didn't mean it literally." Luz smiled faintly. "I was trying to describe the feeling, the mood."

"If you say so."

A salt breeze from the ocean fanned her heated skin. Luz felt like a well-fed cat lazing in the winter sun, purring softly. It was quiet and peaceful, the only noise the rustling of palm fronds stirring in the wind, and the tumble of the surf rushing onto the beach on the other side of the Kincaid winter estate. She opened her eyes to gaze at the landscaped lawn of her parents' home, its towering palms and flowering shrubbery bronze-tinted by her sunglasses. This place had never seemed like home to her, maybe because she wasn't raised here. For Luz, Virginia was home.

A figure dressed in capri pants and an oversized broadcloth shirt approached from the direction of the estate greenhouse. A floppy wide-brimmed hat completely shaded the face, but Luz had no difficulty recognizing her mother. A shallow basket filled with cut flowers was hooked over her arm.

"Here comes Audra," she said.

"Right," Mary acknowledged in a dry voice.

As Audra walked onto the sandstone deck that aproned the round pool, she glanced their way. "You girls had better get out of that sun before you ruin your skin. A little gives you a healthy glow, but too much and you'll look like old saddle leather." Without a break in stride, she continued to the umbrellaed tables near the low, geometrically designed house.

Luz and Mary exchanged a silent look and pushed out of their lounge chairs. "I wonder if I'll ever be able to sit by a pool without hearing her say that," Mary murmured as both women slipped on long caftans. "Oh, well, it was getting too hot."

A uniformed maid was at Audra's side when they joined her at the table. Once Luz had believed servants stood by windows watching for their employer's return or else possessed some uncanny sixth sense. It had been disappointing to learn they were usually warned in advance by a phone call, such as now—the gardener had likely called the house to advise the staff that Mrs. Kincaid was on her way back.

Audra handed the basket of flowers to the maid. "Be sure to put them in water immediately. And bring some tea."

"Yes, ma'am." Then she disappeared through the sliding doors on the glass-walled side of the house facing the pool and lawns.

Within minutes, she returned with a pitcher of tea and tall glasses of ice. After the drinks were poured, the talk flowed easily into family news. With everyone so spread out and the grandchildren in school, Audra insisted on these weekly visits so that they could all remain in touch with what was happening.

"I mentioned to Michael your decision to let Rob skip college this fall," Audra said. "He agreed with it. Rob is so serious. Michael felt it would teach him to relax and have fun."

"The change in Rob is remarkable since I told him that Drew had agreed to let him sit out a year. He had a party that weekend to celebrate. It must have been some party," Luz declared with a laugh. "He phoned the following Monday and said he was broke—and could I deposit some more money in his checking account."

"I know at the moment he's keen on polo, but I hope that you'll see that he does some traveling."

"I think I've found a way for Rob to do both. You remember I promised to take Trisha to Paris in June, as a graduation present. June is also the month when England's polo season is in full swing. So I'm trying to arrange, through some of Jake's British polo friends, for Rob to play on one of their teams. We can all three fly to London first, then Trisha and I can go to Paris. It will be perfect for both of them." She was pleased with her plans.

"That's very clever. I'm surprised you thought of it, Luz," her mother remarked, then continued, "Speaking of plans, I have decided to close the house in Virginia permanently. I've spoken to Frank about possibly selling Hopeworth."

"Oh, no," Luz murmured.

"I know. We all have a sentimental attachment to the place, but I thought it was a shame to let the house sit vacant, unused." Audra had never approved of waste. Luxury was one thing and waste was another. "However, Frank reminded me how advantageous the stud farm is as far as taxes are concerned and advised me to keep it."

"Bless Frank," Mary muttered under her breath, and Luz silently agreed.

"Now comes the matter of actually closing the house. I was hoping that one or both of you girls would supervise the packing that needs to be done. There are paintings that should be crated and stored. I don't know how many trunks are in the attic, a lot of them filled with things you children had when you were small. You might want to sort through some of them to see if there is anything you want to keep. You can check with Michael and Frank to see what they might want done with their things." Audra took their agreement for granted.

Luz glanced at her sister. "It might be fun."

Mary nodded, but seemed hesitant. "It isn't a small project. It's likely to take a couple of weeks to do it right. With my brood, I don't know if I can be gone that long. Do you think Drew can survive without you for two weeks?" she teased.

"He has to go to New York sometime in the middle of February. I had planned to go with him, although on these business trips, I rarely get to spend much time with him. Maybe I could go to Virginia instead. I'll talk to Drew and see what he thinks." Two weeks ago she wouldn't have bothered to consult him, she would have simply gone ahead and made her plans, but things were different between them now. "I'll let you know next week. In the meantime, see what you can arrange."

Finding the time to discuss the trip with Drew was not as easy as Luz had expected. Both were so busy the next few days, Drew with business appointments and men's club meetings and she with a charity auction, that during the few moments they saw each other they joked about passing one another in the driveway.

At seven o'clock on Friday evening, Luz returned from her appointment with the beauty salon and noticed that Drew's brown Mercedes wasn't parked in the garage. Frowning, she entered the house and went straight to the morning room, where she found Emma sitting at a desk located in an alcove.

"Have you heard from Drew?" She paused inside the room and set her purse on the round breakfast table.

Emma turned, removing her bifocals. "He called a half hour ago to say he was going to be late and not to wait dinner."

"But what about the concert tonight? We have tickets." She unfastened the single-buttoned jacket of her ruby-red suit and shrugged out of it. "Am I supposed to meet him there?"

"No. He said for you to go without him, that he wouldn't be able to make it."

Disappointed, Luz sagged a hip against the table and thoughtfully fingered the gathers at the neckline of her silk charmeuse blouse. "I don't really want to go by myself," she murmured and sighed dejectedly. "You're welcome to use them if you like, Emma. I think I'll just spend a quiet evening at home for a change."

"Thank you. I think I will go."

Luz gathered up her jacket and purse and left the room to go upstairs and change. She had plenty to do to make the evening alone pass. She wrote letters to the children, assuring Rob that she exercised his horses regularly and suggesting to Trisha that they might spend a weekend together when she went to Virginia. All the while she consciously listened for the sound of Drew's car coming up the driveway.

The later it became, the more troubled she became. At ten o'clock, she called his office, using the private number that didn't go through the switchboard. There wasn't any answer. Thinking it meant he was on his way home, she fixed some fresh coffee. An hour later, Luz knew her assumption was wrong. Her mood alternated between worry and irritation. It was half past eleven when she finally heard his car outside. She was at the rear entrance waiting for him when he came in, her arms folded in front of her.

"Well, hello." He smiled in surprise and bent to kiss her cheek. "I didn't expect you to be up still. How was the concert?"

"I didn't go. Where have you been? I tried the office but no one was there."

He curved an arm around her shoulders and drew her along with him as he walked to the living room. "I took Claudia to dinner. It seemed the least I could do after keeping her so late at the office. I would have called to tell you, but I thought you were at the concert. I'm sorry if I worried you."

"You did." Now that her fears were calmed, irritation was left. "You must have had an awfully late dinner."

"Not really. I'm afraid we got to talking and lost all track of time," he admitted.

"I see."

"No, I don't think you do." Drew paused, letting his briefcase rest atop the backrest of the lemon-yellow sofa. "I don't know if I can explain how much I enjoy talking to Claudia. I can discuss things with her that I can't talk to you about. Granted, you would listen, but you couldn't respond intelligently. Claudia is a lawyer, so we can converse on the same level. Conversations with her are always so stimulating." He glanced at her. "Do you understand?"

"Yes."

"I hope your feelings aren't hurt." He appeared suddenly impatient with her. "I mean, it is business."

"I understand." It was part of his life she didn't share—a large part. And legal shoptalk bored her, she knew that. Since he couldn't talk to her about it, that left a void between them. Now another woman was filling that void. To say it didn't hurt or that she didn't feel that she had somehow failed him would be to lie.

"I'm sorry for causing you needless worry and for unknowingly keeping you up." He swung his briefcase back to his side.

"I made coffee."

"No thanks. I'd just as soon go to bed. I'm supposed to meet John Randolph at the golf course bright and early in the morning so we can play a round before the course gets crowded."

"But there was something I wanted to talk to you Luz said.

"Can it wait? I'm really beat." A minute ago talking about Claudia he hadn't acted tired. H animated with the pleasure her conversation

"All right." But she trembled with the

ment, a resentment centering around Claudia Baines. She resented her for giving Drew what she couldn't, and she resented Drew for taking it. And she resented herself for feeling the way she did about both.

"Thanks." He kissed her lightly. "Good night, dear."

All honeymoons end sometimes, even second ones. Luz wondered if this was the end of hers as she watched Drew pass through the doorway to the entrance hall where the oak staircase rose to the suite of rooms on the second floor.

Over the weekend, Luz didn't mention to Drew that Audra wanted her to go to Virginia. She had no reason. If Drew remembered that she had wanted to talk to him about something, he didn't bring it up. The first of the week, Mary called to schedule the trip and Luz suggested the last two weeks of February.

That evening, Drew excused himself from the dinner table. "I'm going into the library. I have to make some phone calls."

After he left, Luz lingered at the table over a second cup of coffee. The mirrored ceiling reflected the flickering yellow flames of the candles on the table. So romantic a setting, she thought, but not for one. She blew the candles out, then took her coffee into the living room.

The door to the library-den was not tightly closed. She heard Drew laugh, and gravitated toward the sound. She wandered into the room, thinking she'd sit and have her coffee there and tell him about her coming trip to Virginia once he had finished his phone calls. But she didn't have a chance to sit down in _____ ___ wingback chair by the fireplace.

___ ___ ___w said into the phone, "Just a ___ ___ ___ and over the mouthpiece of the ___ ___ ___ething, Luz?"

___ ___ ___ her head.

___ ___l and waited, not removing his ___ ___ esume his conversation. It took ___ ___ected her to leave the room. He ___ ___ what he said. She felt strangely ___ ___g told her company wasn't wanted ___ ___f-consciously, she retreated, un- ___ ___s so obviously not welcome. But

about,"

when he was
e'd been very
gave him.
orce of her resent-

00

once outside the room, Luz stopped, wondering why she had let him prod her into leaving.

As she turned to go back inside she heard Drew say, "Sorry, Claudia. You were saying?"

Abruptly, she swung away from the door and crossed the living room to the liquor cabinet behind the wet bar, where she poured a liberal amount of whiskey into her coffee. Claudia. She was growing to hate that name. It was so obvious to Luz that the woman was playing up to Drew. How many times had she heard others say that most successful career women slept their way to the top? The woman was using Drew. Surely he knew it. Maybe he didn't care. Her insides felt twisted, and the whiskey didn't seem to smooth them out.

She didn't know how long she nursed her whiskey-laced coffee nor how much time passed before Drew emerged from the den. What little of her drink remained in the bottom of her cup was cold when he joined her at the wet bar.

"I think I'll fix myself something," he said, walking behind the counter. "What are you drinking?"

"Just coffee," she lied.

"I think I'll have something stronger." He picked up a glass and added cubes to it from the icemaker. "Isn't there anything worth watching on cable tonight?"

"I don't know."

"I think I'll check." He splashed some soda in with the whiskey and picked up the glass. "Are you coming?"

"No." As he started to walk away, Luz called him back. "Drew. I'm going with Mary to Virginia. Audra wants us to close up the house. I'll be gone about two weeks."

"When?" He appeared unconcerned that this was the first he knew of it.

"The middle of February. We leave the fourteenth."

"I leave the same day for New York. I rescheduled the trip and moved the departure time ahead a few days. I was going to tell you, but it slipped my mind. What time does your flight leave?"

"We haven't made reservations yet. Mary's handling that."

"It would be convenient if we could go to the airport together. It would mean one less car parked in the lot."

"Yes." Luz didn't know what she expected his reaction to be, but it wasn't this near indifference.

*        *        *

The airport was crowded with winter-weary northerners seeking the tropical clime of Palm Beach. Through the flood of fur-wrapped arrivals milling by the doors, Luz saw her sister directing a porter laden with luggage to the ticket counter where she waited.

"I've already checked my bags," Luz said when Mary joined her.

"Good." The porter set her cases on the scale, and Mary handed him a tip. While she waited for her luggage to be tagged and the claim stubs to be stapled to her ticket envelope, she turned to Luz. "Where's Drew? Has his flight left already?"

"No. He went to the newsstand."

After the baggage was checked, they moved away from the congestion at the counter. "Should we wait here for Drew or go to the gate?"

"Here he comes." Luz saw him walking toward them, a winter topcoat thrown over his arm. He was carrying a briefcase along with a folded newspaper and a package.

"What do you have there, Drew?" Mary nodded at the heart-shaped red box peeking out of the plastic sack and sent a sly glance at Luz.

"Some Valentine chocolate for Claudia," he replied smoothly and appeared not to notice the way Luz visibly stiffened. "She's a chocoholic. I would have bought you a box, Luz, but I know you don't like candy."

"No, I don't, but I suppose it's the thought that counts." She was mouthing phrases all the while she was wondering why he'd bought Claudia a gift when he was on his way to New York . . . why he was buying Claudia a gift at all, especially a Valentine present.

"She should be here." Drew searched the throng of travelers. "There she comes."

Luz followed his gaze and located the vivacious brunette, wearing an eye-catching burgundy silk blouse. A long plaid shawl was thrown over one shoulder, a plaid that matched the pleated challis skirt. A thin black leather briefcase swung from her hand. She smiled and quickened her step when she saw Drew.

"Well, I'm all checked in, ready to go," she said to him before acknowledging the presence of the other women. "Hello,

Mrs. Thomas. You look stunning, as usual. So do you, Mrs. Carpenter."

Actually, Luz felt very drab in her oatmeal-and-brown suit and brown bowler-styled hat with the front brim turned down. She wished she had chosen something more colorful, but the nubby material stood up under traveling so well.

"This is her first trip to New York, so naturally she's excited," Drew volunteered, and Luz felt a second shock wave go through her. Not once had he mentioned that Claudia was accompanying him on the trip. Did he think it was a minor detail?

"Naturally," Mary said, filling the silence that Luz couldn't. No words would come out, and she was afraid of what they might be if they did.

"Can you imagine? All those years living in Connecticut and I've never been to New York City," Claudia declared. "Though I doubt I'll have time to see any sights."

"You're from Connecticut?" Mary asked.

"Didn't Drew tell you? We're from the same town. We even know some of the same people."

"From different eras, of course," Drew inserted dryly. "She wasn't even born when I left there."

"It doesn't matter." Claudia shrugged aside the age difference. "It still proves what a small world it can be."

"Yes, it does," Mary said, continuing to fill the blank spaces.

"Our flight is scheduled to begin boarding in ten minutes," Drew said. "We should go to the gate."

"All right. It was a pleasure seeing you again, Mrs. Thomas." She thrust a hand at Luz.

"You, too." She managed to recover enough poise to shake hands. Then Drew was bending to kiss her cheek.

"Enjoy yourselves," he said.

But Luz couldn't wish him the same. "Have a safe flight," she said instead and felt a growing heaviness as she watched the two of them walk away.

"I take it that you didn't know she was going with Drew to New York." Mary eyed her perceptively.

"No, I didn't." Her voice sounded flattened, void of all emotion.

"It sounds like the honeymoon is over."

"A honeymoon requires two people. Maybe I was the only

one on it . . . and I just didn't know it." Her eyes burned with tears and she quickly blinked them away.

"Luz." The pity in her sister's voice was more than she could stand.

Her chin came sharply up as she determinedly shook off her own hurt and self-pity. "There's a saving grace in all this. Maybe he didn't tell me she was going, but he didn't hide it either. After all, she met him here—with us—and they openly talked about the trip. They wouldn't have done that if there was something to conceal."

"And the candy?"

"Stop it, Mary," Luz demanded angrily. "I don't have all the damn answers!"

After a pause, Mary said, "Let's go to the gate. Did I remember to tell you Stan Marshall is meeting us at the airport?"

"No, you didn't." Luz was grateful for the change of subject as they started down the long, crowded corridor to the departure lounge.

Stan Marshall was the manager of Hopeworth Farm, and his association with Jake Kincaid went back more than twenty years. A jockey in his youth, he was a short stocky man with a craggy face and grizzled hair—and the patience of a saint. He was standing at the gate when Luz and Mary left the plane. His soft, squashy hat, the kind he'd seen the English country gentlemen wear, was in his hand. Luz swore he had on the same tweed jacket with suede patches at the elbows that he'd worn for the last ten years, and wondered if he had a closetful or whether he simply bought an identical jacket when one showed signs of wear.

After he had welcomed Mary, he turned to Luz. "This feels like old times. I still expect to see Jake coming along some-where behind you. You know this is the season the two of you always used to come to the farm."

"Yes." She had loved her father, liked him, but never really respected him as a man. Still, she missed him. "We had some good times."

"It's a sad reason that's brought you here this time. I'm not going to like seeing that grand old house shut up. It needs living in."

"Maybe someday." But Luz didn't expect it to come for a long while.

"We'd better be going to the baggage claim before somebody slips off with your luggage. I've got the station wagon parked right out front. It's a chilly one today, it is." Stan Marshall was a talker—to people, horses, anything that listened. "I had the telephone reconnected in the house and a couple of ladies in to tidy the place. The pantry is all stocked. If there's anything else you need, just tell me."

The Virginia countryside lay barren under bleak gray skies. Barren hardwood trees stood silently along the roadsides and in the brown fields, their exposed branches making a random pattern of dark lace against the low clouds. The white board fences looked out of place in the winter-drab landscape, and the horses grazing beyond them were shaggy-coated and dull. The sleek, shining steeds wouldn't emerge for another two months.

Yet the sights evoked warm memories for Luz, nostalgia for carefree times. She gazed at the foal-heavy mares in the pasture, penned separately from the frisky yearlings and the older horses in training. In the distance, she could see scattered burnished red splotches against the land, part of the farm's Hereford cattle herd. Mainly the beef were raised so that the handful of polo prospects Jake had always had in training could become used to working with animals. These horses spent roughly a year doing stock work before graduating to more advanced stages of training.

When the station wagon swung onto the lane, entering the property of Hopeworth Farm for the first time, Luz glanced ahead to the right, seeking and finding the cupolaed roofs of the stables and barns. A half-mile track, a jumper's course, work arenas, and the manager's quarters were located there. Off by itself to the left sat the main residence.

"There it is." Mary pointed over Stan Marshall's shoulder at the Greek Revival mansion. The shutters were closed on all but a few first-floor windows, protection against summer's heat and winter's chill. The house looked as if it were sleeping.

Stan parked the station wagon in the graveled cul-de-sac in front of the antebellum home. "It's unlocked," he said. "I'll bring your luggage in directly."

Inside her childhood home, Luz paused and glanced about while Mary wandered into the foyer that ran the depth of the house. An Oriental rug, softly colored in rich cream and seafoam green, covered most of the hardwood floor, stopping short of the curved freestanding staircase, which was wide enough so the hooped skirt of the Southern belle wouldn't touch either side. The fourteen-foot-high ceiling was outlined with friezework, and an ornate medallion anchored a crystal-and-bronze chandelier.

"It's different somehow, isn't it?" Mary's glance roamed the walls as if seeking what she sensed. "Maybe it's because no one is waiting."

"Only the house itself." It was completely furnished, lacking only vases filled with flowers to give it that finished touch—like an orphaned child dressed in its best clothes waiting for someone to love it.

Her sister crossed the foyer and paused in front of the long antique bureau. Its mirrored back reflected the Oriental urns and porcelain figurines on the polished wood top. "Would you look at all this?" Mary touched the fragile china model of a pair of goldfinches. "We have ourselves quite a project. Everything will have to be catalogued before we pack it away."

"How many rooms are there?" Luz couldn't remember, but all were like this, ready to live in.

"Fifteen. Or is it sixteen? Either way, that's not counting the bathrooms." Mary looked at her. "Or the attic."

"Two weeks, eh?" Luz smiled wryly.

The front door opened and Stan Marshall trudged in, a suitcase under each arm and one in each hand. He looked as broad as he was tall. "Where shall I put these?" He paused in the foyer, puffing and trying not to show it.

"Shall we sleep in our old room, Luz?" A gleam appeared in Mary's eyes.

"Why not?"

"The top of the stairs, the last room on the right." Mary directed him to the bedroom they had once shared.

"Last room." He shifted the heavy baggage for a better hold and set out to climb the stairs.

"Let's look around." Luz didn't wait to see if Mary agreed as she crossed to the cypress doors leading into the formal dining room.

Their tour of the house was a combination of reminiscences and discussions about where and how they would begin their task. When it was over, they were back at their starting point in the foyer. Stan Marshall came out of the study.

"All your luggage is upstairs, and I've got a fire burning in the study fireplace. Any time you decide you want to go riding, Luz, just call the stables and I'll have Sequoia saddled and ready for you. And I've got some other nice hunters for you, Mary. You're welcome to take your pick," he said. "Mrs. Osgood and her daughter will be here in the morning to help you. When you need some men for the heavy lifting and crating, the stablehands are at your disposal."

"You've covered just about everything, Stan," Luz declared.

"I hope so. Welcome home, ladies." He tipped his hat to them and left by the front door.

Late in the evening, Luz sat in front of the fireplace, sipping a superb aged brandy from Jake Kincaid's private stock. A cranberry wool sweater and charcoal slacks replaced the traveling suit she'd worn earlier, and she was curled comfortably in the oversized leather armchair, her feet tucked under her. Mary was on the floor, leaning against an ottoman and gazing into the yellow flames, her dress changed as well to slacks and sweater.

"This is my favorite room." Luz let her gaze wander over the cypress-paneled study, its walls adorned with paintings by Brown, Snaffles, and Golinkin that captured the color, action, and excitement of polo in a single moment in time. Silver trophies were interspersed with the leather-bound books on the shelves, and gold-framed photographs of people and horses— polo ponies, racers, hunters—were displayed in front of the books.

"Not mine," Mary said. "I like the music room best."

Luz absently shook her head. "Every time I think of that room, I remember the look on Audra's face when I asked her what 'assignation' meant and why Daddy was keeping one . . . and who was Sylvia Shepler. I was eleven."

Mary turned sideways, frowning curiously. "What did she say?"

"She said that Sylvia Shepler was a friend of my father's and he was meeting her. That was what 'assignation' meant."

Luz paused and swirled the brandy in her glass. "And she ordered me never to speak of it again."

"He was a philanderer."

"I wonder if we'll ever know why she put up with it." She stared into the dancing flames.

"Who knows?" Mary settled back into her former slumped position.

"Let's leave this room till last," Luz said.

"It doesn't matter to me."

# CHAPTER VI

On Saturday, Trisha arrived to spend the weekend. The day was sharp and clear, the air brisk and the sun bright. After being cooped in the house all week sorting and packing, Luz welcomed her daughter's visit as an excuse to go riding. Together they tried to talk Mary into coming with them, but she was adamant in her refusal.

"My idea of a horseback ride is a gentle canter across the meadow. I know you, Luz. You plan on tearing across the countryside, jumping fences and leaping ditches. Thanks, but no thanks. I'll stay here and fix some of my special spaghetti sauce instead."

"There goes my diet," Trisha moaned, but with a telltale gleam in her dark eyes that more than approved of the choice.

Stan Marshall had two hunters saddled and waiting when they reached the stables. Luz climbed onto her favorite mount, a golden chestnut Thoroughbred called Sequoia, and waited for Trisha while she swung onto the saddle of her horse, a rangy pinto of a mixed breed, brown with white spots.

"You two look more like sisters than mother and daughter," the stud-farm manager declared.

"That's a compliment, Luz." Trisha's laughing breath vaporized when it hit the nippy air. "It means neither one of us looks her age. You appear younger and I older."

Luz was aware that when you're seventeen, you can hardly wait to be twenty, but when you're twenty, you discover no magical change has occurred. You don't feel twenty or thirty or forty. Age has nothing to do with the way you feel, think, or act. Luz had yet to learn how being old was supposed to feel, but she had a strong hunch that you never *feel* age. All you ever *feel* is yourself.

"Such flattery is likely to turn a girl's head, Stan," Luz said, smiling absently. "Ready, Trish?" She glanced at her daughter to be sure she was settled in the saddle, the stirrup length properly adjusted.

"Whenever you are." She nodded.

"Enjoy yourselves!" Stan backed away and lifted his hand.

"We'll try to make it back in one piece," Luz promised with a wave as she reined her chestnut hunter toward the pasture beyond the stable barns and paddocks.

Fresh and eager, the two horses broke into a rocking canter with little urging from their riders. Luz breathed in the invigorating crispness of the air. Her heavy Irish sweater of hand-knitted wool kept her from feeling any of its chill. The colts in the paddocks raced close to the fence, gamboling and frisking as they rode by. An older group of horses in the adjoining paddock took little interest in their passing, barely lifting their heads to look.

Luz slowed her horse to a dancing walk to look over the bunch. "Stan mentioned there were two four-year-olds in that group that he felt were ready to go into training. A roan with a blaze face and a sorrel with four white stockings," she explained to Trisha while she tried to locate the animals in the small herd. Their dull, heavy winter coats didn't make the task easy. "Rob could use some younger horses on his polo string. Of course, it will take a year or more to train them. Still, it might be worth the time and trouble."

"Rob doesn't have the patience to work with a green horse. He wants everything now. That's his problem." Trisha stated an observation more than a criticism.

"I can do the preliminary training and let Rob take over when the pony is ready for slow practice games." She voiced the alternative that occurred to her.

"You have the patience for it, that's for sure."

"I should." A smile broke across her face. "I raised you two."

"Ah, but can you keep up with us?" Trisha challenged and kicked her horse into a gallop.

With a touch of the heel, Luz gave chase on Sequoia. Both riders angled away from the pasture gate and took aim on the low rail fence. Two lengths in front of the fence, Luz collected the chestnut, preparing it for the jump. As its hindquarters bunched to catapult it into the air, she leaned over its neck, rising slightly in the stirrups. Then they were airborne, arcing over the fence with a free-floating sensation. Luz shifted her weight back to aid the horse's balance as they came down on the other side a stride behind Trisha's pinto, but not for long.

Neck and neck, they raced across the pasture, scattering surprised cows. The whip of the wind in her hair and the thunder of galloping hooves in her ears, Luz exulted in the wild and free sensations. When they neared the wooded end of the pasture, Trisha let her take the lead. Upon entering the trees, the horses slowed to a fast canter to follow the trail wending through the woods. Well familiar with the hunt course, Luz dodged the bare branches of low-hanging limbs and jumped the Thoroughbred over the fallen logs across the trail.

A low stone wall cut across the clearing in front of them. Beyond it lay open fields, winter-brown and gently rolling. The chestnut hunter cleared the wall easily and set out on the cross-country run at a steady gallop. The pinto came up to range alongside, Trisha's face showing the same eagerness Luz felt. All that was missing was the bay of the hounds following the false fox scent laid down for them, and the summoning call of the huntsman's horn to signal the chase was on.

On top of a grassy knoll, Luz slowed her mount to a walk and let it blow, and Trisha followed suit. This spot was roughly the halfway point on the hunt course, and a favorite of hers. The exhilaration of the run left her puffing slightly, her blood heated and racing fast. She stroked the chestnut's arched neck while she gazed at the rolling Virginia countryside, dotted with the dark skeletons of winter-bare trees and patched with plowed fields.

"This is a beautiful view in the autumn," she told Trisha. "All the fields are golden and the trees are brilliant reds and oranges. It looks all afire."

"I'll bet it does, but right now it only looks like so much kindling," Trisha remarked wryly. "We were never here much in the fall. Rob and I were always in school when you came."

"I wish I'd brought you both with me to experience the thrill and the tradition of the hunt. It always seemed there was plenty of time." She sighed ruefully. "The annual blessing of the hounds was always done at Hopeworth. Then after a bracing toddy to warm the blood we'd all start out in search of the fox. It's quite a sight with everyone gathered on the front lawn, dressed in proper attire—white ascots, black hunt jacket and hat, and white breeches—except, of course, for the huntmaster and the master of the hounds, who wear scarlet jackets. And off we'd go on a harum-scarum ride through cornfields and over fences and ditches . . . after the fox."

"It all sounds fun right up to the last part, then it turns a little bloodthirsty. I think I'd root for the fox."

It was so like Trisha to root for the underdog. "Actually, there aren't many foxes around anymore. It's rare for the hounds to start one. Mostly, they follow a drag, which is the scent of a fox dragged over the ground ahead of the hunt. That was true even when I was your age. As a matter of fact, I wasn't blooded until I rode to a hunt in England."

Trisha grimaced in distaste. "That's the disgusting tradition of smearing the blood from the fox onto the face of a rider participating in his first kill, isn't it?"

"It was rather gruesome," Luz conceded. "I remember that I had trouble eating when we all went back to the manor for the big hunt breakfast. The tables at those affairs are always groaning with food. It always reminds me of that scene from *Tom Jones.*"

A thoughtful frown claimed Trisha's face as she eyed her mother. "You really love the life here, don't you?"

"Yes." It was Luz's turn to grow thoughtful. "I used to wish your father would open an office in Washington or Richmond so we could live here. But he already had an established practice in Florida, so it didn't make much sense. He used to talk about the possibility of expanding his practice, but he never mentions it anymore."

"Maybe he will in a few years."

"I doubt it." Luz knew that Drew didn't share her love for this part of the country and possessed only a tolerance for what he called "the horsy set," an attitude he had carefully concealed around Jake Kincaid. His support of Rob's desire to play polo for a year was obviously given to please her—or, at least, to avoid arguments.

"He might," Trisha insisted. "Especially when he takes on a new partner."

"A new partner?" Her spine stiffened as Claudia Baines flashed through her mind. The steady clop-clopping of her horse's hooves suddenly sounded like a hammer pounding in her head.

"Yes." Her dark eyes were agleam with some secret knowledge when she glanced at Luz. "Me."

"You?" Behind her confusion, there was immense relief.

"Yes. I've just received notice that I've been accepted at Harvard this fall." A proud smile of satisfaction curved her wide mouth.

Surprise and shock traveled through Luz. She was suddenly at a loss to know what to say. Her two children were so different. Rob always talked to her about his problems, told her his hopes and aspirations, but Trisha was a mystery. Half the time, Luz couldn't guess what she was thinking, let alone what she wanted. She'd always had the impression Trisha took the world lightly and never cared much about anything. This sounded very much like an impulsive decision, made without thinking things through.

"Trisha, are you sure that's what you want to do? Do you realize what it entails?" Luz doubted it. "Four years of college, plus another three years of law school. Clerking for other attorneys and passing the bar. Do you seriously intend to do this or is it just a passing fad of yours?"

"It's what I want. It's what I've wanted for a long time," she stated firmly. "Luz, I can't be like you and just do nothing all the time. I want my life to have some purpose and meaning beyond planning this year's charity auction or a ski trip to Switzerland."

Luz had always wondered what Trisha thought of her. Now she knew, and that knowledge hurt, more deeply than she had ever thought it would. But she successfully hid it, aware that Trisha hadn't said it to wound.

"Then I'm glad you've been accepted. Your father will be pleased when he finds out you'll be attending his alma mater. We'll have to call him tonight and tell him the news," she said and managed a smile. "I think the horses are rested now. Are you ready to head back?"

"Lead the way. I hope Mary has the food on the table when we get back. I'm starved," Trisha declared as they urged their horses out of a walk and posted at a trot.

All the way back, Trisha's words were a weight on Luz's shoulders that she couldn't shake off. It dulled her enjoyment of the ride and took the edge off her previous high spirits. But she was careful not to let on to Trisha that anything was wrong. When they reached the house, she made a point of telling Mary the news and insisted they raid the wine cellar to celebrate the occasion.

After an early dinner, Luz telephoned home to talk to Drew. But it was more than Trisha's unexpected announcement that prompted the call. She had an inexpressible need to hear his voice and know that she was missed. Emma answered the phone.

"Hello, Emma. It's Luz. Let me speak to Drew."

"I'm sorry, but he isn't back yet," the housekeeper replied.

Her wristwatch indicated it was only a little after seven. "I suppose he's just coming off the golf course. Did he say when to expect him?"

"Not until tomorrow. He's still in New York," Emma said, vaguely startled that Luz hadn't known.

"But . . . I thought he was supposed to return on Friday."

"He called yesterday to say that he was going to have to stay over another day. The earliest flight he could get on was Sunday morning. Is anything wrong?"

"No. Trisha is here." She glanced at her daughter, curled cross-legged on the floor watching her. "We just thought we'd talk to him."

"I'm sure you could reach him at the hotel," Emma said.

"We'll try there." She hung up, then dialed the hotel number.

"He's still in New York?" Trisha guessed from what she had gleaned from the one-sided conversation.

"Yes." Luz listened to the telephone ring and carefully avoided glancing at her sister. When the hotel operator came on the line, Luz asked for Drew's room. In her mind, she kept wondering whether Claudia was staying an extra day, too, but she didn't want to see that question expressed in Mary's eyes. Instead she kept telling herself the matter must have been very important, because Drew wasn't in the habit of setting meetings on Saturday when he was in New York.

After the fourth ring, the phone was picked up and she recognized Drew's voice on the other end of the wire. "Hello, darling. I just talked to Emma and she said you were forced to stay a day longer. How's everything going?" Luz rushed her words, not giving him a chance to explain things for himself.

"Fine. How are you doing?" he sounded distant, but Luz blamed that on the connection.

"Mary and I are tearing our hair out, but otherwise fine. Trisha came for the weekend. She has some news. I'll let her tell you herself." She passed the receiver to Trisha and kept a smile on her face while she listened again to the announcement and heard the rest of the hurtful assertion in her mind—"I don't want to be like you, Luz."

"Since Rob isn't likely to keep the family tradition, I decided to follow in your footsteps, Dad. I've been accepted at your alma mater." There was a short pause, filled by his response, then Trisha said, "I received my acceptance notice this week. It's official." That was followed by another break in which Trisha grew quieter, some of her exuberance fading. "I am happy. And I'm glad you are, too." Then she glanced at Luz as she listened to the voice on the phone. "Sure, I'll tell her. Bye, Dad."

As Luz reached to take the receiver so she could talk to Drew, Trisha stood up. Instead of handing it to her, she set it back on its cradle.

"He had dinner reservations, so he had to go," Trisha explained. "He said to tell you he'd call next week when he got back home."

"Oh." Luz regretted not talking to him longer in the beginning. "What did he say when you told him?"

"He was glad . . . proud of my decision. And he didn't sound as surprised as you were," she remembered wryly, then frowned. "When you talked to him, Luz, did you have the feeling someone was there with him?"

She hadn't been on the phone with him long enough to get any definite impression. "There probably was. More than likely his client." Or Claudia Baines, but Luz didn't say that. She didn't want Trisha to get the wrong idea about Drew's relationship with the young female lawyer.

Trisha left early on Sunday afternoon to return to the private girls' school she attended. With her departure, Luz no longer had to keep up a pretense of cheerfulness. When Mary suggested tackling the trunks in the attic, Luz readily agreed, grateful for any activity that might keep her morose thoughts at bay.

The third-floor attic had formerly been used as servants' quarters. The tiny, poorly lighted, unheated rooms had long ago been converted to storage space. Piles of boxes and trunks were randomly stacked amid broken rocking horses and old dress forms, and objects that defied identification. There was an old and dusty smell to the drafty rooms that spoke of long-forgotten things.

"Let's pile the stuff we're definitely going to pitch in the center of the rooms," Mary suggested. "I think that will be quicker."

"Okay."

They began with the bulky, obvious items—the wheelless doll carriage, the padded dress forms with their wire skirts, and the broken sleds and rocking horse. Mary dragged an old phonograph player to the middle of the room.

"Do you suppose this is an antique?"

Luz glanced at it. "I'd hardly describe it as being in good condition." The arm dangled by a wire and the turntable sat at a definite angle.

"I can't believe Audra would keep all this junk." Mary shook her head in amazement as she hauled out an old table radio, knobless and gutted of tubes. "When we were little, she was boxing up our clothes and donating them to some needy organization the minute we outgrew them. So why did she keep this stuff?"

"Jake did. It's the one time I remember hearing them argue about something. Audra insisted the attic was a firetrap and Jake warned her that if she removed one box, he'd . . . actually, I didn't hear what he threatened to do," Luz recalled with a faint smile, then paused to look around the cluttered room. "But I don't think a single box was ever taken out of this attic."

"Neither do I. It's strange how one man could be so sentimental yet so—"

"Yes," Luz interrupted Mary before she could say "insensitive." There was nothing to be gained by speaking ill of the dead.

Conversation lapsed as they ruthlessly attacked the piles of boxes and trunks, discarding most of their contents. An hour into the chore, Luz unearthed an old trunk and discovered the treasure trove of memories it contained . . . a plait of snowy-blond hair she had braided for Jake after her long ringlets had been cut off, her first riding habit for the hunt, and her christening dress.

"It's chilly up here." Mary shivered as she squeezed her hands together to warm them. "Want some coffee? I'll go downstairs and get it."

"Sure," Luz agreed absently, the question barely registering.

In the trunk, she found a box of old photographs. She didn't even realize Mary was gone until she heard the clump of her footsteps on the steep stairs. The sound roused her, and she looked up when Mary entered the cluttered room, out of breath from three flights of steps.

"I need something stronger than coffee after that." Her sister crossed the room and handed Luz one of the mugs of coffee, then collapsed on the floor beside her. "Hey, isn't this what you were doing when I left?" she accused and glanced over Luz's shoulder. "What have you got there?"

"Some old snapshots taken when we were kids," she answered in a musing tone. "Remember this one?" She showed her the black-and-white photograph taken when she was eight years old. A woeful-looking collie was sitting beside her, a rag bandage around its head and one on its leg. "I was going to be a veterinarian when I grew up."

"It wasn't long after that you decided you were going to be a jockey and ride in the Grand National like Elizabeth Taylor," Mary chided. "Then you wanted to be a singer, I think."

"What do you suppose happened to all those dreams?" Luz stared at the scratched old photographs.

"You grew up, thank God." Mary warmed her hands against the hot sides of the coffee mug.

"I suppose." She sighed heavily and laid the pictures back in the box.

Mary tipped her head, angling it toward Luz. "What's bothering you? And don't say nothing. You've been quiet as a cat ever since Trish left."

"Were you surprised by her decision to prepare for law school?" Luz asked instead.

"A little. But after putting seven through college, I've given up trying to guess what they'll do." She took a swallow of her coffee, eyeing Luz over the rim. "It surprised you, didn't it?"

"Yes." But that wasn't what brought the hurt rushing back to tighten her chest and make her throat ache. "Do you know what she said to me when I questioned her about it?"

"What?"

"That she didn't want to be like me and do nothing. In her words, she wanted her life to have meaning and purpose." Her short laugh held no humor. "That's quite a denouncement."

"This is the career-minded generation. The world was different when we were their age," Mary reminded her. "Granted, there were a dedicated few who wanted careers, but they were the exception, not the rule. Our ambition was to marry well and raise a family. Anything else was just a stopgap until the right man came along."

"I know."

"Don't pay any attention to that women's-lib bullshit. It isn't easy being a wife and a mother," Mary stated with a decisive nod.

"It's more than that." Luz shook her head. "It isn't just Trisha. My mother thinks that I'm not very clever. My husband doesn't believe I can carry on an intelligent conversation. And now my daughter thinks my life has no purpose. Mary, I'm forty-two years old and I feel like a failure." Her voice was flat. "This isn't the way I thought it would turn out, Mary. What happened to all the dreams?"

For a minute, Mary couldn't answer. Finally, she put an arm around Luz's shoulders. "I don't know, kid. I don't know."

# CHAPTER VII

A howling March wind prowled around the closed and shuttered antebellum home. When the front door opened, it rushed in, sweeping around the baggage-laden man coming out. The quick and curious wind raced to investigate the shadowed and gloomy interior, billowing under the cloth dustcovers draped over the furniture and lifting edges to take a look. Then the door shut and the wind died in a slow swirl of cold air.

Luz shuddered and burrowed a gloved hand under the collar of her coat, gathering it more tightly around her throat. Her gaze wandered over the barren foyer. Its walls were blank, all paintings and adornments packed away in protective crates. The furniture was hidden beneath shapeless, draping cloths. There was nothing in their drawers or doors, and no objects gracing their polished surface. Overhead, a cloth bag encased the crystal-and-bronze chandelier.

At the sound of footsteps on the freestanding staircase, she turned and watched Mary descend. "Is that everything?" She spoke in a low tone. The house was asleep, its eyes closed and covers drawn around it.

"Yes." Mary's voice was equally hushed.

Together they crossed the length of the foyer. The high heels of their shoes made sharp clicking noises on the bare hardwood floor once covered by the Oriental rug now rolled up and stored away. Luz had a strong impulse to tiptoe, and the last few steps to the door, she did to avoid the hollow echo of the sound.

Outside she waited while Mary locked the front door, her back to the strong March wind tunneling down the long portico. She could hear it rattling the bony branches of the trees that shaded the front yard in the summer. When the deadbolt was securely locked, they walked swiftly to the station wagon parked in the drive, its engine idling, and crawled inside, nodding when Stan asked if they were ready.

"It's a shame," her sister murmured as they pulled away from the house.

But Luz said nothing, and simply gazed at the silent house, framed by a windswept sky. The times in that house had not all been happy, carefree ones. There had been raging fights with her brothers and sisters, moments of anger and resentment toward her parents, and the anguish over minor tragedies that only the young can feel so sharply. Yet, the bad times had a way of fading from memory until they were only dimly recalled. But Luz knew it wasn't all the good things that had happened to her in that house which made this moment so poignant. When she had lived there, all life's expectations had been before her. Now she was faced with the reality of her life, and found it wanting.

The solid and efficient Emma Sanderson met the arriving flight. Drew was tied up at the office and couldn't get away, she explained. Luz watched the enveloping hug Mary received from her youngest and the warm peck on the cheek from her husband, and wished for that kind of a welcome.

"Mrs. Kincaid telephoned this morning," Emma told her. "She wants you to come for lunch on Friday."

Before Luz could acknowledge the message, Ross Carpenter informed her sister, "You received the same invitation."

"No thanks." Mary's lips thinned into a grim line of rejection. "All she wants is a report. You can give it to her, Luz. After being away for two weeks, I can guess at the chaos that's waiting for me at home. I can do without a cross-examination from Audra until I get it straightened out."

"Aren't you lucky to have such a devoted sister?" Luz mockingly chided Mary for expecting her to take the brunt of their mother's demand for a thorough report.

"I think so," Mary said and laughed.

After claiming their luggage from the carousel, they went their separate ways. An hour later, Luz entered her home, weary from the long flight and feeling vaguely despondent. Behind her, the caretaker carried in her luggage.

The phone started ringing as her foot touched the first step of the oak stair. She paused, letting the caretaker go around her, and glanced back at her housekeeper and secretary. "Answer that, Emma. If it's Mrs. Kincaid, tell her I'm upstairs changing and that I will be there on Friday."

As Emma went to pick up the living-room extension, Luz started up the stairs. A moment later, the ring of the telephone cut off. Luz was nearly to the top when Emma called up to her.

"Luz! It's Drew!"

"I'll take it up here." She hurried up the last few steps and went directly to the extension in the sitting room. "Hello." The breathy quality in her voice came mostly from pleasure that he had taken the time to call.

"How was the flight?"

"Long," Luz said, glancing absently at the caretaker when he crossed the room to the stairs. "What time will you be home?"

"That's part of the reason I'm calling."

"Oh, Drew." Mixed in with the disappointment was irritation. She knew what that statement meant. It was a prelude to the announcement that he'd be late. She might have been gone for over two weeks, but nothing had changed.

"I'm sorry, Luz, but I have an important client here from out of town. And I really have to take him to dinner tonight."

"Very well." But there was no way she was going to spend the evening alone her first night back. "I'll join you. Where and when shall we meet?"

"Luz, I can't ask you to do that. I know you must be tired from traveling and—"

"You are not asking. I am volunteering." An angry determination had chased most of her fatigue away.

The line went silent for several seconds before he said, "If you're sure, I have dinner reservations for eight o'clock at Le Pavillon, but we'll meet half an hour before for drinks in the lounge."

Promptly at seven-thirty, Luz left her car with the valet and entered the restaurant. The maître d' came forward to greet her. "*Bonsoir,* Madame Kincaid-Thomas." He always hyphenated her name. Luz suspected it was his way of remembering the importance of her social status. *"Votre mari est ici. S'il vous plaît."* He beckoned her to follow him and escorted her to the lounge, where Drew was seated with his guests.

Any doubts Luz might have had regarding the advisibility of including herself in tonight's dinner party vanished the instant she saw Claudia Baines sitting at the small cocktail table. The brunette had usurped many positions Luz had once held, becoming Drew's companion, friend, and confidante, but the role of hostess at this dinner was not one she was going to assume.

All three men politely stood when Luz approached the table. She moved to Drew's side to be introduced to his two clients, Jacques Aubert and Guillaume Poirier. Each took her hand in turn, bowing slightly over it.

*"Enchanté, madame."* Jacques Aubert, the tall and slender one with a decidedly Gallic eye for the ladies, smiled his most charming smile at her. "It is our pleasure to have you with us this evening."

*"Non, monsieur. Le plaisir est le mien."* She graciously returned the compliment in his language.

"You speak French?" His look was skeptical and curious, uncertain whether she actually knew the language or only a smattering of phrases.

*"Oui."* Luz inclined her head in an affirmative manner. "But it has been a while, so I may be rusty."

"My wife is modest," Drew inserted. "She speaks French fluently. She should. She manages two or three trips a year to the Continent or England."

The second man, sharply dressed despite his stoutness, his dark hair thinning at the crown, started to speak. Luz had the feeling he had intended to speak in French before he glanced at Claudia and changed his mind. "This is rare, madame. Few Americans know any language but their own."

"That is unfortunately true, Monsieur Poirier," Luz agreed. "However, as large as this country is, few people travel outside its boundaries. Even if a second language were compulsory in our public schools, most would eventually lose their facility in it from lack of use. That isn't true in Europe, where daily business can be conducted in all languages—French, German, Italian." The list went on, but she stopped there.

"Still, those of us who aren't well enough versed in another language to use it in conversation envy those who possess the ability Mrs. Thomas has," Claudia stated, drawing the attention back to her.

"Ah, but I am certain, Mademoiselle Baines, that you have considerable other talents," the charming Jacques insisted. "Beauty and brains are a rare combination."

As the waiter stopped to take her drink order, Luz wondered if she had unconsciously attempted to assert her superiority over Claudia by responding in French. She wasn't certain whom she had been more interested in impressing—Claudia or Drew's foreign clients.

In the lounge, the conversation remained general, but shortly after they moved into the dining room, it moved to business. As they discussed the legal matters on which they were seeking Drew's counsel, Luz found herself acting more and more frequently as a translator, supplying English words or phrases that eluded the French men or defining words they didn't know. On more than one occasion, she didn't know the French equivalent of some legal term.

Through it all, Luz had a very definite feeling that a "we" and "they" existed. Drew and Claudia were on the "we" side while she was part of the Frenchmen's "they." She sensed an invisible bond between Drew and Claudia, a quickness with which they picked up each other's thought and an easy way they touched each other when they wanted to insert a point or emphasize something. She understood why Drew had said they worked well together, yet when she watched Claudia she had a sense she was observing a territorial intrusion. It made her wonder how much of jealousy was a feeling of possession— that Drew was her private property and Claudia was trespassing.

By evening's end, Luz felt mentally and emotionally drained. When the parking attendant arrived at the front door with her car, she said her *au revoirs* to the Frenchmen and left. Drew would be home later after he had driven the two men to their hotel.

The foyer light was on when she entered the house. She left it burning for Drew and went upstairs. The suitcases had been unpacked in her absence. All signs of her recent trip were gone. She changed into a nightdress and wrapped a kimono around herself, too tired and too tense to go directly to bed.

When Drew arrived home forty minutes later, Luz was in

the sitting room, unwinding with a glass of brandy. He was startled to see her up. "I thought you'd be in bed sound asleep." He unknotted his silk tie and pulled it from beneath his shirt collar. "It's been a long day for you."

"Not that long." She uncurled from her chair, setting her drink aside, and crossed over to stand in front of him. With fingers clasped behind his neck, she tilted her face up to him. "And I'm not that tired. I've been gone for two weeks, or had you forgotten?"

His arms were slow to go around her. "I hadn't," he assured her, but he was slow to accept the invitation of her moist lips. When he did, his kiss held a long, steady pressure, his mouth rocking only slightly across hers.

She wasn't seeking a wild display of passion. Her mood tonight desired the closeness of his body, the warmth of his arms around her, and the comfort of his love, nothing more. Luz was satisfied with what she found in his response.

She nuzzled his lips, breathing into his mouth when she spoke. "Your room or mine?"

"Yours."

She turned within the circle of his arms and pressed his hand against the flatness of her stomach, maintaining shoulder contact with his chest while they walked slowly into her bedroom. They undressed separately and crawled into bed. Little foreplay preceded the sexual act, a decision that was mutual.

Afterward Luz lay alone in the darkened room. Drew had retreated to his own bed within minutes after it was over. There had been something lackluster—almost perfunctory, about their lovemaking tonight, she realized, as if they were performing some duty. Luz suspected she had been more tired than she realized, unable to arouse enthusiasm in herself or Drew. Or maybe it was just another facet of this vague dissatisfaction that had troubled her for days. She sighed and turned into her pillow, shutting her eyes and waiting for the sleep that wasn't far away.

The warm, sunny Florida weather was pushed out by a storm front that lingered for three days. Gray drizzle alternated with tropical cloudbursts that saturated everything, including Luz's spirits.

Virtually confined to the house by the inclement weather

and left alone to fill the long hours Drew spent at his office, she had too much time in which to think about her life and dwell on its idleness. Until now, she had never felt unfulfilled. She had always had everything she wanted. But she couldn't shake the feeling that she had failed those around her. She had not become the bright and clever daughter her mother wanted; she was not the intellectual, career-minded role model her daughter sought. Worst of all, all those descriptions fit Claudia Baines.

It was still raining on Friday. Unlike other luncheons Luz knew this one with her mother would not be canceled because of the weather. After being housebound for most of the week, Luz welcomed any excuse to get out, even if it meant a fault-finding session with her mother. No one ever did things quite the way Audra would have, and endless explanations were usually required to justify the difference. It was a trait of her mother's that seemed to have grown stronger in recent years. Part of growing old, Luz supposed.

The questions began the minute she arrived at the Kincaid oceanfront estate. Luz explained everything—how something was packed, where it was stored and why, what was kept and what was discarded or given away. Few of her answers met with Audra's approval. Luz's nerves were already worn thin. When her mother began complaining because they had packed her Limoges china set instead of sending it here, Luz finally lost her patience.

"Why did you have Mary and me close the house, Audra? You should have done it yourself. Maybe then it would have been accomplished to your satisfaction."

A second later, she was leveled by a long steady look. "When are you going to learn to control your temper, Luz?" It was an autocratically tolerant query posed many times before. "It isn't my fault you and Mary didn't do a proper job."

"But we did." Luz managed to speak evenly, but her voice trembled with the effort. "However, we did it the way we felt it should be done. Since you assigned the chore to us, you'll have to be satisfied with the results."

"That's quite true." Audra's agreement surprised her. "Ultimately, I am responsible for your actions." She turned away, signaling an end to the discussion. "We're having lunch on the glass porch today."

Never had she been permitted to have the last word in any conversation with her mother. Smothering a sigh of frustration, Luz followed her into the ocean-facing room, walled in tinted glass on three sides. Raindrops splattered on the glass, blurring the palm trees swaying in the wind. Leaden clouds drooped low over the stormy green Atlantic, waves churning and frothing and throwing the sea's wrack onto the beaches. The gray, angry turbulence outside seemed to match the mood Luz had been in for days.

They crossed to the rattan table set for two, and she sat in the chair opposite her mother. As she smoothed the linen napkin across her lap, the maid brought a fresh avocado salad to the table and spooned a serving onto their plates. Luz picked at it, her appetite lost in the restlessness that pushed at her.

During lunch, Audra talked about the family, catching Luz up on all the things that happened while she was away. Little response was required from her. Which was just as well, since she hardly listened to any of it. At last, the dishes were cleared away and she no longer had to keep up a pretense of eating. A teapot and warmed cups were placed in front of Audra.

"Really, Luz. You could show some interest in what I've been saying." She poured tea from the ceramic pot into one of the cups and cast a reproving glance across the table.

"I was thinking." Luz took the cup and saucer her mother passed to her.

"Thinking or sulking?" Audra filled the second cup.

"Thinking," she repeated firmly, and stirred a spoonful of crystallized brown sugar into her tea.

"About what? Are you and Drew having problems?" Shrewd dark eyes studied her with a wondering look.

"We're getting along fine. Why would you ask that?" It was a subject that made Luz defensive.

"All couples have problems at one time or another. It's part of marriage. And I know his law practice has been taking a great deal of his time lately. It's natural that you might feel slighted."

"Well, I don't," she insisted. "That isn't the problem. Not directly, anyway." She was reluctant to confide in her mother, but Audra had a way of ferreting out information.

"Why don't you tell me what it is? I may not be able to help, but sometimes it's enough just to talk a problem out."

She settled deeper into her chair, her shoulders squared and her back straight, one hand holding the teacup and the other the saucer.

"It isn't anything earth-shattering." Luz attempted to diminish its importance. "Now that Trisha and Rob are grown, it's only a matter of a year or two before they'll be living away from home permanently. So I need to decide what I'm going to do with my time. I can't continue to do nothing all day while Drew works."

"It seems to me that you have plenty to do." Audra frowned. "You're involved in so many activities now—"

"I'm not talking about social clubs or local charity organizations," she interrupted impatiently. "I want to do something that matters. Sheila Cosgrove has that smart little dress shop and Billi Rae Townsend has opened an art gallery."

"What nonsense is this?" her mother demanded.

"I should have known you wouldn't understand." Luz pushed out of the chair and stiffly crossed to the glass-paned wall looking out to the ocean.

"Perhaps you would care to explain exactly what it is that I don't understand." The command was calmly issued, but a command all the same.

"That I want to do something with my life."

"Something that matters," Audra said, repeating the phrase Luz had used earlier. "And you believe that expensive boutiques and art galleries *matter?*"

"Yes." She thrust her hands into the deep pockets of her gored skirt, doubling them into fists, and hunched her shoulders, fully expecting to hear a lecture on manners. Sometimes it seemed they never talked as one adult to another, always mother to daughter instead. "Although I'm certain you don't believe I'm intelligent enough to operate a business of my own."

"Now that is not true." The teacup rattled in its saucer as the pair were firmly placed on the table. "You are a very capable woman, a good manager and excellent organizer. Your household is smoothly and efficiently run. No small credit goes to your assistant, Mrs. Sanderson, but I'm also aware that you closely supervise everything yourself." Luz slowly turned to face her mother, stunned to hear such praise coming from her lips. "And how many social functions and benefits have you successfully organized? I couldn't begin to count them myself. I may be old, Luz, but I'm not blind."

"You've always treated me—"

"—as a mother treats a child," she admitted freely. "Surely you have learned by now that in a mother's eyes, a child never grows up. You never see them as quite ready to leave home, or to marry, or to have children."

"I suppose not." But Luz was still slightly dazed by what she was hearing.

"And as for doing something that matters, what could possibly matter more than your family?" Audra demanded. "Simply because your children are grown does not mean that they will stop having problems—that they won't continue to need you. What about when your grandchildren are born? Don't you want to be there when they come into the world? How can you do that if you're running a business? Luz, you are the anchor pin that holds the family together. Without you, they'll drift apart. They'll lose the closeness that made them special. It's the family that matters, Luz. The family."

She shook her head slowly as she was drawn back to the table. "I wonder if I'll ever know you, Audra."

"I'm your mother. It isn't important for you to know me. And you'd do well to remember that. Now sit down and drink your tea before it gets cold," she admonished.

Smiling, Luz did as she was told.

Halfway home from her mother's, it stopped raining and a spray of sunlight glinted through a break in the clouds. The smile she'd been wearing for most of the drive was still on her face when she pulled in front of her Spanish-styled home. She left the car parked by the steps and glided up the two steps to the carved entrance door.

"Emma!" she called cheerfully as she swung into the foyer. "I'm home. Have there been any phone calls?"

The day's mail was stacked on the side table in the foyer. Luz stopped to sort through it, skipping the various bills and invoices in her search for a letter from Rob or Trisha. At the bottom of the stack was a slim brown package, addressed to her.

Curious, she picked it up and glanced at the return address, conscious of Emma's footsteps coming from the dining room.

The package came from the hotel in New York where they always stayed. Wondering what it contained, Luz hooked a finger under a folded end of the brown paper and ripped it loose from the packing tape. Inside was a slim box.

"How was lunch?"

Luz half turned at the question, smiling absently at her plump gray-haired secretary, while she finished pulling the paper away from the box. "Actually, it was more enjoyable than I expected. Any calls?"

"Mrs. Randolph phoned to remind you of the luncheon meeting next Tuesday. I assured her that it was listed in your appointment book. She asked you to call her later so she could discuss the order of the meeting with you."

Luz lifted the lid of the box. Tissue paper rustled softly as she pushed it aside to reveal the contents. A folded letter lay atop a silky black garment trimmed in black lace. It looked like a teddy. With a bewildered frown, Luz flipped open the letter. Emma was still talking, but Luz was no longer listening as she quickly scanned the typed note, then read it again, more slowly.

*Dear Mrs. Thomas,*

*Enclosed is an item of lingerie one of our maids found when she cleaned your suite after your recent visit to New York. We took the liberty of having it laundered before returning it to you and hope this delay hasn't caused you any inconvenience.*

*We appreciate your patronage.*

*Respectfully yours,*

A signature was scribbled across the bottom. Luz glanced at the black undergarment again and lifted an edge of the black bodice. It didn't belong to her. She didn't own any black lingerie.

"Is something wrong, Luz?" Emma's question finally penetrated her consciousness.

Something stopped Luz from saying there had been some mistake. "No, of course not." She quickly put the lid back on the box. "Did you say Drew called?" She had a vague recollection of his name being mentioned.

"Yes." Emma eyed her uncertainly, not fully believing that nothing was bothering Luz. No matter how long and closely they had worked together there was still that fine line between employer and employee, and Emma didn't cross it. "He called to say he'd be a little late and suggested that you plan to serve dinner at eight."

"Thank you." She moved away from the foyer table, clutching the box in her hands. "See to the rest of the mail, will you, Emma?" She walked to the stairs.

"What about Mrs. Randolph?" Emma asked as Luz's hand gripped the banister. There was a pounding in her head. "She wanted you to call."

"Later," Luz replied without even turning her head, and climbed the long set of steps to the second floor.

Upon entering the master suite, she closed the door behind her. Quick, reaching strides carried her to the loveseat in front of the tiled fireplace. She removed the letter, put the box and its wrapping paper on the coffee table, then turned to the telephone sitting on the end table. She dialed the number listed on the hotel's letterhead. She had to find out whether there'd been some mistake before her imagination ran rampant.

"Yes, this is Mrs. Drew Thomas calling from Florida. I would like to speak to—" Luz paused to glance at the signature in the letter. "To Mrs. Nash."

"Would you hold one moment, please?"

"Yes." But it seemed much longer than that before a woman's voice identified herself as Mrs. Nash. "I'm Mrs. Thomas . . . Mrs. Drew Thomas," Luz began.

"Yes, Mrs. Thomas. I've been expecting your call. We found the undergarment you left when you were here two weeks ago. It has been mailed. You should be receiving the package any day now."

"I . . . I wasn't aware I had left anything. Are you certain it's mine?" Her fingers were gripping the receiver so tightly her knuckles were turning white.

"I'm quite sure. As a matter of fact, our maid called us from your suite when she found it to ask what she should do. We decided it would be best to have it cleaned and sent to you in Florida." The woman began to sound worried. "It was a black silk teddy with a lace bodice."

"Really." Luz glanced at the offensive garment in the box,

aware of the brittle quality in her voice. "I hadn't even missed it." She shut her eyes, trying to block out the first splinters of pain. "Where did she find it?"

"I believe she said it was between the sheets all the way to the foot of the bed. Which is probably why you didn't see it when you packed."

"Yes. . . . Thank you, Mrs. Nash." She pushed the receiver onto the cradle.

She felt sick inside and hugged her arms about her middle, her body rocking slightly in pain. Tears started running down her cheeks, their taste wet and salty on her lips. Her mind seemed numbed by the shattering discovery, but somehow she knew that wouldn't last.

# CHAPTER VIII

By the time Drew arrived home that evening, late as usual, her pain had given way to an anger that moved from raging hot to icy cold, and back again. Luz stood facing the French doors that opened off their private sitting room onto a sun deck. The darkness outside gave the glass panes a mirrorlike quality. She stared at her reflection, seeing the ravages the tears had wrought, and smoothed the straggly ends of her blond hair into place to repair some of the damage before Drew saw her. There was nothing she could do about the puffiness around her eyes that made the tiny age lines more noticeable. Luz stiffened when the door opened and Drew breezed into the sitting room. She didn't turn around, keeping her back to him.

"Emma said you were up here. Sorry I'm late." His reflection approached hers in the mirroring panes. "It'll only take me a minute to wash up, then we can go down to dinner. How was your day?"

The touch of his hands on her shoulders felt revolting, and the thought of his lips against her cheek was equally repugnant. Luz moved out of his hold before he could kiss her, conscious of his startled reaction.

"Hey, what's the matter?" he chided.

She swung around to face him, her arms crossed while her hands agitatedly rubbed the taut muscles of her upper arms. "That . . . came in the mail today." With a nod of her head, she indicated the unwrapped package on the coffee table.

Puzzled, Drew glanced at the box, then back at her, but Luz knew her expression was too frozen to tell him anything. At the moment, she felt very cold and very hard. He hesitated, then walked over for a closer look. She watched him part the folds of the tissue paper and had the satisfaction of seeing him visibly blanch at the sight of the lace teddy. Something flickered in his eyes when he glanced at her, and Luz guessed that he was wondering where she got it and how much she knew.

"Maybe you should read the letter," she said, drawing his attention to the folded sheet of printed stationery near the package.

He scanned it as quickly as she had, but he seemed better prepared for the contents than she had been and didn't have to reread it. "There must be some mistake," he insisted, but she wasn't about to be bluffed that easily.

"There is no mistake, Drew. I called them myself this afternoon. It seems that frothy piece of silk was found buried in the sheets at the foot of the bed. It obviously isn't mine. I wasn't there, and I don't own anything that even remotely resembles that. So whose is it, Drew?"

He wouldn't look at her. "It was a mistake, Luz."

"You're damned right it was a mistake!" Her anger turned hot. "Who was with you? As if I don't already know. A hooker off the street wouldn't wear something like that. And you can't convince me it was some high-priced call girl. A professional wouldn't leave something like that behind. So whose is it?"

"I don't see the point in answering that," he stated. "I'm the one in the wrong."

"You bastard!" Her voice trembled close to a shout. "Acting so damned noble to protect that bitch! You don't want her dragged into all this, do you? Are you afraid it might hurt her reputation, ruin her good name? I'm your wife! But you don't give a damn about that, do you?"

"Luz, stop it." Drew tried to quiet her. "You have a right to be angry and upset over this, but there is no need to inform the entire neighborhood."

"Then tell me. I want to know whom you were with," she demanded in a not much gentler tone.

"What good would it do to know?" he countered with his insufferable logic. "She's innocent of any blame in this."

"Innocent!" Luz exploded. "I can just bet how innocent she is. And if you won't say her name, I will. Claudia."

"There you go again with those jealous suspicions of her." His continued refusal to admit she was involved drove Luz to the telephone. "What are you doing?" Drew grabbed her arm as she picked up the receiver.

"I'm calling your precious Claudia to see what she has to say about all this." She dialed information. "Claudia Baines, residence number, please."

Drew depressed the switch hook within the cradle, breaking the connection. "Don't make a fool of yourself, Luz."

"You've already done that for me, so I have nothing to lose and everything to gain." Her gaze locked with his.

"But what would you gain?" he argued.

"The satisfaction of knowing I'm right." She stared him down. A second later, he swung away from her, his head bowing in mute defeat.

"All right."

"All right what?" Luz wouldn't let him off the hook with that mute admission. She wanted to hear him say it.

"All right. It was Claudia," he impatiently shot back, and she felt physically sick. "I never wanted it to happen."

"And Adam never wanted to take a bite from the apple Eve offered him," she mocked sarcastically. "Am I supposed to believe that?"

"I didn't take her to New York with the intention of going to bed with her. It just happened," Drew insisted. "I swear to you, Luz, I never meant to hurt you. I love you."

But they were just words, and he'd already shown her how little they meant to him. "How could you do it, Drew? Of all people, why did it have to be her?" Luz wasn't conscious of thinking out loud.

"I don't know if I can explain the attraction I feel." Drew sat down heavily on the loveseat and combed his fingers through his hair. "She makes me feel young. She's fun to be with— and a joy to talk to. And I suppose I'm flattered, too, that she finds me attractive."

"The quickest way to a man's heart is through his ego," Luz said snidely. "And you have enough ego for two men. Can't you see she's just using you? What better way to leap ahead than to become the senior partner's mistress?"

"She isn't like that. You don't know her the way I do."

It hurt to hear him defend her, and she lashed out in response. "No, I don't. But I'm sure what you didn't know about her before you found out when you were in bed. Tell me, Drew, did you enjoy it? Maybe I should take lessons from her. Would you like that?"

"Stop it, Luz," he muttered.

"Come, come, Drew," she mocked. "Don't tell me you wouldn't enjoy a *ménage à trois?*"

"Dammit, Luz, that's enough." He came to his feet and crossed the few steps to the fireplace, half turning his back to her. "You're making it all sound sordid and cheap."

"But that's the way I feel!" The pain was in her throat, making it raw. "I feel cheap and used—humiliated. When I think of that night at the restaurant—sitting at the table with her—with both of you . . ." She couldn't finish the thought.

It was something that almost defied description. Drew and Claudia were lovers and they shared that secret. Drew had betrayed her and never let on. That night he had even made love to her. Looking back, she felt like such a fool. And now Claudia knew things about him, intimate things that only a wife should know. Somehow that knowledge debased Luz. She knew she would never be able to look that woman in the eye again without remembering Drew had lain naked in her arms. All in one blow, she seemed to lose her honor, her self-respect, and her pride.

"Luz, I'm sorry. How many times in how many ways do I have to say it?" The sincerity in his plea made an impression on her.

The anger drained back into its well, leaving her emotionally flattened when she looked at him. "What happens next, Drew?" she asked in a colorless voice.

"I don't know what you mean."

"Are you going to see her again?" Her glance absently took in the silver-tufted mane of his dark hair, the distinctive cleft in his chin, and the masculine contours of his features. Handsome, intelligent—he was all those things—but her trust in him was gone. Without it, he didn't seem to be much of a man.

"I'll have to see her at the office. I can't very well avoid that. As for the other thing"—he deftly hedged naming it—"I promise you, it's over. It was a mistake to become involved with her from the beginning, and it would be an even bigger mistake to continue that relationship. We've had a successful marriage, Luz. I don't want to lose that any more than you do."

She had carefully avoided asking whether Drew had continued to meet Claudia after they had returned from New York or if it had been a one-time fling. But he had just indicated the former. It made his perfidy more difficult to tolerate.

"Then you aren't going to discharge her," she said.

"I can't do that. It wouldn't be fair to Claudia," Drew protested.

"Do you think it's fair to me to go on working with her?" she countered blandly. "I am your wife. Why should I have to endure knowing that you're with her every day and wondering what you're doing together? If you feel you owe her some sort of loyalty, then surely you can find her a position in another law firm. I've heard you say countless times what a brilliant lawyer she's going to be. You have attorney friends all over the country. Get one of them to offer her a better position with more pay."

"I'll see what I can do." But he gave in grudgingly.

"Please do," she said.

He sighed heavily. "Is that your condition?"

She hadn't thought in terms of laying the ground rules under which their marriage could survive, but she supposed that was what she was doing. Divorce had never crossed her mind until now. She shied away from the word that represented ultimate failure to her.

"Yes."

"We'll put all this behind us," Drew said as he came over to stand in front of her. "We'll work it out together."

When he raised his arms to draw her into his embrace, Luz hunched away from them. "No, I—" She needed time to rid herself of the mental image of him making love to Claudia before she'd be able to respond to his touch. "Not yet." Keeping her head down, she backed away. "I'll check on our dinner." Food was the farthest thing from her mind, but she had to pick up the threads of their life somewhere.

The following two weeks were difficult for Luz. She attended all the meetings and luncheons on her calendar, but she always made her excuses and left as soon as she possibly could. Most of her free time she spent exercising Rob's polo string.

She claimed that she was doing it so that when Rob came home during spring break, the horses would be in top condition. But riding soothed her troubled spirits. Sometimes she had the childish wish never to stop riding, but she always did.

Drew was very attentive in the beginning. The first few days he came home shortly after the official closing hours. Then it became later and later every day. Luz never asked what arrangements he had made regarding Claudia, and Drew never volunteered. The black lace teddy had disappeared that first night. Neither of them mentioned it, nor anything else that had subsequently happened.

During the second weekend, Luz had let him make love to her. "Let" was the correct word, because she hadn't participated, merely let him use her body to obtain his satisfaction. She was stunned by how much had been lost, how totally indifferent she had become to his caress. She had never believed love could die so quickly. There wasn't even "liking" in its place—or hate. Nothing was there. She felt nothing for him or about him. She didn't understand how that could happen. It made her wonder if there wasn't something wrong with her.

She couldn't fault Drew for not trying to make everything work out. Every weekend, he'd taken her some place, almost courting her with dates. And he inquired about her activities, attempted conversations in the evenings. She made the effort, too. The difference was her heart wasn't in it.

The Easter holidays signaled the beginning of spring break. With Rob and Trisha home to enliven the atmosphere, Luz wasn't so conscious of brittlely cheerful conversations and forced interest in daily happenings. Still, a certain amount of tension was always there, just below the surface.

Sighing for no reason, she leaned back in the thickly cushioned poolside chaise and closed her eyes to savor the early-evening quiet. A lingering April sun remained in the sky, low on the horizon. Its long, golden rays were pleasantly warm, but they did little to ease the dull, throbbing pain in her forehead. She lifted the squatty cocktail glass and rubbed its cold, wet sides over her brow. Ice cubes rattled against the sides, sloshing the diluted whiskey in the bottom.

A revving motor broke the quiet as it rumbled and roared up the driveway. Unwillingly, Luz opened her eyes and glanced in the direction of the garage, where Trisha's sports car was coming to a stop with a squeal from the brakes. Trisha climbed out of the driver's side, dressed in bright orange jogging shorts and a matching tank top trimmed in hot pink. Rob was only a step behind her, in his riding boots and jeans. They headed toward the back entrance to the house, then spied her and changed their course.

"Hi!" Trisha plopped down on a chair next to her chaise, a wide smile splitting her face.

"Hi yourself." It was fairly easy to smile back. She glanced at Rob standing hip-locked by Trisha's chair. "How was the game?" He'd been playing morning and afternoon ever since he'd been home—friendly games made up of teams of polo-loving amateurs. Players were always needed to fill out a team roster when a regular player couldn't keep the date. So Rob was getting in a lot of practice.

"Good. We won twelve to three."

"Good, he says. Such false modesty," Trisha mocked. "They creamed them."

"Congratulations." Luz lifted her glass in a salute to his victory, then took a long sip.

"Aren't you starting kind of early, Luz?" Trisha frowned with vague disapproval. "You're drinking more lately, aren't you?"

"No, I'm not." But she knew that her predinner cocktail had increased to two to fill the time she spent waiting for Drew to come home. "And it isn't that early. In case you haven't looked at your watch, it's seven o'clock."

"I guess it is." She shrugged her indifference toward the time. "When's dinner?"

"Nine o'clock."

"Why so late?" Trisha protested.

"Your father said he wouldn't be home until eight-thirty, and you know he doesn't like to sit down at the dinner table the minute he walks in the door." Luz stirred the ice cubes in her glass, watching the changing oily shimmer of the liquor.

"How come he always has to work so late?" she grumbled.

Something snapped inside. "Why don't you ask your father?" she flared.

Trisha pulled back in surprise, a mixed frown of confusion and injured innocence on her face. "Well, you don't have to bite my head off."

"I . . . I have a headache." It was a lame excuse even if it was true. "I'm sure your father will try to make it home sooner if he can." Luz forced herself to smile and made a determined attempt to lighten the heavy atmosphere. "I haven't told you my good news."

"Brace yourself, Rob." Trisha was quick to pick up the change, a wicked gleam lighting her eyes. Luz's previous stinging response seemed to have rolled off her back like so much water. "She's going to tell us she's pregnant."

"Hardly." But the outrageous guess surprised Luz into laughing. It was the first unguarded response in weeks. "You two are almost more than I can handle now. Besides, I don't think either your father or I would be interested in starting a second family at our age."

"It was a thought." Trisha shrugged while Rob just shook his head at her. "If it isn't that, what is your good news?"

"I received a letter today from Fiona Sherbourne. She has invited us to stay at their estate while we're in England this June." Luz glanced at Rob. "She said it was only proper, since you are going to be playing on Henry's Seven Oak team for the Windsor Park Tournament. She also said he had been bragging that you were going to be his 'ringer.'" In polo terms, it meant a low-rated player who played above his handicap.

"I hope I can live up to his bragging." His eyebrows lifted in a high arch while the corners of his mouth came grimly down. "It isn't going to be easy when I'll be riding strange horses and playing under a different set of rules."

"There are only minor differences between the Hurlingham Rules and the U.S. Polo Association's. In the study there's a copy of Lord Mountbatten's polo book, which contains both sets. You should study it before we go," Luz advised.

"I will." So serious and intense in his promise, Rob was very positive in his nod. The rare times she saw the light of exhilaration in his eyes always came during fast polo games. His love of the sport was beyond question, equaled only by his determination to excel at it. Luz was glad she was able to give him this opportunity to gain some international experience.

"As for the horses, Fiona wrote that Henry had recently purchased a string of eight Argentine ponies. So I don't think you have anything to worry about when it comes to riding strange horses. It sounds as though you're going to be well mounted."

"Better find out what the Spanish word for 'whoa' is." Trisha poked him in the leg, and hit a bruised spot where a ball had hit him.

"Knock it off, Trish." Rob rubbed at the soreness, never very patient with her irreverent humor.

"One thing I should warn you about, Rob," Luz interrupted, hoping to stop the bickering that would have continued between them. "Henry is very particular about riding in proper attire. Jake played with him a few times, and I remember once how put out Henry was when Jake didn't wear a regulation shirt. So be sure to take plenty of changes with you. Even in practice, he'll expect you to be dressed correctly." Her glance made a pointed sweep of the faded jeans and T-shirt hugging his lank frame.

"How do you suppose Henry will feel about Rob's long sandy locks?" Trisha continued to taunt just to irritate her brother. "If he's such a stickler, maybe he won't let Rob play for him unless he cuts his hair. In polo, they roach the pony's mane. Why not his?"

"You're a pain, Trisha." He pushed the sun visor down across her face, stretching the wide elastic band that secured it around her head. She ducked out of his reach and removed the visor to fluff her shaggy cinnamon curls back into order. "Why don't you pick on somebody else for a change?"

"What are older brothers for?" she mocked.

"Luz, make her lay off," Rob appealed to her as he always had when his sister's needling became too much for him.

Trisha became impatient with him. "Lighten up, Rob. I'm only teasing."

"That's enough, both of you," Luz intervened for the sake of her own peace, and settled her glance on Trisha, who had instigated it all. "Not all of this England trip is for Rob's benefit. Early summer is the Season in Britain, or what's left of it. Which means there will be rounds of parties. I admit there isn't much of a debutante season on either side of the Atlantic any more, at least not on the scale there once was. Since you refused to take part in any of the coming-out affairs here—"

"I think they're crass," she stated contemptuously. "It's all pointless anyway. Supposedly the idea is to meet all the eligible young men, but I already know everybody who is anybody. It's just an opportunity to show off—for the parents as well as their daughters. I much prefer my trip to Paris, especially since it includes my first shopping trip on the Rue du Faubourg St. Honoré."

"That's reassuring," Rob said dryly. "For a minute there, she was sounding so superior to the rest of us, it's a relief to know she's as acquisitive as everyone else is."

A smile tugged at the corners of her mouth when Rob scored one off Trisha, but Luz tried to keep a straight face and continue with the discussion. "I know your feelings on the subject, Trish, but this will acquaint you with the international scene and give you an opportunity to meet new people. Fiona is planning a huge party while we're there, and I'm sure we'll receive invitations to others."

"It probably will be fun." But Trisha knew there was only one person she was interested in meeting again—Raul Buchanan. She supposed it was human nature to want something that was out of reach, greener grass and all that. Maybe if she ever got to know him, she wouldn't like him. But not many men had made such a strong impression on her. "Is Drew still coming with us?" she wondered.

"Our plans have changed somewhat. Now we're going to be gone longer—roughly three weeks. I don't know if your father can arrange to be away from his office for that length of time. He may simply join us in Paris." With that said, she swung her legs over one side of the chaise and pushed out of the chair. "I think it's time for all of us to think about cleaning up for dinner."

"Be there in a minute," Trisha promised and watched her mother cross the patio to the glass-paned doors and enter the house. Beside her, Rob shifted as if to follow. Trisha tipped her head back to glance at him. "Does she seem weird to you?"

He paused. "What do you mean?"

"I don't know. Just sometimes she acts a little depressed."

"She said she had a headache," Rob reminded her.

"Yeah." But Trisha wasn't convinced that was it. On the surface, everything seemed normal, but sometimes she felt bad vibrations and couldn't place the source.

"At the polo office today, I heard you asking around about that Argentine player, Raul Buchanan. How come?"

Trisha feigned a shrug of indifference. "I just wondered where he was playing now."

"What'd you find out?"

"At Retama in San Antonio. They have their fiesta somewhere around this time of year. I wouldn't mind going to it. I've heard it's more fun than Mardi Gras in New Orleans."

"Nice dream." Rob smiled. "But Luz would never forgive you if you missed the Easter gathering of the Kincaids. I bet you'd blow your trip to Paris."

"Easter. It's fitting, isn't it?" She grinned with the humor of her own thought. "The original Kincaids have multiplied like rabbits. It's kinda fun, though, hiding all the Easter eggs for the little ones and seeing everyone again."

It was an ironclad rule that every member of the family gather at the Kincaid estate on Easter Sunday. No exceptions were allowed unless a member was serving in a branch of the military—the Kincaid influence was not always strong enough to obtain a leave. Audra wanted her sons, daughters, and grandchildren home on all holidays, but usually she let it be their decision. On Easter, it was an absolute command.

So they came—children, grandchildren, and now great-grandchildren as well. Events for the entire day were scheduled, starting with sunrise services, the traditional family Easter-egg hunt, a huge brunch, volleyball games on the beach in which all ages participated with each team having its requisite number of youngsters, swimming, and an outdoor barbecue late in the afternoon. By then, everyone was too tired and too full to do anything more strenuous than talk.

Luz often thought the choice of Easter was a symbolic one, representing the resurrection of the family as a unit—laughing, playing, eating, all as one. They were a rolicsome, boisterous group—too loud, sometimes. Which was why Luz had slipped away to the wide sun deck overlooking the beach and ocean, where a volleyball game raged, supervised toddlers played with their sandbuckets, swimmers braved the rolling waves, and others sunned themselves or sat under large umbrellas. Here the shouts, shrieks, giggles, and talk were at a distance, giving her a break from all the noise and confusion and the unaccustomed crush of people.

"Aha, I've caught you sneaking off," a voice accused in

jest, and Luz turned, relaxing when she saw it was Mary. "Shame on you for stealing off like this. Anyone would think you didn't like our company."

"I just had too much of it." A quiet smile curved her mouth. "What's your reason for slipping away, or am I supposed to believe you were looking for me?"

"That's what I'll tell everyone," her sister countered as she leaned her hands on the deck rail. "But I'd lie about anything for this little bit of peace and quiet. Isn't it wonderful to get away from that"—indicating the crowd of family on the beach—"for a little while."

"It is," Luz agreed.

"There goes Julie's little monster heading for the water." A toddler waddled as fast as he could toward the oncoming waves, but a teenage boy, one of several watching the younger ones, scooped him up before his feet got wet. "Remember what that was like, Luz? I swear you needed ten pairs of eyes to keep my brood out of trouble."

"I remember. It's a good thing we were young then or we would have died of heart failure many a time." A breeze curved a strand of hair across her mouth, and Luz turned into its salty current, shaking her head and letting it blow aside her hair.

"Where's Drew? I don't see him."

"He's out swimming." Even at this distance, it was easy to pick him out from the other heads bobbing in the surf. The twin streaks of white hair made him easy to distinguish.

"You seem unusually quiet, Luz."

Sisters could be too perceptive. "Why do you think I'm here?"

"I don't mean now. All day, even in the middle of that, you've seemed just a little bit reserved. Is something wrong?" She looked askance at her, a thought suddenly occurring. "You aren't still bothered by that remark Trisha made?"

"Isn't that odd?" Luz mused aloud. "I had completely forgotten about that."

"Then what is it?"

She had always trusted Mary with her secrets. Although she wouldn't have searched her out to confide in her, now that the opportunity presented itself, she accepted it. "Drew had an affair with that woman Claudia Baines. It happened while they were in New York. I found out about it by accident. It doesn't matter how. He assures me it's over."

"Don't you believe him?"

"I don't know." A long sigh broke from her, before her mood turned wryly bitter. "Claudia. Remember that word-association game? Every time I hear her name, I think of the word 'cloying.' Claudia is cloying. It isn't true, of course. The times that I've seen her—you've met her—she seems warm and friendly. But cloying still comes to my mind. Maybe because it's all so sickening."

"I've never understood why a woman becomes a man's mistress. It's true that she has no responsibilities and no commitments and she doesn't have to go through the day-to-day drudgery of living with him. But there are so many more minuses to an affair. She rarely sees him on weekends, and never on holidays. He may go to bed with her, but it's guaranteed he'll go home to sleep. His wife, children, and job all have priority over her. She's at the bottom of his list, and she sees him only whenever he's so inclined. Women who put up with that must have a streak of masochism in them."

"He's infatuated with her."

"I'd think you would find that reassuring," Mary said. "Infatuations don't last."

"But look at the damage that's been done in the meantime." It saddened her to know how very far apart they were now. She turned to Mary, uncertain why she felt she had to say, "No one else knows this. I couldn't stand it if Rob and Trisha found out."

"I won't tell anyone, not even Ross. I don't want to give the man any ideas," she joked lightly.

"Thanks." Luz smiled faintly, then looked toward the beach, her attention drawn back to the spot where she'd last seen Drew. He was wading ashore. She watched him shake out a beach towel and rub himself dry, then drape it around his neck and jog toward the bathhouse cabana on the beach close by the house.

When he noticed her standing on the sun deck, he waved and cupped a hand to his mouth to shout. "I'm going to shower and change! Afterward, let's have a sundowner!" She waved in acknowledgment, then he disappeared inside the cabana.

It seemed time that she attempt some sort of conciliatory gesture. "I think I'll fix those drinks and take them down."

"I'll just stay here and enjoy the quiet," Mary replied.

After fixing the drinks at the wet bar located in the game room, Luz used the covered, outside stairs that connected the cabana with the main house. Her rubber-soled deck shoes made almost no sound on the board steps as she walked slowly down the two flights of stairs to avoid spilling the drinks in her hands.

It took her a minute to juggle the drinks and open the rear door. As she stepped inside and paused to close it, she heard Drew talking to someone. That's the way it sounded at first, but no one ever answered him. Puzzled, Luz left the door standing ajar and went down two of the carpeted steps leading to the sunken rec room.

When he came into view, his back was to her. He was wearing a thick terry-cloth robe, and a towel was slung over his shoulder. The instant she spied the telephone receiver in his hand, Luz understood why she had been hearing only one side of his conversation. She began paying attention to what he was saying.

"Sure," he said and waited, then, "I will. Bye." The intimate tone, the warmth in his voice, told her more than the meaningless answers. When he hung up the phone, Luz was raging with hurt.

"Who were you talking to just now?" The harshness of her demand rang through the stillness, and Drew swung around in surprise, a stunned and guilty look on his face.

He recovered quickly. "It was the wrong number. Someone wanting the Carlyles."

"You lying bastard!" Her cry of outrage was hoarse and raw as she hurled a glass at his head, ice cubes and liquor spraying the air. He dodged it, and it crashed against the wall in an explosion of shattering glass.

"Luz, for God's sake—"

But she wasn't interested in anything he had to say. "You called her, didn't you? It was Claudia on the phone, wasn't it?" She was trembling with the violence she felt.

"Luz, I told you—"

"I know what you told me." Distantly she could hear the shouts and laughter of children filtering through the glassed front of the cabana. With the recognition came a sense of where

they were and awareness that any of the family might walk in
on them. Luz reached deep inside to get control of her emotions.
"And it's obvious that the things you said meant nothing. But
this isn't the time or the place to discuss it. Not now. Not until
Rob and Trisha leave. Then we'll talk."

"I think that's wise," he said carefully.

"But remember this, Drew. If you can't get rid of her, I
can." She shoved the other drink glass onto a table, the contents
sloshing over the side, then walked stiffly to the sliding doors
that opened to the beach. She slid it half open and paused to
look over her shoulder at him. "You'd better ring one of the
housemaids to clean up the broken glass." She left the cabana
and walked down to the water, letting the seaspray sting her
eyes.

# CHAPTER IX

With riding gloves, hat, and quirt in her hand, Luz left the stable and cut across the patio area around the pool. The physical tiredness was a good feeling, relaxing all her muscles and leaving them loose. She lifted the weight of her blond hair off her neck and let the warm breeze fan her skin, then shook her head to let it fall free.

Early evening was a good time to school Rob's horses, while the sun still lingered in the sky and before the night dew made the grass slick. Even the best-trained polo ponies needed routine practice in the basics—stops, backing, and turns—to correct any bad habits they might acquire. Sessions like today required her concentration, not allowing her any time to think about her problems or feel sorry for herself. Working with the horses was therapy for her.

Possibly she had needed such therapy today more than at any other recent time. Rob and Trisha had left for school this morning, which meant that tonight she'd have it out with Drew. One way or another, Claudia was going out of their lives.

The French doors into the living room were unlocked, and she entered the house through them. Luz was three strides into the room before she heard the clink of ice in a glass and caught a movement out of the corner of her eye. It brought her up short, and she turned toward it. After being outside in the glaring light of a setting sun, her eyes were not completely adjusted to the comparative darkness of the interior.

"Drew." She recognized him in surprise. "What are you doing home so early?" Then a second thought struck her. "Where's your car? It wasn't in the garage."

"It's parked out front." He remained behind the bar, a preoccupied frown crossing his tanned face while he swirled the ice in his drink with a circular motion of his hand.

"Oh." At least that explained why she hadn't seen his brown Mercedes.

"It's time we had that talk, Luz," Drew announced.

"I agree." She tossed her riding equipment onto a chair cushion and walked over to the bar, slipping her hands into the pockets of her tan jodhpurs. "This can't go on."

"I came to that realization, too." He took a swig of his drink. "By the way, I sent the cook home. I knew it was Emma's day off, and I felt it would be better if we were alone."

"It's probably best." She hoped this wouldn't turn into a shouting match.

He braced his hands on the countertop. "I want a divorce, Luz."

The floor seemed to go out from under her feet. Of all the things she'd thought he might say, that bald statement was not one of them. The shock of it left her numb with disbelief.

"No." Her voice was so faint she barely heard it herself.

"It's the hardest thing I've ever had to say, Luz. I've never wanted to hurt you," Drew insisted. "I love you. I'll always love you. That will never change."

"Then . . . why?" The numbness was splintering, and the pain was coming through. It was crazy. It was insane. In these last weeks since she'd learned about the affair, she had told herself there were no more feelings left, that everything was gone, that there wasn't any way he could hurt her anymore. But the pain she was feeling now with those words pounding through her head—"I want a divorce, Luz"—was tearing her apart.

"Because I'm in love with Claudia. I can't give her up. I can't let her go. I've tried, believe me." The push of his body emphasized his claim. "But she and I share something very special, very rare. I can't expect you to understand how much I love her."

"My God, Drew, she's young enough to be your daughter. Don't be a fool!" she cried in protest.

"The age difference . . . doesn't matter. Maybe in the beginning it bothered me, but neither of us thinks of that when we're together. It became insignificant a long time ago."

"What about twenty years from now?" Luz argued desperately. The panic she felt was almost terror. He couldn't mean it! He couldn't throw away their lives like this! "For God's sake, think of what you're saying, Drew!"

"I have thought about it. In these last few weeks, I've thought about little else. This isn't a decision I've reached lightly. Please understand that."

"Understand!" There was a catch in her choked voice, the sobs so close to escaping. "You're throwing away twenty-one years of our lives! Don't they mean anything to you?"

He bowed his head, shaking it slowly. The rocking of those silver wings seemed to mock her. "You're not making this any easier, Luz."

"You're a rotten bastard." She hurt so much inside she could hardly breathe, and she lashed out with the raw anger of a wounded animal. "Am I supposed to make it easy for you to leave me and go to that dark-haired young bitch in heat?"

"Let's leave out the name-calling, Luz. It's beneath you." The aggressive thrust of his chin seemed to carry a warning that he wouldn't tolerate any further deprecations of Claudia.

"What am I supposed to call her?" She heard the shrill ring of near hysteria in her voice, but there was nothing she could do to stop it. There were explosions inside her—waves of pain, panic, and anger. "That charming young woman who stole my husband? She's a scheming, conniving bitch! She may have you fooled, but not me. She got you the same way she got her law degree—on her back!"

His hand tightened around the drink glass. For an instant, Luz thought he was going to hit her. A second later, his expression showed iron calm. "That's an attitude I should have expected from you. You can't accept that Claudia has the intelligence to obtain something on her own, because you've had to have everything given to you. So you fear all professional women like Claudia and try to tear them down. For your information, she graduated *magna cum laude*, and you don't do that by screwing your professors."

Belittled by his words, Luz turned away to hide the tears filling her eyes. She didn't know what to say—how to reach him and stop this nightmare. There had to be a way to save their marriage.

"Don't do this, Drew." She issued the soft plea in a trembling voice as the tears spilled down her cheeks. "I need you."

"You don't need me. You've never needed me."

"That isn't true." He couldn't believe that. But when she looked at him, Luz saw the sardonic twist of his mouth that confirmed he did.

"I'd hate to count the number of times I've been reminded how lucky I was to marry a Kincaid. For years, people used to call me up and ask 'Are you the lawyer who is Jake Kincaid's son-in-law?' But I've finally earned a reputation of my own. You've never needed my name, and God knows you have more money than I'll make in a lifetime. You'll get along fine without me."

"But you're my husband."

"You say that the way you say 'my mink' or 'my diamonds.' I'm not a possession to wear on your arm, Luz," Drew stated tightly. "And after today, I won't be your husband. You can keep the house and everything in it but my own personal items. I'll take my car. As for the rest, I recommend that you retain Arthur Hill. He's represented the Kincaid family for years. Or anyone else you choose to work out a divorce settlement on the other properties and investments we've acquired during our marriage. Have them contact my partner, Bill Thorndyke. He'll be drawing up the separation papers for me."

It all sounded so final, yet none of it wanted to sink in. She couldn't believe that he meant any of this—that he could so coldly walk away from her after all these years. Her world was falling apart, and Luz didn't know how to hold it together.

"The children." She reached desperately for a straw. "What about them? Have you considered how this will affect them?"

She hated the pitying look he gave her. "As you pointed out the other day, they're practically adults. They are old enough to understand that these things happen. Marriages are breaking up all the time."

"But not mine," Luz protested, the sobs coming through and her body shaking with them.

"It's over, Luz. There's nothing you can say that will change it." He tossed down the rest of his drink and set the glass on the counter with a certain finality. "It will be better for everyone if you just accept that."

"How can I?" She wiped at the tears running into the corners of her mouth and appealed to his reason. "You say you love me, Drew. If you mean that, then why rush into a divorce? Right now you think you're in love with . . . her. But what if you aren't? What if it just turns out to be infatuation? Don't you think you should wait and see if it will last before you throw away our marriage? A year from now you may wonder what you ever saw in her. It will all pass. You'll see, and things will be the way they were for us." At the moment, it seemed her only hope—to stall for time.

"No, Luz. You don't understand." Her arguments hadn't swayed him at all. She could see that in his steadfast expression. "Even if I had any doubts about my love for Claudia—which I don't—it wouldn't change my decision. Claudia is pregnant with my child."

"No." Luz recoiled in shock, conscious of the sickening lurch of her stomach.

"I didn't intend to tell you that today, because I didn't feel it was relevant. I want a divorce so that I can marry Claudia because I'm in love with her—not because she is going to have my baby. But I'm telling you to stress the point that even if I didn't marry her and we stayed together, nothing would be the way it was. It would be impossible for either of us to forget that I have a bastard child in this world."

His voice seemed to come from a great distance as her mind reeled with the humiliation and embarrassment the announcement portended—for herself as well as Rob and Trisha. "She . . . she can have an abortion—or move away to have the baby and give it up for adoption."

"It's her body, and it's up to her to decide whether or not she wants an abortion. Not you, Luz. Or me," Drew stated flatly.

"You're a lawyer. Talk her into it," she declared wildly.

"I wouldn't even try." He moved out from behind the bar, a calm deliberation in the way he carried himself. "She wants the baby."

"She wants you!"

"And I want her. And I'd take the child myself before I would let anyone else raise it," he said.

The walls seemed to be crashing down around her. She looked at Drew and felt so helpless, so utterly powerless. It frightened her. She was like a lost child, not knowing which way to turn to find her way out, too scared to cry, all the panicked screams locked inside.

"I'm sorry, Luz." Drew paused, his glance shifting away from her. "I'm truly sorry for both of us that it turned out this way."

It was a full second before she realized he was walking toward the door. Luz ran after him. "Where are you going? You can't leave!"

"I can't stay here." Although he stopped, there was some invisible barrier between them that prevented Luz from reaching out to cling to him. "I've packed my clothes. They're in the car. I'll arrange to pick up the rest of my things another time. . . . Goodbye, Luz."

She stood rooted to the floor, unable to move, as he walked to the front door and opened it. His clothes were already in the car. They had been there when she came home. There had never been any chance of changing his mind. She wanted to die remembering the way she had pleaded with him to reconsider, abandoning her pride and self-respect.

"You're going to her place, aren't you?" Luz accused, loudly and bitterly. "You're going to live with that cheap bitch you knocked up, aren't you?"

Drew paused briefly in the opening and faced her with an impassive look. "If you need me for any reason, contact the office. My answering service knows where to reach me."

"You bastard! Get out! Get out of my house!" She began grabbing things and throwing them at the door when it shut behind him. Vases of flowers and ceramic figurines, magazines and umbrellas, anything she could find, crashed into the general target area while she hurled a string of obscenities after him.

She never heard the slam of the car door or the low rumble of the motor. When she ran out of a ready supply of things to throw, her strength waned. She sagged onto the stairs and hugged the newel post for support. "Don't do this, Drew," Luz whispered brokenly. "Don't leave me."

The weeping began, slowly at first, then with gathering force until her shoulders shook with wracking sobs. The rejection went too deep; it was too total. There was no release for the pain. So she cried herself to a state of numbed exhaustion.

Darkness swallowed the house, and she welcomed its enveloping black cocoon. It was a place to hide away from the world, and that's what she wanted. A shrill sound broke the silence, and Luz was slow to identify the ring of the telephone. It roused her briefly, then she sank back into her torpor, trying to block out the annoying sound.

Belatedly it occurred to her that it might be Drew calling to say he had changed his mind. She hurried to answer it, stumbling over the shards of pottery and glass in the dark foyer, and fearing he might hang up before she could get to the phone.

"Hello?" There was an anxious pitch to her husky voice as she gripped the receiver in both hands and waited for the sound of Drew's voice in response.

"I was beginning to think no one was there," a woman answered with a trace of exasperation. "This is Connie Davenport. Let me speak to Luz." Luz couldn't say anything for several seconds. "Hello?" The woman demanded a response.

"She isn't here." Luz groped for the telephone and pushed the receiver onto its cradle, abruptly hanging up on her friend before she could say more.

The darkness became alien, and she searched for the wall switch and flipped on the overhead light. The phone started ringing again. This time she backed away from it, the debris crunching under her feet. A noise came from the rear of the house, and Luz swung around in vague alarm. The phone was silenced in midring as it was answered elsewhere. Some distant part of her mind registered that Emma had returned. She didn't want to see her. She didn't want to see or speak to anyone. She headed for the oak stairs, seeking to escape the questions she wasn't prepared to answer.

"Mrs. Davenport is on the phone, Luz. She wants—" Emma Sanderson stopped abruptly in the foyer, her usually unshakable composure broken by the wreckage she saw. Luz's haunted and tear-stained face did little to reassure her. "My gracious, what happened? Should I call the police?"

"No," Luz answered dully and faced the stairs, wanting to hide. She didn't know what to say. She didn't know how to explain to anyone that Drew had left her . . . for a younger woman . . . an intelligent woman.

"Are . . . are you sure, Mrs. Thomas?" her secretary said. "If you've been harmed . . ."

"Harmed" was such a gentle word that Luz almost laughed. "Destroyed" was more apt. "No, Emma." She paused with one

foot on the first step. "I don't want to speak to anyone . . . except Drew." She held out the hope that he'd come
to his senses and spare her all this humiliation—that he'd miss
her and come back. "If he calls, I'll be upstairs."

"Shall I try to reach him?"

"No." It was a forceful reply. She had virtually begged him
not to leave. She wouldn't plead with him to come back.

She climbed the stairs to the master suite and shut the door,
hoping to shut out the world a little longer. She ventured as
far as the door to his bedroom. The dresser drawers and closet
doors were open and emptied of clothes. No personal items
remained in the room. It looked bare and abandoned—the way
she felt. She went into her own bedroom and closed the door.

For three days, Luz didn't venture outside those four walls,
refusing all calls and returning her meal trays virtually untouched. None of the household staff commented on Drew's
absence or his missing clothes, not even Emma, but Luz knew
they had guessed that he had deserted her. Sometimes she sat
for hours staring into space. Sometimes she cried until there
seemed to be no more tears left, but there always were. At
night, she prowled the room, bitterness and anger running deep,
hating him and swearing she'd never take him back even if he
came crawling on his knees.

Each time she saw her reflection in the mirror—the pale
and drawn face with its faint age lines deepened by sleeplessness—her resentment toward him grew. All their years together
had been for nothing, thrown away for someone younger. What
man would want her now—a forty-two-year-old woman with
grown children? They all wanted twenty-year-old nymphs who
could make them feel young and virile again. She'd seen those
pathetically lonely middle-aged divorcees, starving for affection, and didn't want to be one of them.

So she waited, half hoping he'd come back before anyone
found out he'd left her and postponing the moment when she'd
have to admit to someone that Drew had walked out on her.
She dreaded facing her friends. Worse was the prospect of
telling Rob and Trisha.

There was a knock on her bedroom door. "Go away!" But
her sharp command was ignored; the door was opened. Luz
glared at Emma. "I told you I didn't want to be disturbed for
any reason."

The plump woman hesitated only briefly, then crossed the room to hand Luz a thick envelope. "This came for you. It looked important." She quietly withdrew from the room, leaving Luz alone to open the envelope.

She stared at the return address printed in the left-hand corner: *Thomas, Thorndyke & Wall—Attorneys at Law.* Mechanically, she lifted the sealed flap with a fingernail and removed the official-looking document. She scanned the first page. There was no need to go farther. It was a notice that Drew had filed for a legal separation. He wasn't coming back.

With the notice in hand, Luz walked out of the bedroom where she'd slept alone for so many years and down the stairs to the living-room bar. The first drink tasted like water, so she fixed a second, stronger, and reached for the telephone.

"This is Luz Thomas calling. Jake Kincaid's daughter. I want to speak to Arthur Hill." She took a swallow of the drink while she waited for the attorney to come on the line. When he did, she explained the facts to him with as little detail as possible.

"I strongly advise against any hasty action, Luz." He'd known the family too long not to speak to her as a father. "A reconciliation is always possible—and preferred."

"No." Her tone was decisive and cold. "I want a divorce as quickly, and as quietly, as one can be arranged. No delays."

The desire for revenge was strong, but she was thinking clearly if only temporarily. She stood to lose more in a messy divorce than Drew did. Dragging a pregnant Claudia into divorce court would likely illicit sympathy for both the woman and Drew, and bare her humiliation to public ridicule. Not to mention how awkward it would be for Rob and Trisha. A quick and quiet dissolution was the way to handle it. Reluctantly, the attorney acceded to her wishes.

The doorbell chimed as Luz hung up the phone. She ignored its summons to take another drink while Emma's footsteps sounded in the long corridor. The minute the door opened she heard her mother's imperious demand: "I have come to find out what is going on here. You have repeatedly refused to put my calls through to my daughter. Now I insist that you take me to her." During the past three days, Luz had not bothered to ask who had called for her, but she wasn't surprised to learn her mother was one.

"I'm sorry, Mrs. Kincaid, but your daughter left very definite orders not to be disturbed—by anyone." Emma stood up well to her, respectful yet firm.

"Emma, I'm in the living room," Luz called to break the stalemate that was bound to occur. She slid off the bar stool as her mother swept by Emma and entered the living room, followed closely by Mary. The wry thought crossed her mind that at least she'd be spared from telling all this twice. "You're just in time. What can I fix you to drink? Gin and tonic, Audra?"

"Two o'clock in the afternoon is much too early to be drinking." Her mother took the glass out of Luz's hand and set it on the counter with a resounding thump.

"This is my house and I drink when I please." Luz grabbed up the glass and stiffly walked behind the bar to replenish its contents.

Audra's lips narrowed in disapproval at Luz's defiance, but she didn't pursue it. "Have you been ill?" Those sharp eyes inspected the wan and haggard face. "No one has seen or talked to you in days."

"No." Luz freshened her drink with ice. "I've simply been incommunicado."

"You should have been out, letting yourself be seen and silencing those wagging tongues spreading rumors that you and Drew are having marital difficulties," her mother decreed.

"Why? They're true." Luz avoided looking at Mary, aware her sister would see through her bravado. "As a matter of fact, I talked to Arthur Hill a few minutes ago and instructed him to begin the divorce proceedings. So you see"—she lifted her glass in a mock salute—"I do have something to celebrate."

"You can call him right back and tell him you've changed your mind."

"But I haven't." She took a swig from the glass, feeling the liquor burn down her throat.

"No Kincaid has ever gotten a divorce," Audra informed her.

"Then that makes me the first, doesn't it?" Luz declared, but she couldn't maintain that brittle facade of indifference, and the bitterness came through. "He doesn't want to be married to me any longer. He's in love with someone else—someone younger. So at least allow me the dignity of being the one to divorce him."

"Love has nothing to do with it. Whether he's in love with you or someone else, it makes no difference. That is no justification for breaking up your marriage. This little affair he's having will pass. For the sake of your family, you must wait it out."

"The way you did with Jake?" Luz did the unpardonable and referred to her father's philandering ways. "Do you think people admired you for letting him make a fool of you? They laughed behind your back and pitied you for being so stupid that you couldn't see what they really thought. Your marriage was nothing but a farce, and you were the fool in it." She watched her mother go pale, but she couldn't stop the vindictive attack. "No matter how miserable I might be, I never want to be like you. The very thought makes me sick to my stomach."

She never saw the arc of her mother's hand, but she felt the stinging blow to her cheek when it struck her. The force of it turned her head, and she kept it turned after the sound of the slap ended in absolute silence.

"I won't apologize, Audra." She breathed in slowly and deeply, struggling for control. "That is how I feel."

"Luz," Mary said to fill the chilling silence. "Aren't you being too hasty? After all, in a few months, Drew may decide that this woman isn't worth giving up his home and family for. There's no need to rush into a divorce."

"You're saying I should give him a chance to make a fool of me again." This time she didn't have to say anything about her parents. Both women knew. "He already had his chance to end it with Claudia. I believed him once and behaved like a gushing bride. Never again. Besides, there is a little matter of a baby on the way."

"My Lord, you mean she's pregnant?" Mary's eyes widened.

"According to Drew, yes." Luz swirled the liquor in her glass, feeling wretchedly bitter and hurt. "Tell me, Audra, did you ever have to deal with any illegitimate Kincaids running around?"

"No. But that changes nothing," Audra stated. "Your duty is to your family. No sacrifice is too great if it keeps a marriage intact and the family together."

"Even if that sacrifice includes losing the respect of our children?" Luz challenged. "I loved you and Jake, Audra, but I never respected you—either of you. I swore I'd never let any man destroy me the way Jake destroyed you—or you, him. I was never sure where the blame properly belonged. On both of you, I guess—Jake for running around and you for putting up with it. I'd rather live alone the rest of my life than endure a marriage that's a sham." She took another drink. Alcohol was a weak comfort, but it was the only one she had.

"I suppose you think you can drown your sorrows with that." Her mother viewed her drinking with disgust.

"Temporarily, Audra. Temporarily." Her smile was as twisted as her humor—and her pain. She wished she were alone so she could cry.

"What about Trisha and Rob?" Mary inserted quietly. "How did they take the news? Or haven't you told them?"

"Not yet." She dreaded facing them, dreaded their questions more than anyone else's. They'd want to know why the marriage had failed. How could she answer something she didn't understand herself? Drew's rejection of her had left her feeling that somehow she was at fault—that she had done something to drive him to another woman's bed.

"You can't wait very long. There's always a chance they'll hear it from someone else," Mary warned.

"I know. But it isn't something I can explain over the telephone. I thought I'd ask them to come home this weekend." She felt a hot flare of resentment. Drew should be the one to explain to them, since he had walked out on her. Why did she have to endure the pain of their questions?

"It's a shame you didn't have a houseful of children the way I did," her sister said, then sighed.

"Why?" She couldn't imagine anything worse than telling twelve children instead of two that their parents were getting a divorce.

"Any man who would walk out on a wife with twelve children would be considered a first-class heel."

Luz frowned at her sister, hearing something that surprised her. "Is that why you had twelve children? So you could hold them over Ross's head in case he ever thought of leaving you?" She saw the dull flush creep into Mary's face.

"I wanted a lot of children. So did Ross," Mary insisted somewhat defensively. "But I admit a part of me recognized that they were a kind of insurance our marriage would last. And stop looking at me as if I've just poisoned an apple. I've had to be realistic. My looks aren't the kind that make a man's heart beat faster and inspire undying love. Even with the Kincaid name and money, I knew I could wind up dumped on some shelf. So I surrounded myself with love the best way I knew how. I reinforced the marriage knot with family ties. Maybe you should have done the same, Luz."

"Maybe I should offer that advice to dear Claudia," Luz murmured and tipped the glass to her lips. Illusions were shattering all around her, it seemed.

"What do you want us to say when people ask why you and Drew have separated?" Her mother refocused the conversation on the matter at hand, requesting the official family response for any inquiries. Luz knew her answer would be passed to her brothers, Michael and Frank, creating a united front.

"Irreconcilable differences. Isn't that the phrase?" And that irreconcilable difference was Claudia. "Tell them it's an amicable divorce."

"What about when they ask about the other woman involved? They will, you know," Audra reminded her.

A sardonically amused smile lifted the corners of her mouth. "I'll probably say, 'How incredibly tacky of you to bring that up,' then walk away."

"Very wise." Audra nodded in approval.

Luz's head began to throb from the strain. It was crazy, but she couldn't allow herself to show her true feelings to either her sister or her mother—not the frightening vulnerability she felt, the awful insecurities, nor the doubts about her self-worth. She had to hide them. Her self-confidence was eroded, leaving only a brittle shell. It couldn't withstand much probing.

"Do you mind leaving?" She avoided looking at either of them as she made her stiff request. "I'd prefer to be alone just now. I—I have to call Rob and Trisha, and I'd rather do that in private."

"If you need me, you will call?" Mary pressed for reassurance.

"Of course." But Luz knew she wouldn't and wondered why she was afraid of exposing her weaknesses to the family. It should have been the one place she found solace. Did she feel she had somehow failed them, too? She honestly didn't know. She simply felt alone—so alone.

\*     \*     \*

A white organza scarf was tied around the band of the navy-blue hat, its long tails trailing off the back of the extra-wide brim. The hat acted as a shield against prying eyes. Luz hid beneath it the same way she hid behind the very dark sunglasses framed in white. Her nerves were coiled as tautly as a main-spring as her glance jumped over the faces of strangers exiting the plane. She unconsciously pressed a hand to her abdomen to quiet the nervous churning of her stomach. The white silk of her navy polka-dot dress felt smooth beneath her palm, so at odds with the rawness inside.

She was aware of Rob standing beside her, studying her with a brooding look that seemed almost sullen. Fortunately, there hadn't been time to talk, since his flight had been delayed and had arrived only minutes before Trisha's. She knew how mysterious she must have sounded when she called them, first assuring them no one was ill or dying, then insisting she needed them to come home this weekend.

Trisha emerged from the line of deplaning passengers and cut across the departure lounge to meet them. Dodging the swooping hat brim, she hugged Luz, then stepped back and viewed her with sharp, curious eyes that reminded Luz of her mother's.

"You look like hell, Luz," she said.

The bluntness was so reminiscent of her mother at times. "Thank you, Trisha. You do such wonderful things for my morale." She realized her ironic remark could invoke questions, and she didn't intend to provide answers in an airport. "The car is in the lot. Why don't I meet you two outside the baggage-claim area?"

"Sure." Their agreement was readily given.

When they temporarily parted company a few minutes later, Luz felt as though she'd been granted a stay of execution. Over and over, she had rehearsed what she was going to say. She worried about how they would take the news of the impending divorce and what they would think of her. She wanted them to think well of her. More than anything, she needed their approval and support.

Parent-child relationships were so complicated. She hadn't sought their advice in making her decision, yet their opinions mattered so very much.

They were waiting at the curb when she drove up. As soon

as the luggage was stowed in the trunk, they climbed into the car. Rob got into the back seat, letting Trisha sit in front with Luz.

"If you don't mind, we'll talk when we get home." She doubted that she could concentrate on the road and their questions at the same time if she tried to talk to them now.

Trisha started to answer, but Rob was a split second quicker. "We don't mind." Trisha appeared to disagree, but she said nothing. Luz was grateful for the way they bridled their curiosity and hoped they would continue to show such understanding.

The Mercedes's convertible top was raised to close in the interior, the air-conditioning vents letting in the only circulation. Luz had always thought a divorce would make a person feel free—would make her welcome the sensation of the wind blowing through her hair. But she wanted to hide, under hats, behind dark glasses, inside cars. Maybe Drew felt free, but she felt naked and exposed. It was as if everyone could see the flaws that she'd taken such pains to hide—like the small cellulite deposits dimpling her thighs or the faint stretch marks on her stomach from two pregnancies.

The drive home from the airport was made mostly in silence. Neither Rob nor Trisha appeared inclined to talk, although Luz was aware that their gazes strayed to her often. She led the way into the living room, entering through the French doors to the patio. She removed her hat and dark glasses and laid them with her purse atop a bar stool.

Her blond hair was pulled severely back and coiled in a bun at the back of her neck. Its style stretched the skin across her face, eliminating the crepy look around her eyes and the lines of strain recently etched near her mouth as well as smoothing her brow and tautening a sagging chin. The total effect was a mock facelift. More than once since Drew had left her, Luz had considered cosmetic surgery. She no longer believed there was such a thing as aging gracefully. She didn't want to look old and hear unkind comparisons between herself and the youthful Claudia. It all came from insecurity, she knew—from not believing anyone could care for her the way she was.

The tension in the air was thick. Luz sensed the waiting, and she walked behind the bar. Liquor had become a crutch, a false support to help her deal with unpleasant things. Depending on it only proved how weak she was. She knew that and poured a drink anyway.

"I know you're wondering what is so important that you had to come home this weekend," she began.

"We already know about the divorce, Luz," Trisha said quietly. "Dad called us."

The announcement was like a blow knocking the wind from her. She hadn't the strength to hold the glass anymore and set it down before she dropped it. "Drew called?" Shock was in her voice, but it quickly receded under a rush of resentment. "The swine! He could have let me know he'd talked to you. I've been through hell wondering how to tell you." All her carefully built emotional defenses were shattered. Blindly, Luz moved around to the front of the bar, where Trisha was perched on a stool and Rob stood awkwardly.

"He called the day after you phoned us," Trisha explained.

"He told you about the divorce over the telephone? How could he do anything so cold and impersonal?" His insensitivity made her want to cry. She touched Rob's shoulder, feeling the rigidly flexed muscles.

"We wanted to hear your side," Rob said.

My side. Your side. It was beginning—the dichotomy of a family. Luz ached inside, for herself and for them. "Did he tell you that he'd found someone else?" Tears blurred her eyes when she saw the confused and pained look on Rob's face that said he knew.

At the sight of her tears, he reached and gathered her into his arms, crushing her tightly against him. He turned his face into her hair and muttered half-smothered words of anger. "How could he do this to you, Luz? The dirty son of a bitch—" The rest was choked off.

But it didn't matter. This was the first physical comfort she had known. She closed her eyes, feeling the strain of his body as it tried to absorb her anguish. She held him tightly, needing him, crying softly, yet reassured by her son's fierce embrace. It was some minutes before she slowly pulled away, careful not to notice his reddened eyes while she wiped away her own tears.

"Maybe I should ask what he told you," Luz suggested in a soft, emotionally charged voice.

"Nothing much really," Trisha said. "Just that he'd found

someone else and the two of you had decided to get a divorce. Naturally he hoped we'd understand. Marriages just sometimes break up, he said."

"It happens all the time." To others, Luz thought. She had never expected it to happen to her.

"Have you met her?" Despite her frequent questions, Trisha seemed unnaturally contained. Rob was usually the quiet one, showing all this reserve Luz saw in her daughter.

"Yes."

"What's she like?"

"She's young and beautiful." Luz tried not to let her own jealousies color her reply. "She's a lawyer, so she and your father have a lot in common."

"Maybe if you'd shown a little interest in his work instead of confining your dinner conversation to such scintillating topics as the current theme of your latest bazaar, this wouldn't have happened."

The stinging criticism hurt, however innocently disguised it was. "I have tried to talk to him about his work, but when he gets too technical, I can't follow him. I imagine he grew tired of explaining everything to me all the time." She was conscious of the defensive edge in her voice.

"You could have tried to learn." It was a half-muttered complaint, and Luz resented being singled out for blame. This whole issue had been a touchy subject for too long, so she naturally reacted to it.

"You think I should have studied law, even though I wasn't personally interested in the subject, simply to please him?" Luz challenged. "Don't you think that's a slightly antiquated idea, Trisha? A marriage consists of two individuals who live together. The idea is not for one person to impose his interests on the other. To share them, yes, but not to force the other to like them."

"Luz is right." Rob spoke up on her behalf. "I can't think of anything more boring than spending an evening talking about writs, supoenas, and litigations."

Trisha hopped off the bar stool in a sudden burst of impatience. "Well, it just seems to me if a man is happy at home, he doesn't go out looking for someone else to love. I just want to know what went wrong. What did you do to send him away?"

"I don't know," she answered sharply. "Why don't you ask

your father? Then you can tell me so I won't have to keep wondering."

"I suppose it was your idea to sleep in separate bedrooms," Trisha accused.

Luz slapped her. "Your remarks are becoming too personal, young lady." When she saw the white mark her hand left on Trisha's cheek, she felt sickened by what she'd done. Her temper died as quickly as it had flared. Trisha was young and could be forgiven her impetuousness, but Luz was an adult and should have known better than to react in kind.

When Trisha turned and grabbed up her purse to walk to the door, for an instant Luz couldn't move or speak. "Trisha." She watched her daughter pause near the door, not turning. "You once asked me what I had ever lost. I think I can answer that question now. I lost my illusions. Nobody lives 'happily ever after'—not even a Kincaid. Please . . . I don't want to lose you."

Slowly Trisha swung around to face her mother. "You won't, Luz. But I have to go see him. He's my father, and I love him, too."

"Of course." Luz understood, but that didn't silence that little niggling fear. Trisha had always been Daddy's girl. It wasn't fair. Drew had Claudia, and she was alone. She needed the children, and he was starting another family.

Trisha hesitated by the door. "Are you coming, Rob?"

"No." After she'd gone, Rob walked over to Luz and stood near her, his hands self-consciously shoved into the side pockets of his slacks. "I can't face him yet. All I want to do is hit him right now." He shuffled away, his head down, while he muttered in a barely audible voice, "The bastard. The dirty, rotten bastard."

For a long time, Luz stood alone in the middle of the room, then she walked back to the bar where she'd left the drink.

Later that evening, Luz was in the kitchen fixing a pizza, something she hadn't done in years. She'd given all the help the weekend off so that she could be alone with Rob and Trisha. She wondered if the pizza was such a good idea as she placed the anchovies atop the mounds of shaved mozzarella cheese. It was a remembrance of happier times when the four of them were together. She placed the finished pizza on a rack in the refrigerator, ready to pop into the oven as soon as Trisha came back.

When she walked out of the kitchen to join Rob on the patio, she heard Trisha's voice. She didn't mean to eavesdrop, but she knew that neither of them would talk freely about their father to her. They wouldn't want to be accused of carrying tales, nor would they intentionally want to hurt her.

"He wants to talk to you, Rob. Won't you at least call him?" Trisha urged.

"No, dammit, I won't. And I don't see how you can have anything to do with him after the way he walked out on Luz!"

"He had his reasons."

"Yeah, and I know the reason. A cute little piece of ass half his age."

"Rob, you haven't even met her. Don't you think you should wait to condemn him at least until you've seen them together?" Trisha argued, then her voice turned thoughtful. "I've never seen him look so happy. He's always smiling or laughing—something he rarely did at home. His face seems to shine every time he looks at her. He loves her, Rob. I think even you would like her if you gave yourself a chance."

It hurt to hear the way Trisha described them. It sounded so idyllic, and she was going through hell. Hate and envy mixed with bitterness. It wasn't fair. Every divorce had winners and losers, and she was the loser in this one—her youth gone and her self-esteem shattered. Luz remembered again what she'd told Mary that evening in the study of the Kincaid manor—this wasn't the way she thought her life would turn out.

"I don't have to listen to this shit!" Rob's angry declaration was followed by the scrape of a metal chair leg across the patio tile, then the sound of footsteps.

It was only a matter of seconds before she would be discovered. Luz quickly stepped forward into their view. Rob stopped when he saw her and glanced quickly back at Trisha. Her facial muscles felt the strain of holding a pleasant expression as she joined them.

"If I had known you were back, Trisha, I would have put the pizza in the oven," she said. "I hope you're hungry. I fixed a giant one."

"Aren't you going to ask how Dad is?" Trisha's previous irritation with Rob was now extended to include Luz.

"Why don't you keep your mouth shut, Trish?" Rob demanded. "She'll ask if she wants to know!" Just as suddenly, he seemed to retreat behind a brooding expression and took a long stride in the direction of the house. "I'm not hungry."

"Don't go, Rob." Luz called him back, and unwillingly he returned, his back and shoulders hunched.

"Well, aren't you?" Trisha persisted defiantly.

Luz obliged. "How is he?"

"Fine. So is Claudia. I know this will probably sound as traitorous to you as it did to Rob, but I happen to like her."

"I thought you would." But it didn't help to know she'd been right. "Did they tell you their news?" Luz asked, very casually.

"Yes." The quietness of her answer caught Rob's attention. "What news?"

"Dad wanted to tell you himself, but you won't talk to him, so I suppose it's up to me to tell you before somebody else does. Claudia is pregnant. Sometime around November, we're going to have a little brother or sister."

"A half brother or sister!" Rob shot back. "No wonder he didn't give a damn about walking out on us. He's already starting another family."

"That isn't true," Trisha protested.

"Then what the hell else do you call it?"

"I don't know." She ran a hand through her shaggy chestnut hair. "I'm so confused."

"I think that makes three of us," Luz stated. "It happened so suddenly for all of us, I guess."

"You must have had your fill of arguing and fighting," Trisha realized.

"You could say that," she admitted wryly. "At least, toward the last. Before that, I don't suppose we talked that much— not about important things anyway." She felt drained, empty, and very tired. "I'd better put that pizza in the oven if we want to eat tonight."

"Luz," Trisha said when she turned to leave. "Dad wants to pick up the rest of his things. He wondered when would be a good time for him to come over."

She wasn't ready to see him. She knew that. Everything was too painful and too fresh. At the moment she hated him too deeply for what he'd done to her—the way he'd destroyed her and turned her into a shell of a woman.

"Rob and I have a date to go riding in the morning. Why don't you call him and see if he can come over then?" She was being cowardly, but she didn't care. She didn't want to see for herself how happy he was without her. Luz suspected the bitterness would be with her for a long time. "By the way, I've changed the dates of our European trip. We'll be leaving as soon as you two graduate. I think we'll all be ready for an extended vacation by then."

"Do you think he'll come to the graduation exercises?" Rob's jaw was tightly clenched.

"I can't imagine him missing it."

"Will he bring her?"

"I don't know."

"If he does, I'll—"

"—do the same thing that I will, Rob," Luz interrupted, weighted by a dull ache inside. "You'll be civil."

But it wasn't the easiest thing to do. When the graduating class walked down the aisle, Luz could hardly bear to stand next to them. Claudia looked so youthful and radiant, and Drew fairly beamed. She managed to avoid saying more than a few words to them, lingering until they had congratulated Rob before she approached him. It was the same awkward scene all over again at Trisha's commencement. So different from the way she had envisioned it months ago—no celebration dinners, no large gatherings. It was all separate and strained.

A property settlement had been quickly agreed upon, neither side wanting to fight over it and prolong the granting of a divorce decree. The final divorce papers had been signed only a week before Rob's graduation. And Luz's so-called friends had been quick to inform her that Drew and Claudia had set their wedding date. All she could do was smile and nod—and pretend it didn't hurt.

# Part II

Part II

# CHAPTER X

The polo fields at Windsor Great Park had a distinctly British look, precisely manicured and evenly green. Each blade of grass on the smooth, hard surface appeared to be clipped to the proper height, with no variation allowed. The effect was clean and neat, the product of decades of care and tradition. The "sport of princes" had been imported to the western world by the British Tenth Hussars in the latter part of the eighteenth century after they had watched a visiting tribe of horsemen from Punjab, India, demonstrate their skill on horseback with a stick and ball. The game gained immediate popularity with the horse-loving British.

From a lawn chair on the sidelines, Luz watched the game in progress, the Round Tower of Windsor Castle in the background. A straw boater and sunglasses shaded her face from the glare of a June sun. The weather was perfect, a faint breeze wafting through the trees in the park, a pure azure sky above. The drizzling rain that had bogged the turf the previous week and made the playing surface slick and treacherous had finally moved out. Now the field was fast and hard, and the play matched it.

She lifted the powerful binoculars and focused on the column of riders racing toward the far goal. There was always something about rough sports that conjured images of war, whether it was football pitting burly men against each other, or polo with its dashing cavalrylike charges by columns of horses and riders.

The sunlight glistened on the shiny-coated horses, stretched in a flat-out run and colored in rippling shades of browns and blacks with a dun thrown in, providing a splash of dark gold. She centered the focus on the front pair of riders jostling for position on the ball and saw the neck shot Rob made, his mallet swinging in front of his horse, under its neck, and hitting the ball at an angle for the goalposts. Lowering the binoculars, Luz watched for the signal from the white-coated goal judge, positioned on the ground behind the posts. He waved a flag over his head, indicating a score.

"I believe your son is going to be a better player than his grandfather was," Fiona Sherbourne remarked as the riders slowly trotted their horses back to the center of the field. "Henry has kept it very quiet that he has a Kincaid playing on his Seven Oak team. Strategy, he says."

Luz glanced at the Englishwoman who had been their hostess for a little over two weeks. She was seated in the chair next to Luz, her posture flawlessly erect, yet managing to appear relaxed. Although she was ten years Luz's senior, her soft dewy skin looked firm and young. More than once since she'd been in England, Luz had covertly scanned the brown hairline for a hint of surgical scars, but they were well hidden if they were there.

"I'm glad Henry is pleased. Rob has been very anxious about playing up to the caliber of the rest of the team." The opposing players faced off at midfield, angling toward the sidelines. The umpire bowled the ball among them, and play resumed with a clash of hooking mallets.

"Anxious isn't the word." Tired of sitting, Trisha stood up and slipped her hands inside the large pockets of her green skirt. "He's become so obsessed with the fear he might forget some minor rule difference that he's been driving me crazy."

A melee ensued once the ball was knocked clear of the throw-in. Three times it was sent in different directions as red- and blue-shirted riders fought for control of it, horses stopping and spinning to lunge after it. The bell rang ending that chukkar of play. The riders pulled in their horses and headed for the pony lines to change mounts and, if there was time, spend a moment together in the small team pavilion discussing tactics.

"I think I'll walk around and see who's here." Trisha was never content to remain on the sidelines for long, preferring action to observation. "The Royal Family is in residence at the castle. Who knows? Maybe I'll run into a prince."

Fiona watched her leave. "I wondered how long she'd be content to sit with us. Young people always want to be doing something, have you noticed?"

"We all were like that at her age." Personally, Luz had preferred the nonstop round of outings, teas, and parties that had filled their days since they'd arrived in England. The frenetic pace seemed to suit the quiet desperation that drove her.

"It amazes me how those two have grown up in three short years. They're practically adults. No doubt they believe they are." She smiled.

"Don't remind me." It seemed the whole world was conspiring to make her feel older.

"Dear Luz." Still smiling, now with a secretive quality, she leaned closer and pressed a hand on her forearm. "What you need is the name of my doctor."

The remark confirmed her suspicions, but she wasn't tempted by it. To Luz, cosmetic surgery was more than an admission of vanity. It was a statement that a person had to look young in order to be accepted and admired—and loved. She resented that truth she had so painfully learned for herself, insisting that she preferred the martyrdom of age and loneliness to the appearance of false youth.

"What I need is a Pimm's No. 1," she replied.

"That does sound refreshing." Fiona lifted a gloved hand and discreetly wagged a forefinger to summon the uniformed servant hovering in the background. She requested the chauffeur to fetch a drink for each of them from the well-stocked bar built into the Rolls-Royce. "Did I tell you I received orders from Henry that champagne was to flow like water at Saturday night's party? I believe he hopes to get the opposing team drunk. Originally, I had scheduled the party to take place the following evening as a celebration for the tournament victors, but Henry wanted it on the eve of the final match. It's all part of his grand scheme of psychological warfare. He goes to such lengths to win a polo tournament. And all he receives is a silver cup to add to the already extensive collection in his display case."

"I doubt that I'll ever understand why people glorify youth, beauty, success . . . and winning polo games." Her smile was tainted with bitterness.

"Luz, you are becoming a dreadful cynic."

"I suppose I am."

* * *

Windsor Castle sat in a grand sprawl along the banks of the Thames an hour outside of London. Its gray mass of stone walls, turrets, and ramparts was dominated by the great Round Tower, its mast flying the Royal Ensign to signify that her majesty was in residence. The massive stone walls enclosed thirteen acres of ground, symbolically protecting the State Apartments, home of the monarchy, and St. George's Chapel, the embodiment of the Church of England, while the town of Windsor sat within their shadow. Outside the battlements stretched the eighteen hundred acres of green meadow and trees that composed Windsor Great Park, connected to the castle by an elm-lined avenue known as Long Walk. Located within the boundaries of Great Park were the polo grounds.

Trisha strolled up the sidelines, gravitating toward the pony lines where grooms and horsemen were gathered. She had no specific purpose in mind. She recognized faces among the scattering of spectators waiting for play to resume. Unable to put a name with every face, Trisha simply nodded and smiled at all of them, but didn't stop to strike up a conversation. She wasn't in the mood for company.

On the whole, the trip had thus far exceeded her expectations. On previous visits to England she had still been a child, but now she was free to go and do as she pleased. She was of age now, no longer a schoolgirl. And every day had been party and play time. She'd thrown herself into the fun with a kind of wild abandon.

Walking alone on this grassy field with the sun warm on her back, Trisha realized she hadn't escaped the thing she'd run so hard from—her parents' divorce. Part of her wondered why she let it affect her at all. She was not to blame for the split. Even if they didn't love each other anymore, she still loved them both.

But that was it. She was caught in the middle, her feelings for neither of them changing while she watched them change. Her father looked younger, acted younger, and dressed less conservatively. When Trisha had visited him the day before they left for England, he'd been wearing jeans. Her father in jeans!

As for Luz, the change had been more subtle—a retreat into some bitter dark world while she continued to show an insouciant face to those she met. Most people didn't notice the new sharpness of her tongue or the brittleness of her smile, but Trisha did.

One new trait her parents shared was this pretended lapse of memory for the last eighteen years. Each of them acted as if Trisha had been born, full-grown, a month ago. Neither wanted to talk about the past, reluctant to recall even happy times. Trisha had learned not to mention Luz when she was with her father, especially if Claudia was there, and Luz usually changed the subject if she said anything about her father. The divorce had strained her relationship with both of them, because she and Rob were reminders of the past, especially for her father, who was starting a new life with a new woman and a new family on the way.

At least she understood what was happening. Trisha doubted that Rob ever tried to. All he cared about was polo. And his dedication to the sport was something Luz appeared to be absorbing as well, as if it gave her a purpose. Trisha supposed it was natural, since Rob had always been Luz's favorite. As a result of their increasing closeness, she felt more estranged from the family group. It created a loneliness, and Trisha guessed it was the loneliness she was trying to fill that prompted her to party so much, accepting every invitation that came her way.

Play resumed on the field to complete the game's last chukkar. Trisha paused a minute to watch the action, but it didn't hold her interest despite her brother's participation on the leading side. Her glance strayed from the contestants as she started walking again. It passed over the two men dressed in riding breeches and boots lounging against the front fender of a car parked roughly ten yards ahead of her. Something familiar about one of them pulled her attention back to the pair.

A stunned second later, Trisha recognized Raul Buchanan. That strong, angular profile and smoothly cropped brown hair couldn't belong to anyone else. She didn't need a glimpse of those light blue eyes to confirm that it was Raul. Her downcast spirits soared, and her steps lifted as she approached him unobserved, his attention on the field of play.

"Did you see Sherbourne miss the ball again?" The remark was addressed to the man with him, the faint accent and resonant pitch of his voice so familiar to her again. "He is unable to hit a backhand shot on the near side. If the back had followed him, he would have had an easy goal."

"Should I warn Rob that you are scouting his team?" Trisha spoke and smiled in satisfaction when his glance settled on her with a flicker of recognition.

"I knew I had played against the rider in the Number One position before, but I failed to recognize him without the Kincaid string of ponies. Thank you for identifying Sherbourne's ringer." He inclined his head slightly in her direction while his gaze stayed on her face. "Let me introduce my teammate, James Armstrong. James, this is Miss Trisha Thomas, granddaughter of Jake Kincaid."

"This is indeed a pleasure, Miss Thomas." The English rider formally shook hands with her. He was a slightly built man with a narrow face and high forehead, his hair bushing thickly from a thinning top. "Your grandfather was a superb competitor. I am glad to learn your brother is following in . . . his boots, shall we say."

"Thank you. I believe Rob loves the game even more than Jake did," Trisha said, then turned back to Raul, conscious that his gaze hadn't left her. "This time I don't think you'll be able to accuse him of saving his horses."

"Not this time." He remained attentive yet slightly aloof, with a hint of warmth that kept Trisha hoping.

A jetliner thundered overhead on its flight path from Heathrow Airport not many miles distant. It briefly disrupted the flow of conversation as they waited for its roar to abate.

"I take it you and your brother are visiting the Sherbournes at Seven Oak." The comment came from James Armstrong.

"Yes. We arrived a little over two weeks ago." She wondered how long Raul had been here.

"How are you finding England so far? You couldn't have chosen a better time of year—Ascot Week, Wimbledon."

"It's been a never-ending round of activities," Trisha admitted and belatedly wished she had spent more time with her brother on the polo fields. She might have learned earlier that Raul was in England. "I'm having a marvelous time. Although it is a treat to see a familiar face."

"I presume you two met while Buchanan was playing in the States," Armstrong guessed.

"We did," Raul replied.

An impish light crept into her eyes. "Unfortunately, at the time, Raul thought I was too young for him." She sensed a ripple of impatience as the furrow in Raul's brow deepened and his glance swung away from her.

"Is that right?" Armstrong feigned a cough to conceal a chortling laugh and clapped a hand on Raul's shoulder. "I'll leave you to settle this, old boy. Meet you later at the pub." He moved away.

For long seconds there was only the background noise from the field—the gruntings of horses straining for speed and the thudding of hooves on the grassy sod. Trisha wandered over to lean against the car hood near Raul and feigned a brief interest in the action. Then she turned back to Raul. "Are you sorry he left?" she asked.

"No. His presence would not have prevented you from making some outrageous comment," Raul said. "Sometimes I forget how aggressive American women can be."

Trisha experienced a warm rush of satisfaction that he had finally called her a woman. "All women can be aggressive," she declared. "I don't think it has anything to do with nationality."

"Some are bolder than others, then." The long grooves on either side of his mouth were deepened by a small smile.

"Perhaps," she conceded. "I told you we'd meet again."

"Since your brother plays polo, it was likely our paths would cross."

"But I didn't expect to see you here—in England." She turned thoughtfully curious.

"Why not? Britain is practically the home of polo. The British are the ones who exported the game throughout the hemispheres."

"But you are Argentine. There is that matter of the little fuss over the Falklands," she reminded him.

"Polo has nothing to do with national politics. I am not here to play for the honor of Argentine, but for the victory of my team—which happens to be British."

"Will you be playing against Rob's team?"

"It appears we may meet in the finals." His attention again centered on the game in progress. It never strayed from it for long, Trisha had noticed. Those keen blue eyes always seemed to be assessing the play of horse and rider, seeking out weaknesses and strengths.

"Then I'll have to cheer for both sides."

"Your host will not be pleased by your decision. Sherbourne prefers undivided loyalties."

"I would love to be accused of consorting with the enemy," Trisha declared, deliberately being provocative, but the faint twitch of his lip didn't reveal whether he was amused by her or the idea. "You'll be coming to the party Saturday night, won't you?" All the participating teams had been invited, as well as a horde of other guests.

"Yes."

"Will you be bringing someone?" She felt tense when he met her look.

"The final match is scheduled for the following day. I will have to leave the party early to be rested. It would not be fair to ask a lady to accompany me, then expect her to leave the festivities when I must."

Trisha released a long breath of relief. "No, it wouldn't."

"You are too transparent, Miss Thomas," he said dryly.

Her head turned sharply toward him, his mocking criticism coming as a surprise. "Why?"

"When you show your feelings, people will invariably hurt them." His level gaze contained a warning, but she was more intrigued by why he so consistently kept her at arm's length.

"Have you been hurt?" Trisha wondered.

"Not in the way you mean." He'd been poor and hungry and ridiculed. Those were feelings completely outside her experience, feelings she could never understand. The struggle for survival rarely allowed time for sensitive emotions. The bell rang to end the game, and Raul straightened away from the car. "You will want to go congratulate your brother on his team's victory."

Before he could take his leave, Trisha reached quickly for his hand. "Come with me. I want you to meet Rob."

At the pressure of fingers, he glanced down at her soft hand, so golden pale against his darkly tanned skin. "Another time." Briefly, he admired her persistence, but he knew that for all her pseudo-worldliness, she would still expect more from a relationship than he could—or would—give.

"Later at the pub then." She observed the arch of his eyebrow. "Sooner or later you're going to learn that a Kincaid doesn't take no for an answer."

"I thought you once told me you were more Thomas than Kincaid."

She was encouraged by his recall of a past statement. "I'm not sure what I am anymore." Mostly because she didn't know what a Thomas stood for—certainly not constancy. Her father had changed too much from the man she'd thought he was. "I heard James Armstrong say he'd see you at the pub. That should be a neutral ground to meet my brother even if you do end up opposing each other again. Which pub is it?"

"The Cygnet."

"Then we'll see you there later, too." Trisha elected to quit while she had an affirmative response from him.

As Luz approached the picket line, grooms were walking down tired and sweaty horses. Among the dismounted riders, there was a lot of backslapping going on, and hearty voices filling the air. Rob's face was wreathed in a smile of exhilaration. He was an emotional player, and this time he'd won.

"Congratulations, Rob."

"It's the Argentine horses Henry bought. They are the best ponies I've ever ridden." He shook his head in a marveling gesture as he glanced at a sweat-slick bay being led away by a groom. "I thought the gray couldn't be beaten in his prime, but these mounts . . . someday I hope I can have a couple of them on my string."

"Maybe we'll look into the possibility."

"Do you mean it, Luz?"

"A player is only as good as his ponies." Luz didn't feel she was indulging him in a whim. Rob had already proved to her that he was serious about the sport. As in any other sport, he needed the proper equipment and coaching. She had discussed the latter on several occasions with Henry Sherbourne, getting his recommendations on possible mentors. But this wasn't the time to tell Rob of her future intentions. After the tournament, she would talk to him about them.

"Good game, Rob." Trisha joined them.

Her congratulations didn't make much of an impression. "Can we start looking as soon as we get home?"

"Looking for what?" Trisha asked.

"Rob needs to improve his polo string. He's so impressed with these Argentine horses of Henry's that I suggested we might buy some."

"I know who you should talk to, Rob."

"Who?" He looked skeptical.

"Raul Buchanan. He and a bunch of other players are stopping at a local pub for a beer. I was going to ask if you wanted to go there with me." She knew Rob was aware he was being used as a means of seeing Raul again.

"You don't mind, do you, Luz?" Of late, Rob had become reluctant to be away from Luz for long, behaving as though he had to make up for Drew's absence.

Maybe that was normal under the circumstances. And maybe Trisha resented Luz's turning to Rob for comfort instead of her. She didn't know. She simply didn't think it was wise of her mother to let her life revolve around Rob so much. Maybe it was too soon, but she still felt Luz should go out on her own more.

"I don't mind," Luz insisted blandly. "Go enjoy yourselves." But it was her expression—or lack of one—that made it seem like a sacrifice. Not for a minute did Trisha believe it was deliberate.

"You should start dating, Luz," she said impulsively.

The snapping sharpness was suddenly there. "Which old fart would you suggest I pursue? Simon Thornton-White, who belches like a foghorn, or maybe old Mr. Tynsdale, who wheezes climbing two steps? In case you haven't noticed, there is not exactly a surfeit of unmarried men my age. Although I suppose I could always take a young lover."

"Luz, I—"

"You meant well, Trisha. I shouldn't have . . ." The anger dissolved in a weary sigh. "It's the sun. It's given me a rotten headache. I think I prefer a quiet evening. And if I'm lucky"— her lips twisted in a wry, humorless smile—"Fiona won't ask me to be the fourth at bridge tonight."

"We don't have to go to the pub," Rob said.

"Maybe some of his string will be for sale. These Argentines are always selling their ponies. Henry would like it if you bought some of the opposition's mounts before the big game. You two have a good time tonight. And don't come early or

I'll think it's my fault," she declared and walked away before Rob could protest further.

"I guess we have our orders," Trisha murmured as she watched her mother leave. The hat, the gloves, the flat-heeled shoes all created the proper image of sophistication and poise, yet something was missing.

"Have you noticed how frightened and lost she looks sometimes when she doesn't know you're watching her?" Rob observed grimly. "That's what he's done to her."

"It must be like losing half of yourself," Trisha guessed. "Do you think Dad will ever come back?" The possibility seemed so remote that her question was almost a childish wish, but Trisha longed for the even tenor of her former life.

"No, and good riddance to the bastard," Rob muttered and caught at her arm. "Let's go to your pub."

The public house was on a narrow, winding street, cobblestoned and old. Above the timbered door of the wood-and-stone building was the weathered sign depicting a young swan, the royal bird that inhabited the noble Thames. The popular meeting place was half filled with customers and there was a low but steady din of voices. Heavy old furniture and raftered ceilings and bulky wood trim, all darkened by age, combined to give a certain gloom to the ancient drinking establishment, an aura that wasn't improved by the dusty-paned front windows and inadequate lighting.

Trisha scanned the room, searching the tables in the dark corners, skipping over the locals in their workclothes and worn business suits. A handful of men in riding clothes sat at a far table. "There they are." She pointed them out to Rob, then led the way across the planked floor, dodging tables, chairs, and milling customers.

The air was pungent with the smell of ale and stout, spiced with pipe smoke. They approached the far corner where Raul was seated with his polo-playing friends. When he saw Trisha making her way to his table, he pushed his chair back and rose to meet them. He clasped her hand in greeting, and she felt a tingle of excitement at his firm, warm grip.

"My brother, Rob Thomas. Raul Buchanan." As she watched the two shake hands, she noticed the stark differences between them.

Only an inch or so separated them in height, yet Rob looked smaller, more wiry and slim, while Raul had a filled-out completeness, his chest and shoulders flatly roped with muscle. Maturity and experience were stamped in Raul's dark face, but her fair-skinned brother looked young and untried. Rob had been the older brother for so long that she had expected more equality between the two, but Rob was a boy next to a man.

"There is no room at this table. Shall we sit over here?" Raul suggested the adjacent empty table.

"That's fine." Trisha sat in the chair he pulled out for her, while Rob dragged out the wooden chair on the opposite side of the table.

The barmaid came by as Raul transferred his mug of ale from the other table and took the side chair, placing Rob on his left and Trisha on his right. "What'll it be for you, luv?" The barmaid's red-lipped smile was automatic, matching the boredom in her eyes.

"A Guinness," Rob ordered. "How about something to eat? I'm starved. Do you have Cornish pastry?"

She nodded affirmatively, then glanced at Trisha. "And you, miss?"

"A bitter." Which was the English name for the standard draft ale Raul was drinking. Before leaving, the barmaid looked at Raul, but he shook his head, declining to order. His glass mug was still half filled. "I think this may turn out to be an opportune meeting. Rob was just discussing the possibility of buying some Argentine ponies for his polo string. I thought you might be able to offer him some advice or recommendations if you didn't have any horses for sale yourself."

"I always have horses for sale, but much depends on matching the horse with the rider—and the price you are willing to pay." Raul directed his response to Rob.

"That's true, but a player is only as good as the pony he rides," he said, repeating the phrase Luz had used.

"The reverse is also true. A pony is only as good as the man who rides it." Raul's long brown fingers gripped the glass handle of the mug and lifted it in Rob's direction. "I did notice today that your game has improved since we played." He raised the glass to his mouth and took a drink.

"I plan to improve a lot more," Rob asserted. "I'm taking

a year at least to concentrate on polo. That's why I want to get some better ponies."

The barmaid returned to the table with their drinks as well as a plate holding a half-moon-shaped pie stuffed with meat, onions, and vegetables. Rob took pound notes from his pocket and laid the necessary amount on the table for the girl. While she made change, he took a bite of the savory regional specialty and washed it down with a swallow of the Irish stout.

"Who is your coach?" Raul asked as Trisha sipped at her dark ale. She didn't mind being ignored in the conversation, since it gave her an opportunity to study Raul more closely without being observed.

On the surface, his face seemed to give away little. Yet there was a hard, relentless quality about the set of his jaw that she'd seen matched by his play on the field. And there was little softness about his mouth or the deep slashes that flanked it. Perhaps most revealing of all were his keen blue eyes with their trace of aloof arrogance. He was a dispassionate man, viewing life from atop his horse and untouched by it. Trisha smiled to herself, wondering if she wasn't becoming fanciful because he seemed so indifferent to her pursuit of him.

"I don't have one—at least, not at the moment. At the academy the team coach worked with me privately on my game, and I've taken classes at the polo club with various professionals." Rob shrugged.

"If you mean to improve, you need someone to criticize your play and point out mistakes before they become bad habits. You should have your own coach to work with you every day, both on your form and in team play."

Trisha brightened at his advice, the possibility occurring to her that something might be arranged whereby she could see Raul on a regular basis instead of these hit-and-miss meetings. "Do you give private instruction to young players?"

"I have in the past." There was a knowing glint in his eyes when he met her look as if he was fully aware of the direction her thoughts had taken. "Now, I mainly give courses in advanced polo for the serious player at my rancho in Argentina. The minimum course is two weeks and the longest is three months. We work on form, technique, and tactics. All lodging, meals, and horses are furnished, so you need only bring your riding clothes. The course begins in the spring—our spring, which is, of course, your autumn," he explained, switching his attention back to Rob. "You might consider enrolling. Either way, I recommend that you come to Argentina if you intend to purchase our ponies. There are several polo *estancias* that specialize in raising and training horses for the sport, including my own. It is our high-goal season as well, so you will have an opportunity to see polo played at its best."

"You Argentines unquestionably have the best polo team in the world," Rob conceded almost grudgingly. "Your record in defeating the Americans in the Cup of the Americas competition proves that. I probably could gain a lot from taking lessons from the best. And I'd have firsthand knowledge of the methods your gauchos use to train the horses."

"The true gaucho vanished long ago, the same as your cowboy. Only the myth remains," Raul stated dryly. "You are likely to find the gaucho of today driving a tractor."

"Or riding a polo pony?" Trisha suggested.

A dark brow arched briefly. "The comparison could be made, I suppose." Raul leaned back in his chair, an arm sprawling over its back while he absently stroked the mug handle. "The gaucho of old had little regard for life and limb. His only need was a horse to ride, and he usually had a string of thirty so he could travel far and fast. Danger was his companion, and he loved her. It was said about the gaucho that his wants were few and basic. His bed was his saddle. And he ate with a knife, because a fork would mean a plate and a plate would require a table, and a table would mean a dwelling with a roof and walls."

"Much of the same could be said about a professional polo player." Trisha was intrigued by the analogy she saw. It made her wonder how much of his attitude was inbred, a throwback to the past.

"I remember Jake's saying that poverty was the only cure for polo," Rob recalled with a half-smile quirking his mouth. "And that didn't always work."

"It gets in the blood and leaves little room for anything else," Raul agreed.

"That isn't very encouraging," Trisha protested.

"It wasn't meant to be," Raul informed her.

Her tongue had an acid taste, and she let it taint her mood.

"Since you're never in any one place too long, what's your next stop after England?"

"I leave next week for France."

"What a coincidence! We seem to be on the same itinerary. We'll be in Paris next week as well." Trisha was amazed by her luck.

"I'll be in France, not Paris," Raul corrected pointedly. "Staying in the country at the chateau of a friend . . . playing polo."

"But surely there's a way we can get in touch with you while we're there," she reasoned.

"For what purpose?"

She glanced at her brother as he lowered his glass and wiped Guinness from his upper lip. "If Rob is interested in any of your horses or wants to attend your polo school, he'll need to contact you somehow."

"Here." Raul took a business card from inside his pocket and handed it to Rob. "My address in Argentina. Hector Guerrero will supply any information or make any arrangements you might need. And he knows where I can be reached, if necessary." He signaled the barmaid for another round of drinks.

"I've heard about these polo colleges in Argentina." Rob studied the printing on the card. "But it's game experience I need."

"That is a slow way to learn, because you cannot control what the other side does and no two plays are ever alike. In practice games, we can recreate a sequence of events to show how and where you got out of position and teach you to anticipate the actions of your teammates as well as the opposing players. Polo is more than just skill with a mallet and a horse. It's knowing where every rider on the field is at a given moment and where he is likely to go next. I am certain your previous coaches have explained this."

"Yes." He combed a hand through his hair, then rubbed the back of his neck in a thoughtful gesture. "I know I could use a coach, but maybe I should mention this school of yours to Luz and see what she thinks."

"Raul is coming to Henry's party on Saturday. You can introduce them." Trisha guessed that their mother would agree to anything Rob proposed.

"Hey, Buchanan." One of the men at the next table rocked his chair backward to intrude between Raul and Trisha. "What was the name of that Aussie bloke who took a header in yesterday's match? A spectacular crash, it was."

"Carstairs."

"Bart says he ended up with a concussion."

"He was lucky," someone else said. "They had to put his horse down."

"Reminds me of the time old Sawyer went down with me. You were there, Buchanan. Hell, it was your black horse that rode us into the ground. Raining, it was, and slippery. Three of us went down at once. You talk about a tangle of bodies and thrashing legs. When I opened my eyes, there sat Buchanan, astride his horse, as calm as you please, waiting to see who walked away from the mess. I swear that damned black horse he rode that day had webbed feet."

Conversation jumped between the two tables after that as past falls were recounted and injuries compared. Soon pints of beer and bottles of stout were commandeered and used as pawns to reenact the placement of riders, and the circle of chairs was widened to encompass both tables. As the only female present, Trisha found herself slowly crowded out and forgotten. Finally she left her chair on the periphery, took her pint of ale, and stood against the back wall to watch and listen.

Once she caught Raul's eye and felt the pulsebeat of his attention center on her, but it was soon claimed by someone else. A woman would have a difficult time fitting into his world, she realized. There was so little room in his life for one beyond warming his bed wherever he happened to be sleeping that night. She was intelligent enough to recognize that as part of his attraction, but it didn't lessen his appeal.

Shortly before ten o'clock the barmaid came around to warn them the pub would be closing in a quarter of an hour and it was time to order their last drink and settle their accounts with her. As the gathering began to break up, Trisha rejoined her brother. Raul was standing beside him.

"Can Rob and I offer you a lift?" she asked.

"No. I have a car at my disposal."

"Then why don't you drive me back to Seven Oak?" She tipped her head to the side, faintly challenging him with her look. His hesitation lengthened as he appeared to weigh her suggestion against some inner suspicion.

"It's probably out of your way . . ." When Rob ventured the beginning of an excuse, Trisha could cheerfully have belted him, but it wasn't necessary.

"That is of no importance," Raul interrupted. "I will drive your sister safely back."

"Good night, brother dear." She pointedly signaled him to get lost. Rob glanced at her uncertainly, then took his cue and left the pub ahead of them.

They were delayed a few minutes while Raul took leave of his companions, then they crossed the smoky, ale-rank room to the door. Trisha waited while he opened it for her, then stepped outside. The air was fresh and cool. She paused to breathe it in, listening to the muffled voices in the pub disrupting the night's stillness. The quiet encouraged hushed tones. When the light touch of his hand directed her up the cobblestoned street, Trisha stole a sideways glance at him.

"Are you angry with me?" she questioned lightly while their footsteps made a companionable echo in the night.

"Because my friends will think I am robbing the cradle. That is the phrase, no?" The Spanish accent seemed slightly more pronounced, a certain thickness in his low voice, perhaps caused by irritation.

Actually, she had meant because she had maneuvered him into giving her a ride home, but she let it pass. "If it arouses anything, it's likely to be envy. If you think you are old enough to be my daddy, you should see the woman my father is going to marry."

"If it is permissible for your father, it is permissible for you?"

"Something like that." She waited for him to say he wasn't her father, but he made no response. Rectangular patches of light spilled from the windows of houses along the street. "After ten o'clock, nothing moves in these small English villages. It isn't like London."

"The car is here." He directed her into a shadowed side street where a cream-colored car was parked at the curb.

"An Aston Martin." She trailed her fingertips over its smooth, hard surface in appreciation of its sleek power and beauty, as Raul unlocked the passenger door.

"It belongs to a friend." His hand assisted her into the left front passenger seat, then he walked around and slid behind the wheel.

"I'd rather have this than a Rolls any day." She caressed the smooth leather upholstery, liking the rich feel of it under her hand. "Now I know the second thing I'm going to buy with my inheritance. Imagine tootling around campus in this." Her laugh was quickly drowned by the rumbling purr of the engine springing to life at the turn of the ignition key.

The headlamps illuminated the cobbled street and the old stone buildings that loomed on both sides. She felt the surge of power when the car accelerated forward, cornering like a cat at the intersection and turning onto the main street. The buildings seemed to fall away. Within minutes, they were outside the sleepy village and speeding along an empty road, the gentle English countryside hidden in darkness.

"Turn left here," Trisha said when they approached a crossroads.

"I am familiar with the way to Seven Oak," he informed her. "I have played at Sherbourne's field on the estate before."

She settled back in her seat. "It feels so strange sitting on this side—and the car going down the wrong side of the road." She smiled and glanced at the dashboard in front of Raul. "And looking at the speedometer and seeing the needle pointing at a hundred and thirty. I have to keep reminding myself that's kilometers."

"It can be unsettling." But he appeared untroubled by it.

It was too dark to see anything out the window except the road ahead of them. Trisha partially turned in her seat to gaze at Raul, the faint illumination from the dash lights highlighting his features.

"Where did you learn to speak English so well? Were you educated over here?"

"No." She saw the small lift of a corner of his mouth that hinted at a smile. "I assure you my name was not entered on Eton's registry at my birth. Although many of my countrymen have attended college in Oxford, Heidelberg, or the Sorbonne."

"Then how did you learn to speak so fluently?"

"There are suburbs of Buenos Aires—Hurlingham, Belgrano—where once a man could live his whole life and never hear a word of Spanish spoken. The British influence in Argentina is very strong. They owned great *estancias* on the pampas, sheep ranches in Patagonia. They built our railroads. They brought their language, their culture, their sports, like soccer and polo. They encouraged our independence from Spain. Most became Argentine in the end, instead of just making their fortunes and returning to Britain as they did in Australia and India."

"I didn't know that. But I know very little about any of the South American countries."

"I remember. Once there was great wealth to be had in Argentina. The phrase 'rich as an Argentine' meant something. Now people say 'rich as an Arab.'"

"I think a trip to Argentina is definitely in the offing," Trisha announced with a determined lift of her chin. "Rob will attend your polo school. It's merely a matter of going through the formality of getting approval from Luz. My mother has practically given him a blank check when it comes to polo. That should interest you."

"And you feel I should be grateful for the business you have directed my way, no?" Again that tautness of voice seemed to thicken his accent.

"I suppose I did you a favor of sorts." She knew very well she had, in both school fees and potential horse sales.

"So you feel I'm in your debt. Should I guess what form the repayment is to take?"

She didn't like his tone. "Who says I expect any repayment?"

"My driving you to Seven Oak was not the price? Or perhaps I should say the first installment?" His attention shifted from the road long enough for him to glance at her.

"Perhaps I hoped that you had finally recognized that I'm of some value to you."

And perhaps her action was slightly calculating, but Trisha felt it was justified. She was determined that he was going to notice her. Thus far, it was working. She had gotten him to take her home. The rest was up to her own persuasive wiles.

The headlight beams illuminated the massive stone pillars that marked the entrance to the country estate. The iron gates stood open. Raul turned the car onto the long circular drive, slowing its speed. The lights shining from the windows of the large manor house just ahead were visible through the spreading branches of the ancient oaks. Six of the number that had given the estate its name remained standing, scattered over the wide lawn. Raul stopped the car beneath the enveloping shadows of one of them and switched off the engine. They were still some distance from the front entrance of the imposing stone mansion.

He turned sideways in the driver's seat to face her, an arm resting along the back of the seats. "I am not obligated to you in any way. Whether you speak favorably on my behalf or not, that is as you choose. I owe you nothing."

She was irritated that her attempt had failed. "What is it going to take for you to notice me?"

"I have noticed you. You are a young, charming woman. But I am not interested in you," he stated flatly.

"What's wrong with me? Do you like your women meek and submissive? The kind that trembles when you touch her?" She glared at him. "Or maybe it isn't women you like. Maybe I've been throwing myself at a homosexual all this time."

"I see. Now you challenge my manhood."

"Maybe you're so partial to the British because, like them, you can go either way." Trisha needled the one sensitive spot she'd found.

"Take your clothes off." His mouth thinned into a long, straight line while the dark center of his eyes seemed to bore into her.

"What?" She almost laughed the word.

"I said to take your clothes off. You told me once that you are not a virgin, so take your clothes off. How else can I prove anything to you? That is what you want, no?"

"Yes." Still, she hesitated, her lower jaw moving to the side as she warily contemplated his impassive face. Her bluff was being called, and Trisha wasn't sure what her next step should be. She wanted him to make love to her. Not quite like this, but . . .

Keeping her eyes on him, she began unbuttoning her blouse. He held her gaze while she shrugged out of it. Her pulse beat a rapid tattoo in the vein along her neck as she unfastened her front-buttoned skirt and wiggled out of her half-slip. At that point, she hesitated, waiting for some reaction from him.

The tip of his finger ran under the edge of her brassiere strap. "All of them."

She slipped out of her bra and panties and added them to the little scrunched pile on the car seat beside her. She felt slightly uncomfortable with her nudity, yet excited by it at the same time. When he began to lean toward her, the blood seemed to roar in her ears. Her stomach muscles tightened as he slowly leaned closer, stretching out the moment.

Suddenly she heard the click of the door latch and felt the rush of cool air when it was pushed open. It was a full second before she realized Raul had done it.

"Get out of the car." He remained motionless, only inches from her. Confused, she stared at him, searching for some explanation. "Get out," he ordered roughly.

Stunned and totally bewildered, she backed out of the car, automatically covering herself with her hands. She half expected him to follow her, but the edge of the door brushed her arm as he pulled it shut. A second later, she heard the engine start up. She couldn't believe it.

She grabbed at the car door. "My clothes!" But it was locked. She pounded on the glass, running alongside as he shifted the gears and reversed onto the road. "You bastard, give me my clothes!"

The driveway's sharp gravel jabbed into the tender soles of her bare feet, and Trisha limped to a halt as the car completed its tight turn, the headlights pointing to the gate. Rage had her close to tears while the cool night air chilled her skin, raising the flesh. With a spin of the wheels, the car backed up to draw level with her. She stood hunch-shouldered and shivering, glaring at the driver.

As he rolled the window down, she spit out the stream of abusive language that she had clamped on her tongue. "You dirty rotten sonuvabitch! I'll kill you for this! You're a bastard. A mother—" Her clothes were thrown out the window, hitting her. Trisha grabbed at most of them before they fell to the ground.

She could not see Raul's expression in the darkness, but his tone showed indifference to her impotent anger. "Humiliation is a cruel teacher. Perhaps you will be less quick to take your clothes off for the next man."

Again the tires dug into the gravel, spinning out chunks.

She picked up a shoe and hurled it at the window as the car shot forward. "Bastard!" The shoe bounced harmlessly off the cream-colored side and the car roared down the drive, red taillights mocking her. Clutching her clothes to her breast, Trisha watched it disappear, then moved gingerly over the sharp stones to retrieve her shoe, hot tears burning her eyes.

# CHAPTER XI

An envelope rested on a silver salver sitting on her vanity table. Luz noticed it when she started to set her whiskey glass down. Idly wondering how long it had been there, she picked it up. It looked like a wire of some sort. The envelope's cellophane window partially obscured the close-typed printing naming the addressee, but it appeared to read "Mrs. Thomas."

"Madam?"

Turning, Luz glanced at the Sherbournes' maid. She was holding up three of Luz's gowns so that she could select which she wanted to wear to the party tonight. Luz took a quick sip of the drink, then motioned toward the bed with the glass. "Just lay them on the bed. I'll decide later." The hour was getting late, but Audra wasn't here, so who would give a damn whether she was late or not?

"Very well, madam. Will there be anything else?"

"Yes, another drink," Luz ordered, then sat down on the velvet-covered vanity bench. The silk of her dressing robe rustled softly as she crossed her legs. Curious as to the sender of the telegram, she set the drink aside and turned the envelope over to open the flap.

She scanned all the coded and abbreviated information of date, time, and place and came to the body of the message. But it was addressed to Trisha. A word caught her eye, and she kept reading.

"TRISHA," it read.

CLAUDIA AND I WERE MARRIED TODAY STOP WE KNOW YOU WANTED TO COME TO OUR WEDDING STOP BUT WE

FELT IT WAS BEST THIS WAY STOP WE LOVE YOU STOP
LOVE, DAD

Married. She lowered her hand to her lap, her fingers losing
their grip on the telegram. It slipped from them and floated to
the floor. No matter how many rumors she'd heard about his
wedding plans, none of them had seemed real. She hadn't
accepted it was going to happen. But it had. Drew had married
Claudia.

It was over. It was really and truly over. He belonged to
someone else now. Luz reached for the whiskey glass and
paused to stare at her left hand. Moving in slow motion, she
took off the large diamond wedding ring and laid it in the very
bottom of her jewelry case on the vanity. Her hand felt bare,
a part of her gone. She missed the weight of it. It was like
losing something.

Quickly she reached for the glass and drank it down, nearly
choking on the fiery alcohol as she swallowed. It burned, but
it didn't make her feel warm inside. She was now just the
former Mrs. Thomas. Another one had taken her place—
younger, prettier, more intelligent.

"Your drink, madam." The maid set a full glass of whiskey
and soda in front of her.

"There's no ice in it. I want ice in it."

The music from a small string orchestra in the Great Hall
below drifted up to the second-floor corridor, accompanied by
a low hum of voices. Trisha caught the soft strains as she
emerged from her room. The party—or ball, as Fiona Sherbourne preferred to call it—was in progress, the first guests
already arrived.

She paused on the green-and-rose runner in the hallway and
made another mental check of her appearance. With her fingertips, she touched the gold filigreed combs holding the tousled mop of rust-brown curls away from the sides of her face
and the filigreed loops dangling from her earlobes. She double-
checked the amethyst brooch to make certain the safety latch
was hooked, pinning it to a shoulder of her turquoise silk gown,
then adjusted the draping folds of its low neckline so that it
hung properly. The line of the gown was simple and, she hoped,

elegant. Tonight she felt in need of all the sophistication she could contrive.

Nervously smoothing the silky material over her hips, Trisha crossed the hallway to the tall door of her mother's suite and knocked lightly on the heavy wood door. Her lips felt slick from the extra coats of gloss. She waited, listening for footsteps from inside the suite. Emma Sanderson opened the door. Her tight-lipped expression relaxed slightly when she saw Trisha standing in the hallway outside.

"Is Luz ready? I thought we go could downstairs together," Trisha said.

"No." Behind the exasperation in her glance, there was something else, but Emma looked away before Trisha could identify it. "So far, she's changed clothes three times. Now she's trying on the first gown again."

Trisha understood. Luz wasn't normally indecisive about such things, although lately this uncertainty had become fairly common. The divorce appeared to have shaken her confidence in a variety of ways.

"I'd better go down before Fiona sends out a search party," Trisha said.

"You probably should. Luz will join you shortly, I'm sure." The assertion had a slightly doubtful ring to it.

She started to suggest that she speak to Luz, but she suspected Emma could handle the situation better than she could. She invariably said the wrong thing to Luz. It had gotten worse since the divorce. She couldn't believe her father was totally at fault for the breakup; some of the blame had to belong to Luz. Or maybe it was simply that she loved her father and wanted to forgive him, while Luz didn't, and wouldn't. The bitterness just grew.

She shied away from her thoughts of the past to concentrate on the present. "How do I look?" She made a half-turn to give Emma a full view.

"Stunning." The smile of approval was genuine. "You've grown up before my eyes this year."

"Thanks." She didn't feel mature. She felt vindictive, wanting her pound of flesh.

A loud thump came from an inner room of the suite, followed by Luz's angry voice. "Dammit, Emma, if there isn't

any more ice in this place, get me some champagne. I know
the British serve it chilled."

Trisha frowned. "Is she drinking already?"

Pursing her lips, Emma cast a hurried glance over her shoulder, then gave Trisha a quick, worried look. "Keep an eye on
her tonight if you can."

"I'll try." Although she didn't know what good it would do.
Her mother's drinking was becoming a problem, she realized,
and she didn't know how to cope with it. For God's sake, she
was the daughter. The door closed, and Trisha swallowed the
half-formed protest.

When she turned, she saw Rob coming down the hallway
from his room. Her brother always looked so different in formal
wear, more the Lord Fauntleroy with his sandy-blond locks
than a long-haired rebel. But she had always regarded Rob as
being self-centered, so her impression was likely colored by
her own opinion. Admittedly, she was occasionally jealous and
resentful. Rob was the male offspring and everything seemed
to revolve around him. It was all natural, she supposed. And
there were times when even she was guilty of deferring to his
wants.

"Luz isn't ready," she informed him. "Shall we go down
together?"

The small swagger left his walk, part of a remaining cock-
iness from that afternoon's victory that had gained his polo
team a place in the next day's final match. His complacent
expression flickered as he glanced at the door to the suite.
"Anything wrong?"

"She can't make up her mind what to wear." Trisha shrugged
aside the delay.

"Oh." Satisfied by her explanation, Rob continued down
the wide corridor, and Trisha walked with him to the upper
foyer where the staircase went down to the main floor.

As they descended the stairs, the hum of brittle voices grew
louder, nearly drowning out the background music of the orchestra. The larger main foyer was congested by the steady
flow of arriving guests and the bustle of servants checking the
expensive stoles and wraps. Rob and Trisha slipped around the
slow-moving line of people entering the manor's Great Hall,
where they were formally welcomed by their hosts.

Lights from the chandeliers glittered off the recently restored fresco ceiling—and the jeweled bosoms of matrons who had little else to show off. As they wandered into the mixed crowd of old and young and in between, Trisha kept an eye out for one face in particular, staring at the back of dark heads until her angle changed and she could see it wasn't Raul Buchanan.

The double set of doors leading onto the lighted terrace and the Elizabethan knot garden beyond stood open to maintain a continual flow of fresh air through the huge crowded ballroom. A scattering of guests had already strayed outside to stroll along the formal terrace.

"Champagne?" A uniformed servant proffered a tray laden with glasses of the sparkling wine, and Trisha paused to take one.

After Rob had taken a glass, the stiff-lipped servant inclined his head and moved on to the next guests. Sipping their drinks, they drifted over to an empty space close to the wall not far from the opened terrace doors.

"As many people as we've met this trip, I only see a half-dozen familiar faces," Rob murmured.

"I know."

"Hello." A slinky brunette fastened her green eyes on Rob, her svelt body swaying provocatively as she paused before him. "We met at the Guddreaux's party last week. Lady Cynthia Hall." She supplied the name, and title, that Rob had so obviously forgotten. "Call me Cyn. Everyone does."

"Lady Cyn." Rob bowed slightly, taken aback and trying not to let it show.

"And I do try to live up to my name," she assured him, then slid a cool glance at Trisha. "You're his sister, aren't you?"

Therefore, a nonentity whose company wasn't wanted, Trisha thought. "I am." Stubbornly she remained beside her brother, not liking this haughty feline.

The young brunette ignored her. "You were a sensation on the polo field today, Rob." And her brother visibly preened under the praise. "Tell me, do you dance as well as you play polo?"

"Almost. Would you care to find out?" he invited.

"Delighted." She hugged an arm around his and led him toward the dance floor. But not before Trisha heard her say, "I'd love to discover everything you do . . . almost as well."

Alone, Trisha idly sipped at her champagne while her gaze

made a long, slow sweep of the room's occupants. She stiffened when she noticed Raul standing a few feet to her left, feeling the impact the sight of him made on her senses, not all of it negative. The formal attire seemed to blunt the rough edges while the black material combined with his dark coloring to create a stronger contrast with his blue eyes. All the arrogance and virility she usually noticed about him was there, this time enhanced by a touch of elegance.

The wave of anger receded under the sobering memory of her reaction a moment ago to Lady Cynthia Hall and the disgust she had felt over the way the brunette had fawned over Rob. It gave her a clearer image of herself, but it didn't lessen the wound to her pride.

She walked over to Raul in a falsely sauntering stride, meeting his measuring gaze without flinching. Inwardly, she felt the seething heat of embarrassment and indignation, but she maintained an outward poise.

"Good evening, Miss Thomas." His glance drifted briefly down to take in her gown. Her fingers tightened on the glass stem. She wasn't sure if that look was a deliberate reminder of her previous nudity or an unconscious act.

"I'm torn between throwing this champagne in your face and simply laughing at the whole ridiculous episode." She held her jaw stiffly as she spoke while she struggled to raise the flash point of her temper.

"I would prefer that you not throw the champagne. The suit does not belong to me."

"When I noticed how poorly it fit you, I guessed it was either that or an inept tailor," she retaliated, seeking to make him uncomfortable with the sleeves that were a half-inch too long and the fullness of the jacket through the chest. "But since you are seldom in one place for long, I decided you were probably the kind who travels light."

"That is true."

She had not meant to acknowledge how thoroughly he had frustrated her, but it welled beyond her control. "Not many men have ever gotten the best of me the way you have. You are becoming quite a challenge."

"I have no wish to challenge you," he countered smoothly.

"Maybe not," Trisha conceded. "But I admit to wishing that I'm around the day some woman forces you to your knees."

"If you had attended today's game, you would have seen me flat on the ground when my mare threw me." A lazy, half-amused smile curved his mouth.

"I was thinking in terms of the two-legged kind." Trisha lifted the champagne glass, using it for a distraction.

A rich, deep-throated laugh came from a nearby cluster of guests. With the glass to her lips, she half turned, spying Luz among them. Briefly she felt shadowed by her mother's stunning looks and sophistication. The metallic fabric of her evening gown, the color of dark steel, shimmered in a thousand rippling shades over her slim body. The long sleeves were held together by a crisscrossing lattice all the way to the high-throated neckline, hinting at bare arms and shoulders. Her hair was pulled sleekly back in a chignon at the nape, and crescents of diamond baguettes glittered on her earlobes. Trisha glanced again at the gown, recalling its distinctive feature. It was backless, plunging low on the spine.

When Luz noticed Trisha, she extricated herself from the laughing group and glided toward her, a half-empty champagne glass dangling from her hand. Trisha spared a glance at Raul, murmuring, "You haven't met Luz, have you?" Then she was turning back to greet her mother.

"Trisha. I wanted to see you before you came down," Luz declared, but after an appraising look, a smile widened her lips. "Not that there was any need. You look beautiful." Trisha detected a faint slurring of words and remembered Emma's warning, especially when the champagne glass was raised for another swallow.

"So do you," she returned uneasily.

"I noticed Rob has already been stolen away by a young lady." Luz glanced in the direction of the dance floor.

"A lady by title only," Trisha inserted.

The comment elicited a lifted brow from Luz. "I shouldn't be surprised," she said. "It appears Fiona took her guest list from the pages of *Debrett's Peerage* and *Burke's Landed Gentry,* with a few notable exceptions such as ourselves." She drained the glass, then noticed Raul looking silently on. "I don't believe we've met. I'm Luz Kincaid Thomas . . . and I'm trying very hard to forget that my name was once Mrs. Drew Thomas until a few short weeks ago." She held out her hand, level, in the Continental fashion that required it only be clasped, not shaken. "Which count or lord are you?"

"*Señor de nada*, lord of nothing." Raul leaned slightly over her hand, a mocking smile on his lips.

The servant appeared with filled champagne glasses balanced on his tray. Luz motioned for him. "I'll have another."

"I don't think you should, Luz," Trisha cautioned.

"Never mind my daughter," she instructed the servant and traded her empty glass for a full one, missing the sharp glance Raul directed at the pair of them. He was seeking a resemblance without finding an obvious one. "She mistakenly believes I've had enough to drink."

"Yes, madam."

"What is your name?" she asked the servant.

"Simms, madam."

"Well, Simms, do you see this glass?" She showed him the one she had just taken from the tray. "I want you to keep your eye on it this evening, and when it starts getting empty, I want you to see that I have a refill. Will you do that for me, Simms?"

"As you wish, madam," he acknowledged, nodding politely.

"That *is* what I wish. Thank you, Simms." With a shift of her attention, she dismissed him.

"I don't think that's wise, Luz," Trisha repeated.

"Why must I behave wisely?" Her shoulders lifted in a careless shrug before she turned to Raul. "What my daughter fails to understand is that tonight I want to get drunk. I don't want to be responsible for the things I say or do."

Raul watched her take a drink from the glass, vaguely surprised that she was aware of what she was trying to escape. It was apparent that the alcohol she'd already consumed had loosened her usual restraint, or she never would have admitted such a thing. Odd bits of information fit into place—Trisha's assertion that her father was marrying a considerably younger woman and her mother's desire to forget her former married name. The divorce was evidently very recent . . . and the bitterness very fresh. He'd seen it before, although this woman, even half drunk, had a certain class about her.

"Are you married, my lord of nothing?" Luz inquired.

"No."

"Divorced, then?"

"No."

She frowned, narrowing her eyes to examine him more closely. "How old are you?"

"Thirty-seven."

"You have made a mistake, milord." Luz wagged her glass at him in a scolding fashion. "You should have married the daughter of some wealthy, influential family, had a couple of children, preferably a son and daughter, and used the family connections to make a name for yourself. Once you have the fine home, important friends, and the money, you can dump your first wife. She'll be old by then. With wealth, power, and status, you can have all the pretty young things you want. That's how it is done, milord."

"I see." It was an old story, retold countless times.

"You would be amazed how easy it is to fool a woman." She bolted down a swallow of champagne, then stared at the sparkling wine left in the glass. "She's invariably the last one to guess anything's wrong. All your friends will see it. Even your family. But not her."

"Luz, please," Trisha urged while she glanced uncomfortably at Raul.

"Luz, please—what? Don't make trouble?" she mocked. "You can count on that. How can a woman make trouble without appearing to be a bitch? It isn't fair. He divorces her for someone else—and she becomes the social outcast. Friends suddenly don't want you around for fear what happened to you might rub off onto them. Or else they're afraid you'll go after their husbands." She looked around the room with bitter, knowing eyes. "Worse is going to a party alone."

"Luz, why don't we go out on the terrace and get some fresh air?" Trisha suggested.

Luz drew away from the hand that reached to take hold of her arm. "I told you I don't want to be sober tonight. Or . . ." She paused to glance ruefully at Raul. "Am I boring you?"

"Not at all." He felt a certain curiosity, a detached interest in this little byplay. These formal affairs didn't appeal to him, so he had no desire to mingle and engage in boring small talk with some guest.

"Do you know what the saddest thing is?" She appeared to address the question to the nearly empty champagne glass. "Realizing you'd be better off if he were dead."

"How can you think that?" Trisha demanded angrily.

"Because it's true," she flashed. "If he were dead, I could at least have his memories to hold on to. But now I look back on twenty-one years and see the waste. It was all for nothing. It's been thrown away—like my life. What do I have left? Where do I begin again? I've always been a wife. You warned me, Trisha. My life has no purpose, you said. Well, it doesn't. Not anymore." She downed the rest of the champagne and swung away from them. "Where's Simms?"

She took an unsteady step forward and hooked the hem of her gown, nearly tripping. In a reflexive move, Raul was at her side, a supporting hand on her waist to right her. "Thank you," she said.

Her head remained downcast, a slight flush staining her cheeks. Over his shoulder, Raul caught the look of silent appeal Trisha sent him; she was plainly at a loss to prevent the certain embarrassment she knew would come.

"I believe Simms has gone for more champagne, Mrs. Thomas." Raul had no idea where the servant was. "I am rather tired of standing around myself. Would you care to dance? At least until Simms comes back."

She looked at him, a degree of sobriety in her brown eyes, but he could feel the uneven sway of her body; she needed his support. "Are you trying to save my pride so that I won't look the fool in front of all these people?"

"Yes." He smiled faintly at her astuteness.

"You are the most gallant lord here tonight," she mocked. "I would curtsy at the honor, but you understand, my lord of nothing, that if I sank to the floor, I would likely stay there."

"I understand." His smile deepened.

With his arm firmly around her slim body, he guided her through the milling guests to the small dance floor. She held her head high, smiling and nodding to two or three people along the way. When they reached the cleared area, he took the empty wineglass from her and gave it to a bystander, then gathered her into his arms. As he spread his hand over the hollow of her back, he was surprised by the heat of her bare skin. She had given him the impression of coolness, yet her flesh felt almost feverish. The fiery warmth stirred him, and he frowned thoughtfully, aware of the exotic fragrance scenting the curve of her neck.

"It's been a long time since I danced with a stranger," she mused aloud. "I suppose I'll have to get used to that."

Her attempts to follow the slow pattern of his dance steps were uncoordinated. The champagne had affected her sense of balance, and she had to rely more heavily on the muscled band of his arm. When it tightened to bring more of her weight against her body, she relaxed in his hold. Dancing with him felt different somehow—the pressure of his hand on the hollow of her spine, the movement of his legs against hers. This wasn't what it had been like to dance with Drew. It was all strange and new. Luz didn't know whether to blame the sensation on the man or on the alcohol.

Her hand rested on the ridge of his shoulder. It was wider than Drew's, muscled but not bulging. Almost idly, she ran her hand along it, stopping at the darkly tanned column of his neck. She noticed the sinewed cords and traced one from collar to jaw before lifting her gaze to his face. She was conscious of his blue eyes looking down at her, but they made no impression on her. Her tactile exploration was almost abstract, the way one would explore the contours of a statue. Her stroking finger followed the high ridge of his cheekbone, then made a slow sweep down the slashing groove by his mouth and stopped on the point of his chin.

"My husband had a deep cleft," she murmured absently.

On the sidelines, Trisha watched the pair, appalled by her mother's behavior. Luz was practically draped all over Raul. And the way Luz was touching his face, like a lover—it was too intimate. She knew Luz was drunk, but that made it all the more embarrassing. Trisha scanned the other couples on the dance floor, looking for Rob so that she could signal him to cut in.

"May I have this dance, Trisha?"

The inquiry took her by surprise, but she recognized the young man with the acne blotches on his smoothly shaven face. She'd met him several times at various parties, although his name escaped her at the moment. He was the third son of some viscount or earl—and a lot of fun, she remembered that much.

"Not right now. I'm looking for my brother. Have you seen him?"

"I think I saw him duck outside a few minutes ago." He grinned. "Our sin-loving Lady Cyn had him in tow, I believe."

"Thank you." Her smile came and went swiftly as her attention reverted to the dance floor. Silently she swore at Rob for disappearing at such an inopportune time while she watched helplessly, wondering how much longer that slow, seductive song was going to last.

When Luz's reference to the cleft in Drew's chin elicited no response from her partner, she wasn't troubled by his silence. She was in a champagne mist. And if her living statue were to speak, it would likely have jarred her. As it was, nothing disturbed the swirling fog.

With the rounded point of a polished nail, she outlined the lower curve of his mouth. Lately she had tried to imagine what it would be like to have another man hold her and make love to her. All these years there had been only Drew. One or two times she had met men who had briefly tempted her, but she had never needed the stimulation of an outside affair. Now she wondered if that meant she'd been a coward all this time, afraid to try something new and different.

She had tried to imagine the passion of another man's kiss devouring her lips—the taste of his tongue. She had gone so far as to visualize his hands roaming over her body, cupping her breasts, spreading across her hipbones and up the curve of a bent leg. Yet when she tried to see her imaginary lover's face, he had none, and her fantasy was lost. A body could not make love to her. It had to be a person with a face.

And here was a face. She liked his clear eyes, the way they looked at her so steadily. And his hair, so thick and dark—she wondered if it was coarse like Drew's. She hadn't thought about a man's hair before. She touched a smooth side, discovering its fine texture, so soft, almost silken. She slid her fingers into it, and decided it was more like velvet, hundred-dollar-a-yard silk velvet.

Of all the eligible men she knew, she had finally met one whose face could fit with the body of her fantasy lover. The man had admitted being a bachelor. Dimly Luz also recalled that he'd claimed his age as thirty-seven. He was younger than she was.

"How old do you think I am?" she asked, but when his glance sharpened on her, it almost pierced the alcohol veil that protected her. "No. Don't look too closely." Quickly, Luz lowered her chin and rested her head on his shoulder, partly hiding her face near the curve of his neck so that he couldn't see the fine lines that had begun to appear.

This was better, not looking at him. Everything was becoming hazy from the champagne, and it was difficult to concentrate on more than one thing at a time. At the moment, she was satisfied with the sensation of his hand on her lower back, the pressure of his thumb on her spine and the alternating touch of his fingers on her waist. Luz felt loose and warm. Everything had been so wrong in her life for so long; this was the first time in months anything had seemed right.

His jaw and throat gave off the heady scent of a male cologne. She breathed it in each time she inhaled. At the same time, she could feel the warmth of his breath on her eyelids and knew his mouth must be somewhere near her eyebrow. Little things, yet they were so disturbing they made her ache inside. She wanted to cry, but she wasn't sure why. Drinking did that to her sometimes. Tears would flow from her eyes on their own.

"Mrs. Thomas." His voice seemed to prod her, and she wished he had kept silent.

"What?" she said impatiently. So little effort had been expended in movement that Luz was slow to realize they had ceased dancing. In her eyes, the room was still swaying.

"The song has ended," he told her.

She listened and could hear no music, only the uneven hum of accented voices. With a push of her hands, she reeled away from him, and the room started to spin. Luz stopped and pressed a hand near her eyes, trying to clear her head and her vision. She felt his arm go around her ribs in support of her tottering body.

"The song ended." When she looked up, her fantasy died, too. Men like her lord of nothing wanted young girls. A bitter laugh rolled from her arched throat. "I almost forgot. All men are bastards." She badly needed a drink. "God, where's Simms? Damn him anyway." She shrugged away from the arm holding her and lurched forward to look for the servant. As he crossed the room with a drink tray, Luz saw him. "Simms." But someone stopped her before she could go after him.

"Luz, you're drunk." At the low and angry denouncement, she frowned, while Trisha's face kept going in and out of focus. It was true.

"More champagne, madam." A sea of glasses swam in front of her eyes, all filled with amber-pale liquid.

"No, thank you, Simms." Luz formed her words carefully, making an effort to speak clearly. "I believe I am sufficiently inebriated. Would you be so kind as to escort me to my room? I should not like to pass out in front of . . . all these people."

"As you wish, madam." He offered her a dark-sleeved arm, which she tightly gripped with both hands.

The incongruous pair crossed the room at a slow, stately pace. Trisha watched them, angrily ashamed yet grudgingly admiring the measure of dignity Luz was able to maintain. "Only Luz could get away with that." She hadn't intended to think out loud, and glanced quickly at Raul. "I'm afraid my mother—"

"No apology is needed for her," he interrupted. "If you will excuse me." He turned and walked toward the terrace doors.

Trisha stood uncertainly, then swung in the opposite direction and came face to face with the young man who had asked her to dance earlier. "I didn't think those musicians could play anything that had a beat to it," he said, drawing her attention to the up-tempo song. "Want to try it?"

"Sure." She didn't glance in the direction of the terrace as they walked onto the dance floor.

In a secluded corner of the terrace where the shadows were thick and deep, Raul paused and took a thin cheroot from his inside pocket. He struck a match and cupped the flame to the end of the narrow black cigar. Blue smoke swirled in front of his face as he exhaled.

He was unsettled by what had happened. He had danced with countless women over the years. Some had aroused his lust, but few his interest. Yet this woman was different. The reaching out for love and comfort had touched something inside him—and the way she had bitterly rejected what she couldn't have had enforced the feeling. He sighed heavily and took another drag of the cheroot, wondering why she had gotten into him for even that brief time and why he still thought about her. Forgetting came easy to him. He'd forget her, too.

Beyond him lay the formal patterns of the knot garden, the hedges and plants arranged to create intricate knot designs. But the light from the terrace couldn't penetrate it, and the garden was a dark blur, black shadows dissolving into one another. A hedge rustled nearby, and Raul caught muffled sounds, groaning whispers and heavy breathing. He dropped the half-smoked cheroot onto the stone terrace and ground it beneath his heel. He wasn't interested in listening to some couple make love. Besides, it was time he went back inside and made his presence seen so he could leave this obligatory party.

The thin material of her gown offered little barrier to the sensation of the nubby point of her breast under his hand. Its outline was as definite to Rob as it would have been if he were actually touching her flesh. The wild little sucking sounds she made while he drove his tongue deep into her mouth stimulated his own building excitement, and the hands kneading the muscles in his shoulders and back needlessly urged him to do more. He was almost half crazy now. The bulge in his pants had stiffened into a rod after the first kisses had exploded in passion. He could feel his throbbing penis straining against his trousers. He felt hot enough to pop right now.

He rocked his mouth off her wet lips and dragged it across her cheek to lick at the opening of her ear, his rough and labored breathing sounding loud in his own ears. "God, you're beautiful." He meant it the way that anything with two bumps where a pair of breasts belonged and a hot quivering cavity between a pair of legs was beautiful to an aroused male. Only Rob knew she wasn't some ugly cunt a bunch of horny high school boys had persuaded to spread her legs for them. This girl was some sexy bitch, and she was hot for him.

"So are you," she whispered rawly, kissing the side of his jaw and neck with an abandoned eagerness. "So are you."

But when he tried to force her onto the grassy carpet of the garden, she resisted. "The grass. I'll get green stains all over my gown." Rob groaned in agonizing frustration, thinking quickly and desperately.

"Let me take off my jacket. You can lie on it." He urged with his hands and his nuzzling mouth, trying to keep her as aroused and wanting as he was.

"No, silly." She laughed and pulled a half-step away from him. When he reached out to gather her back, Rob noticed her hoist her long skirt up around her waist. "I'll just climb on and neither of us will get soiled. Unzip your pants."

The shadows from the hedges and the overhanging branches of a tree made it seem as if he were moving in a dream. And everything was centered on the ivory paleness of her legs and hips. He could hardly take his eyes off of them. Then she was too close, a hand on his shoulders and another holding up her skirt in a bundle while a long, slim leg hooked itself high around his hips. Instinctively he lifted her.

"Jeezus," he swore at the ease with which he was swallowed into her hot, tight hole.

Her legs locked around his hips in a scissor hold, the strength of their muscles surprising him as she began rocking against him. But there wasn't any one thing he could concentrate on, not with that hot little tongue darting in and out of his ear and driving him wild. He felt the slap of her bottom against his pumping hips.

"Yes. Yes." Her urging moans were getting louder.

"Sssh. Someone might hear." From where he was standing, he could see the smokers on the terrace and glimpse the guests milling inside the Great Hall. But there was no way he could stop now.

"Do you suppose someone's watching us?" She sounded excited as her fingers dug into his hair, clutching him tighter. "I hope so. Let them watch. Let them watch," she moaned.

It ceased to matter as he drove into her, thrilling with each shuddering sensation until it was all pumped out of him, weakening his knees. There was nothing left but a pleasant tingling ache. He wiped himself with his handkerchief, then belatedly remembered to offer it to her.

"You were fantastic." Rob never quite knew what to say to a girl afterward.

"I know." There was a smug, feline quality about her smile as she tossed his wadded handkerchief under a bush. "Let the gardener wonder about that in the morning. Or did you want to keep it for a souvenir?"

"No." Such coarse remarks didn't appeal to him.

"I told you I wanted to find out everything you did well." She came over to him. "And it was good, wasn't it?"

"You know it was." Standing close to her this way, he remembered the heat of her and the things it did to him.

"I know something better," she said.

"There is nothing better," Rob retorted. Except maybe the

thrill and excitement of polo—that stimulating chill of danger—but she wouldn't know about that.

"You disappoint me." She unfastened the clasp of her beaded evening purse and removed a mirror and a tube of lipstick. Turning so the light from the manor reflected on the mirror, she redrew the outline of her mouth with the red lipstick. "I thought all you rich American boys knew about stardust."

"What?"

"Stardust. Spelled with a *C*—as in my name, Cyn." She shook her head at him, doubting that he understood her. "Cocaine, darling boy." The lipstick was tucked back inside her purse, but when she took her hand out, a vial of white powder was between her fingers.

Rob felt a surge of excitement, and stiffened to resist it. The pull of that remembered feeling was hard to fight.

"Haven't you ever tried it?" she chided his apparent innocence. "I promise you it will make you feel good."

"Yeah, I've . . . snorted it before." He hadn't had any since his folks split.

It sounded stupid and superstitious, but everything had been fine at home until he started messing around with cocaine. Things had gone to hell so quickly, he'd sworn off using it. It had only been an occasional thing with him anyway—not like some of the guys he knew who were tooting every chance they got.

Besides, it was expensive, and Rob wasn't sure how much of his own money Luz was going to expect him to spend to finance this year of polo. Christ, additional horses for his string, "made" ponies, were going to cost five to ten thousand dollars each, and a pro usually had thirty or more ponies in his string. Add to that the grooms, stabling and feed, veterinary bills, horse trailers, traveling expenses to tournaments around the country, a coach, and sponsorship of a team, and the investment started to get near the million-dollar mark.

Money wasn't the problem. He'd spend his own inheritance if necessary. Polo was what he wanted. The exhilaration of playing and winning, like this afternoon. It was a sensation like no other. Except, maybe, the glory of cocaine.

"Then you know what it's like," she said, smiling. "I have enough for two. I think it's always better when you can do it with someone. It's like the difference between masturbation

and making love. It's never as much fun getting off by yourself." She took his participation for granted, and Rob couldn't
make himself say anything to correct her as her hand delved
inside the purse again. "I have everything—mirror, razor
blade . . . damn." She began frantically digging through the
scant contents. "Where's the straw?"

"No problem." Rob took a fifty-pound note from his money
pocket and rolled it into a small cylinder. It was a trick he'd
learned from his buddies at school; if they were searched, they
wouldn't get caught with drug paraphernalia in their possession.

She tucked the purse under her arm and handed him the
square makeup mirror. "Hold this." Rob held it level while she
carefully tapped the white powder into a small mound on its
shiny surface. Then she used the single-edged razor blade to
divide it into thin lines easily sniffed through a straw.

"Ladies first," she said and took the rolled bill from him.
Bending over the mirror, she pressed one nostril closed and
inserted an end of the makeshift straw into the other side of
her nose, then lowered the bottom of the rolled paper to the
white line and inhaled. Rob saw the look of pleasure that spread
over her face when she straightened.

"My turn," he said and waited impatiently for her to hold
the mirror.

He breathed in through the money straw, catching first the
bitter taste of the cocaine, then that slow-spreading numbing
sensation and the warm glow of energy. It was wonderful, great.
The whole world was his for the taking.

"Are you coming to the polo match tomorrow afternoon?
It's going to be a helluva game," he declared exuberantly.
"Those ponies I'm riding are the best I've ever played on.
Sometimes it's like they know what I want them to do next
before I ask them. That bay horse with the four white stockings?
I was riding him in the third chukkar today, and I swear, I
barely pulled on the reins to stop him, and in the next second,
he had reversed his field and we were racing hell for leather
the other direction."

"When I met you at the party last week, you were so quiet.
But when I saw you play today, I said to myself, 'I'm going
to get to know him better.' I planned this whole evening, and
it worked perfectly."

Rob laughed. They talked eagerly, about everything and

nothing. But the exhilaration was too fleeting. In less than ten minutes, he could already feel himself coming down. It never lasted long enough.

After a little while, she removed the other vial from her purse. "Have you ever free-based?"

"No." A guy he knew at school did it all the time and swore by it.

"You have to try it sometime," she said. "It's really more potent that way. And the high it gives you is better than anything."

"Maybe I will someday." At the moment, he was only interested in recapturing the previous feeling as he watched her painstaking division of the powder with growing impatience.

"Once you have, this will seem like kiddy stuff," she warned. "And you won't want to settle for it. A friend of mine can show you how to do it if you're interested."

"We'll see."

"No more," Trisha protested when Don Townsend—she had finally remembered his name, although she still couldn't recall his father's title—tried to drag her back onto the dance floor. "My feet need a rest." She'd been dancing solidly for the last hour.

"I haven't stepped on them that many times. Come on," he urged.

"I don't think you stepped on them at all, but they're worn out," she insisted. "And I'm thirsty."

"All right. What would you like to drink? I'll get it."

"Something tall and cold—and nonalcoholic," she told him. "Done."

As he walked away, Trisha fanned her flushed skin with her hand and moved toward the terrace door where the air was fresher and cooler. All that dancing had made her tired, but it was a good feeling—the blood flowing through her body, her muscles loose and relaxed. She admitted, although only to herself, that a lot of her tension had left when Raul did.

"There you are, Trish. I was just looking for you."

"Rob." Her brother's sudden appearance took her by surprise. Her glance swept over his slightly rumpled hair. "You've been gone so long I don't think I'd better ask where you've been—or what you've been doing. Where's the siren? Did you lose her?"

"Cyn?"

"Cyn's her name and sin's her game." Trisha mockingly repeated the catch-phrase Don Townsend had used to describe her.

"She's in the powder room." Rob ignored the snide remark as he stretched his neck to scan the room. "Where's Raul? I saw you with him earlier."

"Much earlier. He's already left to rest up for tomorrow's game."

"I wanted to introduce him to Luz." His shoulders sagged in a disappointed slump. "Did he meet her?"

"Yes, unfortunately."

"What happened? Did he talk to her about the polo school?"

"I don't think he had a chance. I doubt if it would have sunk in if he had."

"Where is she? Do you know?" He looked around the room again. "I think I'll talk to her and see what he said."

"She's upstairs in her room—probably passed out," she informed him grimly. "She was quite drunk, Rob."

"No." His expression turned somber, that troubled moodiness settling over him again. "I'd better go check and see how she is."

"She's fine," Trisha insisted, but Rob didn't accept her word for it and walked quickly away to see for himself. "At least," she continued, speaking only to herself, "she was fine an hour ago when I looked in on her." She lost sight of Rob in the crowd of guests, then saw him going out the large doors into the main foyer.

"Something tall and cold—and nonalcoholic." Don Townsend gave a mock bow as he stopped beside her and presented a tall glass of soda to her, a wedge of lime floating on top.

"I'll love you forever for this."

"Promises, promises."

# CHAPTER XII

The ball took a wild bounce on the cut-up turf and bounded into an open area as the momentum of the players carried them past it. Raul's inside position blocked his opposite number from any attempt at the ball and gave him the closest angle to the ball. Checking his pony's speed, he urged it into a tight, fast turn and aimed for the ball, his mallet aloft.

"Leave it!"

The shouted instruction came from a teammate who had a better angle for a shot at the ball than he did. Now his team duty became to block the closest opposition between his teammate and the goal. Only one rider was in that position, already racing his pony to intercept the anticipated flight of the ball and defend against a score.

Instinctively, Raul waited a split second until his chocolate-colored horse had the necessary pivot foot on the ground to change angles before he signaled with legs and reins to alter direction. That fractional hesitation gave a fluidity to the movement, an effortless grace with hardly any break in speed. If he hadn't waited that pulsebeat, the horse would have attempted to obey the signal, but off-balance, on the wrong lead, it would have appeared lumbering and awkward.

Control was the key. Control of a mind and body other than his own and knowing the exact second to exercise it. And it all had to be reflex. There was no time to consciously check which hoof was down or which lead the pony was on, he had to know. The animal had to be an extension of himself, two highly skilled athletes playing as one.

He heard the *clunk* of a mallet striking the ball behind him.

Out of the corner of his eye, Raul saw the ball flying by him
and made a mental note of its path as he bore down on the
horse and rider angling toward the ball. He identified Rob
Thomas as the rider, but it made little difference beyond knowing the level of skill of his opponent.

Raul closed on the young rider at an acute angle, approaching on Rob's mallet side. At this speed, anything wider would
be not only dangerous, but a foul as well. The distance shortened. And the impact of two tons of horses and riders colliding
at a combined speed between fifty and sixty miles an hour was
coming. His horse knew it as well as Raul, but the animal
didn't shy from it.

The danger of the collision had to be ignored. Controlled
recklessness was an integral part of polo. It was definitely a
contact sport, and those who feared it had no business on the
field.

Timing and leverage were the dominant factors, and Raul
planned both so the impact was made by his horse's shoulder
driving into that of his opponent's mount. Wham! He felt the
bone-jarring hit and saw the sorrel head of Rob's pony dip
down, stumbling, nearly knocked off its feet, but the horse
recovered stride and balance.

Still, the collision had given Raul the advantage. His knee
was in front of Rob's—the angle was his—and he kept the
weight of his horse leaning into the other galloping animal,
successfully riding Rob off the line of the ball and leaving it
clear for his own teammate to send it through the now undefended goalposts.

Raul looked back as Hepplewhite made the scoring swing,
but he didn't ease the pressure on the horse and rider running
stride for stride with him. Even when the ball went sailing
through the air toward the posts, he rode off the opposing
player, keeping him away from the ball.

There was always the chance of a wild bounce, a freak
ricochet that could stop it short of the goalposts. Raul didn't
let up until both had gone over the endline. Only then did he
pull up to go back, prepared to give further assistance, but it
wasn't needed. The ground judge waved the flag over his head,
indicating a point scored, and Raul reined his horse in.

Rob's sorrel acted up, wildly tossing its head and fighting
the restraining pressure on the bit. Such misbehavior wasn't

normal in a horse of the sorrel's caliber of training and game experience. Instinctively, Raul's horseman's eye attempted to locate the reason as Rob forced the sorrel alongside to return to the center of the playing field. His glance fell immediately on the blood-flecked foam at the corners of the horse's mouth. He looked back at Rob, ignoring his mixed expression of grudging respect and resentment over being ridden off the play.

"His mouth is cut," he said bluntly, leaving the choice to Rob whether he should play out the final minute of the chukkar on a pony suffering pain. If Rob took the precious time to change horses, he would leave his teammates one man short when play resumed with the throw-in. In Raul's opinion, fair play did not include giving advice to the opposing side.

A second later, Rob swung his horse away and spurred it toward the picket line. Raul doubted if the young rider would have made that choice six months ago. His absence on the field for a few seconds of playing time would not be as harmful to his team as a full minute of play on a disobedient pony.

His horse pushed at the bit, and Raul gave it more rein. Its chocolate head bobbed low as the horse blew out a rolling snort, clearing its distended nostrils. Absently, he listened to the familiar noises of the horse as he posted back to midfield at the regulation trot.

It was four against three in the ensuing throw-in. Raul's side got control of the ball and drove quickly for the goal. On a fresh horse, Rob raced onto the field, but he was too late to even out the numbers and prevent the scoring of a goal.

As the two teams regrouped in the center of the field, Raul heard Sherbourne berating Rob for his decision. "What the hell did you think you were doing? There was less than a minute! Why didn't you wait until the damned chukkar was over to change horses?"

Raul smiled humorlessly at Rob's initiation in playing for someone else. Regardless of how wrong he was, the team owner or captain was always right. The desire to win was fierce. And having two quick goals scored on them in succession was hard for a man like Sherbourne to accept. Rob, indirectly involved in both plays, suffered the brunt of his sour temper. It was an unpleasant by-product of the game, like fatigue and injuries.

Before the umpire had a chance to bowl the ball between

the staggered line of riders, the bell rang to end the chukkar, with Raul's side ahead by three points and only one period left to play. He rode to the picket line and dismounted. The groom, a chunky young girl, took the reins from him and led the sweating horse away.

Pulling off his helmet, Raul breathed in tiredly and temporarily laid his mallet, crop, and helmet across the armrests of a lawn chair. There wasn't time between chukkars to grab more than a few seconds of rest before he had to check the saddle and equipment on a fresh mount. There was a soreness in the thigh muscle of his right leg, the result of being accidentally hit by a stick early in the match. It showed signs of stiffening if he didn't keep moving.

Raul fought off the exhaustion that pushed him toward the chair seat and reached for the wet towel draped over the back. He wiped the sweat from his face and ran it over his damp hair, then let it cool the back of his neck. Blood had dried along a cut on his arm, although he didn't remember how he got it. It wasn't hurting him, so he didn't bother to clean it.

Someone handed him a drink. He lifted it to his parched mouth and downed half of it before pausing to walk again and keep that leg muscle from tightening up on him. The groom came back, leading a saddled horse. He'd saved the black so he could use its lightning speed in the final period. Raul walked to the horse rather than wait for the female groom to bring the animal to him.

As he rechecked the tightness of the saddle girth and the length of the martingale, Hepplewhite rode over, already mounted on a fresh pony. The tiredness in the team captain's face was overshadowed by the gleam of a victory within reach.

"Speed, didn't I tell you that was the key?" he declared. "Every time the tempo picked up we got control. Sherbourne's style of play is steady and deliberate. A fast pace rattles him. This period, you and that black horse have to run their legs off. You do what I say and, by damn, we'll win this trophy."

Raul nodded, fully aware the pressure was on him more than the others. He was the professional in their midst. He was getting paid to play, so results were expected. And the only result that counted was winning. The invisible pressure was always there, sometimes wearing on him. But polo was his profession and Hepplewhite's avocation. Excellence was expected—demanded—from him, and little leeway allowed for the bad days everyone had sometimes.

"I will need the longer stick," he told the groom as he walked to the lawn chair and retrieved his helmet and whip.

After he was in the saddle, she handed him the alternate mallet. The black horse was taller than the brown pony he'd ridden before. To compensate for the difference in their heights, he used a longer stick so he wouldn't have to adjust the reach or rhythm of his swing. Holding the mallet upright, like a warrior's lance, he reined the black horse toward the long, wide field of green.

"Good luck," the groom called.

From the sidelines, Luz watched the play resume. Last night's champagne had left her with a miserable hangover, and the supposed stimulation contained in the gallons of caffeine-rich coffee she'd consumed this morning hadn't improved her condition. She still felt rotten. Her head felt heavy, in need of support, and there was a dull pounding in her temples. Despite the shade of her hat and dark glasses, the brilliant sunlight hurt her eyes. Everything jarred her senses—sounds, smells, movements.

Part of the dullness came, too, from Drew's telegram informing them of his marriage to Claudia. This morning, she had given it to Trisha and Rob. Typically, Rob had said nothing and walked out of the room. Trisha had been equally subdued, murmuring something about buying them a wedding present.

Luz tried not to think about it and watched the game instead. The action on the playing field happened too fast for her to follow all of it, so Luz concentrated on keeping track of Rob. She wasn't altogether successful at that, frequently losing sight of him amid the flashing sticks and galloping ponies. At the moment, he was racing at the head of a charging line of players, chasing a ball toward the goal line. Luz was fairly certain it was the opponents' goal, although she might have missed a change of ends.

"Go, Rob! Go!" Trisha urged him on.

Luz winced at the encouraging shout, wishing her daughter wouldn't yell so loudly. A black horse came streaking out of the following pack after Rob. The rider leaned way forward over the horse's neck, stretching in his stirrups and reaching

with his mallet. When Rob swung at the ball his mallet head
hooked the other man's stick, and he had no chance to hit the
ball through the posts.

"Damn him," Trisha swore.

"Who was it?" With her slowed comprehension, it was all
Luz could do to identify her own son.

"Raul Buchanan. Who else?" Trisha muttered while she
looked through the binoculars.

"Who else," Luz agreed dryly—and quietly. The Argentine
had been Rob's nemesis the last time they'd played against
each other, and today appeared to be a repeat.

"If looks could kill, Rob just buried him. Wanta see?" Trisha
offered her the binoculars.

"No." It was all she could do to hold her head up, and those
field glasses were heavy. Besides, she doubted if she'd be able
to see any better through them anyway.

And she had already guessed which one he was. Even at a
distance he had looked familiar to her, so she had identified
him from the start of the game. These last couple of days, Rob
had talked about Raul Buchanan incessantly. Supposedly she
had met him at last night's party, or so Rob claimed at breakfast
this morning, but Luz didn't remember that.

Most of last night was a haze to her, although she had a
vague, lingering sense that she'd made a fool of herself. She
had seen and talked to a lot of people, mostly English lords
and gentry, but no Latins that she recalled. Actually, she was
grateful Rob had let the matter of her memory lapse drop.
Maybe he knew she'd had too much to drink, but she hadn't
wanted to admit that to him.

The game moved swiftly with none of the fouls that had so
frequently halted the action in the first half of play. Privately,
Luz was glad it wasn't dragging out, although for Rob's sake
she was sorry time ran out while his side was still behind.

"Poor Henry." Fiona sighed. "He won't be fit to live with
for a week."

"I suppose we should go console Rob," Trisha said.

Luz would have preferred to go straight back to Seven Oak
and lie down with an ice pack on her forehead, but she knew
Rob would expect her to come by. Before the game, he had
said he wanted her to meet Raul Buchanan. Now that the
Argentine player had beaten him again, he might have changed

his mind about that. God, she hoped so. She wasn't sure if she was up to meeting the man who was fast becoming Rob's polo idol.

"We'll be back shortly," she promised Fiona Sherbourne, and carefully pushed out of the chair.

Together, Luz and Trisha proceeded up the sidelines toward the picket area. Luz kept her head down so that the brim of her hat could shield her from as much of the glaring sun as possible. Silently, she wished for some of that notoriously foul English weather—some heavy thick clouds would be nice.

They skirted the spectators, most of them there in hopes of catching a glimpse of some member of the Royal Family, either playing in the game or observing the action. Passing the parked horse trailers, mainly the old-fashioned horse boxes instead of the goose-necked kind so common in the States, they approached the riders' pony lines. They had to watch where they were going and avoid the piles of horse droppings that dotted the rear area.

"There's Rob." Trisha pointed.

Luz glanced in the direction she indicated. Rob was in the company of another man whose back was to them, the polo helmet tucked under his arm to reveal dark, rumpled hair. The color of his sweat-darkened shirt identified him as a member of the opposing team, obviously being congratulated by Rob on their victory.

"Hey, Luz!" Rob called to her, his expression seeming unusually earnest in the face of his loss. A second later, Luz recognized the black horse standing to one side of the rider, and it all made sense. That was Raul Buchanan with him. "You've met my mother, haven't you?" he said to him as she walked up, Trisha lagging slightly behind her.

When the man turned, shock rippled through her. That face belonged to the man she had danced with at the party. The clothes were wrong—the dirt-smudged white breeches, the tight-fitting polo shirt, and boots. In black evening suit, she would never have guessed that he played polo for a living— that he was Argentine.

A second thought hit Luz with sickening force. She'd been so drunk. The impression she must have made on him was sobering. She looked at his level blue eyes, deeply lined at the corners. He probably saw her as a bitter, self-pitying divorcée, afraid of growing old alone. That wasn't really who she was. And she wouldn't have him looking down at her.

"Yes, I've met Mrs. Thomas," he said.

"You have the advantage on me, Mr. Buchanan," Luz asserted coolly. "Last evening you only identified yourself as the 'lord of nothing.' A memorable title—and a curious one under the circumstances."

"It seemed appropriate at the time. The phrase was once used to describe the gaucho—the cowboy of my country. *Señor de nada,* lord of nothing. As you said, Mrs. Thomas, it's memorable although the humor may be weak." The explanation was smooth and aloofly made.

"Part of the fault for this mix-up may be mine." Trisha stepped forward. "You see, the other evening, Luz, I likened Raul to a modern-day gaucho."

A combination of things registered simultaneously on Luz—Trisha's familiar use of his given name, the way she looked at him, and the memory that her daughter had been with him when Luz first saw him. The nearly twenty-year age difference came last, but Drew had proved to her how irrelevant that was to a man. Luz shuddered inwardly when she recalled how very close she had come to making an utter fool of herself and indulging in absurd fantasies. The dark glasses she wore were a blessing.

"Well, *señor de nada*—or should I call you Mr. Buchanan? I don't know which you prefer." Her brittle, forced laugh, like her smile, had a trace of sarcasm that mocked whatever nobly romantic notions he had about himself.

"Mr. Buchanan—or simply Raul."

Luz suspected the latter familiarity was offered because he had already given the privilege to her daughter. "My son has spoken at length about you, Mr. Buchanan." Belatedly, she realized that Rob probably called him by his given name, too, but she preferred to keep this new distance. "Naturally he talked about your polo school."

"He is a good player. With training, he could improve his handicap rating. I admit I would like to see him enroll in the program. I think he would benefit greatly from it."

"Before we made a decision of that nature, I would have to know more detailed information about it—the duration of the training, the time frame. And the costs involved—I'm sure you don't do this for nothing," she added cynically. "Many things have to be considered."

"I understand." Raul's expression had become very remote. "I have supplied your son with my address in Argentina. You may direct your inquiries there for information, or any arrangements you may wish to make. He also has the name of the man to contact regarding the school."

"I was under the impression it was your school. Do you actually do any instructing, or have you simply lent your name to it?" Luz challenged.

"It is my school," he stated firmly. "And I will be involved in the instruction of the finer points of the game, but there will be others teaching as well, so the young player will have the benefit of the expertise of others."

"I hope you don't think I was accusing you of misleading us." She smiled.

His mouth curved in response, its line containing the same knowing expression as hers. "It never crossed my mind, Mrs. Thomas."

"Then you will understand when I say that I'm accustomed to dealing with the person in charge, and that appears to be you." She wasn't about to be shunted to some underling. "It seems only fair that if we are prepared to invest both time and money in your program, you take time to answer our questions personally."

"I would do so now, Mrs. Thomas, but unfortunately they will be making the trophy presentation shortly. And I have the feeling your discussion would be a lengthy one. Previous commitments will take me out of the country the first of the week, so I cannot be certain how soon I could arrange to meet you. I gave you my associate's name as an alternative. It would be poor business practice—and rude—to indefinitely postpone supplying the information you seek before deciding whether Rob—your son—may wish to attend this year's session."

"It starts the latter part of August," Rob volunteered. "That's less than two months away."

The obvious deadline irritated her. She felt she had to take a firm stand to establish some kind of authority. Her pride insisted on it.

"Raul is going to France," Trisha supplied.

"Yes, I will be there approximately a month before I fly home to Argentina."

"Perhaps that's our answer, Mr. Buchanan," Luz stated. "We—that is, Trisha and I—will be in Paris for the next ten days. Rob will stay on here and join us later. Surely we can arrange to have dinner one evening."

"I am staying in the country." He began what sounded like a refusal, then appeared to change his mind. "But I could arrange to come into the city for an evening."

"We will be staying at the Hotel de Crillon. What day would suit you? Our plans are flexible." Again, she forced the issue, seeking a firm date rather than leaving it open.

"Shall we say Tuesday, the week next?" he suggested smoothly.

"That will be fine," Luz agreed. "Dinner at eight."

"I will leave the choice of restaurant to you," he replied. "If any conflict arises, I will leave a message at your hotel, but I anticipate none." A movement on the field distracted his attention. "You will excuse me." He collected the reins of his horse and swung onto the saddle.

When Luz tipped her head back to look up at his now greater height she looked directly into the sun, its light no longer blocked by her hat brim. Not even the dark lenses of her sunglasses could shield out all the force of its blinding glare. She averted her face and instinctively raised a hand to cover her eyes.

"In Paris, Mrs. Thomas." The firm tone of his voice promised a future meeting. A second later, she heard the heavy step of the black horse, its shod hooves carrying him away. Wary of the sun, Luz chanced another look at the rider, this time careful to keep her head down, and watched him ride back onto the field to join the other members of his team.

She was conscious of the silence on both sides of her. "Is anything wrong?" She glanced first at Rob, noting his moody dejection.

One corner of his mouth was pulled down in a rueful line. "It didn't sound as if you thought very much of his school. It really is a kind of polo college," he asserted.

"It may be, but I don't have any of the facts. At this point, I have no opinion one way or the other," Luz insisted.

"He's the best polo player I've ever met. I could learn a lot from him." The stubborn jut of his chin reminded Luz of Drew, always so very definite about his ideas. "Remember when I changed horses just before the end of the next-to-last chukkar? Henry crawled all over me for that, because they scored a point while we were short. Raul told me, before you came, that I had made the right decision. I didn't have control of my pony, so I was useless to the team anyway."

"What happened to the pony?" A frown flickered across Trisha's face.

"It was my fault, I guess." He shrugged self-consciously. "I never checked over the equipment. The bit was too tight and it cut up his mouth. Henry isn't going to be too happy about that either."

"It was a regrettable oversight. I'm sure Henry will understand." Luz smiled with bland encouragement. "If he doesn't, I'll simply have to remind him of the time he was playing in a game with Jake and forgot to check the saddle girth. The first time he went to make a shot, the saddle twisted, and he did a rather ungainly swan dive onto the grass."

"I would have loved to see his face." Rob laughed. "As red as he gets, it must have looked like a ripe tomato."

"Close." The empty smile remained in place as she glanced at Trisha. "Fiona will be ready to leave. We'd better go back."

"I'll see you there," Rob said. "I want to check on the sorrel before I have to face Henry."

As she and Trisha left the picket area to retrace their steps, Luz felt the dampness of her armpits. Her palms were clammy with nervous perspiration, too. She realized how much the confrontation with Raul Buchanan had shaken her. She had to get control of herself and put last night's performance behind her. It was best forgotten. All of it.

Gradually she became aware of Trisha's silence. Her expression was unusually pensive as she gazed at the little ceremony being conducted on the field, the presentation of the winner's trophy. Any hope that the subject of Raul Buchanan had been dropped faded from Luz's mind.

As if sensing her study, Trisha turned to look at her. "It must have been embarrassing."

"What?" Luz looked to the front, pretending not to understand her reference.

"I didn't realize you didn't know his name last night. I guess

I thought he'd told you." She stared at the ground as they walked. "It had to be really awkward for you finding out like that."

"Why should it? I don't have to account for my actions to him—or to anyone," Luz added stiffly to include her daughter, then went on the attack. "You seem to know him quite well."

Her head came up to meet Luz's glance. "Not as well as I would like."

"Don't get involved with him, Trisha. He's too old for you."

"Luz, I—"

"And don't bring up your father. There is no comparison. You are barely eighteen, and that is too young to be getting involved with an older man. I don't care who he is."

There was no answer from Trisha, but Luz didn't expect one. Nor did she believe that her daughter was going to listen to her.

Shortly after they returned to Seven Oak, afternoon tea was served in the relatively informal sunroom. Luz sampled the small sandwiches, avoiding the cucumber in favor of the lighter watercress, but concentrated mainly on the tea. Her stomach wasn't up to digesting the sweet rich delicacies on the polished silver tray. It wanted to turn when Luz watched Trisha biting into one of the cream-filled brandy snaps, so she was careful not to look at Rob when he helped himself to a cream dariole, a custard tart topped with red currant jelly and whipped cream.

Her host ignored the light repast altogether, she noticed as a disgruntled Henry Sherbourne tossed down another swallow of Scotch, then hobbled away from the window overlooking the garden, nursing a sore hip and shoulder bruised in a fall during the polo match. Luz suspected that defeat had only added to the pain of his injuries. He was a stocky, florid-faced man with what Jake had been fond of calling "donelap's disease," meaning his stomach "done lapped" over his belt. His presently tucked-in chin and the downward droop of his mouth corners emphasized the jowling of his cheeks. As Fiona had predicted, he was in an ill temper and had said barely ten words since he'd joined them.

"Excuse me." The butler made one of his silent entrances; he was a properly sober-faced and formal man, young by the standard image, in his middle thirties, but exuding quiet authority. "There is a telephone call for Mr. Thomas."

"Me?" Rob said in surprise and question.

"Yes, sir." The dark head inclined in an affirmative nod. "A young lady, sir. Cynthia Hall."

"Oh." He appeared vaguely flustered.

"Would you care to take it in the library, sir?"

"Yes, that's fine. Thank you, Tobin." Recovering, he set aside his Haviland plate with the half-eaten cream dariole and dabbed at his mouth with the linen napkin.

"Hurry, Rob," Trisha teased. "You don't want to keep *Cyn*thia waiting."

His look glittered with brotherly irritation as he rose from his chair, then he pointedly ignored her to follow the butler out of the room. Trisha stared at the door through which he'd gone, a bemused expression on her face.

Then she stirred, announcing generally, "It's time I was getting ready."

"For what?" Luz frowned.

"Didn't I tell you?" She paused on her way to the door. "Don Townsend is coming by to pick me up. We're going dancing somewhere. With him, who knows where we'll end up? It is likely to be Annabel's in Berkeley Square. You don't mind, do you?"

Luz knew she wasn't really seeking her permission. "No. But try not to be too late," she called after her.

With Trisha gone and Rob on the telephone in the library, that left just the three of them in the room. "A quiet evening at home seems to be in store for us," Fiona remarked, then glanced in her husband's direction. "It's probably just as well."

Luz smiled wanly in agreement, although she knew there were a couple of things she had to do before she could enjoy that implied peace. "Henry, what do you know about Raul Buchanan?"

There seemed no better time to begin gathering background material on the man. She knew little about him beyond his surface credentials as a high-goal polo player, and Rob was too prejudiced in the man's favor for his judgment to be reliable And there was the problem of Trisha's interest to consider. Personally, she wanted nothing more to do with him, but she wasn't likely to succeed in imposing her dictates on Rob and

Trisha. Since a decision had to be made after she met him again, she wanted it to be a rational one. To do that, she needed information from sources other than Raul Buchanan.

"Don't mention his name to me!" Henry took another swig of his Scotch, trying to wash out the bad taste.

"I wasn't trying to rub salt into your wounds." She had her own smarting memories of him, although it was her own behavior that was to blame for them. "But I understand he has a polo school in Argentina. You know how interested Rob is in improving his game. He has been talking to Buchanan about attending his school. Most of my experience, personally and through Jake, has been in club polo—the lessons and occasional seminars they give. I felt you would know more about the professional level of play, and advanced training of this nature, specifically Buchanan's and how well it's regarded."

"I see." It was a harrumphing response, grudgingly accepting the subject matter. "I can't tell you much about the man personally, but I know our British pros are keen on him. There are some good training schools around. As a matter of fact, there's one in Ireland. But I can't speak specifically about his. However, there's no doubt Argentina has some of the best players in the world. One would think that would be the place to learn. I could make some inquiries, if you like."

"Please. I'll be meeting with Mr. Buchanan a week from Tuesday to talk about his schooling program. I would like some information beforehand."

"That shouldn't be a problem."

"Thank you, Henry. I do appreciate it."

After tea, Luz went up to her suite. In the hallway, she met Rob coming out of his room. The smell of his after-shave was so strong, she wondered if he had splashed the whole bottle on his face.

"Going out?" she guessed.

"Yes. Cyn is on her way over now. Cynthia Hall, the girl who phoned earlier," he added quickly. "We're just going out for a couple of hours."

"Enjoy yourself." She didn't want Rob to feel guilty for leaving her alone. Since the separation and divorce, he'd been very sensitive about that, often making sure she had plans of her own.

After she went by him, he seemed to hesitate before continuing down the hall. As she entered her rooms and turned to shut the door, she couldn't help thinking that everyone was paired. Fiona and Henry were downstairs. Trisha was off with her date, and Rob was meeting his. Now Drew and Claudia.

"Two by two," she muttered.

"I'm sorry. What did you say, Luz?"

Emma's voice startled her. She pivoted around to face the room and saw Emma sitting at the small desk by the sitting room window. "Nothing." She walked forward, her attention resting thoughtfully on the plump woman who seemed so well adjusted to her own single status. She frowned curiously. "How do you cope with loneliness, Emma? You've been a widow for ten years or more."

They worked so closely together, their lives entwining, yet they had never become confidantes. Luz doubted that there was much about her private life that Emma didn't know, yet they never talked about it. And she knew nothing about Emma's, beyond the names of a few friends and relatives, and odd bits about her late husband—superficial information.

"I stay occupied, involved in my work and interested in people and places," she answered matter-of-factly. "It's a matter of keeping busy at something, I guess." As if to prove it, she reached for the note pad on the desk. "I have verified our airline reservations to Paris, and a limousine will be waiting for us at the airport when we arrive. They have our flight number and our scheduled time of arrival, so there shouldn't be any mix-ups."

"Good." Luz crossed to the window and looked out at the tree-shaded lawn, so vibrantly green in the light of the late-setting sun. She supposed Emma was right. That fine line was better not crossed. Someday it might prove awkward to both of them.

# CHAPTER XIII

As the long limousine entered the whirl of traffic around the Place de l'Étoile, renamed Place Charles de Gaulle, where twelve avenues converged like spokes of a wheel, Luz was certain the sight could be enjoyed only from the luxury of a rear seat. From the window, she glimpsed the majesty of the Arc de Triomphe rising from the center of the star, the flame to the unknown soldier of the First World War flickering at its feet.

A moment later, the limousine was swinging onto the wide boulevard, the Champs Élysées. This was Paris. Each time she saw it, she knew she had arrived in the City of Light. The busy avenue seemed to symbolize everything Parisian with its crowded streets and sidewalk cafés. It widened at Rond-Point, and chestnut trees shaded either side of the street, planted long ago to create a fashionable promenade for ladies in horse-drawn carriages when the Champs Élysées was a garden stretching to the Louvre.

As they approached the end of the avenue, Luz looked for the famous horse statues of Marly and saw them emerge from the green foliage. But there wasn't time to admire again their graceful power and beauty. The perfectly refined symmetry of the Place de la Concorde was before her, the ancient Egyptian obelisk piercing the heart of the large square, harmoniously balanced by two Roman fountains, two Grecian temples, and eight statues. Beyond lay the Tuileries, the entrance marked by a pair of equine statues by Coysevox to match those of Marly.

It was impossible to take in all the familiar landmarks at

once. Sighing, Luz settled back in the velvet-upholstered seat and glanced at her traveling companions. Trisha and Emma appeared only mildly interested in the scene, indifferent or immune to the sights of Paris that always excited her.

The limousine slowed to a stop in front of the hotel's unpretentious entrance. Luz gathered her purse from her lap and waited for the door to be opened for her. Extending a hand to the uniformed doorman, she let him assist her from the rear seat. As soon as Trisha joined her, she left Emma to make certain all their luggage was unloaded from the trunk and entered the lavishly marbled lobby of the regal hotel, the building formerly part of two palaces commissioned by Louis XV and sold to the Comte de Crillon, from which it took its name.

The concierge recognized her and came forward to greet her. *"Bonjour,* Madame Thomas. Welcome to Paris. It is good to have you with us again."

"Thank you, Georges." She smiled warmly. "It is wonderful to be in Paris, as always."

"Your suite is all prepared for you." He escorted her to the desk and spoke in rapid French to the clerk, testing Luz's fluency in the language. The registration slip was presented for her signature, all the necessary information already supplied. Luz signed it and passed it back to the clerk. "Monsieur Thomas will be joining you on the weekend, *non?"* the short, friendly concierge stated when the clerk stepped away to get her key.

*"Non."* Luz realized she had never changed the original reservations, which had included Drew for the latter part of their stay. "There will only be myself, my daughter Trisha, and Emma Sanderson, my secretary. My son will be joining us, as planned, this weekend, but not my husband. We are divorced."

For so long, she had avoided volunteering the information, but this time she felt a sense of relief in admitting it. She and Drew had been frequent guests of the hotel. Some of the older staff, like Georges, were likely to ask about him, and she didn't want to go through the act of letting them believe he simply wasn't joining her on this trip. It would have been easy to do, and the divorce wasn't any of their business. Still, it was better this way. Now the word would likely spread through the hotel staff, and no one would ask about him.

"I am sorry, madame. I did not know."

"Apologies aren't necessary, Georges," Luz assured him. "You couldn't know."

"*Mais oui.*" He shrugged, then peered at her with a compassionate twinkle. "It is good you come to Paris. It is a place for the heart, *non?* A place to forget the old love and find a new."

"I doubt it." She laughed softly.

His hands lifted palm upward in an imploring gesture. "A beautiful divorcée such as madame will have all of Paris at her feet."

"*Non,* Georges." She shook her head, amused by his flattery. "It is likely to be my daughter who has all of Paris at her feet."

"*Oui,* she is beautiful," he agreed. "But French men prefer the mature women. It is only the foolish *americains* who want the blandness of youth."

"*Merci,*" Luz declared with a wide, deeply grateful smile. "I always knew I loved Paris." It made her feel like a woman, and it was a glorious feeling.

The clerk returned, and the concierge quickly reached for the large manila envelope in his hand and offered it to Luz. "This packet was delivered for you, madame."

Frowning in surprise, she took it and glanced curiously at the writing on the envelope, but the sender wasn't identified.

"Émile will show you to your suite, Madame Thomas. And I will see that your luggage is sent directly to you. Call me if there is anything you require during your stay with us."

"Thank you." She noticed the bellman standing to one side with the key. Her curiosity would have to wait until she reached her suite.

"*S'il vous plaît.*" The uniformed bellman bent slightly at the waist, directing them toward the elevators.

Luz hesitated, looking around. "Where's Emma?"

"She's coming." Trisha nodded toward the hotel entrance and the round figure in the beige raincoat bustling across the lobby to join them, her stubby-heeled shoes echoing loudly in the marbled magnificence of the former private palace.

Luz nodded to the bellman to proceed, assured that her secretary was directly behind them. As they reached the elevators, the doors slid open. Luz stared at the couple who stepped out with startled recognition.

"Diana, you are the last person I expected to see in Paris," she declared.

"Luz." The platinum blonde embraced her with equal surprise, then stepped back. "What are you doing here? I haven't seen you in ages. It was the Fasig-Tipton sale in Kentucky, wasn't it?"

"I think so." Luz interrupted their meeting long enough to greet her husband, Vic Chandler. "It's good to see you again, too, Vic." They exchanged kisses on the cheek.

"You're as beautiful as ever," he insisted, but it sounded like an empty compliment after the concierge's flattery.

"I called when I was in Virginia last February. I thought we could get together, but you were gone," Luz said.

"California. I'm just sick about Hopeworth Farm. Every time we drive by and I see that beautiful old home all boarded up, I want to cry." Diana Chandler looked compassionately at Luz. "I wish you could have talked Audra out of closing the place."

"It was the only practical thing to do." But Luz regretted it more than anyone.

Impulsively Diana reached out and caught her hands, clasping them tightly in a gesture of sympathy. "It's been such a difficult year for you, Luz . . . losing your father in the fall, and now this mess with Drew."

"It's that time of life, I suppose." She shrugged, rejecting the pity she saw in the eyes of her old friend. "You grow up thinking everything's going to stay the same, the people you love will always be there. But everything and everyone changes, and there isn't anything you can do about it. It simply happens."

An uneasiness flickered in Diana's eyes, so artfully shadowed to accent their china-blue color. Luz understood that involuntary shying away from such talk, that half-formed fear that maybe it was true and her emotional security might prove to be as tenuous as Luz's had been.

"I suppose so." Diana took a deep breath and deliberately looked bright. "What brings you to Paris?"

"It's my graduation present to Trisha, a shopping spree in Paris." She angled her body slightly to include her daughter in the conversation while Emma remained to one side with the increasingly impatient bellman. "We have appointments at three *haute couture* houses."

"This is Trisha," Diana declared, then greeted her with an embrace, pressing her cheek to Trisha's and stepping back to look at her. "So grown-up. She's beautiful, Luz," the blonde asserted with a quick glance in her direction.

"Thank you, Mrs. Chandler." Trisha smiled politely, but there was a muted sparkle of irritation in her dark eyes.

"Where's Rob?" Vic Chandler asked. He was a tall, thickly built man whose high forehead had become more pronounced as his hairline receded.

"Playing polo in England. He's flying over to join us next week." In time to be on hand for her meeting with Raul Buchanan. "You never said what you're doing in Paris. Is it a business or pleasure trip?"

"Both," Vic answered.

And Diana elaborated. "Do you remember that yearling colt we bought from Jake? The one you liked so well?"

"Sully Maid's colt sired by the Minstrel?" Luz started to smile. "The ungainly chestnut Jake always referred to as the dud?"

"That's him," Diana admitted with a remembering laugh. "Well, Vagabond Song is racing at Longchamp this weekend. He didn't do all that well as a two-year-old, but he's really improved this year. His workouts have been exceptional, according to our trainer. So we decided we wanted to see him run. And I convinced Vic that if we were going to come to Paris, we might as well spend some time here and do a little shopping. If it had been August, I wouldn't have suggested it. I swear all of France goes on vacation in August."

"True. Vagabond Song. It certainly has a better ring to it than 'the dud,'" Luz said. "I always thought he'd be a horse slow to mature."

"Wait until you see him," Vic advised. "He doesn't look like the same horse. That ragged colt turned into a sleek, powerful horse."

"You must come to the race with us and watch him run," Diana insisted.

A Sunday afternoon spent in the atmosphere and elegance of Longchamp appealed to her, but the deciding factor was the chance to watch a colt foaled at Hopeworth Farm. "We'd love to, wouldn't we, Trisha?" She turned to her daughter.

"Sounds fun," she agreed.

"Then it's settled," Vic declared. "You'll be our guests."

"Listen, we'll talk soon." Luz moved toward the elevator doors, still held open by the pale, dark-haired bellman. "We've only just arrived. We haven't even been to our rooms yet."

"We have to run, too." Diana edged in the opposite direction toward the lobby proper. "Don't spend all your time on St. Honoré. There are some very smart boutiques in Les Halles."

Acknowledging the advice with a smiling nod, Luz stepped into the elevator. The doors slid shut the minute Trisha and Emma were inside, and they were whisked silently up to their floor. The bellman led the way to their apartment suite, unlocked the door, and showed them inside. Luz paused in the ornately decorated sitting room and temporarily laid her purse and the manila envelope on the intricately inlaid top of a marquetry table. Already familiar with the amenities in the suite and the view of the National Assembly building on the opposite bank of the Seine, she let the bellman point them out to Emma while she removed her hat and lightly pushed at the flattened crown of her hair with her fingertips.

"God, I hate it when people talk like that." Trisha's low explosion drew her glance as Luz picked up the manila envelope to satisfy her curiosity about the sender. "'She's beautiful, Luz.'" It was a stinging imitation of Diana's voice. "I could have been a dress instead of a person. 'It's a beautiful dress, Luz.'"

"She didn't mean anything by it." She ripped open the manila flap as Emma gave the departing bellman his tip.

"I know, but it irritates me anyway. I'm not an inanimate object that belongs to you. I think it's rude to talk like that," she insisted, then noticed the printed pamphlet complete with photographs that Luz removed from the envelope. "What's that, a brochure?"

"So it seems," she confirmed after a cursory glance at the contents, and the signature on the note clipped to the brochure and accompanying fact sheets. "Raul Buchanan sent them." She removed the attached note to glance through the printed photographs in the brochure while Trisha tried to look at it over her shoulder. "It's his polo school." The pictures depicting practice sessions in polo were common, as were the "pretty" shots of ponies, provided for the students, grazing in a green pasture. It was the ones showing the buildings that attracted her attention. "It doesn't look very impressive."

"Luz, it's a school, not a luxury hotel," Trisha reminded her and reached for the brochure. "May I see it?"

"Of course." Luz handed it to her, then read the handwritten note that had been clipped to it.

*Dear Mrs. Thomas,*

   *I have enclosed a brochure and an information sheet listing the available courses and their prices. I thought you would wish to study it before we meet on Tuesday.*

                           *Raul Buchanan.*

The brevity of the note did not surprise her, nor its forthright tone, lacking any embellishing salesmanship. It seemed in character. But she frowned at the handwriting. She had expected a bold, slashing style. Although there appeared to be strong pressure on the pen, the lettering was tightly formed, almost crude in its style.

"What did he say?" Trisha asked.

"Nothing." She quickly wiped away the small frown and shifted the note underneath the fact sheet to peruse it. "He just thought I'd want to look over this information before we met."

"I heard Henry tell you that he talked to some players who highly recommended Raul's polo school."

"Yes." It seemed that a lot of professional players went there to refine their skills and work on their particular weaknesses in the sport.

"Do you think Rob will end up going there?"

"It's too soon to say. After all, it isn't the only one of its kind. And Argentina is awfully far away—at the other end of the world. I don't know if I like the idea of Rob's going there alone when the area is politically so unsettled. There are so many kidnappings in those South American countries."

"That happens all over. Look at Italy. With that kind of reasoning, what are we doing in Europe?"

The logical argument irritated Luz. It sounded so much like something Drew would have said. "I'll study this later." She reached for the brochure in Trisha's hands and returned it all to the brown manila packet. "Emma, would you ring down to room service for coffee? And we'll need a maid to unpack the luggage."

The light drizzle pattered softly on the umbrella as Luz paused at an intersection on the Champs Élysées and waited for the traffic light to change. Trisha stopped beside her, their umbrellas overlapping. The gentle shower was just steady enough to send the umbrellaless pedestrians scurrying between the drops, holding newspapers, shopping bags, or jacket shoulders over their heads.

Car tires made a squishing sound as they traveled down the rainwashed streets. Luz glanced at the set of traffic lights fastened to the street post, positioned shoulder-high to a pedestrian so drivers in their low-built cars could see them and their view wasn't blocked by the car roof. The first time she'd ever seen them, it had been in Paris. They had become a distinctive feature that she always associated with Paris in her mind—like the water towers in Manhattan.

The light changed, and Luz stepped off the curb, avoiding the narrow stream of water washing the litter of street and sidewalk into the city's famous sewers. She was briefly separated from Trisha by the oncoming flow of people hurrying across the crosswalk. They met again on the other side and turned toward the striped awning of a café terrace.

All but two of the sidewalk tables were empty, all the rest of the café's patrons choosing to be inside out of the warm drizzle. Luz found two dry chairs close to the building and sat in one of them, closing the umbrella and propping it against the side of the chair. Trisha checked the table before she set her small paper bag on top of it, a purchase she'd made when they had ducked into an English bookstore to escape a sudden heavy shower. It had been years since Luz had been in a bookstore, and she had browsed idly through the various sections separately from Trisha.

A waiter stalked out of the café and approached their table, a look of "those crazy *americaines*" on his face. "*Que voudriez-vous, madame?*" he asked curtly.

"*Vin blanc.*" Placing her order for white wine, Luz ignored his rudeness. Big cities seemed to breed it. She had encountered it just as often in New York as she had in Paris.

"The same," Trisha said.

*"Deux."* The waiter pivoted stiffly and walked away. The iron-legged chair scraped across the concrete as Trisha scooted it closer to the table. "The more I think about that dress you selected, the more I like it," said Luz. "Its line is simple and elegant. You can achieve all sorts of looks with it by varying your accessories. A well-designed dress can be a permanent part of your wardrobe. I'm still wearing the Dior gown I bought the year after you were born, and I don't think anyone has ever noticed."

"I thought the dress was chic," Trisha replied.

"Chic is *passé.*" Luz mockingly reproved the use of the overworked adjective. *"C'est très élégant.* And elegance never goes out of style."

"I'm not sure whether I should have bought that silk blouse, though." Trisha frowned, chewing on an inside corner of her lip.

"As I told your father in the past, you can never be too rich or too thin—or have too many silk blouses," she joked.

The waiter returned with their wine and set the glasses sharply on the table, then left just as abruptly. As Luz sipped at the dry wine, she realized how infrequently she'd thought of Drew in the last three days. She had been afraid being in Paris would bring back painful memories of past visits she'd made to the city with Drew. But her time had been too crowded with things to do—shopping, concerts, *son-et-lumière,* festivals—and Paris had its own forceful personality that dominated the senses. She was slowly breaking the habit of making mental reminders to tell Drew about this or that. Perhaps, Luz thought, that was it more than the other things. And there was distance. No people around to remind her about the divorce or Drew's quick remarriage.

Resting her elbows on the table, she absently held the wineglass in both hands and gazed at the passing pedestrians. She liked Paris when it rained. The low gray skies blended with the old buildings and the mirror-wet streets shined like onyx. The air smelled fresh, rinsed of its exhaust fumes, and the gentle shower washed the city dust from the trees and shrubbery, revealing the green brilliance of their leaves. As she looked down the Champs Élysées through the blur of the drizzling rain, the scene reminded her of a painting by Pissarro, all impressionistic and indistinct yet capturing the essence.

The rustle of paper distracted her, and she turned her head as Trisha removed a book from a sack. Still holding the wineglass, she rested her forearms on the table and watched Trisha scan the first few pages.

"What's it about?" she asked curiously and lifted the glass with one hand to take another sip of wine.

"It's a travel book on Argentina," Trisha replied without looking up.

Luz frowned. "Why did you buy that?"

"Just curious." She shrugged and continued to read. "There's been so much talk about it lately I thought I'd find out more about it."

"I see." She took a swallow of wine and held it in her mouth for a short minute before letting it flow down her throat.

"Did you know Argentina is the eighth-largest country in the world, behind India?" Trisha looked up.

"No, I didn't." Luz smiled tightly.

Trisha read on. "It says here, the population of the country is ninety-seven percent white, nearly all of European descent."

"That's very fascinating." She unsnapped the clasp on her purse and took out francs to pay for their drinks. "Since it's raining, why don't we spend the rest of the afternoon at the Louvre? We could wander through the Grande Galerie." Luz preferred to visit the museum by sections; otherwise she became overwhelmed by so many priceless paintings and sculptures and ceased to appreciate any of them.

"Raul told me there were many similarities between Argentina and America. Listen to this. The Parana River is the equivalent of our Mississippi, and the pampas are like our Kansas prairies. The Andes are their Rockies, except they're a mile and a half higher."

Breathing out a sigh of resignation, Luz adjusted the knot of the silk Hermès scarf higher on the side of her neck. She stopped listening and started remembering what Henry had told her about Raul Buchanan. He came from a working-class background and owned a small ranch, about the size of Hopeworth Farm, on which he raised horses and cattle and operated his polo school. He was solvent although hardly wealthy. There was nothing earth-shattering in any of it. The only problem with him was of her own making, and she could hardly hold that against him.

* * *

The famed Longchamp racetrack was located in the sprawling, tall-treed Bois de Boulogne inside the city of Paris. Luz stood in the restricted-access area of the inner paddocks where all the prerace excitement took place and watched the sleek Thoroughbreds being led by their grooms into the white-railed enclosure. The spreading limbs of the towering trees created a leafy canopy, blocking out the sun and adding a shady coolness to the light breeze that flirted with the loose folds of her skirt, blowing softly against the material, then dancing away. It was an idyllic setting, lush green grass carpeting the ground, a champagne bar under the trees, a lattice-pillared glass booth for the weighing in of jockeys, betting windows and closed-circuit television for the exclusive, well-dressed crowd. The atmosphere of old-world aristocracy was strong.

"Here he comes." Diana Chandler laid a hand on Luz's forearm to claim her attention.

Luz glanced down the line of horses being led into the saddling area. The only chestnut-colored horse she could see was a tall animal with a bright golden coat and a white streak running down the center of its delicately shaped face. She remembered that "the dud" had a white facial marking, but the three-year-old bore no other resemblance to the gangling colt she remembered.

"See him?" Diana said excitedly. "That's Vagabond Song."

All doubt vanished when Luz saw the Chandlers' trainer, an Englishman renowned on the European racing circuit, walk forward to meet the groom leading the chestnut stallion. "He's magnificent," she exclaimed.

"Isn't he?" Her friend beamed with pride.

As the groom and trainer brought the horse to its assigned saddling spot, where Luz waited with Trisha and Diana while Vic Chandler stood to one side with the French jockey, she had a chance to observe the horse more closely. The young stallion exhibited none of the agitation shown by other prancing, sidestepping horses. Its ears were pricked forward, interested in the commotion of the crowd, and its large, wide-spaced eyes looked calmly about the paddock.

"Look at the chest and shoulders," she said to Trisha as the groom walked him up to them. "He's built like a Greyhound. Bred for speed and long distance."

The chestnut horse curiously pushed its nose toward Trisha. "He's spectacular," she murmured, smiling as she rubbed the velvety muzzle.

"Bloody fine horse he is, mum," the grizzled groom asserted. "Tractable, too."

"He gets that from his dam." Luz stroked the sleek neck. "She has a wonderful disposition and the heart of a lion." Scratching the horse's poll, she murmured, "I wish Jake could see you now. Wouldn't he be surprised at the way you turned out? Some dud you are."

Conscious of the trainer hovering anxiously by his charge, Luz stepped back to let them get on with their preparations. The call to saddle up would soon be made. Trisha moved back with her.

"I think we should place a bet on him for good luck," Trisha announced and hooked an arm over Luz's. "Come on."

"How do you know it won't be bad luck?" Luz countered, but she let herself be guided out of the paddock. "You aren't supposed to bet on your own horse."

"But he isn't our horse," her daughter reasoned.

"But we bred him." Theoretically, she had been involved in the decision only to a very minor degree, but a Kincaid had bred him and she was a Kincaid, so it amounted to the same thing. "Smart horsebreeders know better than to bet on the horses they raise. It's enough of a gamble bringing them into the racing world."

"I'm going to put some money on him even if you don't." Trisha directed her through the milling crowd of onlookers outside the paddock, propelling her in the direction of the betting booths.

"Go ahead. I'll wait here for you."

It was well in advance of post time, and the line of bettors was short. Trisha rejoined her within minutes, wagging the win tickets she'd purchased. "All or nothing," she said, laughing.

"I hope it's all," Luz replied, then noticed a bright green hat in the crowd. A minute later, Diana Chandler saw them and came over.

"Ewan is superstitious about owners being in the paddock when the horses are saddled," she explained.

"Where's Vic?" She glanced behind Diana to see if he was coming.

"He went to the bar. I told him I'd find you and we'd meet there." As they started in the direction of the champagne bar nestled under the trees, Vic approached, awkwardly juggling four glasses of champagne. Trisha hurried forward to rescue two of them before he spilled all four. She gave one to Luz.

"I thought we should drink a toast to the winner." Vic lifted his glass.

"Aren't you being premature?" Luz chided, carefully holding the glass away from her to keep the wine that had spilled over the rim from dripping onto her dress.

"To Vagabond Song, then."

"To Vagabond Song." She raised her glass in an agreeing salute, then carried it to her mouth, cupping a hand underneath it to catch any of the drips.

Trisha never got hers drunk. "Luz, look. Isn't that Raul?"

She turned to look in the direction Trisha was staring, certain she was mistaken until she saw him walking under the trees. There was no mistaking the figure in the light gray blazer, his shirt opened at the throat. Trisha hurried forward to intercept him, the sudden action breaking the invisible grip that had held Luz motionless.

"Who is he?" Diana murmured, tilting her head toward Luz in a secretive fashion.

"Raul Buchanan, a professional polo player from Argentina," she managed to reply evenly.

"Is he a boyfriend?"

The question startled Luz; the first thought in her mind was that Diana meant hers. "Pardon?"

"Has Trisha been seeing him?" Diana patiently repeated her question.

"No." Her answer was quick. The minute she said it, Luz was not altogether certain of her facts. "At least, not to my knowledge. We met him in England."

# CHAPTER XIV

"Raul, what are you doing here?" Trisha's voice carried clearly across the intervening space to Luz. He showed no surprise at meeting Trisha. "You weren't supposed to be in Paris until Tuesday."

"My plans changed," he replied, and Luz noticed his glance travel past Trisha to make an apparently idle sweep of the crowd, but it stopped when it located her. Briefly unsettled, she wished she didn't have the damned champagne glass in her hand.

Trisha followed the shift of his attention, then asked, "Are you here alone?" to reclaim it for herself.

"I am."

"Then you must join us." She possessively linked an arm with his and led him across the grassy lawn. The familiarity of the action seemed to confirm Luz's earlier suspicion that there was more to her daughter's relationship with this man than she knew. She didn't like it.

"This is a surprise, Mr. Buchanan," she greeted him coolly when he reached them. Trisha continued to hold his arm and stand close to him, further enforcing her claim, with no objection from him. "Vic and Diana, I'd like you to meet Raul Buchanan from Argentina, a polo player *extraordinaire*. Victor Chandler and his wife, Diana, friends of ours from the States. They have a three-year-old running in the next race."

After Raul and the Chandlers had exchanged pleasantries, Luz said, "It's somewhat unexpected seeing you here at Longchamp, Mr. Buchanan. I wouldn't have been surprised if we were at the polo fields near Bagatelle. Weren't you supposed to be playing somewhere this weekend?"

"I was," he admitted. "But a sprained wrist prevented me from taking part." The slight movement of his right hand drew her glance to the bandage visible below his jacket sleeve.

"Is it serious?" Trisha's concern was instant as she shifted her hand to support his lower forearm and inspect the injured area.

"No, but it will keep me out of active play for a while, so the team found someone else to take my place." His glance shifted to Luz. "The injury does mean that I will be returning to Buenos Aires sooner than I had planned. I hope we can reschedule our meeting so we can conclude our business before I leave."

She sensed Diana's curious glance. "Mr. Buchanan gives advanced training courses to polo players. Rob is interested in attending his school," she explained.

"How wonderful!" Diana exclaimed.

"Rob is flying in tomorrow morning. I know he wants to be present when we talk. Perhaps we could meet tomorrow afternoon at the hotel."

"That will be fine," he assured her.

"It's such a coincidence running into you here," Trisha declared, then shrewdly guessed, "Have you been by the Crillon? Did they tell you we were here?"

"Yes," he confirmed. "I left a message for you at the desk."

The riders-up call sounded in the paddock, creating a stir of activity and heightened tension. "They'll be making the parade to the post soon. We'd better be going to our box," Vic Chandler said and raised his champagne glass in a final toast. "To the race."

"To the race," Luz echoed faintly and self-consciously lifted her glass. A second later, she reminded herself that it didn't matter what Raul thought of her behavior. In a gesture of defiance, she downed all of the champagne in her glass, aware of his steady regard.

"Please join us, Mr. Buchanan," Diana invited.

He hesitated as if waiting for Luz to second the invitation, but it was Trisha who spoke up. "Yes, why don't you, Raul?" she urged.

"*Gracias,*" he accepted with a polite tip of his head.

They joined the throng strolling from the paddock area toward the viewing stands. As they made their way to the owner's box, Trisha trailed behind to walk with Raul. Luz couldn't hear what they were saying, but she recognized that intimate tone in her daughter's voice, the one used by a woman trying to attract a man's interest. When they reached the private box and settled into their seats, Luz found herself sitting next to Raul with Trisha on his other side.

Luz focused her attention on the racehorses prancing onto the famed oval track. The colorful silks of the jockeys perched in the high-stirruped saddles were bright splashes against the emerald-green turf and the sleek, shining mounts parading past the noisy crowd.

"Did you receive the pamphlets I left at the hotel for you?"

Abruptly, Luz turned her head to look at him and found herself staring into his face, remembering every detail from the angled jawline to the straight-bridged nose—and the sensation of touching him. She wondered if he looked at her and recalled those moments on the dance floor. She glanced away before her expression gave away her thoughts.

"Yes, I did. They were most helpful." As she determinedly directed her attention to the field of horses, she spied the golden chestnut pacing calmly alongside its lead pony. "There's Vagabond Song, the Number Seven horse."

"He's a handsome animal," Raul remarked.

From her seat behind them, Diana Chandler leaned forward to insert, "If he does well in this race, we're considering entering him in the Arc this October."

The Prix de l'Arc de Triomphe, commonly known as the Arc in the international racing circle, was the most important and prestigious Thoroughbred racing event in France. The mile-and-a-half contest, open to three-year-olds and older, frequently decided the year's international champion. It was also an international event of the breeding world and *haut monde*, rivaled only by the Prix Diane at Chantilly and the Royal Ascot.

"My interest in today's race is more than just cheering on a friend's horse," she said to Raul. "Vagabond Song was foaled at my father's Thoroughbred farm in Virginia. As a matter of fact, I was there when Jake booked the mare to the Minstrel, his sire. Jake never thought much of the colt, but I always liked him. So my interest is of a very personal nature."

As he listened to her explanation, his gaze made a more thorough study of her as if he was seeking something that he sensed was behind the sophisticated facade. "You seem to have an eye for horseflesh, Mrs. Thomas."

"Hopeworth Farm was my home when I was growing up, so I've always been interested in horses." While she deftly handled his compliment, she felt she gained a degree of respect from him, and that pleased her.

The horses were being led into the starting gate. The mile-and-an-eighth race was only minutes from beginning. The crowd sensed it, and the steady din abated as the voices became subdued by the air of expectancy. Seconds after the last horse was locked in, the bell clanged and the gates sprang open. A roar went up from the crowd as the racers leaped out.

For the first several yards, the field of ten horses appeared to run abreast, a confusing blend of jockeys' bright silk colors and the horses' myriad browns. By the first furlong, the leaders emerged from the close-running pack bunched along the rail. Luz strained for a glimpse of the distinctive blue-and-green silks of the Chandler Stables as the horses began to string out along the oval's backstretch.

"I see him." Vic Chandler had his binoculars trained on the racers. "He's running fifth and in the clear."

Glancing at the middle of the pack, Luz located the chestnut horse running easily and close to the leaders. She lost sight of him when the horses made the turn into the final stretch. Then she saw him passing the fourth-place horse. The jockey was making his move, his hands pumping with the stride of the horse, urging it to greater speed. There was no perceptible increase, yet the stallion was effortlessly overtaking horses one by one.

Coming down the final stretch to the finish line, only the race favorite remained ahead of Vagabond Song, and the distance between them closed with each running stride. The crowd was on its feet, cheering the stretch duel. But Luz held her breath, straining with the chestnut the last few yards. Two lengths from the finish line, he caught the favorite, ran neck and neck for a stride, then pulled in front, crossing the line in first place.

"We won! We won!" Diana clasped her husband's arm in excitement while the jockey stood up in the stirrups and raised the whip he'd never had to use, in a gesture of victory to the crowd.

"Congratulations." Luz turned to hug Diana, sharing the ebullience of victory and pride of ownership she saw in their faces.

"I knew he would win." Trisha joined the glad-handing celebration going on in the owner's box.

The race board flashed the official results, confirming the order of finish. "Come on, Diana." A buoyant Vic Chandler put an arm around his wife to guide her out of the box. "They'll be wanting us down in the enclosure for the presentation."

"And I've got winning tickets to cash in!" Trisha laughingly produced them with a flourish. "I told you to bet on him, Luz. Kincaids always win, and Vagabond Song is a Kincaid horse." As the Chandlers made their way out of the private box, Trisha turned to leave, then paused and touched Raul's arm. "I'll be right back."

Luz stiffened at the intimacy implied in such an assurance. Her glance flashed to Raul, seeking any indication that he responded in kind, but he merely nodded a brief acknowledgment. After Trisha left them, Luz let the postrace noise and confusion fill the silence in the owner's box and watched the presentation of the winner's purse to the Chandlers in the enclosure below. The chestnut's sweat-slick coat glistened in the sunlight, its neck proudly arched in triumph, and its trainer by its side.

"I wish Jake could have seen this," she murmured absently, recalling the sense of personal accomplishment he had always felt when one of the horses he'd bred did well in a race.

"I'm certain he would be proud." His response startled her into recalling she had voiced the thought.

"Yes, he would." Her glance slid away from his. "After the action of the polo field, horseracing must seem like a tame sport to you. A bunch of horses running around an oval track."

"Perhaps a little, but I enjoy the noise and excitement of the track." A faint smile edged his mouth as he looked over the crowd.

It was a mixture of disgruntled bettors with torn losing tickets, winners shoving their way to the pay windows, and optimists picking out the winner of the next race. Those on the field, the horses and the jockeys, the almost-made-its and the also-rans, were heading back to the stables, the jockeys hoping for a better horse in the next race and the horses wanting the kind hands of a groom and a portion of grain.

"The atmosphere arouses a bit of nostalgia for me." His attention came idly back to her. "When I was growing up, I worked as a stableboy at the tracks in Buenos Aires, so it is all familiar to me—the anticipation, the letdown, and the rare jubilation."

His response piqued her curiosity. "Where did you learn polo, then?"

"An owner hired me to work at his stables. He also played polo. I learned the game the long, slow way—and often the wrong way."

"But you made it to the top."

"Not to the top," he corrected her. "I have yet to earn the ten rating."

"And you aren't willing to settle for less," she realized intuitively.

"Given a choice, Mrs. Thomas, would you settle for less than the best? I think not." There was a knowing quality to his lazy smile, but no unkindness. It was almost a sharing of ideals, and it moved her in a strange way.

"You're probably right," she admitted, responding to that smile.

"I did not expect you ever to admit openly that I might be right about anything." His smile turned gently mocking, to hint at her previous mistrust.

"I sometimes speak rashly," Luz admitted, stimulated by this subtle wordplay that had sprung between them. It was an almost forgotten sensation that reminded her of high school and college days. She thought she had forgotten how to play the game, but flirting was obviously like riding a horse—no one ever completely lost the knack.

"Which is not always wisely," Raul suggested dryly.

"Not always," she agreed.

Trisha breezed back into the owner's box, her return scattering the faint undercurrents Luz had sensed. She grasped the clutch purse with her winnings tightly in her hand. "It won't buy a Dior original, but it will finance another trip to that divine shop on the Rue du Faubourg St. Honoré with all the leather and suede," she declared, then laughed. "Remind me to send a basket of apples to Vagabond Song when we get back to the hotel. And I'll have them throw in a bunch of carrots, too. It's only fair, since he did all the work."

"That's true." Luz smiled, but she felt oppressed by Trisha's vivacious humor, its youthful vigor more than she could match.

She welcomed the arrival of the Chandlers, both of them still glowing from their horse's victory. "Remember that drink we were going to have to the winner?" Vic said. "Well, I think it's in order now. What do you say?"

There were more races on the afternoon's program, but they would be anticlimactic after this one, so Luz agreed with Vic's suggestion. They left the owner's box and retraced their route to the inner paddocks while Vic related the jockey's account of the running, naturally filled with praise for the horse.

He was still talking when they reached the champagne bar under the trees, but paused in his story long enough to ask, "Champagne all around?" His glance singled out Raul, who nodded affirmatively; he took the ladies' answers for granted. Once the order was placed with the bartender, he went back to his story, hardly skipping a beat. "Ewan wants to try the Song in a mile-and-a-quarter race to see how he fares before committing to the Arc. I say the breeding is there and we should go for it, but he likes to play it cautious. He's brought the Song along this far, so I have to go along with him. As Jake always said, you can't argue with success." The bartender set the filled glasses in front of him, and Vic handed them to Raul to distribute. Luz was conscious of the brush of his fingers when he passed one to her. "To the winner, Vagabond Song." Vic raised his glass in a repeat of his prerace toast.

"To the winner," they all echoed.

The race remained the topic of conversation, the race and its winner. Through it all, Luz caught herself watching Raul, especially when Vic questioned him about Thoroughbred racing in Argentina and the caliber of the horses compared to the American and European horses. Then she could study him without being obvious.

The conversation came around to a discussion of fillies competing with colts in their same age group. "I have a two-year-old filly that I picked up last year at the yearling sale in Deauville for next to nothing. She has been doing exceptionally well in her races. She won the last two going away. I've been talking to Ewan about running her against some colts. I think she could beat the ones I've seen."

"You're better off waiting until the fall," Luz said. "It's been my experience—through Jake—that fillies always fare better against the colts in the fall than they do in the spring when they're in season."

"A good point. I hadn't considered that." Vic nodded thoughtfully, while Luz caught a glimmer of respect in Raul's look and experienced an odd rush of pleasure.

Then his glance shot past her. A split second later, his right hand gripped her arm above the elbow and pulled her closer to him, out of the path of a man shouldering his way to the bar before she was jostled by him. She looked up to thank him and saw the pain in his expression. She realized he had used his injured arm.

"Your wrist—" she began.

*"De nada."* He brushed aside her concern, insisting it was nothing, but there was something warm in his look.

It unsettled her, though, just as her growing fascination with him unsettled her. Maybe it was as simple as being in the company of a man who was a stranger to her compared to Drew, whose every gesture and expression she knew so well she could almost anticipate what he was going to say next. But she didn't know Raul well enough to guess what he was thinking or what a particular look or movement meant.

That unknown always spiced a relationship, never allowing a person to be sure of her footing until the time came when everything was learned and disenchantment or boredom set in. That's obviously what had happened to her marriage. She and Drew had grown apart, and he had become bored with her. That level of interest necessary to make a relationship last had to be based on more than just caring or wanting something to be so. Maybe it required common interests such as Drew shared with Claudia.

The weight of her depressing thoughts began to crush her. Luz took a drink of champagne to throw them off. She was enjoying this afternoon, and she wasn't going to let herself be buried by endless wonderings of what she'd done wrong. Paris was a place to have fun—to enjoy being a woman.

"I have the most perfect idea," Diana declared. "Let's all go out to dinner this evening and celebrate in style."

"I think it's wonderful," Luz seconded it and turned to Raul. "You will come, won't you?" It was less a question than a statement.

"I have no wish to intrude on a private celebration among friends," he declined politely.

"Nonsense," Diana dismissed his reasoning. "The five of us watched the race together. We should all dine together, too. You can't abandon the party now, Raul. What kind of celebration would that be with one of us missing?"

"Don't be difficult, Raul." Trisha lent her voice to the others, cocking her head at him at a provocative and challenging angle. "Why do you always have to play hard to get?"

Luz watched the smile come into his eyes as he looked down at Trisha. There was obviously a hidden meaning in that phrase known only to them. She liked it even less than the other times she had intercepted such intimations.

"It seems I cannot refuse the invitation." He bowed slightly to his evening's hostess.

"That's settled. Now the problem, where to go? So many of the fine restaurants are closed on Sunday, even Maxim's." Diana waited for suggestions. When none were forthcoming, she offered her own. "There is that popular restaurant in the Latin Quarter. It's always filled with actors, writers, and artists."

"Please," Luz objected. "Let's not spend an evening surrounded by intellectuals."

"What about the Tour d'Argent? The food is superb, the wines are excellent, and the decor is very elegant," ventured Diana.

"The food is so rich," her husband objected.

Raul took no part in the ensuing discussion over the merits of various proposed restaurants, some rejected on the ground that one or another of them had eaten there in the past few days. There were any number of establishments in Paris that served fine food, although not all were high-priced or expensively decorated. But the wealthy, he'd observed, tended to equate price with quality. Sometimes it seemed they spent more time deciding where to eat than which horses to buy. He'd sold horses to wealthy amateur players on sight alone. If he'd ridden a horse in a game, that was sufficient for them. Looking at Luz Kincaid Thomas and Trisha, he realized they had never in their life wondered *how* they were going to eat—only where and what. It was something he never could shake, and he felt his distance from them and viewed their conversation with the disdain of reverse snobbery.

"What about the galleon moored opposite the racecourse?" Vic suggested. "It has excellent food and a great view overlooking the Seine. Maybe we can get a table outside."

There was a lull, but no objections were forthcoming. "Do you suppose we can get reservations?" Diana wondered.

"Georges can get anything," Luz insisted.

# CHAPTER XV

Reservations were made for dinner at nine o'clock, and two chauffeur-driven cars picked them up at the hotel in advance of that hour. The Place de la Concorde had a magical quality at night, the towering obelisk and the surrounding statuary illuminated by spotlights and diamond waters dancing in the lighted fountains. At the other end of the wide boulevard, Napoleon's triumphal arch stood in all its glory, bathed in light.

"After dinner, perhaps we should be terribly touristy and take the Evening Road up to Montmartre so we can view the lights of Paris." The heavy pearl dangling from an ear swung against her neck as Luz turned her head to glance at Trisha in the shadows of the car's interior.

Trisha leaned forward to touch Raul's arm, which was draped along the backrest of the front seat. The sheen of her black satin dinner suit reflected the light from a streetlamp.

"Have you seen the view from Montmartre by night before, Raul?" she questioned when he turned.

"Yes."

"Who with? I know a gentleman would never tell, but I have my doubts that you are a gentleman," she mocked playfully.

"That is your choice." He briefly lifted his hand from the seat back in a gesture of indifference. Before he faced the front again, his glance lingered an instant on Luz in the opposite corner. She was impressed by the way he'd deftly handled Trisha's deliberately provocative comment, turning it away so easily.

She glanced at her daughter, whose flirting had been so idly rebuffed. Trisha looked the young sophisticate tonight. The black satin jacket with peplumed waist, puff sleeves, and notched lapels in contrasting white satin covered a close-fitting strapless sheath with a sweetheart neckline, trimmed in white satin. The crowning touch was the nothing of a hat, a V-shaped black band coming to a point in the center of her forehead with a pouf of black veil. As Luz had advised her, it was impossible to be overdressed in Paris, where even the shop clerks dressed with style and élan.

The car pulled to a stop in front of the moored galleon, its lights silvering the waters of the Seine. The driver opened the rear door for Luz, taking her hand as she swung gracefully out of the car. Straightening, she smoothed the shimmering material of her slim, straight skirt, dotted black on black, and adjusted the flared waist of black-belted jacquard blouse, a contrasting match of white dots on white.

A car drove up behind them, bearing the Chandlers. Together they boarded the galleon, refurbished to house a first-class restaurant. Although the summer night was mild, they chose to dine inside instead of taking a table in the open air. The maître d' showed them to a quiet area away from the noise and congestion of the kitchen entrance. Raul held the chair for Luz as she sat down, then took one facing her. The menus were waved aside for the time being as they ordered aperitifs. When the drinks were served, another toast was drunk to the horse whose victory had brought them together.

"Tell me, Trisha." Vic Chandler sat at the head of the table while Trisha occupied the chair on his left next to Raul. Leaning an elbow on the table, he bent toward her, appearing intrigued by her blossoming sophistication. "Have you left some young man pining away back in the States for you?"

"No." The edges of the hat veil came no lower than the tip of her nose, the fine mesh creating a provocative see-through mask for her dark eyes. "There is no special one. I prefer playing the field."

"The polo field?" he teased with a pointed glance at Raul.

"Speaking of polo . . ." Luz took a sip of her Cinzano, then lowered the glass, holding it at the top with her fingers. "Rob tells me that you also train and sell polo ponies. Is that right, Raul?" She decided to discard their previous formality; a social evening was no place for it.

"Yes. I presently have approximately twenty ponies with game experience for sale as well as many others in various stages of advanced training."

"I know that after riding the ponies Henry bought there, Rob is very interested in purchasing some Argentine-bred horses for his string."

"We spoke of it." Raul nodded.

"Yes. That evening at the pub," Trisha inserted.

"Regardless of what we decide about your school, we will probably be coming to Argentina in the near future anyway to look at horses, including yours," she said.

"I would welcome the opportunity to show you my ponies, and I always recommend to prospective buyers that they ride them, preferably under game conditions." He paused, smiling slightly. "With the school to draw from, we never lack for players to make up a team for an impromptu game. Although I believe my ponies are among the best in Argentina, if you don't find all that you want in my herd, I will introduce you to other stable owners with made ponies for sale."

"How kind of you."

"Kindness has little to do with it, Mrs. Thomas."

"Please," she interrupted. "I would prefer that you call me Luz." She felt his gaze move over her face, touching hair, eyes, and lips. The line of his mouth curved faintly as if satisfied by what he saw.

"As you wish," Raul said and picked up from before. "My offer is a matter of business. You will see my ponies first and have a standard by which to judge the others. And if you come before the end of August, you'll have an opportunity to look over the school's facilities and still allow time for your son to enroll."

She had to smile at his strategy, despite feeling a twinge of disappointment that he hadn't addressed her by name after she had invited it.

"We'll be there in August," Trisha stated. "It can't be any later than that or it will interfere with the beginning of fall term. And I'm not about to let Rob and Luz go without me. Argentina fascinates me."

"She's been reading all about your country." The glass was close to her lips as Luz spoke, eyeing Raul across its rim. "She's made all sorts of interesting discoveries, such as that

the Constitution of the United States was the model for your
own."

"August. Why, you'll barely be home a month before leaving on another long trip," Diana realized.

"You always did love to travel," Vic recalled. "Although
Drew was never particularly fond of it. Since you broke up
with him, you seem to be making up for lost time."

"It might appear that way, but actually this European trip
has been planned for some time. Our party is simply smaller
by one," she said, the taste of the aperitif strong on her lips.

"You need to find yourself a man," Diana stated, and Luz
unconsciously looked at Raul, remembering, however vaguely,
when he'd held her in his arms and they had danced so close.

"She will," Vic asserted. "Luz has the right idea. New
places, new faces. See what life has to offer and go after it.
The best way to put out the ashes of an old fire is with a new
one."

"Please," she protested laughingly. "The divorce was just
recently final."

"How long has it been since you and Drew split up?" Vic
asked.

"Three months." Sometimes it seemed much longer than
that. It had all the echoes of a bad dream. And there was a
part of her that still expected to wake up some morning and
everything would be the way it was.

"You know what they say, Luz—'Eat, drink, and remarry!'"
Vic laughed at his own pun. The waiter stopped to inquire
whether they wished to see the menus yet, sparing Luz a response. "Yes. And a round of drinks for everyone except this
young lady." He patted Trisha's arm. The drink in front of her
was barely touched. "Send the . . . uh . . . *sommelier* to our
table. We'll want to order some wine."

After the menus were distributed, Luz noticed that Raul
spent little time studying the selections. He laid the menu aside
after one quick perusal. Trisha angled her body toward him,
the raised menu shielding much of her face from Luz's view,
and pointed to an item, asking his opinion.

Luz pretended to study her bill of fare. "Have you already
made your choice, Raul?" she asked, breaking up the murmured
conference.

"Yes," he replied, straightening away from Trisha.

"Do you always make your decisions so quickly?"

"About some things I do."

"And the important ones?"

"They take longer," he admitted, smiling dryly.

"And you don't consider the choice of food important," Luz guessed.

"Some dishes taste better than others, but food is food, no?" A dark brow was arched with amused question.

"It is almost sacrilegious to say such a thing in France." She laughed. "If the waiter hears you, he'll have you thrown out."

Eventually all decided what they wanted and their orders were given to the waiter along with the selections of wine recommended by the wine steward to accompany the various courses. In French fashion, the meal was a leisurely affair with time between each course. All the while, the wineglasses were kept filled by an attentive waiter.

As the main course was being served, Luz noticed Raul bending his head to catch a murmured aside by Trisha. She opened her mouth to say something that would reclaim his attention. Then it struck her what she was doing—what she had been doing all evening. She was vying with her daughter for Raul's attention—competing with Trisha woman to woman. She wasn't trying to protect Trisha. She wanted Raul for herself.

"Is something wrong, Luz?" Diana questioned the shocked look on her face.

The words were slow to register, but when they did Luz answered quickly, "No," and reached for her wineglass.

She barely tasted the fish, washing each bite down with wine from a glass that was never allowed to become empty. Each time she looked across the table and saw them talking, a rawness went through her, the simmering anger of jealousy. She hated herself for it. It was so wrong to resent her daughter's youth and beauty, yet the terrible envy was there.

The cheese was served in advance of the sweet. It tasted like chalk in her mouth. When she tipped her head to take a drink of wine, she felt woozy. She had no idea how much she had drunk, but it was too much. Determined not to embarrass herself a second time, Luz set the glass down and pushed her chair back from the table.

"Would you all excuse me?" She stood up, holding on to the chairback for balance. "I'm afraid I've had too much wine tonight. I think I should leave." There was a movement, but Luz wasn't sure which member of her party had started to move. "No. You stay here and finish your meal. I'll be fine. The driver's waiting outside. He can take me back to the hotel."

"I'd better go with her." Trisha folded her linen napkin and laid it alongside her place setting.

"I don't want you to come with me." She was the last person Luz wanted, afraid of what her wine-loosened tongue might reveal. "I am not helpless, Trisha." The harshness of her tone seemed to push Trisha back into her chair. "Please, all of you stay and enjoy yourself," Luz insisted tautly. "I'll be fine."

Before more protests could be made, she left the table and walked as quickly as she dared to the exit. Once outside, the fresh air hit her and the vague feeling of dizziness became suddenly overwhelming. She pressed a hand to her head, trying to stop the spinning inside it while her other hand groped for any kind of support until this merry-go-round in her mind stopped turning.

An arm went around her at the same instant that she felt a body beside her. She leaned gratefully against its solidness. *"Pardon, monsieur. Un moment."* Luz breathed in deeply, filling her lungs with the warm night air and letting it sober her. *"Merci."* As she moved away from the supporting chest and shoulder, she looked up and recognized Raul as her kind Frenchman. "Well, my lord of nothing has come to rescue me again." It was hurt pride that made her mock him. She angrily pushed his arm away from her. "I don't happen to need your help this time."

"I will see you safely into the car," he stated, and motioned to the drivers lounging by a rear fender of one of the hired cars.

As she looked anywhere but at him, she began to notice the silvery sheen of the Seine, the bright pattern of lights shining out from the huge galleon and the faint dusting of stars overhead. A summer night in Paris should be filled with gaiety and laughter. She longed to be carefree again. Young and foolish. Why not?

It was almost with defiance that Luz faced Raul, indifferent to the approaching car. "I want to dance. Everyone who comes to Paris should dance, and I haven't yet."

"The car is here." Raul nodded toward the waiting vehicle.

She heard the opening of a car door and glanced impatiently at the capped chauffeur ready to assist her into the rear seat. "He'll wait. He's getting paid for it. Dance with me," she ordered, holding out her arms. "You're Argentine. We'll do the tango. You must know the tango."

There was a trace of double-edged sarcasm in her voice, some of it coming back to sting her. Yet she'd gone too far to stop. When he failed to move, she took a hand and placed it on his waist, then slipped her hand into his left one and extended his arm out from his side.

"Are you ready? One. Two. Three. Ta da-da-dum da-da-da." But he made no attempt to follow her steps. "Don't you like the tango?" Luz challenged. "It's so appropriate." She choked back the laugh in her throat to keep the fine edge of hysteria from bubbling through. "The Last Tango in Paris." But he found nothing humorous in her feeble joke. "All right. If you won't dance with me, I'll ask the chauffeur." Releasing his hand, she turned toward the car and the waiting driver.

He stopped her. "We will dance, but not the tango."

"Very well. Not the tango," she agreed, this time waiting for him to take her in his arms and begin the dance.

The pressure of his hand on her back was familiar, and she let it guide her. After several steps, Luz recognized the formal pattern of the waltz. She hummed a melody as they danced along the street, the night turning glorious. The feel of his arms and the scent of his cologne stirred up longings she had thought were buried. She closed her eyes to shut them in, but the dance's sweeping turns began to affect her shaky equilibrium. She lost a step and staggered against him, breaking the rhythm and the spell of the dance.

"I think we'd better stop," she said with her head down, then lifted it to look blindly around, her bearings lost. "Where's the car?"

It was some distance behind them. Raul signaled the driver to bring the car to them while he kept a supporting hand under her arm. When the car stopped beside them, he opened the rear door and helped her inside. Luz sat back in the seat and leaned her head against the curved back. She shut her eyes, feeling more lonely and hurting than before and still unable to come to terms with the jealousy she felt toward Trisha.

The rear door opened on the other side. She lifted her head in surprise when she saw Raul slide into the passenger seat beside her.

"You don't need to come with me," she protested. "The driver will take me back to the hotel."

"And where will you have him stop along the way?" Raul challenged.

Luz had no argument to offer and turned away to look out the window. "I suppose you think I'm drunk. I wish I were—then I wouldn't know what I was doing."

"To the hotel, *monsieur?*" The French driver looked at their reflection in his rearview mirror.

"Yes."

As the car traveled along the street, Luz stared at the deep-shadowed woods of the Bois de Boulogne that loomed beside the boulevard. A scattering of faint light was dimly visible through the thick foliage, marking the roads and avenues that wound through it.

"Driver." She leaned forward and tapped him on the shoulder. "Take us through the Bois."

"*Le Bois de Boulogne? Non, madame,*" he protested vigorously as he stared at her through the mirror. "It is not safe at night. It is filled with the lowlife—the prostitutes and the crazy Brazilians who dress in woman clothes. *Non, madame.*"

"I want to see them. Drive through the park." This time Luz made it an order, and settled back into her seat, ignoring his grumbling in French. Under protest, the driver obeyed, turning the car into the park at the next entrance.

The centuries-old trees towered on either side of the road, one of many winding through the large park on the west side of Paris. The lights from the staggered streetlamps illuminated the massive trunks, but could not penetrate the leafy roof overhead or the deep shadows beyond the roadside. Everywhere there was darkness and a sense of isolation, kept at bay by the overlapping streams of light from the car's headlamps.

At a lighted intersection with another of the park's meandering avenues, a car was stopped close to the curb. A woman in a tight, short dress with stiletto heels stood near the passenger side, bending at the waist to talk to the driver inside. A man was beside her, while under the streetlamp two more women waited, their clothes and heavily made-up faces marking them as prostitutes.

The chauffeur barely slowed the car as he swung it around the parked vehicle and checked for crossing traffic at the intersection. In that brief moment, Luz saw the man, obviously a pimp, open the passenger door and give his hooker a shove inside. Then they were past the car and her peek into that other world ended.

A match flared in the shadowy corner Raul occupied. Luz turned and watched the play of yellow light over the hollows and planes of his face as he lit one of those slim black cheroots. The flame was blown out along with a stream of smoke. Briefly the air inside the car was tainted with the smell of burned sulfur before the swirl of tobacco smoke asserted its aroma. Luz sensed the unspoken disapproval in that glimpse of his sternly drawn features.

"Aren't you amused by this tour of the seamier side of Paris?" she mocked.

"No." His attention appeared to be centered on the burning tip of the slender cigar between his thumb and fingers.

Luz turned her gaze toward the road ahead of the car, the area now dotted with more prostitutes, some with pimps, some alone, standing and smoking or talking to one another, or strolling singly or in pairs, but all eyeing the car as it approached them. They all seemed to have the same bored expression.

"You can get anything you want here," she said cynically. "Drugs, sex—twenty minutes worth of love. All for a price, of course."

They came up behind a car creeping along the road while the driver perused the selection of sexual goods for sale. The grumbling chauffeur was forced to slow down, but even the reduced speed didn't allow much reaction time when the vehicle in front of them suddenly braked. Cursing, the chauffeur yanked on the wheel and slammed his foot on the brake pedal, tires squealing as the car stopped crosswise in the road. Luz was thrown sideways against Raul. Instinctively, he held on to her.

Sensations flooded her, from the hard strength of his arm and the strong smell of tobacco smoke on his breath. Her hand was flattened onto his chest from bracing herself. She could feel the smooth texture of his jacket and the lapel edges. Beneath it was the strong beat of his heart. All she had to do was tip her head and his lips would be on hers.

With more smothered cursing, the chauffeur maneuvered the car back onto its original course. "Are you all right?" Raul's low-pitched voice seemed to vibrate against her.

Luz closed her eyes, wanting to say no she wasn't, but of course she couldn't. There was nothing wrong with her—nothing at all.

"Yes." Her hand stiffened to push herself away from him and back to her own side of the seat while she kept her face averted and looked out the window instead. She lifted her chin in an unconscious assertion of fierce pride.

Outside, fewer prostitutes lingered under streetlamps until they finally traveled through an area where there were none. When the car turned onto a connecting lane, they seemed to pass from one section to another. Again she saw women along the roadside, only these appeared better-dressed than the last. Higher-priced whores, she guessed with vague indifference.

After they had passed several, she sensed something was wrong. It became a very definite feeling when Luz noticed a tall, slim girl with long dark hair that hung almost to her waist walking a Doberman. No hooker would do such a thing. The reputation of that dog's breed would deter any prospective customer from approaching her. Surely a woman alone, even with the dog to protect her, wouldn't choose this area for an evening stroll.

Her curiosity aroused, Luz took special note of the next pair they passed. Again, her eye was initially drawn to the better quality of their clothes. Although the accessories were slightly garish, the style of dress drew attention away from the obvious flaws of their figures—thick waists and narrow hips.

"They're men," she realized.

"*Oui, madame,*" the chauffeur replied. "The so-called Brazilians who all the time dress up in women's clothes and parade through the Bois. Some try to pretend they are prostitutes, then rob the man. *Les policiers,* they try to get rid of them. They come back—like the rats in the sewers of Paris."

She'd seen female impersonators before in clubs, but she had never encountered any transvestites. They hardly traveled in the same circles, she thought wryly. As they approached three more men in drag standing beneath a lamppost, Luz

noticed one of them had on a particularly fetching dress, but
the silk scarf knotted around the neck like a bandana exhibited
a definite lack of style. It ruined the whole effect of the dress.

"Stop the car," she said.

*"Madame—"*

*"Halte!"* It angered her the way he argued over her every
request. With great reluctance and objection, the chauffeur
stepped on the brake.

"What are you going to do?" Raul demanded, but Luz saw
no reason to explain her intention to him.

She opened her own door and started to climb out of the
car. Raul caught at her arm to stop her, but she twisted free
and stepped into the street. "Wait here," she instructed the
driver. "I won't be long." Muffled cursing came from inside
the car, this time in Spanish, when she shut the door.

With no traffic in sight, she started across the street, angling
toward the female-clad trio under the streetlight. Her steps
quickened when she heard the slamming of the passenger door
on the opposite side. Before the sound of running feet caught
up with her, Luz approached the transvestites, who were eyeing
her with suspicion.

*"Un moment,"* she requested, and pointed to the one on the
left, wearing the sandy blond wig. *"L'écharpe."* She indicated
the scarf knotted around his throat. *"L'écharpe n'est pas chic
comme ça."* The footsteps halted somewhere behind her as she
reached for the silk knot to show him the proper way to tie it.
False-lashed eyes looked at her with mistrust as he drew back.
*"S'il vous plaît,"* Luz insisted and reached again for the scarf.

This time he didn't pull away. Adroitly she loosened the
knot and fluffed the silk print material until it lay in a soft ring
around his neck. She retied the knot, less tightly, and let one
end of the scarf trail down his back while the other fell to the
front.

*"Voilà."* Luz stepped back and gestured to the others to
view her handiwork. They nodded their approval.

*"Merci."* But the man still appeared skeptical and confused
by her action.

*"De rien."* She shrugged aside his thanks and backed away.
*"Bonsoir, mesdames."* Luz caught her mistake and laughed.
*"Bonsoir, messieurs."*

When she turned to walk back to the car, Raul was beside

her in a single stride. His fingers dug into the soft flesh of her upper arm. There was no eluding this grip that propelled her across the street to the car parked with its motor idling.

"*Idiota,*" Raul muttered, and no translation was required, though Luz knew only a few words of Spanish.

The chauffeur hopped out of the car to open the door for her, while throwing wary glances toward the three transvestites, who were conversing in murmurs beside the lamppost. Raul made sure she was inside and the door was shut before he walked around the car.

When he slid onto the seat beside her, Luz said, "If they're going to dress like women, they should know how to do it properly."

"To the hotel," he said to the driver. "There will be no more stops."

"*Oui, monsieur,*" the man replied with obvious relief.

"I don't know why you're so angry anyway." She flashed an impatient glance at Raul. "What were you afraid they were going to do? Rob me? I left my purse in the car, so all they could have taken was my jewels and they're insured. Rape wasn't likely. I'm sure they know it usually takes two hands to pull down a pair of panty hose, which makes it rather difficult to hold the victim." Silence was her only answer. Sighing heavily, Luz tipped her head back to rest it against the seat. "All right. So maybe it was a stupid thing to do."

The car emerged from the park onto a busy Paris street. She closed her eyes, wishing . . . she didn't know for what. That she wasn't so confused, so lonely? The glare of streetlights flashed across her closed eyelids. She let her thoughts drift, not focusing on anything except the lulling motion of the car.

When they arrived at the hotel, Raul went inside with her, obtained her key from the room clerk, and escorted her to the elevators. Luz supposed she should resent his actions, but she rather liked this solicitous concern to see her safely to her suite. Her earlier pain and anger and defiance were fading as her mood turned wistful and a little sad.

At her suite, Raul unlocked the door and pushed it open for her. She walked straight into the sitting room and deposited her purse on a chair. Unconsciously she reached up and began pulling the pins to free her hair from its French pleat.

"The key is on the table."

Turning at the waist, Luz glanced back to the door, where Raul stood just inside the suite. His hand motioned toward the kingwood bureau standing against the wall, indicating where he'd left the room key.

"Fine." She stared at him, drawn by an attraction she couldn't deny. She was conscious of his leanly muscled physique and the steel-blue eyes. He looked so strong and capable.

"If there's nothing else . . ."

"No." She squared around, turning her back to him once again, and dropped the hairpins onto the chair beside her purse. Her glance strayed to the door of her private bedroom. The prospect of climbing into that bed and lying alone made her ache. She wanted to be held and loved and needed by someone. Hugging her arms to ease their empty feeling, Luz absently caressed her shoulders. "I want someone to make love to me." The declaration seemed to echo through the room.

"Do you always get what you want?" Raul demanded harshly.

Luz swung around to face him. "I'm a Kincaid." She had always had everything she wanted until now.

"I should have guessed. You expect people to perform according to your command, no?" he challenged, and she was too sensitive to rejection not to see it in the iciness of his expression.

Angrily, she hurled words at him, hurting inside. "Just get out! Get out and leave me alone." She bolted across the room to the small refrigerator where the miniature bottles of liquor were stored.

"Shall I ring for a maid to assist you?"

"No!" She wanted him to take her to bed—not a maid. Her fingers closed tightly around a gin bottle as she braced herself with one hand flattened on the refrigerator top. "I don't need you. I don't need anyone. Just go away!"

For a moment there was no sound in the room except for the harshness of her own breathing. Then she heard the door shut. She shook with quiet sobs. Her gaze fell on the small liquor bottle in her hand. She swept it away from her, along with the glasses and ice canister. All went crashing onto the carpeted floor, bouncing and rolling across it with a muffled clatter. Her hands clutched the edges of the refrigerator as she sank to her knees.

"Good gracious! What's going on out here?" Emma came

bustling out of her room, tying the sash of her long cotton robe, a satin scarf around her head to protect her hairdo while she slept. "Are you all right, Luz?"

"Yes." She scrubbed a hand across her cheeks to wipe away the tears, then pulled herself up.

Emma's slippered foot accidentally kicked a glass and sent it rolling against a chair leg. "What's all this mess?" Her gaze narrowed suspiciously on Luz.

"It's not what you're thinking, Emma, although, Lord knows, I've given you cause to think I'm always drunk. But no more. It never helps. It only makes things worse. I realized that and—" She waved indifferently at the drink items strewn across the carpet. "What you see is the result of that discovery." She watched Emma pick them up and stack them back on top of the small refrigerator.

"Where's Trisha?"

"With the Chandlers. I . . . I left early." She ached inside, and it was a heavy, hollow feeling. "It's hard to get used to being alone, Emma. I don't know what I'll do if Rob and Trisha stop loving me, too."

"That isn't likely. You're their mother. What you need is a good night's rest. Nothing ever looks quite as gloomy in the morning."

But Luz thought of Audra. Did she love her mother? Or was it duty and obligation that forged the link? Was there any real closeness? Rob and Trisha were all she had. She couldn't stand the thought of losing them. They had to care about her as much as she did about them. She didn't want them resenting her the way she sometimes resented Audra. What an awful irony that would be.

"Are you coming to bed?" Emma paused halfway to the door of her own room.

"Yes." Alone. She'd sleep alone, the way she always had.

Awakening slowly, Luz rolled onto her back and lay there for several seconds, waiting for the dull pressure to begin pounding in her head, but it didn't come. The only dullness she felt came from sleep, not the aftereffects of alcohol. She stretched, arms reaching, back arching, legs moving beneath the bedcovers, then relaxed and let her eyes come open to look about the drape-darkened room. For another moment, she lay motionless, then swung her legs off the edge of the bed, the sheets rustling, and reached for the silk robe lying at the foot of the bed.

Sunlight was trying to force its way through the thick folds of the drapes, its brightness glimmering about the edges. Luz slipped into the robe, the silk material gliding across her skin, and she crossed from the bed to the window. The plush carpet was soft beneath the bare soles of her feet. She located the draw pulls and opened the drapes, letting the sunlight pour into the room.

Below, the Place de la Concorde was swarming with traffic, creating a muffled hum of noise. As she gazed at the octagonal square, once skirted by a moat fed by the river Seine, Luz tied the inside strings of her robe at the waistline, then reached for the outer silk cords to secure the front. It was over by the statue to the provincial capital of Brest that Louis XVI had been beheaded. Later the guillotine stood near the gates of the Tuileries, where it served its bloody three-year reign, severing the heads of some thirteen hundred victims.

Looking at the classical proportions of the square, so symmetrically balanced, it was difficult for Luz to imagine the terror the square had known. Built as the Place Louis XV to proclaim his glory, it was fittingly renamed the Place de la Concorde, consecrated to concord between men, and the venerable Luxor Obelisk had been erected in the center where the statue of Louis XV had stood. Luz wondered when she would again find concord, an internal calm, in her life.

There was a knock on the connecting door to the other rooms of the suite. "Room service!"

Recognizing Trisha's voice, Luz smiled. "Come in." With a final pull to tighten the knot of the cord belt, she turned toward the door as it opened. Her robe-clad daughter wheeled through a serving table, draped in a white linen tablecloth and laden with a coffee service, juice, and a basket of croissants. There was a miniature assortment of jams and marmalades and a small vase of fresh flowers.

"I heard you stirring about and thought you might like some coffee," Trisha said as she pushed the wheeled table over by a painted fauteuil chair of the Louis XV period.

"I would." Luz moved to the table and poured the steaming

coffee from the silver pot into a cup. As it cooled, she sipped her orange juice.

"How do you feel?" Trisha helped herself to one of the croissants.

"I don't have a hangover, if that's what you're wondering," she replied dryly, combing fingers through one side of her sleep-tousled hair to push it away from her face. As Trisha moved to sit cross-legged on the bed and nibble at the flaky croissant, Luz picked up the coffee cup and saucer and carried it to the damask chair.

"What happened to Raul last night? He left to check on you and never came back."

A fine tension rippled through Luz as she studied the deep brown color of the coffee, so close to the shade of Raul's hair. "He came back to the hotel with me. After that, I don't know where he went."

"Well, he never showed up back at the restaurant. We waited almost an hour before we decided he wasn't coming back." She picked at the crumbs that had fallen onto her lap. "Last night you seemed to get along with him better. Have you finally started liking him?"

She glanced sharply at her daughter, wondering if Trisha had realized that she had been competing with her last night for Raul. But the question seemed to be as casual as it sounded. "I don't dislike him," she said and sipped at the hot coffee, hoping Trisha never learned of her jealousy.

"Well, you've gotta admit he's all male," Trisha declared, a smile crooking her mouth and dimpling a cheek. It was apparent that even while mocking the attraction she felt she was enjoying it.

"That he is," she agreed. She knew it too well. "But I still don't think he's suitable for you. And that's a mother's pre-rogative," she stated to check the protest forming on her daughter's lips. "I don't want to see you make a fool of yourself over him. It hurts too much. I should know."

A small silence followed. Luz was conscious of Trisha studying her. She sipped at the coffee, giving her attention to the cup and saucer instead of to the girl on the bed. "You were referring to Drew when you said that, weren't you?" Trisha said quietly. "I know you must still miss him."

The statement prompted Luz to attempt to analyze her present feelings toward her ex-husband. The bitterness and pain of the divorce were still too fresh for that to be true. "I'm not sure. Mostly I miss not knowing what tomorrow will bring. I always knew what I was going to do, what was going to happen, what to expect. Now I don't know what it's going to be like. It's scary sometimes," she admitted.

"If things didn't work out for him with Claudia, would you and Dad go back together?"

Luz breathed in deeply, then exhaled in a heavy sigh. "That's a loaded question," she hedged. She doubted if any direct reply was possible. Maybe two months ago it might have been, but now, it didn't seem likely. "There's a lot of pride and hurt feelings involved—and he's married."

"I know Dad loves you and always will. He's told me that. Don't you still love him?" Trisha frowned.

Although she understood exactly the dream her daughter was cherishing, she didn't believe it would ever come true. So much was destroyed that she wasn't sure how much love she had left for Drew. "You've always been the practical one, Trisha. You surely don't believe that Drew and I could pick up where we left off if something happened between him and Claudia."

"No, I guess not." She absently pulled off a piece from the croissant.

Luz watched her, afraid that she had somehow failed Trisha, that she hadn't been all a mother should be to a daughter—perhaps she was too much like her own mother. Or like last night, when she'd actually treated Trisha as a rival.

"I know we've had our differences in the past, Trisha," she began hesitantly. "And I haven't always understood. But I do love you. You know that, don't you?"

"Yes." An impatience seemed to push Trisha off the bed, her pajama-clad legs uncurling and carrying her to the serving table, where she brushed the pastry crumbs from her hand onto a plate. "Sometimes I just wish you'd let me grow up. You let me make my own decisions about some things, but I have to make my own mistakes, too, Luz."

"Like Raul, I suppose." A certain hardness entered her voice.

"If Raul is a mistake, then yes," she asserted, then made a determined attempt to throw off the grimness. "It's after nine already. Rob should be arriving from the airport anytime now.

I'd better get dressed." She moved away toward the connecting door.

"Thanks for the morning coffee."

"Sure."

It wasn't a very satisfactory conclusion to their conversation. Luz rested the cup in its saucer, wondering why she could never say the right thing to her daughter. She could talk to Rob, but with Trisha she always came away with the feeling she had failed to make herself clear.

Outside her mother's door, Trisha paused. No matter what Luz said, she was convinced her mother objected to Raul solely because he was older. It wasn't fair. Luz was letting her bitterness and resentment over Drew's marriage to a younger woman color her opinion. All that business about a mother's prerogative was simple jealousy of any relationship between a younger woman and an older man. In a way, Trisha felt sorry for her, but that didn't alter her determination to pursue Raul.

The lock clicked and the main door to the suite opened. Rob walked into the sitting room, followed by the porter with his luggage. Trisha noticed his drawn, irritable look as he swung impatiently toward her.

"Which room is mine?" he demanded.

"That one." She pointed to a door. "And hello to you, too, brother dear."

"Sorry. Hello." Immediately after the perfunctory greeting, he glanced at the porter and motioned to the door she had indicated. "Put the bags in there." Rob turned away from him and ran a hand over his hair, then wearily rubbed the back of his neck.

"Heavy night?" Trisha guessed.

His head came up slightly, his hand stopping its motion. There was an instant of sharpness in his expression, then he crooked his mouth in a rueful grin. "You could say that."

"Don't tell me. Let me guess. You had a farewell fling with Lady Cyn last night and sampled more of her sinful delights."

Rob looked at her askance. "What do you mean by that?"

"Come on, Rob," Trisha mocked. "You were with her, weren't you?"

"Yeah. So what?" he challenged.

"So I doubt that you sat around and held hands if half of

what I heard about her is true. I'll bet she even taught you a few new things," she teased.

"A few," he admitted with a faintly secretive air.

"Is she as kinky as they claim?" Trisha asked.

Hesitating, Rob glanced at her. "She's not into whips and chains if that's what you mean. And I didn't find anything particularly kinky in her methods of getting turned on." He sounded defensive.

"Rob, you aren't serious about her, are you?" She frowned warily.

"Hardly," he scoffed. "She showed me how to have a good time and turned me on to some new ways. We got a little high together and had a little fun. That's it." He closed the discussion. "Where's Luz? Is she up yet?"

"Yeah. She's in her room having breakfast." She indicated the door behind her.

"I'd better let her know I'm here."

Trisha watched him walk by, then finally headed for her own room to shower.

The waters of the Seine reflected the colors of the buildings and trees that stood on its banks, and the sightseeing boats, the *bateaux mouches*, that traveled its wandering course. Luz strolled along the cobbled quay, Trisha keeping pace with her while Rob ranged ahead of them. After a delicious and filling lunch at a restaurant next to the quay, a leisurely walk back to the hotel suited her perfectly.

Her gaze wandered from the river to inspect the massive stone blocks that rose from the water level to form a solid retaining wall for the river's banks. A line of trees and shrubbery softened the imposing dimensions of the wall and provided a parklike atmosphere along the water's edge. Here and there ivy crawled across the stone to cloak the huge blocks in green. Great iron rings adorned the wall, remnants of another age when the Seine had been a river of commerce.

"What time is it?" Rob stopped and waited for them to catch up with him, his body taut with impatience.

"Almost two." Luz glanced at her wristwatch.

"Don't you think we should be heading back to the hotel?" he questioned as they approached a set of steps leading to the street level, some thirty feet above.

"We have plenty of time," Luz assured him, climbing the steps at a leisurely pace. "Raul won't be there until three, so there's no need to hurry. The hotel isn't more than fifteen or twenty minutes from here."

"Did you have a chance to study the information he left? I only had time to glance at it before you two dragged me off to have lunch," he complained.

"Yes, I read it over." On the street level, the stone-walled bank was lined with more trees, leaning toward the river below while spreading their leafy shade over the row of bookstalls.

"What did you think of it?" Rob wanted to know.

"I thought it was all very interesting." She preferred to put this discussion off until later, although she knew she couldn't postpone it for long. But at least when the time came, she had her priorities all set, and personal reservations were not going to dictate her decision.

Trisha lingered at one of the stalls to look over the books and magazines. "Look at this," she said, and Luz paused to glance at the comic book she was holding, a French version of Bugs Bunny. After returning it and assuring the seller she didn't wish to purchase it, Trisha moved on to the next stall, browsing over the titles as she went.

"We aren't going to stop at every one of these, are we?" Rob protested.

"Why not?" she gently chided him for being so impatient. "They're all so quaint and picturesque."

"You've had a whole week in Paris. Why couldn't you have looked through this junk before? Why today? I don't see why we came out at all," he grumbled. "We could have had lunch at the hotel. I didn't think that restaurant was all that great. The menu was in French. I couldn't even read it."

"The restaurant was French. We are in Paris," Luz reminded him.

"My brother, the world traveler," Trisha mocked.

"I don't care." There was a mutinous set to his expression as he shoved his hands into his pockets. "And I still don't see why we had to come out."

"Rob, you arrived at the hotel at nine in the morning. Our meeting with Raul isn't until three this afternoon. Surely you didn't expect us to spend five hours sitting around the hotel," Luz reasoned.

"Your mistake was in not suggesting that we go by the polo field in the Bois de Boulogne. Rob would have been in favor of that," Trisha said.

"If we'd stayed at the hotel, I could have studied the information he gave you. Maybe that doesn't mean anything to you, but it's important to me. I don't care what you do, but I'm going back to the hotel." He walked off without waiting to hear their response.

"He's such a jerk when he gets in these moods." Trisha stared at her brother's retreating figure, irritated by his juvenile behavior.

"It is important to him," Luz offered in his defense. "Rob has a lot he wants to prove."

"Don't we all," Trisha murmured.

Surprised by the comment, Luz eyed her curiously. She had never considered the possibility that there was something Trisha felt she had to prove.

Promptly at three o'clock, the doorbell to the suite rang. "I'll get it." Trisha sprang quickly to her feet and crossed to the door that opened to the hotel corridor.

Luz remained seated in the painted and gilded chair, her legs crossed, front-buttoning chemise opening to show a slice of knee and thigh. In an attempt at a pose of controlled calm, she rested one hand on the back of the other.

Opening the door wide to admit him, Trisha greeted Raul with a warm "Hello."

Luz's eyes rushed to him when he walked into the suite. Tall and lean, he moved with a rider's easy grace. His fine, yet thick hair lay smoothly against his well-shaped head, its dark color accenting the blackness of brow and lashes and the piercing blue of his eyes. The broad and angular features of his deeply tanned face wore an impassive expression as he responded to Trisha's greeting.

An instant later, Luz observed the glance he directed toward her and wished she had taken the time to put her hair up in a French twist instead of simply tying it back with a black scarf. The more sophisticated style would have provided an added poise, which, judging from the erratic beat of her pulse, she needed. Then Rob came between them.

"It's good to see you again, Raul." He extended a hand

toward him, then pulled it back. "I forgot about your wrist. Trisha told me you had injured it. How is it?"

In a testing motion, Raul flexed the fingers of his right hand. The white tape bound around his wrist for support was clearly visible below the cuff of his jacket. "It's improving."

After shutting the door, Trisha moved to stand at his side. "What happened to you last night? We waited and waited at the restaurant, but you never came back."

The female interest, so apparent in the way Trisha looked at him, reminded Luz of her earlier resolve. She was not going to compete with her daughter for any man. Their relationship was too precious to her to risk damaging it because of some purely physical attraction. No man was going to come between them. Luz intended to do all she could to discourage Trisha's attachment to Raul, but not because she was jealous and wanted him for herself. Regardless, she still believed the difference in age and experience was too great. If she could keep Trisha from being hurt, she was going to try.

Lowering her gaze, she listened to the faintly accented timbre of Raul's voice as he responded to Trisha's question. "After seeing your mother safely back here, I saw no point in returning to the restaurant, so I went to my hotel. I regret if I caused you undue concern."

"Well, you did," she informed him pertly.

"Then you have my apologies," he said and turned to face Luz once more.

"Come sit down," she invited politely, motioning to the Louis XV couch that matched her chair. "I don't believe I properly thanked you for seeing me to the hotel last evening."

"It is not necessary." He crossed to the gracefully curved sofa, supported by the period's distinctive cabriole legs, and sat down. Trisha joined him, sitting at the opposite end of the sofa.

Luz took him at his word, glad to drop the whole thing. "May I offer you some coffee?" She glanced at the gray-haired woman lingering in the background. "Emma, would you pour?"

"Of course," she replied and walked over to the inlaid bureau where a tray with cups and silver coffeepot waited in readiness. "Do you take cream or sugar, Mr. Buchanan?"

"Neither, thank you."

"I don't care for any coffee, Emma," Rob said as he pulled

a chair closer to the sofa and sat down, leaning forward in an attitude of intense interest.

Emma placed two cups of coffee in their saucers on the round marble-topped table in front of the sofa for Raul and Trisha, then went back for the third. "What more would you like me to tell you about my school?" Raul reached for his cup.

"I believe Rob had some questions after looking at your brochure." Luz took the cup and saucer from Emma. "Thank you."

"What was it you wished to know?" Raul directed the question to Rob.

While they talked, Luz sipped at her coffee, but it burned her tongue. She set it down to cool and stared absently at her shoe to avoid looking at Raul while he talked. She listened to the two of them, paying little attention to the actual content of their discussion. Polo was a subject Rob could go on about for hours. She could hear the eager quality of his voice, his earnest absorption with the topic, and that hunger to know more. When she lifted her gaze, it was to study him.

His sandy hair, a couple of shades darker than her own, grew long in the back, curling over the collar of his jacket. Although he shaved daily, his cheeks still had a boyish smoothness. His features were so serious—even in animation they had an intensity of purpose behind them, like his eyes, dark coals burning with an inner fire she didn't understand. She knew that look on his face, that wanting of something so desperately that he hurt inside. She recognized it, but couldn't comprehend it.

There was a lull in the conversation. Luz started to take a sip of her coffee and discovered that sometime in the interim she'd drunk it all. Emma had withdrawn to her own room to let them talk in private. She stood up, then paused to ask, "Would anyone care for more coffee?"

"No, thank you," Raul said, and Trisha shook her head negatively.

"What do you think, Luz?" Rob asked as she crossed to the long table.

"About what?" She hadn't been listening, so she couldn't be sure of his reference.

"The school, of course. It sounds ideal to me—just the kind

of learning experience I need." He pushed out of his chair and walked over to where she was standing as if seeking some way to impress upon her the certainty of his feelings.

The demanding appeal of his gaze left her with little doubt, but Luz asked anyway, "Are you sure this school is the one you want to attend?"

"Yes. We're going to Argentina to buy horses anyway, so why not make one trip count for both? Why should I go somewhere else? This is one of the best," he argued.

"Don't you think it might be wiser to wait until we get to Argentina and you have a chance to see the school, before you make the decision?" she reasoned as she refilled her cup.

"Why? After I get there, if it turns out that I'm not learning all that I could, I can always leave. It isn't as though I have to stick it out if it turns out to be something other than what we believe. Which I don't think it will."

"I see." She walked back to her chair and sat down, poised slightly on the edge of it and holding the cup on her lap. "It appears my son has made up his mind. As he said, your program has been recommended to us as one of the best. That's what I want for him." She faced Raul squarely, meeting his eyes. This had nothing to do with anything other than polo. She hoped she was making that clear to him.

"I do not believe you will be disappointed in your choice," he stated.

"I will be accompanying him," she continued. There were too many unknowns for Luz to allow Rob to go there alone. "I'm not certain how long I'll be staying. That's a decision I'll make after we get there."

"I'm coming, too," Trisha asserted.

"You are welcome, of course," Raul said. "But I must tell you that our accommodations may seem spartan to you. While we do have a swimming pool and tennis court on the grounds, our facilities are mainly designed around the school. And the household staff takes care of the basic necessities. The *estancia* is not a resort."

"I understand. I believe I'm capable of roughing it for a while," Luz assured him, a tiny sting in her voice. "And I don't expect to be entertained while I'm there."

"What's the weather like in August where you live, Raul?" Trisha wanted to know.

"The climate is similar to northern Florida's. The days are mild, but the nights can be cool." It was an offhand answer, most of his attention centering on Luz.

"According to your brochure, you are located southwest of Buenos Aires," she said.

"Yes. It's approximately a three-hour drive by car. I would recommend that when you make your travel plans, you arrange to spend your first night at a hotel in Buenos Aires. You will be tired after the long flight from the States."

Now that the decision had been made, there were more details to be discussed. This time, Luz took an active part in the conversation, but she found it difficult to talk with Raul without that female part of her being stirred.

Later, when she watched Trisha walk him to the door, she realized just how difficult this trip to Argentina could turn out to be. She was committed to it—because Rob was committed to it. This was what he wanted more than anything. Maybe it was wrong to live her life for the children, but they were all she had. She needed them.

# CHAPTER XVI

The Florida sun was still making its morning climb into the blue summer sky, but its heat was already felt on the green practice field near the private stables on the house grounds. Luz could taste the salty sweat on her lips as she galloped the pinto horse after the ball. She lined the pony so that the ball would be on the right when they approached it, allowing her a simple offside forehand stroke.

Rising in the stirrups to brace for the shot, Luz put her full weight on the irons and gripped with her knees and thighs to maintain her position on the horse's back. As her hand cocked the long stick above her head, she twisted her body from the hips, pointing her left shoulder at the ball, and leaned out to the right. She kept the hand holding the stick well above her head so the mallet head could gather speed when she made the downward swing.

With her eye on the ball, she timed her swing to begin when the ball was a couple of feet from the point of her shoulder. At the moment when her shoulder, arm, and stick were in a straight line at the lowest point of the swing, the broadside of the mallet made contact with the ball, a solid *thunk,* the impact vibrating up her arm. She completed the follow-through of her swing as the ball sailed ahead, bouncing toward the near side of the field, where the groom, Jimmy Ray Turnbull, was standing. Someone was with him, she noticed. The pinto's sides heaved beneath her as it blew out a rolling snort. At almost the same instant, Luz recognized that trimly built figure with a flash of silver-gray in his hair. A sudden tension raced through her. Instinctively, she checked the pinto, obeying her initial impulse to turn and run rather than face Drew, but that was countered almost immediately by a surge of pride, and she urged the horse on. The conflicting signals had the horse side-stepping nervously.

The last time she'd seen him had been at the graduation exercises over two months ago, and then only briefly. And Claudia had been with him. What was he doing here now after all this time? It wasn't to welcome her home. They'd been back from Europe for three weeks. Why was he here? What did he want? Her nerves suddenly felt raw, the wounds re-opened.

Fighting the suffocating memories of the fool she had been, Luz let the polo mallet dangle from its wrist strap, unhooked the chin strap of the helmet, and pulled it off, trying to clear her head. With the back of her hand, she wiped at the per-spiration that had collected on her upper lip and realized what a mess she was. No makeup, sweat streaming down her face and along the creases of her eyes, her hair flattened to her head—this wasn't the way she wanted him to see her again after all this time.

Damn him for catching her out like this! Why hadn't he called? Did he think this was still his home and he could drop by whenever he pleased? Angrily, Luz rode over to the sideline where he stood with Jimmy Ray and stopped the pinto in front of the groom, not even acknowledging Drew's presence with a look.

"Hello, Luz." His tone was as casual as if it had been two days instead of two months since they'd last spoken. "That was some good form out there."

Dismounting, she kept her back to him and handed Jimmy Ray the helmet and stick. "Take these to the equipment room," she ordered, then turned toward the house, tugging off the riding glove she wore on her right hand to avoid blisters. "If you came to see Rob or Trisha, they aren't here," she informed Drew with a half-glance his way.

"I didn't. I wanted to speak to you, privately."

The clop-clopping of the pinto's hooves as Jimmy Ray led the horse toward the stable seemed to echo the sudden loud thumping of her heart. Her mind raced wildly over Drew's possible reasons for wanting a private talk with her. The set-tlement agreements and the divorce documents, even the tax returns, had all been completed long ago. And their lawyers would have handled anything related to that anyway.

So it could only be personal. Luz refused to allow herself to think he might be having problems in his relationship with Claudia. The possibility frightened her in a strange way, as if it made her vulnerable all over again. When Trisha had asked her if she and Drew would go back together again, the chance seemed so remote. But if he did want to come back to her, what would she do? Did she want that marriage again? She didn't think so. But what if . . .

"Why don't we go to the house?" Luz said and started forward, still avoiding his eyes. Drew moved with her. Walking with him was such a familiar pattern that it tugged at her. It would be so easy to fall back into old habits, she realized. Reaching up, she unclasped the wide barrette securing the knot of hair atop her head and shook out its damp length. She knew it didn't improve her appearance. "You should have called."

"I did. Emma told me you were out with the horses, so I came over." Drew lagged behind her as they skirted the swimming pool.

There was little protest she could make without admitting that she hated being caught looking like this. Obviously, while they were married, he'd seen her looking worse. But things were different now.

Until she had returned from Europe, Luz hadn't realized how much of an escape that trip had been. Now, in this close-knit community, she was "poor Luz" again, rejected by her husband for a younger woman. That's what made it so horrible to have him see her in this disheveled state—naked of makeup, smelling of horse and sweat, her hair straggly and unkempt. She was hardly a sight likely to kindle regret.

They entered the house through the French doors to the living room. "Excuse me while I freshen up a bit," Luz said over her shoulder as she continued through the room. "Emma will bring you some coffee."

"Take your time."

He probably thought she needed it, Luz guessed angrily and ran up the oak stairs to her private rooms. She entered the bedroom, stripped off her blouse and bra, sat on the bed long enough to tug off her riding boots and socks, then shed her breeches and panties and headed straight for the shower.

In fifteen minutes flat, she had showered, shampooed, put on makeup, and styled her wet hair in a French braid. She grabbed a white smocked cotton dress with drop shoulders from the closet and pulled it over her head, then slipped her feet into a pair of sling heels. She headed back downstairs, belting the voluminous dress at the waist as she went, somewhat fortified by the transformation.

When she walked into the living room, Drew was pouring himself another cup of coffee. A second cup was sitting on the tray. "Want some coffee?" he asked.

"No thanks. After that workout on the practice field I need something tall and cold." Luz crossed to the bar and went behind the counter, taking a glass from the shelf and adding ice cubes to it.

"Isn't it a little early in the day to be drinking?" Drew eyed her critically as he wandered over to a stool, coffee cup in hand. He didn't see the green Perrier bottle until she plunked it on the counter with a glare of defiance.

"You sound like Audra." She popped the cap off and poured the water over ice cubes in the glass, then added a wedge of lime from the bowl in the bar's refrigerator.

"I'd heard you'd been drinking heavily. I'm glad to see you're laying off the booze," he said, and Luz guessed a little bitterly that Trisha was the source of his information.

"Don't tell me you're here to talk about my alleged drinking problem?" she mocked. "'Alleged.' That's a legal term, isn't it? I guess I must have picked up some of your jargon after all." She realized how very bitter she sounded and knew this was no way to begin the conversation, with her emotions so exposed. She looked at the green citrus wedge floating atop the cubes. "Maybe we should start this over, Drew. How have you been?" It was a poised, polite inquiry. "You're looking well."

Indeed he did. Trim and tan, handsome as always, he was exactly as she remembered. Maybe not quite, she revised. He didn't seem quite as preoccupied, and there was a more youthful quality about him, or maybe she was imagining that.

Yet something was troubling him. After living with him for twenty years, she could sense when something was wrong. The impression lost some of its strength when he smiled at her.

"I'm fine. How was Europe?"

"Wonderful, as always," Luz replied. "How's the law practice? Have you been keeping busy?"

"Yes." He lifted his coffee cup to take a drink. "And yourself?"

"Of course." Which wasn't precisely true.

"I've heard you're dating Fred de Silva." The vague disapproval in his voice caught her attention. Luz couldn't help wondering if he was jealous.

"I've only been out to dinner with him twice in two weeks. That hardly constitutes dating," she replied.

Actually she didn't know Fred de Silva that well, only having met him socially. A rather good-looking man in his late forties, a natty dresser, he had the reputation of being, if not a playboy, at least a ladies' man. When she'd run into him at the polo club and he'd asked her to dinner, the invitation had sounded like a welcome change from her usual evenings. Truthfully, Rob and Trisha could not give her all the company she needed, and attending social functions alone didn't satisfy her need for companionship.

The dinners had been just that—a change of pace. She couldn't even say that she liked the man. In some ways, he was too flamboyant and overly charming for her tastes. When she had complained to her sister, Mary, about the gold chains around his neck and the huge diamonds on his fingers, Mary reminded her that Kincaids came from old money—and old money frowned on overt displays of wealth.

So far, there hadn't been a third invitation from him, but Luz doubted that she'd accept if it came, mostly because she didn't want to start something. In a way, going out with him had been a means to get Raul Buchanan off her mind. If she didn't see other men, it would be too easy for her to fantasize about him.

"I hope he didn't talk you into anything, Luz," Drew said grimly. She sharply probed his expression as she searched for signs of jealousy.

"If you're wondering whether I slept with him, that isn't any of your business." Other than a few heavy-breathing kisses, nothing had happened, but Luz hoped it bothered him to imagine her in the arms of another man. She knew the hell that her images of Claudia and him together had been for her, and she wanted him to have a taste of it.

"I recognize that you are free to see whomever you please." He seemed grim, and he was slow to look at her. "I'm concerned that you might have put some money into one of his ventures."

"My evenings with Fred were purely social." She resented his implication that she had to buy companionship. Moving out from behind the bar, she rubbed a hand across the cold, wet sides of the Perrier glass, her temper needing its cooling effect.

"From what I've been able to learn, de Silva is in considerable financial trouble. That big real estate development deal of his isn't panning out."

"That has nothing to do with me," she declared, irritated that he believed she would be gullible enough to invest in something solely on a man's word, without checking into it. After all, she was Jake Kincaid's daughter, which meant she wasn't a total fool even if Drew had made one of her.

"Some of his investors have been threatening to pull out of the project, but now the rumor is that Kincaid money is coming in to bail it out." Drew absently swirled the coffee in the cup, then looked over to her. "De Silva obviously made sure he was seen with you. I'm afraid he's using you, Luz, to stall for time—or to set you up for an investment pitch."

Inside, she was trembling with hurt and anger, but she held herself stiffly motionless. "It was so clever of you to figure that out, Drew. Of course, you had the advantage of knowing that my company is far from scintillating, so if it wasn't that Fred was seeking, it had to be the Kincaid fortune—or my share of it. Am I supposed to be grateful that you've taken time from your precious law practice to warn me about him?"

"That isn't the only reason I'm here," he replied impatiently. "I know you won't believe me, but I happen to still care about you. I don't want to see you hurt any more."

Confusion pounded at her temples. First he slapped her own, then held out his hand. She gripped the glass tightly, so damned unsure of her position. "Tell me, Drew," Luz challenged. "Does Claudia know that you've come to see me this morning?"

"Of course." But the mention of her name seemed to make him uncomfortable. Covering it, he finished the coffee in his cup, then set it aside. "We have no secrets from each other."

"I'm so glad to hear that you don't lie to her the way you

lied to me. You've obviously learned something." Bitterness and sarcasm mixed together in her words. "The sin isn't in making a mistake, but in repeating it."

"I don't think it's wise for us to get into a discussion about our past differences. That isn't why I came."

"Isn't it? I never would have guessed. Everything we've talked about so far has dealt with my shortcomings. I mean, you've criticized my drinking habits, found fault with my dinner partners, and, in your own way, cautioned me against mentioning Claudia. Just what is it you want to discuss, Drew?" Luz demanded tautly.

"I wanted to talk to you about the children."

She swung away from him, fighting her anger and tension. "I suppose you think I'm to blame because Rob still won't come to see you. I can't, and I won't, force him to do it."

"I am concerned about this trip to Argentina you have planned," he asserted. "When I went along with Rob's decision to sit out college for a year, no mention was made about a three-month sojourn in Argentina."

"He has enrolled—" she began as she turned back toward him, but got no farther.

"Trisha told me all about this famous polo college."

"I thoroughly investigated it before I agreed to let him attend." Luz reacted to the disdain she heard in Drew's voice.

"But you didn't consult me about this trip, and I happen to be their father," he pointed out curtly. "Although, God knows, you've always made sure Rob got anything he ever wanted, you could have gone through the motion of discussing it with me. But it isn't the trip I resent so much as Trisha's participation in all this. Do you realize that she is considering waiting until midterm to start college just so she can make this trip? She's putting her acceptance at Harvard in jeopardy, for God's sake."

"I wasn't aware of it. Or, at least, the times she's mentioned it, I haven't taken her seriously." She looked at the glass in her hand, conscious of the inner turmoil this subject aroused. "If she decides to wait, it won't be with my approval. Personally, I would rather she didn't go with Rob and me to Argentina. But she is of legal age, so there's little you or I can do to prevent her from going." She took a drink of the water, for the first time in a long while wishing it were liquor-laced. With a sardonic tilt of her head, she glanced at Drew. "You see, she's wildly infatuated with Raul Buchanan."

"Yes, I had that impression when she talked about him."

"He's much too old for her, but I can't make Trisha see that. It's all your fault, you know. You've set a fine example with Claudia. If it's all right for Daddy, it's all right for her," Luz taunted. "Tell me, Drew, how do you feel about a thirty-seven-year-old man seducing your eighteen-year-old daughter? Maybe that doesn't bother you?"

"Of course it does. She's too young."

"Then why don't you tell her that? Instead of always being the understanding, doting father, why don't you play the heavy for once?" she challenged angrily.

"I'd be more than happy to talk to her, Luz," he assured her, and she hated that placating tone in his voice, that patient reasoning of an adult talking to a child. "But I'm in a somewhat awkward position."

"You're in an awkward position? My God, that's rich!" She pushed the glass onto the counter near him, shaking too much with anger to hold it any longer. "What about me? Don't you think I'm in an awkward position?"

"Of course—"

"Anything I say to her sounds like the bitterly prejudiced opinions of a jilted wife whose husband left her for a younger woman! She won't listen to me. Can't you see that?"

"I understand what you're saying."

"I don't think you do," Luz snapped and pivoted sharply to walk away from him, but he reached out to stop her. She went rigid at the touch of his hands.

"Let's not argue, Luz. It isn't going to help," he insisted while his hands continued to hold her shoulders, the pressure gentle and affectionate. The charm was being turned on, but she was buying none of it. "I know these last months have been difficult for you, and believe me, I regret that. We had some good years together. Let's try to remember them and put this bitterness behind us. We'll never get anywhere in solving this problem if we keep blaming each other for what happened."

"I can't turn my emotions on and off like a faucet the way you can, Drew. I can't pretend nothing has happened." He was expecting too much to believe they could ever sit and discuss Rob and Trisha as parents without also remembering that they once were man and wife. She couldn't wash away the bitter taste of the divorce. No one was that selfless.

"I'm not asking you to pretend merely to—" He was distracted by the small click of a door latch followed by a rush of warm, humid air from the outside.

When Luz glanced toward the French doors, she saw Trisha standing motionless a foot inside the room. Dressed in tennis clothes, a visor around her chestnut hair and a tennis racket in hand, she stared at the two of them. A split second later, Luz realized how it might look with Drew holding her like this and immediately backed away from him.

"I picked a bad time to barge in, didn't I?" Trisha murmured.

"Of course you didn't," Drew denied.

"I saw your car parked out front and I . . . I never considered that you might be here to see Luz," she ended lamely. "I'm sorry."

"There's no need to be sorry."

"Close the door, Trisha," Luz ordered, irritated with Drew that he either could not see the construction she was placing on their being together or was simply not doing anything to squash it. "You didn't interrupt anything. Your father and I were just arguing about our trip to Argentina. He doesn't approve of your going."

"That isn't exactly true," he denied. "I simply felt I should have been consulted about it before the plans were finalized. After all, I am your father, and that makes me an interested party."

"There you go again twisting things around so you come out looking good!" she flared bitterly, then angrily swept a hand toward Trisha. "He's been blaming me because you've been hinting you may not start college until midyear."

"I was merely expressing my concern—"

"And I suppose next you're going to claim you approve of her interest in Raul Buchanan!" Luz accused.

"Since I've never met him, I can't very well approve or disapprove. At this point, I can only trust that Trisha is discerning enough not to be taken in by a possible fortune hunter."

"Damn you." She dug her nails into her palms in helpless frustration. "And you want to become a lawyer, Trisha. Be sure to take lessons from your father in how *not* to give a straight answer!"

"Stop it! Both of you!" Tears shimmered in Trisha's eyes. "Why do you always have to argue with him, Luz?"

"It's always my fault, isn't it? No matter what happens, I'm to blame." It was a battle she'd never win, and it was useless to try, she realized. "You know where the door is, Drew. I suggest you use it." She bolted from the room, tears of impotent rage burning her eyes.

Minutes after she reached the privacy of her room, she heard the front door open and close, followed by the deep rumble of the Mercedes engine starting up. After all this time, she still recognized the sound of that motor. She waited, hoping Trisha would come upstairs so that she could explain all that had happened before she arrived, but she never came. Later, when she saw her at lunch, no mention was made of Drew's visit.

A dark starling took wing into the coral-tinged sky, its iridescent neck feathers flashing with the dying light of the sun. Rob briefly tracked its flight as he climbed the stairs leading to Jimmy Ray's quarters above the stable. When he reached the door at the top, he instinctively glanced over his shoulder to see if anyone was watching, but the stable itself blocked any view from the house and the surrounding acreage placed the other domiciles at a distance.

Inside, a television set blared the sound of screeching tires and crashing cars. Rob knocked loudly at the door, then looked anxiously behind him in a guilty reflexive movement. A second later, the television volume was turned down.

"Who is it?"

"It's me. Rob." He didn't try the doorknob. Jimmy Ray always kept it locked.

After what seemed an interminable wait, the slow-moving man opened the door. He stood there in his loose-fitting tan pants and matching workshirt and sized up Rob. "Want some, do you?" An understanding nod accompanied the drawled summation.

"Yeah, and it better be good. I don't want the shit you sold me last week," Rob stated.

"Be down with it directly." He swung the door closed, shutting Rob out. Rob was never invited to wait inside while he was making a buy. The old man was careful not to reveal the location of his drug stash.

Within seconds after the door closed, he heard the click of the deadbolt sliding home. Rob turned and hurried down the outside stairs. At the bottom, he swung around the rail post and entered the stable through the side entrance.

The interior was cloaked in shadows with only patches of fading sunlight filtering onto the runway from the top half of the stall doors. Rob flipped on the string of overhead lights to illuminate the wide corridor, then wandered down it. A horse whickered in one of the closed stalls. From various points came the soft rustle of hay and the crunching chomp of horses chewing on it, and the occasional stamp to chase away a pesky fly. A breeze stirred through the open halves of the doors facing the paddocks and drifted into the stable, its fresh tang picking up the smell of hay and horse.

The gray horse, Stonewall, thrust its head into the corridor and snorted inquisitively at Rob. He wandered over to it and let the soft gray-white nose investigate his shirt pockets for sugar while he scratched the underside of its jaw. The aging gray horse was growing whiter. A man had made Rob an offer for the horse today. He wasn't much of a rider or a polo player, but he liked the image of himself astride a horse cantering across the field on Saturday afternoon and making showy swings with his mallet. An inglorious end for a good game horse, but it would be an easy old age, Rob decided.

A door shut outside the stable, followed, after a long pause, by the measured thud of footsteps on the outer stairs. Rob reached inside his pants pocket and removed the folded bills, the amount already counted, then tucked it under the taut string of a hay bale sitting on the concrete runway between the closed stalls.

Jimmy Ray ambled into the stable, a slouch hat covering his bald pate. His long-sleeved shirt was buttoned at the cuff despite the subtropical heat of a humid July night. He walked over to the gray horse and nonchalantly passed the packet to Rob.

"How's the old man tonight?" he crooned to the horse, never even glancing at the hay bale that had become the money pickup. From what Rob had been able to learn since he'd begun dealing with him regularly, the groom only pushed enough stuff to pay for his own needs, and he only sold to people he knew well. Not that Rob had ever seen anyone else make a buy from him.

"I'm selling Stonewall," Rob said, slipping the cocaine packet into his pocket.

"To Greble?"

"Yes."

Jimmy Ray rubbed the roached forelock of the animal. "Be the same as gettin' put out to pasture, old man," he drawled to the horse. "Difference is, you'll get to parade once't in a while."

"That's true." He fed the gray horse the sugar lump he'd denied him earlier.

"You be takin' anything with you on this trip? I'll be needin' t' know." His attention returned to Rob.

"Too risky."

"Could be," Jimmy Ray conceded.

"It isn't like I can't do without it for a while," Rob asserted.

"None of us *got* to have it," he agreed, but his mouth slanted in a knowing smile.

Rob wasn't worried. He wasn't hooked on cocaine. You couldn't get addicted to it like the hard stuff. A guy didn't go through agonizing withdrawal if he didn't get it regularly.

The groom patted the gray horse one last time then shoved away. "Night."

Out of the corner of his eye, Rob saw Jimmy Ray pause beside the hay bale and remove the money with a quick twist. He stayed by the gray's stall until the man had left the stable and he heard his footsteps on the wooden stairs outside. Only then did he slide away from the horse and head for the privacy of the tack room.

Once inside, he carefully and quietly shut the door and locked it, then crossed to his saddle rack and crouched down to remove the free-base kit he'd purchased a couple of weeks ago at a head shop in Lauderdale. After he set it out on the small work table where Jimmy Ray repaired broken tack, he took the package of cocaine from his pocket and emptied part of it into a small container. Careful to avoid inhaling the odorous ether fumes, he added enough to the cocaine to make a paste. He performed all the steps the way Cyn's friend had shown him in England. Once the ether-coke paste was lit, he settled back in the high-backed rocking chair in a corner of the

tack room and smoked the pipe, inhaling the vapors. Tooting
was kid's play. This was the only way to do it, he realized as
his world became right and his self-confidence soared.

"Helen, I would love to work on the committee for you,
but I'm leaving for Argentina in a little more than two weeks
and won't be back for at least a month, if not more, so I don't
see how I can be of much help to you." While Luz patiently
explained her refusal to the woman on the telephone, Trisha
absently listened. She was still smarting from the bitter scene
she'd witnessed that morning between her parents, and especially the role her mother had played. "I don't consider it to
be running away, Helen," she heard her mother say tautly. "Rob
wants to buy some polo ponies there and take some training
under one of their top professionals. That's why I'm going. It
has nothing to do with the divorce or Drew."

The very mention of the word "divorce" drove Trisha from
the room. It was over, so why couldn't Luz make peace instead
of holding such a bitter grudge and lashing out every chance
she got? Her father had attempted to justify her behavior after
she had stormed out of the living room that morning.

"Your mother's been deeply hurt by what's happened," he
had said. "It's understandable that right now she's going to
take anything I say to her personally. I wasn't attempting to
criticize her, although that's what she believes. You and Rob
are important to me. I merely wanted to express my desire to
remain involved in decisions that affect your lives."

At least her father was trying to establish some sort of
workable relationship for the family's sake, which was more
than Trisha could say for Luz. She spied Emma coming out of
the kitchen.

"Where'd Rob go? Did you see him leave, Emma?"

"I think I saw him walking to the stables," she replied.

"Thanks." She headed out the French doors to the pool and
patio area and cut across the grounds toward the stable, not
that she had much hope Rob would understand what she was
feeling, but she wanted to talk to him. He'd take Luz's side,
as always.

Dusk purpled the grounds, deepening the shadows cast by
the palm trees, buttonwoods, and shrubbery around the house
area. There were lights shining inside the stable, reaching out

like beacons into the growing night. Trisha walked toward them, conscious of the dew on the grass dampening her canvas shoes.

As she neared the long building, she could hear muffled voices and laughter. She frowned, then realized the sound was coming from Jimmy Ray's television set. He always had the volume on so loud. There was something about that man she didn't like no matter what anyone else thought.

She crossed to the main door and pulled it open. The hinges squeaked as she walked in and let it swing shut behind her. Trisha walked past the closed tack-room door to the wide concourse that ran down the middle of the building. But there was no one there.

"Rob?" A horse shuffled in its straw-covered stall. She wandered down the row, glancing inside the opened tops of the doors. "Hey, Rob, where are you? Are you here?"

A faint sickly-sweet smell drifted in the air. Trisha wrinkled her nose at the odor and guessed Rob was doctoring one of the horses. She heard a loud noise and turned, certain it had come from behind her.

"Rob?" Trisha paused to listen, then noticed the slash of light at the base of the tack-room door. She retraced her steps and stopped in front of the door, but the knob wouldn't turn when she tried it. "Rob, are you in there?" she demanded, jiggling the knob. From inside, she could hear soft scurrying sounds. "Rob!" She rapped on the door.

"Just a minute." The closed door muffled his answer.

Frowning, she waited. A second later, she heard the flush of the toilet in the half-bath located off the tack room, then the sound of his footsteps approaching the door. The lock clicked open a second before the knob turned, and Rob stepped out.

"Why did you lock the door?"

"It's always supposed to be locked," he chided her. "We've got some expensive tack in there. You may not care whether your saddle gets ripped off, but I do." He curved an arm around her shoulder, turning her away from the door while he shut it. "What brings you down here?"

"What's that funny smell?" The fanning action of the door made the odor stronger.

"Some of Jimmy Ray's liniment, probably."

She took a deep breath. "It's too sweet," she said first, then caught something else. "I smell smoke."

"Trish, you're crazy." He laughed at her. "Hey, did I tell you that I'm selling old Stonewall? You'd better say goodbye to him, 'cause I'll be calling the guy tomorrow to accept his offer."

The pressure of his encircling arm forcibly guided her in the direction of the gray horse's stall. Her frown deepened as she looked up at him. This mood of his wasn't natural. He was in such high spirits.

"What's got into you, Rob?" she wondered. "You're acting like you're on something." The minute she said it, everything seemed to fall into place. "Are you?" she demanded. "That smell—have you been smoking pot?"

"What are you talking about?" He paused, giving her an amused look.

"Rob, that's stupid. You know how dangerous it is to smoke in the stable."

"Who says I was?" Rob countered, that lazy grin still curving his mouth.

"I'm not buying that innocent act. It might work on Luz, but not on me." Trisha shrugged his arm off her shoulder and stepped away from him. "That door was locked because you didn't want anyone to walk in and catch you smoking a joint."

"It was locked because I was in the john," he retorted easily. "You may be my sister, but I still don't want you—or Jimmy Ray—to walk in and find me sitting on the can. Or shitting on the can." Rob laughed.

"All you had to do was shut the bathroom door."

"The light bulb was burned out."

"You've got your story all worked out, haven't you?" she accused grimly. "When we were kids, you were always making them up to protect yourself from getting into trouble, but I always knew when you were handing me one. And you're doing it now." Irritated, Trisha swung away and started toward the door. There was no talking to him now, not when he was flying high like this.

"Hey, where are you going?" Roughly he grabbed her arm and pulled her back around to face him. Trisha shrank from the bite of his fingers into her arm, faintly surprised by her brother's strength.

"What's the matter, Rob?" she challenged that wary and suspicious look in his expression. "Are you afraid I'm going to tell Luz?"

"You'd better not." This time there was no smile on his thin mouth. "Because if you do, I might have to mention the time Raul left you standing naked in the driveway at Seven Oak. Didn't think anybody saw you, did you? Well, I did, when I was walking back from the garage after parking the car. Wanta bet your trip to Argentina would go down the tube?"

"Rob, you're a real bastard," she declared angrily. "In the first place, I don't carry tales, and you should know me better than that. And second, I'm eighteen and I don't need Luz's permission to go to Argentina or anywhere else I want to go. Last, but not least, I don't give a damn if you saw me or not—or who you tell. So roll that in your paper and smoke it!"

"Don't come snooping around here anymore. I don't like people checking up on me."

Her look was saddened with disgust. "Believe it or not, Rob, I came here because I wanted to talk to you. I should have known you aren't interested in anybody's problems but your own." His hold loosened as he appeared taken aback by her reply. Trisha jerked her arm and headed for the door.

# Part III

# CHAPTER XVII

After approximately seven hours of flying time, the huge jet-liner was descending to make its approach to Ezeiza, the international airport on the outskirts of Buenos Aires. Luz glanced idly out the airplane's porthole at the tame, gently rolling landscape below. It reminded her of the south of England, with considerably fewer signs of habitation.

Trisha occupied the window seat directly in front of Luz in the first-class cabin. She turned to look back at her through the gap between the seat and the cabin wall. "Uruguay," she identified the country below them, then directed her attention out the window again, eager for the first glimpse of their destination. Luz absently studied her daughter's profile, all her misgivings about this trip returning to trouble her. None of them related to Rob. She was confident their stay would accomplish all he wanted to achieve. Her uneasiness revolved around Trisha and Raul Buchanan—and to be honest, herself.

"Look." Trisha leaned closer to her window. "The Rio de la Plata, the river of silver."

Turning, Luz gazed out her own porthole at the body of water over which the jet flew. It was neither a river nor silver in color. The River Plate was a long, wide estuary, the meeting place of the currents of the feeding rivers and the tide of the Atlantic Ocean. Its sluggish, silt-heavy waters were a dark muddy brown. According to the travel book Trisha had repeatedly quoted from, both the Rio de la Plata and Argentina, which means "silvered land," were named centuries ago by the first Spaniards who mistakenly believed they had found the source of the rumored Inca riches, and the brown estuary would carry the silver to be shipped back to Spain.

Out of her window, Luz could see the haze hanging over the modern city of Buenos Aires, its skyscrapers and factory chimneys thrusting upward against the landscape. The crowded sprawl of its buildings spread out from the muddy banks of the Rio de la Plata, situated some 120 miles from the Atlantic. On the surrounding three sides of the city of "fair winds," the land stretched in a flat checkerboard pattern of large fields, intersected by a network of roads and railroad tracks that fanned out from the population center. From the air, Luz found the view of the countryside bland and uninspiring.

The no-smoking light came on, and Luz rechecked her seatbelt, hearing the grinding thunk of the landing gear being lowered. A fine tension traveled over her nerves. She reminded herself that after landing, there was still passport control to go through and the customary long wait for their luggage at the baggage claim before they met Raul.

With a bending stretch of his wrist, Raul glanced at his watch and tried to estimate how much longer it might take. The flight had landed over thirty minutes ago. Standing well back from the crowd gathered outside the exit doors of the baggage-claim section, he took a deep drag on his narrow black cigar, then impatiently blew out a long stream of smoke.

He was a man who seldom had second thoughts about any of his actions, yet a thousand times he'd cursed himself for not letting this matter drop when it was in its infancy. Each time he had argued that it was business. Rob Thomas represented not only profits as a buyer for his horses but also a considerable fee as a pupil in his polo program. And he was not so well fixed that he could afford to turn away that income. But Raul knew instinctively that a packet of trouble was coming along with Rob Thomas—two packets of trouble.

He had no doubt Trisha would continue her pursuit of him. Dealing with the unwanted attention of a client's daughter was always awkward and troublesome, but when the client was a woman, the matter was complicated further. Raul had never worked for a woman before, and he knew damned well it was Luz Thomas he had to satisfy, not her son. It was not a situation he liked. He was Latin enough not to relish taking orders from a woman. And Luz Kincaid Thomas was used to getting what she wanted. He knew that, as well as he knew that it was the cause of the friction that always rubbed its way to the surface whenever they met. It did not help that he had seen the soft woman in her, and the source of her daughter's boldness.

Arriving passengers, some carrying their luggage and others pushing it in carts, began filing through the exit doors. Raul dropped his cheroot in an ashtray and straightened from his relaxed posture to keep a closer watch on the people coming through the doors. He remained well back from the crush of the crowd as it surged forward against the railed walkway. The babble of voices around him, predominantly Spanish, grew louder, snatches of phrases and shouts sounding above the droned announcements over the public-address system.

Finally, he caught his first glimpse of the Thomas party over the bobbing heads of the crowd—a sable hat set over sleek, honey-colored hair. Even before Raul saw the distinctive profile of Luz Kincaid Thomas, he recognized that proud bearing. It was a quality he both resented and admired. Ambivalence seemed to mark his attitude toward both the Thomas women; one minute he was stirred by their uniquely different beauties and in the next turned cold by their commanding natures.

A moment later, he had a clear look at Trisha through the milling crowd. Her dark gaze, lively and sparkling, scanned the faces of the crowd gathered outside, in search of him, he knew. Rob trailed them, pushing a wheeled cart stacked with luggage, his ruddy features serious and intense in their expression.

Raul waited on the outer edge of the crowd, not moving forward to meet them, instead letting them make their way through the tangled throng of passengers. When Luz paused where the crowd thinned to look around, Raul noticed the flicker of impatience in her expression. Still, he hesitated another second.

As she shifted the full-length sable coat to her other arm, she turned to glance back to her trailing daughter and son. In that instant, she saw him and became motionless. Raul had the impression of a beautiful fragile bird about to take wing, but the image didn't last. A remote coolness seemed to sweep through her. Warm then cold, he thought, unlike her daughter, who seemed warm or hot nearly all the time. Yet that coolness was a defense; somehow he understood that.

Again struggling with his mixed feelings, Raul strode forward to meet them just as Trisha emerged from the crowd and saw him. She said something to Luz, who nodded, then moved toward him. As he approached her, the dark gold lights shining in her eyes appeared to challenge playfully.

"I was beginning to think you had forgotten we were coming." She linked an arm with his to escort him back to her mother, now joined by Rob. "How is your wrist, by the way?"

"It is well. And your flight—was it a comfortable one?"

"Long, but uneventful." Trisha relinquished her possession of his arm when they reached the others.

*"Bienvenida."* He offered the Spanish welcome to Luz and reached out to shake hands. The warmth of her soft skin briefly surprised him; the aura of coolness was so definite that the sensation of heat was unexpected. He released her hand to greet Rob. The noise and congestion in the area did not encourage prolonged conversation. "If you have everything, my car is parked outside. I will take you to your hotel so that you can rest after your long flight," Raul suggested.

"For once, all of our luggage arrived with us." Luz indicated the suitcases stacked two deep on the cart Rob guarded.

After summoning a baggage porter to bring the luggage cart, Raul escorted the three of them outside to his car. He unlocked the doors and assisted Luz into the front passenger seat, then made certain all the suitcases were stowed in the trunk before tipping the porter and sliding behind the wheel.

"How far is the hotel from the airport?" Luz inquired as he edged the car away from the curb and into the flow of traffic.

"Your hotel is located in the center of the city, which is some distance from here. The traffic should not be bad. As in any other major city, all the people leave the city for the suburbs in the evening, so we will be going against the flow." He felt obliged to make the explanation and fulfill his duties as host.

Dusk came early to the southern half of the world in August, a winter month in the reversed seasons of this hemisphere. Little of the city could be distinguished in the gathering darkness, except the glaring headlights of oncoming traffic on the freeway, the lighted signs along the route, mainly in Spanish, and occasionally a streetlamp illuminating graffiti painted on some wall.

Conversation was sporadic during the drive into the city, most of it coming from Trisha with comments by Rob, but Raul noticed that Luz said almost nothing. Up close, he could see no signs of fatigue from the long plane journey. She appeared alert and fresh. Her glistening wine-red lips lay firmly together, their straight line suggesting silent disapproval of something, and revealing a certain tension as well.

"This almost reminds me of Paris," Trisha remarked, drawing Raul's glance to the rearview mirror, where he could see her reflection. They traveled down one of many tree-lined boulevards into the heart of Buenos Aires. "It has a very European flavor."

A smile pulled at the corners of his mouth. "It is natural, no? Argentina was settled by Europeans. When they built the city, the design was influenced by their heritage."

"You're right, of course," Trisha conceded. "Every new culture brings pieces from the old or attempts to emulate it. Look, Luz, they even have sidewalk cafés."

"I noticed." The response was uninterested as Raul felt the rake of her dark glance, but when he turned, she was looking to the front.

Within minutes, they arrived at the hotel. Raul stopped the car in front of the entrance. While the uniformed doorman assisted Luz out of the front passenger seat, Raul opened the rear door for Trisha. She stepped out, then paused in front of him, blocking the opening so that he couldn't close the car door.

"Do we have to leave tomorrow, Raul?" she questioned. "I'd love to see the city. What would be wrong with having a short tour of it? It would be much more interesting if you took us around instead of a guide."

"We are expected at the *estancia* tomorrow afternoon." Out of the corner of his eye, he caught the glistening sweep of dark fur. He glanced across the top of the car at Luz, standing on the other side. The black sable coat was draped around her shoulders, the front held shut at the throat. She looked angry. Raul half expected to be the object of her glare, but it was focused on Trisha.

"Luggage, señor?" A uniformed porter waited by the curb with his baggage rack.

"*Sí.*" Raul moved away from Trisha to unlock the trunk.

"Trisha." Luz's call prompted her daughter to accompany her into the hotel.

After shutting the passenger door, Trisha walked around to the rear of the car, where Raul was supervising the removal of the luggage. "Are you coming inside, Raul?" She ignored her mother to stop beside him.

"It is unlikely there will be any difficulties with your reservation, but I will come in to make certain," he replied.

"Don't say that. The idea of being stranded without a hotel in a city where I didn't know a soul and couldn't make myself understood doesn't bear thinking about." But she laughed when she said it, as though she actually believed it might be an exciting adventure.

"I think there would be no fear of making yourself understood. Many people here are bilingual." Again, Raul was conscious of the impatient look Luz was sending their way. "I believe your mother is waiting for you."

That didn't appear to concern her. "I'll see you inside," she said, smiling as she moved away to join her mother and Rob on the hotel steps.

He watched them enter the hotel, then turned back to the porter. When the last large suitcase was lifted out of the trunk, he closed the lid and checked to make certain it was locked, then followed the porter into the lobby. Familiar with the hotel's layout from previous visits, he went directly to the registration desk. Luz was filling out the necessary forms while Rob leafed through a magazine listing the city's entertainment. Trisha was looking through some brochures on the counter and didn't immediately notice him.

Raul paused next to Luz. 'Are your reservations in order?"

'Yes.'' She slid the form and the accompanying passports back to the clerk and turned to face him. "What time would you like us to be ready to leave in the morning?"

"I would like to start at ten o'clock, if that is not too early for you," he replied, aware that both Rob and Trisha had come over to join them.

"Ten o'clock will be fine," Luz stated as the desk clerk interposed to give the room key to the bellman.

"You will be joining us for dinner, won't you, Raul?" Trisha asked.

The instant the invitation was issued, he noticed the reproving glance Luz gave her.

"You will have to excuse me this evening. I have other plans. And I am certain after your long trip, you would prefer a quiet dinner," he stated.

"You're quite right," Luz agreed. "We will probably have a meal sent to our rooms."

"I will meet you tomorrow morning in the lobby at ten o'clock, then. Have a good evening." The statements were directed to all three of them.

There was an echo of goodbyes as he turned and started across the lobby to the exit. "Mr. Buchanan?" Luz called out to him before he was halfway across it. Pausing, Raul swung back. "I'll be there directly," she said to Rob and Trisha, who were being escorted to the elevators by the bellman. "I just want to have a quick word with Raul . . . Mr. Buchanan."

The almost imperceptible slip reminded him of the times she had called him Raul, and the way her lips had formed his name, slowly, lingering over it. He waited while she approached him, her high heels clicking over the tiled floor.

"Was there something else?" Raul checked the impulse to use her given name even though she had once given him permission to do so. Some instinct had guarded him against establishing such familiarity, and he obeyed it now.

"Yes." The sable coat hung loosely about her shoulders, like a cape, a high collar framing her face with luxurious dark fur. Its color seemed as dark a black-brown as her eyes. "I'm sure you are aware that my daughter is very attracted to you. I would greatly appreciate it if you would not encourage that interest. You are not at all suitable for her, and I would not like to see her hurt. That's all, Mr. Buchanan." She dismissed him and walked back to the others.

Stunned, he stared after her, anger slowly rising in him. She'd spoken to him as if he were a servant, treated him as something less than an equal, coldly informed him that he wasn't good enough for her daughter. Raul pivoted sharply on his heel and strode out of the hotel.

* * *

The next morning, the inner-city congestion slowed the traffic in the streets, but there was more of Buenos Aires to see in the daylight, so Luz didn't object to the slower pace. It allowed her to gain more of a sense of the city with its formal squares and broad avenues. The wide boulevards sometimes seemed severe. There hadn't been enough time for age to give them the grace and charm of their European counterparts, although when the jacaranda bloomed, Luz suspected much of its cold line would be softened. She hadn't noticed any narrow, winding streets. All of the avenues seemed to run endlessly block after block toward some distant vanishing point.

Most of the buildings appeared to be modern, decades rather than centuries old. She noticed an old Corinthian-columned cathedral that dominated one of the many plazas. Its architectural style was reminiscent of La Madeleine, the church that graced the Place de la Concorde in Paris. She made some reference to the cathedral when they passed within sight of it. Raul explained that it was one of the oldest buildings in Argentina, constructed in the eighteenth century, and held the mortal remains of General José de San Martín, the liberator of Argentina, who had led the revolt against Spain to gain his nation's independence, as well as that of Chile and Peru.

That was one of the few times he'd spoken since he'd picked them up at the hotel promptly at ten. Luz knew she was responsible for his present chilly attitude. Last night, she had bluntly stated her wishes and not allowed him to reply. She hadn't wanted Trisha's infatuation with him to become a subject for discussion. Perhaps she should have appealed to him as a concerned mother and possibly gained him as an ally, but it was too late. Besides, she didn't want him as an ally. She simply wanted him to stay away from Trisha, and she knew she had made that clear to him last night.

Her glance trailed over his profile. Unexpectedly, Raul turned his head, meeting her look. Beneath that bland expression, she knew there was anger. His eyes were a glacier-blue, yet burning the way hot ice did. They challenged her, but Luz refused to regret the action she'd taken despite the heightened tension it had created.

"Was there something you wanted to say, Mr. Buchanan?" she murmured.

A horn blared, drawing his attention back to the road. "Perhaps you have already read my mind," Raul suggested smoothly.

"Perhaps I have." Luz faced the front as well, her chin up.

"Then there is no necessity to express my feelings on the matter," he replied. "The problem is not mine, but yours."

"What did you say, Raul?" Trisha leaned forward from the rear seat. "I didn't hear."

"Maybe because he wasn't talking to you," Luz suggested, fully aware that if Trisha learned of the warning she'd given Raul, she'd be furious.

They hadn't gotten along all that well since she'd had that argument with Drew in front of Trisha. Maybe she shouldn't have interfered in this, but she couldn't stand idly by and watch Trisha make a mistake. When she had been Trisha's age, Jake had warned off two of her boyfriends on the basis of their less than respectable reputations. Since Drew refused to intervene, Luz felt she had no choice except to handle it on her own.

"I thought maybe you were pointing out something." Trisha leaned over the top of the seat back, close to his shoulder. "Have we passed the place where you lived after you moved to Buenos Aires?"

"I lived many places." The skyline of the city's towering buildings was behind them. They had recently traveled past an attractive residential area with English-style gardens and hedges, and now had entered a crowded area of tenement blocks.

With her forearms crossed on top of the seat back, Trisha rested her chin in the cup of her fist. "I was thinking about when you were a boy and the kind of house you lived in then. It's hard to imagine you as a skinny little kid with dirty pant knees and toads in your pockets. I have the feeling your mother had her hands full with you."

"Is your mother living?" Luz wondered.

"No."

"Your father?"

"I don't know. He packed up and left one day, and we never saw him again."

It reminded her too much of her own similar abandonment and rejection by a husband she loved. The hurt it left went too deep and left too much loneliness. That was something Trisha couldn't understand. Her bitter feelings toward Drew were a touchy issue between them, and certainly not a subject she was going to pursue in front of Raul.

"Where did you attend school?" Trisha tilted her head sideways to look at him. "I'll bet you were popular with the girls."

"I know this will come as a shock to you, Trisha," Rob said, "but there are other things in life besides sex."

"There are plenty of other important ones, but it puts the life in living," she replied with a provocative candor intended to stimulate Raul's interest. With difficulty, Luz kept her mouth shut, remembering when she had said things about sex to shock people and assert her maturity.

"Where did you get that clever bit of wisdom, Trish?" Rob mocked her. "Out of some book of witty sayings?"

"At least I read, which is more than I can say for you," she retorted. "If a book isn't about horse care or polo, you never open it at all."

"I presume you don't have any brothers or sisters, Mr. Buchanan," Luz inserted with forced smoothness.

"No."

"You missed out on so much bickering." Her comment silenced the sniping pair, for the time being, at least.

The rows of tenement blocks began to thin out as they continued south. In their place, hovels sprang up like weeds. Luz stared at the acres of rusting roofs of corrugated metal sheets that slanted atop huts which appeared to be constructed from a collection of wood, sticks, and cast-off lumber. The grim shanties were crowded on top of each other with a few feet of ground in front fenced with wire, tin sheets, or rotting wood. Some were yards where children played, and others were patches of vegetable gardens. She noticed round-shaped women hauling buckets, with fat youngsters toddling behind them.

"Isn't that sad?" Trisha murmured.

"It reminds me of a refugee camp," Luz said, unable to look away from the sight.

"That is partly true," Raul said. "They are *campesinos*, rural people who come to Buenos Aires to find work in the factories, but there is no place for them to live. The government builds housing, but there is never enough for the numbers who come."

"Do they find work?" Luz wondered.

"Some. Some have enough money to live in a house or apartment if one were available. If you look, you will see television antennas on the roofs of some of the shacks. But it isn't always easy to find a job. Most of the *porteños*—the people of Buenos Aires, the port dwellers—work two, sometimes three jobs to earn a decent living. We have a large middle class in Argentina. But jobs can be scarce. There is not much left for the unskilled." His gaze strayed to the shantytown, his expression unreadable. "Still, they come—in hope. They call this *villas miseria.*"

"Isn't there somewhere else they can go?" Luz protested faintly.

"You must remember Buenos Aires is our largest city. One out of every three people in Argentina live here. We have other cities, but their populations number in the hundreds of thousands, not in the millions like Buenos Aires. It is difficult for you to comprehend the significance of that, but try to imagine a land that stretches from the Canadian provinces of Alberta and Manitoba all the way to the Yucatan Peninsula of Mexico with only one major city. That is Argentina. It is natural that someone from the rural area would look at Buenos Aires and say to himself, 'There will be work there for me.'"

"I suppose it would," she conceded.

She was relieved when the grim dwellings were left behind them. They turned onto a hard-surfaced highway that angled in a southeasterly direction across the countryside. For a time, the monotony of the scenery lulled her into indifference, vast tracts of pasture alternating with alfalfa fields or wheat and sometimes bare cropland waiting for spring seeding.

Slowly Luz became conscious of the unbroken sky all around the car. Its blue reaches were the walls and the roof over this flat floor of earth, and the flatness went on for miles, virtually treeless. The pencil-thin lines of a wire fence became an intrusion, and the pylons and blades of a windmill thrusting into the horizon seemed an event.

"This is the Pampa, isn't it?" she said.

"Yes," Raul answered.

No description of this fan-shaped prairie that spread out from Buenos Aires for three or four hundred miles had prepared Luz for this awesome sight. It was so immense, like the ocean without a shore in sight, just an unending flatness—no hills, no streams, all level ground. She breathed in deeply, her lungs filling with air, then she couldn't seem to release it, so awed was she by the bigness of the land.

Suddenly, in the far distance, she could see a long row of trees standing like a column of lonely sentinels. As they drew closer, she could make out the peaked rooflines of buildings beyond another stand of trees planted as a windbreak. The sight was alien to the surroundings, like a treed island alone in the middle of an ocean.

"What are those buildings ahead of us?" she asked Raul.

"An *estancia*."

When they drove by it, Luz saw that the double row of trees flanked the road leading to a large chateau with barns and other outbuildings. Through the clipped shrubbery, she had a glimpse of a vast lawn, but it was the nearly eight-foot-tall stand of pampas grass that caught her eye. In late summer the high clumps of long-bladed leaves would be topped by towering ivory plumes.

"You recognize the pampas grass, no?" Raul said.

"Yes." It was a plant landscapers frequently used in many of the Southern states, including Florida.

"More than a hundred years ago, all of the Pampa was covered by this tall grass."

It was a thought that staggered the imagination. The minute the *estancia* was passed, they were once again enveloped by the high, wide sky and the flat, flat land. No matter how many times they passed small farms or large *estancias*, Luz never lost that feeling of isolation—nor her fascination for this enormous Argentine prairie, its level expanse not marred by even a gully.

At a halfway point in their trip, they stopped at one of several small towns on their route to have lunch and stretch their legs. There was a sameness about these country villages, Luz discovered. The Spanish influence was evident in the pattern of a main square in the center of town, flanked by a church and a town hall housing the local authority. In addition to a movie house and cafés, there was always a railroad station. In the larger villages, there was also a statue in the square of General San Martín on horseback.

At the small café where they ate lunch, Luz was stunned by the quantity of food on her plate. "Argentina is known as the land of the stretched belt," Raul reminded her. "Like your country, we are accustomed to having plenty, which is why we are reluctant to tighten our belt even when the economy is poor."

After traveling for roughly another hour and a half, they turned off the main road onto a lane lined with towering eucalyptus trees. Their blond trunks had shed much of their stringy bark to stand like pale columns while their branches interlaced to form a living arch over the road. Until the driveway curved in front of it, all Luz could see of the *estancia*'s main house through the trees was a mass of gray stone. She stared at the two-story monolith with its double row of square windows. The photograph in the brochure seemed cheerful compared to the stark, cold dwelling before her. Nothing relieved the severity of its straight lines.

When Raul stopped the car, Luz hesitated before climbing out. She carefully refrained from making any comment about the house, but she suspected her host had sensed her dislike of it as he escorted the three of them inside. Her eyes had barely adjusted to the gloom of the large entry hall when she heard the strike of crutches on the hardwood floor. Turning, Luz saw a crippled gray-haired man wearing leg braces approach them.

"Welcome to Le Buen Viento," he greeted them with a wide friendly smile.

"May I present Hector Guerrero." Raul made the necessary introductions, then said, "Hector will show you to your rooms. If you will excuse me." He dipped his head politely.

"Of course," Luz murmured, although she knew he wasn't asking her permission.

A moment later, there was the sound of the door closing, then Hector Guerrero claimed her attention. "If you will follow me, I will take you to your rooms. The house, she is big and old, but it is easy to find your way in it."

Using one crutch for a pivot, he turned and headed toward a massive wooden staircase leading to the second floor. Luz had a brief glimpse at some of the other ground-floor rooms. All seemed austere with their bare walls and ponderous furniture. She had little hope their rooms would be better. And they weren't.

# CHAPTER XVIII

"Good morning, Hector." Luz paused as she entered the large dining room. The wizened, mustached man was the only person seated at the long table. "It seems that I'm the last one down."

*"Buenos días, señora."* The man's cracked and lined face resembled a saddle exposed too long to the elements, but a smile broke across it when he saw her. "You slept well, yes?"

"Yes." She saw him slip his arms into the metal bands of his crutches and heard the dragging scrape of his leg braces. "Please don't get up, Hector," she insisted and crossed to the coffee urn sitting atop the long bureau. A depleted stack of cups and saucers and the accompanying cream and sugar servers sat beside it.

But the old man didn't listen to her and hauled himself upright, putting most of his weight on the crutches instead of his paralyzed legs. He reached down and locked the braces that permitted him some mobility.

"You will want some breakfast," he said when he straightened. His iron-gray hair was thick and curly, salted with white like the thick brush of his mustache. "I will get Anna to bring a plate for you."

"No, Hector," Luz said quickly to halt that rocking swing of each hip to propel a braced leg forward while he maintained his balance with the crutches. He managed to move agilely, but it looked awkward to her. "Coffee is all I want this morning." Slightly uncomfortable with his handicap, she faced the coffee urn and placed a cup under the spigot.

"Señora, it is no trouble," he replied as if guessing part of the reason for her refusal.

"Honestly, I'm still full from dinner last night," she assured him while letting her cup fill with coffee. "The food was very good."

"*Gracias, señora*. Ramón, the cook, will be most pleased." He altered his course and maneuvered toward her in his waddling walk. "Sunday, we fix *asado*, a big feast for when the others come. You have had this, no?"

"No, I haven't." Luz picked up her cup and added cream to the strong brew, aware that Hector was referring to the impending arrival of the other polo students. She understood there were to be ten in all, counting Rob. Some were spending only two weeks and a few were remaining a month. Considering the fees for the program, it represented a respectable income.

"*Asado* is a roasted meat cooked over an open fire." He touched his fingers to his lips, kissing them, in a gesture that seemed more Italian than Spanish. "You will like it."

"It sounds delicious." Luz sipped at the steaming coffee, still hot despite the addition of rich cream.

She wasn't exactly sure of Hector Guerrero's position at the *estancia*. When she was first introduced to the crippled man the day before, she had thought he was probably a charity case, someone Raul had felt sorry for and invented a job for to make him feel useful. But from what she had observed since, that impression was wrong. Hector appeared to be something of a general factotum, the majordomo of the house as well as stable manager—or at least he was extremely familiar with the operations of both.

After Hector had shown them to their rooms, he pointed out the location of things, informed them about the household routine—mealtimes, the maid's cleaning hours, and so on—and saw that their luggage was taken to their rooms by one of the stablehands. Last night he had dined with them and talked at length to Rob about individual horses in the stable. Not that Raul showed ignorance about any of these things. He hadn't. The impression was they were not his responsibility.

Obviously, when Raul was gone, someone had to run the place. Luz was simply surprised by his choice, although her opinion of Hector was being revised. He was friendly and talkative and had a good command of English. His age was impossible to guess, but she suspected it was ten years on either side of sixty.

"Where has everyone gone?" she asked. Breakfast had been scheduled between seven and eight, and it was only a few minutes before the latter.

"Señor Rob, he was anxious to see the horses." With a swing of his crutches, he turned toward the table and forced his legs to follow. He stopped next to a chair and supported himself on one crutch to pull it out for her. *"Señora, por favor."*

*"Gracias."* It was one of the few Spanish words she knew.

"They have gone to the stables," Hector explained as he hopped backward two steps after she was seated. "I will take the señora there when you have finished, if you wish."

"Yes, I would like to see the horses, too." She wished Rob hadn't been so impatient. They had all planned to go together this morning, which was why she had dressed in her riding pants and boots and worn a thick pullover sweater against the morning coolness. She listened to the sequences of thumps and drags as Hector walked to the coffee urn. "I presume Rob went with Raul . . . I mean, Señor Buchanan."

"Raul is easier, no?" Carrying the coffee cup made his return trip to the table much slower. Luz resisted the impulse to carry it for him. As she'd witnessed on several occasions last night, Hector preferred doing things himself regardless of how awkwardly he did them. "He is Raul. I am Hector. We are all friends."

"Then I am Luz," she said, responding to his friendly overture.

He set his cup down on the table, then paused with his hand on a chair back to glance curiously at her. "Luz, this is a Spanish name."

"It is? Actually, my name is Leslie. When I was born, my older brother couldn't say it correctly. He kept calling me *Luz*lie, and it stuck," she explained.

"Ah," he said with a slow nod of his head. "In Spanish, it means 'light.' María de la Luz, that is how my aunt was called. It translates to Mary of the Light."

"I have never heard the name," Luz admitted.

"You are not Argentine. You are *yanqui.*" He grinned, a row of snowy white teeth showing beneath the curving salt-and-pepper mustache. He pulled out the chair, then maneuvered sideways to sit down.

"Did my daughter go to the stables with them?" She hadn't

checked to see whether Trisha was in her room before coming down.

"*Sí, la señorita,* she goes, too." Hector sipped noisily at the scalding hot coffee, cooling its temperature as he sucked it in. "The coffee is good."

"It is." Luz took another drink from her cup.

"But it is better when someone else is at the table in the mornings. When Raul is gone, I don't drink so many cups."

"How long have you known Raul?"

"Many years. Before this." He slapped his hand against a lifeless thigh to indicate his paralysis.

"What happened?" Luz immediately regretted the impulsive question. "You don't have to answer that if you'd rather not talk about it."

"*No importa.*" With a wave of his hand, he assured her he didn't mind. "This man, he wants me to break this young horse to ride. He is crazy, this horse. When I get on, he throws himself back." Hector mimed the action of a rearing horse falling over backward, then shrugged with an open-handed gesture. "I jump the wrong way. He falls on my legs, and they die."

"It must have been very difficult for you." Self-consciously she clasped her hands around the cup, not knowing what to say without it sounding like pity.

"*Sí.*"

"I can't imagine what it would be like not to ride, let alone walk unaided," she admitted.

"I can still ride, señora . . . Luz," he corrected himself with another wide smile. "I must strap these useless legs to the saddle, but I can ride a horse. I can no longer train them to play polo, but it is enough to be in the saddle."

"You trained horses? Then you must have played polo with Raul. Is that where you two met?"

"I have played with Raul when there was no one else. I was a good *entrenador*—trainer—but not a good player. Training a green horse is a talent of its own. A good polo player may not be able to teach a horse how to be a good pony, but he knows how to ride one. *Comprende?*"

"Yes. Teaching requires a patience that an expert will not necessarily have." Luz smiled, never having considered that aspect before. "Then how did you two meet?"

Hector studied her for several seconds, the dark glint in his eyes assessing something. "We worked for the same man. I trained his horses. Raul was a groom in his stables. It was a long time ago."

"Before he started playing polo," she realized.

"*Sí*. Then later, when he was rated in high goals and people paid him money to play on their team, he bought his own horses to ride and I trained them. Many times, I traveled to Norte América and England with him to look after the horses. Then Raul wants to buy land so he can keep horses and raise them. When we look, we find this place. We want to buy only the land, not this big, gray elephant." The wave of his hand indicated the massive dwelling they were in, and Luz smiled at the appropriate description of the hulking manor. "The man would not sell only the land, so Raul buys this, too. He had been giving polo lessons to players at clubs, so we started this school."

"That's quite a story, but there must be more. You've only given me the highlights." Luz doubted that it had been as easy as he made it sound.

"It is Raul's story. I should not tell it for him," Hector said after hesitating, giving the impression that perhaps he thought he had said too much already.

A burning log crumpled in the fireplace, making a little crashing sound that was followed by the renewed crackle of flames. Luz glanced at the ponderous oak mantel that crowned the stone fireplace. The log blaze gave off enough heat to take the night chill from the room and added a cozy touch to the otherwise austere decor.

There were fireplaces in all the rooms Luz had seen, including the bedrooms, providing the only source of heat for the great stone house, which was not equipped with a central system. For the most part, the mild climate didn't seem to demand it. After seeing the house, Luz understood Raul's cautions about the living accommodations. The house had all the comforts but few of the luxuries.

The rooms were sparsely furnished, containing only the basics—like this dining room with its long table that seated twenty and the massive sideboard along one wall for serving dishes. Nothing broke the severe blankness of the wallpaper covering the top half of the hip-paneled room, except for one wide mirror and the climbing stone of the fireplace. There was even a starkness about the large chandelier, suspended from the ceiling by a heavy brass chain, its curved wooden arms holding etched-glass chimneys shaded with brass. The fireplace mantel was unadorned, and only a brass stand for the poker, broom, and shovel stood beside it.

This same plainness was repeated throughout the house, and the overall effect was impersonal. In Luz's opinion, there was a marked absence of trophies and prizes or photographs. Raul might live and work here part of the year, but it wasn't his home. She remembered the den in her own home, and the way Drew had surrounded himself with his own things—an extra set of law books, golf tees on the desk, a putter in the corner, photographs of the children, and a tennis trophy prominently displayed. He had imposed his personality on the room, but Raul hadn't done that here.

Her curiosity was aroused. Luz drank the last of her coffee and set the cup in its saucer. "As many rooms as this house has, I expected Raul to have a trophy room displaying all the prizes he's won and photographs of famous people he'd played with during his career. Is there one and I haven't seen it?"

"There is no trophy room," Hector told her. "I tell Raul— in the head, you must know you're good."

"That's true." But she wondered if Hector objected to the idea, regarding it as bragging.

"Of course, Raul he is not satisfied with good. No, for him, it has to be *perfección*, nothing less," he said and sighed.

"I don't understand." Luz frowned.

"He chases the ten, señora," he explained quietly, almost sadly, referring to the highest status a polo player could obtain—a ten-goal rating.

"I see." But she wasn't sure that she did, even though she knew it had been attained by only a rare few in the history of the sport.

"More coffee, Señora Luz?"

"No, thank you." She pushed the empty cup and saucer away from her, indicating that she was finished. "Whenever you're ready, I'd like to go to the stables."

"*Uno momento, por favor*. I will tell Anna where we will be." He levered himself out of the chair, adjusted his crutches and leg braces, and left the room by a side door.

After he'd gone, Luz lingered in the dining room for a few minutes, then walked into the large entry hall to wait for him. Her boots made a hollow sound on the polished hardwood floor when she crossed it. The swinging pendulum of a tall, scarred wooden clock ticked off the seconds, its rhythmic ticking loud in the silence. Her glance traveled over the large hall with its open stairwell to the second floor, again noting its bareness that the clock, an area rug inside the front door, and a side table couldn't alleviate.

She tried to shake off the observations she'd made about Raul's personal life. It was no concern of hers how he lived or what the details of his background were.

She heard the sound of Hector's approach and turned to meet him. No hat covered his curly gray hair, but he wore a light jacket, the curved metal bands of his crutches puckering the sleeves where they half-circled his forearms. Luz noticed how broad and muscled he was in the trunk and shoulders— and how skinny and emaciated his legs appeared, little more than tapering sticks jutting against the pantleg material and stiffened with metal braces. Yet there was nearly always a smile shining from his dark eyes.

"We are ready," he announced and insisted upon opening the door for her.

Outside, Luz paused to wait for Hector to join her. The two-story house towered behind her, a huge rectangular box of massive gray stone blocks, unrelieved by decorative elements. No shutters framed the square windows and no overhang shaded the top row of stone. The low plantings in front of the house could not break the intimidating severity of its form.

"It needs a shawl of ivy," Luz decided.

Hector leaned on his crutches to look back at the house. "It needs something."

As they started out, Luz shortened her stride to compensate for his laborious walk, but it wasn't necessary. Hector moved out at a normal pace, forcing Luz to hurry to catch up with him.

They followed the eucalyptus-lined driveway that curved close to the house, then swung around the side of it. A tennis court and pool were located behind the house on a grassy expanse of lawn, a stand of poplars providing a windbreak for the house. It was unlike the layout at Hopeworth Farm; the outbuildings of the *estancia* were not separated from the main house by a wide green belt. A row of trees shielded the stables from obvious view, but it was a living fence that divided the house lawn from the stableyard.

As they approached the stables, Luz noticed the polo field on the opposite side of the road, and farther on a practice field before the paddocks began. The road looped through all this and came out on the other side of the house, Hector informed her, where the sheds for the haying machinery and other vehicles and trailers were located.

Luz spied Rob first, inspecting a flashy bay horse held by a young groom in front of the first stable row. Raul stood to one side, holding the lead to a chestnut that Trisha was petting. She saw the way Trisha was looking at him. "Making eyes at him" seemed such an appropriate phrase. Irritated, she pressed her lips tightly together.

Hearing their approach, Raul straightened. "Good morning."

"Good morning." She managed a smile, although it cooled some when she directed it at her daughter. "You're up and about early this morning, Trisha."

"I couldn't sleep." She shrugged. "New surroundings, I guess." But her glance strayed to Raul, as if he were the real cause for her sleeplessness.

"I trust you slept well last night, Mrs. Thomas," Raul said. "And that your accommodations were not too unsatisfactory."

"My room is very comfortable, thank you." Her glance skipped over him as she tried not to notice the rough weave of his slate-blue sweater or the way it gave bulk to his leanly muscled torso.

"You haven't tried the shower yet," Trisha declared, a wicked light dancing in her eyes. "When I went to take mine this morning, it nearly scared me out of my wits. I turned the faucets on and the water pipes started rattling and clanging so loudly I had visions of the bathroom being flooded. Nothing happened, but it's the first time I've ever been serenaded by a shower. Although I have to admit it was wonderful. There was tons of hot water. I could have stayed under there for hours."

Luz was disgusted at the way Trisha encouraged Raul to form mental pictures of her naked in a shower. She considered it a tasteless and cheap ploy.

"The plumbing in the house is old," Raul said.

"The house is old," Luz inserted, criticizing its condition instead of her daughter's behavior, which she refused to do in front of him.

"I did warn you, Mrs. Thomas, that you might find conditions here less than luxurious," Raul reminded her stiffly.

"It wasn't really a complaint, merely an observation, Mr. Buchanan," she informed him coolly and turned away, encountering Hector's puzzled look as she did so. "Would you ask the groom to walk the bay horse around for me, Hector? I'd like to see how he moves."

The request was repeated in Spanish, and the teenage groom led the flashy animal in a wide circle. "You know horses, Señora Luz?" Hector wondered aloud.

"Believe me, she does," Rob stated positively, and the pride he took in her knowledge gave a much-needed boost to her ego.

They spent the morning looking over the selection of polo ponies for sale and deciding which ones Rob definitely wanted to ride before making a final decision. At noon, they returned to the house for lunch. Afterward, Raul had horses saddled for all of them and they rode out to the pastures to look at some of his young stock.

As they cantered through the tall grass toward the distant herd of grazing horses, Luz felt her horse tug at the reins. She eased the pressure on the bit, letting the animal increase its stride and draw slightly ahead of the others. The freedom of the wind in her hair and the vastness of the horizon were powerful sensations. She longed to gallop her horse until she came to the end of that earth and sky.

As she approached the herd of young horses, they spooked friskily and began a mock stampede, charging away from her. Sighing with regret, Luz reined in her horse and stopped to watch as the mixture of yearlings and two-year-olds wheeled and came racing back to investigate the intruders in their pasture, curiosity overcoming their mock flight. She heard the muffled pounding of hooves coming up behind her as the others rode up to join her, but the limitless land claimed her attention. Its distance strained her eyes, almost making them ache with its immensity.

When a horse and rider came alongside her, Luz didn't even

turn to look. "Tell me, Hector, how do you resist the urge to gallop as long and as far as you can across this land?"

"It is difficult," Raul answered her, and she stiffened at the sound of his voice, her gaze running to him in surprise. Ever since they had started out from the *estancia*, Hector Guerrero had ridden at her side. "You are enjoying your ride," he observed, and Luz guessed her face was still flushed with the pleasure of that fast canter. She scraped a strand of windblown hair off her cheek.

"There's just so much open country," she said. "Texas is flat, but it's nothing like this."

"No. The Pampa is special. Every Argentine, whether he is born in Patagonia, the Andes, Buenos Aires, or the Chaco, feels an identity with it. For one born here, there is no other place."

"Were you born in the pampas?"

"*Sí*. Many miles from here." Raul's horse sidled into her liver-colored chestnut, and his booted leg rubbed against her. "*Che!*" he exclaimed and spoke sharply to his mount in Spanish. The horse shifted away and the contact was broken, but for Luz the sensation lingered.

When Trisha rode up on the other side of Raul, the vague truce that had seemed to exist between them ended. "What do you think of the young ones, Luz?" She stood up in her saddle for a better look at the horses as a brave yearling trotted toward them, reared in a mock feint, then dashed back to the safety of the group.

"*Sí*," Hector said, encouraging her to give her opinion. "You have an eye for the young ones, Señora Luz."

"I think you have me mixed up with Raul," she murmured tautly and squeezed with her legs, ordering her mount forward at a walk to take a closer look at the young stock.

"Ahh." The long, comprehending sound came from Hector, then he slid a knowing glance at Raul and said in Spanish, "Now I know why she spits at you like a tiger cat protecting her kitten. She thinks you will harm it."

"She is wrong," Raul responded in the same language, aware their exchange in Spanish was attracting Trisha's attention. "I am not interested in her kitten."

"In the tiger cat, perhaps?"

"*No. Los caballos*," he snapped.

"*Caballos*—horses," Trisha translated. "I know that one. It appears I'm going to need a Berlitz course in Spanish."

"It was rude to converse in Spanish when you cannot understand the language. My apologies," Raul said, reverting to English.

"It's all right. I just always wonder if I'm the one being talked about." She smiled, unconcerned, and turned to watch her mother approach the young herd, guiding her horse in a long arc that steadily swung closer to the yearlings.

"Your mother, she is good, señorita," Hector said.

"Luz is great at handling horses, but she's lousy with people."

"Maybe that's because you can trust horses," Rob suggested dryly. "People can hurt you, but horses can only break your bones."

Raul saw the quick glance Trisha darted at Hector. "Rob, you are tactless."

"No, señorita, Señor Rob, he is right," Hector inserted, pointing to his lifeless legs strapped to the saddle. "This does not hurt me as much as unkind remarks about a cripple."

"I'm sorry, Hector," Rob mumbled, his neck reddening. "I wasn't thinking."

"Sometimes I wonder if you ever do," Trisha accused.

Raul ignored their bickering to watch Luz work her horse close to the herd of young animals, then stop to study them. She was good. The wind ruffled her hair and let it catch the gold of the sun. He remembered how vibrant and flushed with excitement she'd looked when he'd first ridden up, her gaze fixed on the land. It was an image that stayed in his mind.

It was late afternoon when they rode back to the *estancia* and left their horses with the grooms at the stables. At the house, Luz went directly to her room to shower and change before dinner. She paused inside and leaned against the door to look about the plain room.

The double bed had a heavy carved headboard and foot rails. There was a nightstand and lamp beside it. A straight-backed chair sat in the corner, and a tall chest of drawers stood against an otherwise bare wall. Fresh logs and kindling were arranged in the brick fireplace, waiting for a match. The stark, ivory-plastered walls were outlined by heavy, stained molding and wood trim. The braided rug on the floor next to the bed was the only real patch of color in the room.

She pushed away from the door and walked over to the bed, where she sat down and tugged off her riding boots. In her mind, she kept seeing Raul lifting Trisha down from her horse after they'd all ridden into the stableyard. Trisha had asked for his help in dismounting, which made it all the more frustrating.

With her boots off, Luz stripped out of her clothes and left them piled on the chair seat, then entered the connecting bathroom she shared with Trisha. The noisy water pipes reminded her of this morning's incident when Trisha had been so provocative, telling Raul about the shower. Luz didn't remain under the hot spray for long, not caring for the knocking, banging song of the water pipes.

After wrapping the long towel around her like a sarong, Luz opened the connecting door to her room. Her glance fell on the empty chair seat where she'd left her riding clothes. A noise came from the closet area. When Luz turned toward the sound, the housemaid, Anna, who bore a striking resemblance to Brunhild, stepped out. Her hand went to her chest in a gesture of shocked surprise when she saw Luz standing there.

"I put clothes," she explained in her halting English, thickly Spanish in accent. "Okay?"

"*Sí. Gracias.*" Luz came the rest of the way into the room and shut the door.

"*Por favor.*" Anna appeared to struggle for the English words and stalked over to the nightstand where a glass filled with ice and a pale brown liquid sat on a tray. "*Maté.* Tea." With her hand she gestured toward Luz, indicating it was for her.

"*Gracias,*" she said again.

"*De nada.*" Her curtsying bob appeared out of character. The big-boned, big-bosomed woman backed to the hall door, then turned and left.

Luz walked over to the nightstand and took a drink of the iced *maté*, a native herbal tea laced with lemon. She had tasted it the previous afternoon when Hector had provided refreshments for them after they arrived. Then she crossed to the closet and traded her towel for a robe.

A door opened and closed in the outer hallway. When she heard someone moving about in Trisha's room, Luz hesitated, then walked to the door of the connecting bath and went through to the opposite door.

"Trisha?" She knocked twice, aware it might be Anna instead of her daughter.

"Yes. Come in," Trisha called in answer. "You're just in time to help me get these boots off," she said as Luz walked into the room.

Luz hesitated, then walked over to the chair where Trisha sat and tugged off first one high boot, then the other. Stepping back, she brushed the dirt from her hands.

"Thanks." Trisha peeled the sweater over her head and tossed it aside. "I smell like horse," she said, sniffing at her hand. "That shower is going to feel good. I hope you didn't use all the hot water."

"Trisha, I want to talk to you," Luz began.

"About what?" Trisha unsnapped her pants and zipped down the fly.

"About the shower, for one thing," she snapped, irritated by her daughter's indifference to her presence.

"It's noisy, isn't it?" She laughed and sat down in the chair to kick off her jeans.

"Trisha, I'm serious."

"About the shower?" She looked at her skeptically, and Luz wondered if she was deliberately being obtuse, or whether she was simply making a mess of this discussion.

"No. Not about the shower. About the way you're behaving around Raul. You're making a fool of yourself, Trish." She saw the hard, stubborn light flash in Trisha's eyes and knew she was taking the wrong tack. She had not intended to start out by accusing. She had wanted to explain—to reason.

"Is that right?" Trisha challenged.

"Yes." Luz attempted to get control of her anger. "I don't think you realize how obvious you look and sound. I find it embarrassing."

"I don't know why you should."

"It's one thing to ask a man to help you off a horse you're perfectly capable of dismounting, but it's quite another to talk about taking a shower. You deliberately invited him to imagine what you look like stark naked in a shower. I'm sure you think it's cute and provocative to arouse a man's interest like that, but I find it coarse and tasteless."

"You do?"

"Yes, I do!" she declared angrily.

Clad only in bra and panties, Trisha stood in front of her and rested her hands on her hips. "What makes you think Raul hasn't already seen me naked, Luz?"

Shock drained the blood from her face. "You're lying." But that cocky look in Trisha's eyes made her doubt that.

"Am I? Why don't you go ask Raul?" she invited.

Luz backed away from her, then turned sharply and retreated to her bedroom. The minute she stopped, the trembling started. She couldn't believe it. Somehow she had been so certain that this was all one-sided. But she always knew when Trisha was lying. And that hadn't been a lie.

She closed her eyes, and her head swam with images of Trisha and Raul lying naked together. She recoiled from those mind pictures. She didn't want to visualize them together. She didn't want it to be true.

She started laughing and crying at the same time. After all this time, she had still been subconsciously entertaining hopes that someday he might hold her. That face was still part of her secret fantasies.

It was so terribly ironic—so hilariously sad. The first man to arouse her interest after the divorce was involved with her daughter.

It hurt. It hurt almost as much as losing Drew. There wasn't any new beginning, just a repetition of the past. Luz walked blindly to the bed and sank onto the quilt-covered mattress. She rocked back and forth, silently crying. She could never accept this situation between Trisha and Raul. The jealousy would always be there, making it hell. She didn't know what to do. Her life was so confused. If this was what it was like to grow old, she'd rather be dead.

# CHAPTER XIX

The sun warmed the half of her face not shaded by the brim of her lacquered straw hat as Luz stood on the sidelines and watched the action on the polo field. With the afternoon temperature soaring to springtime heights, she had removed her ivory-and-gold sweater and let it hang down her back, tying the sleeves in front. She was conscious of its heavy weight pulling on her shoulders, but it wasn't the cause of her leaden spirits.

A horse and rider broke away from the player they were guarding and charged the oncoming ball. It was Rob who was playing the Number Four position as defensive back for the white-shirted team. He'd had the inside position on the opposing forward, perfectly placed to turn back any pass to a red-shirted rider. Instead he had turned to meet the ball, leaving the player free and the goal exposed. It was an incautious move that Luz viewed with dismay. He had only one chance at the ball, and if he missed . . . but he didn't. He made a splendid neck shot, driving the ball upfield toward the center.

The bold save was taken from him as the ball landed directly in front of an opposing player. He lofted it toward the goal, where his free-running forward had an easy knock-in for the score. Rob was too far out of position to prevent it.

"Rob, why did you do that?" Luz murmured critically, regarding his deflated posture in the saddle as rightfully deserved.

"It is always this way, Señora Luz." Hector Guerrero stood a few feet from her, most of his weight centered on one crutch. A stopwatch was in his other hand, and a whistle hung at the end of the cord tied around his neck. He was acting as the timekeeper, scorer, and the third man, the referee on the sidelines who casts the deciding opinion when the two umpires on the field disagree on a foul or the point at which it occurred. "When new riders play the first game here, they always try to prove how good they are. Raul says he has eight men on the field playing solo polo. That is why he always has them play a game before the training starts so they can show off for him and he can see all the things they do wrong. When one tries too hard, one often looks foolish."

"That's true." She smiled wanly at his consoling remarks.

Yesterday, Saturday, had been the arrival day for the rest of the students participating in the polo program. "Students" was a misleading word, since most of them were in their early to late twenties and two were over thirty. The class was international in scope, composed of four Argentines, a Mexican, a German, two Americans, the son of an Arab sheik, and a Texan. The polyglot conversation at dinner last night had been confusing for nearly everyone. Fortunately English was the language in which they could all make themselves understood—eventually.

A fluttering of white near the picket lines caught her eye, and Luz turned her head slightly to identify the source. Trisha had wandered in that direction some time ago, although she wasn't in sight now. The flash of white had come from the two Arabs, garbed in their native flowing caftans and ha'iks, who had accompanied Hanif, the sheik's son. Luz wasn't sure whether they served as his bodyguards, valets, or what, but one of them was always present wherever the Oxford-educated Hanif was. Scanning the picket line, she finally noticed Trisha sitting on the ground talking to the red-shirted Texan Duke Sovine.

A horse and rider crossed her line of vision, then cantered toward the sideline. Luz recognized Raul and felt the wary tautness take hold of her. But he didn't look her way, directing his attention at Hector as he reined his horse in with a barely perceptible check on the bit.

It was difficult not to admire the continuous flow of invisible communication between the hard-breathing horse and the man on its back. Raul said something in Spanish to Hector, who looked at the stopwatch, then responded. Without a break in the animal's stride, he turned the horse in a tight arc and rode to the center of the field, where the players were gathering. In this game, Raul was an umpire, not a player.

"Only three minutes left," Hector said to Luz. "It will be over soon." She nodded to acknowledge she'd heard him, but continued to watch Raul, her errant thoughts visualizing those wide shoulders and tapered back without a shirt—as Trisha must have seen them. "He rides as one with the horse, no?"

Startled, Luz glanced at Hector and realized he'd noticed her watching Raul. Quickly, she looked back at the field, struggling against the sudden self-consciousness. "Yes, he does."

"Do you know the legends of our gauchos? It is said they were half man and half horse. Your cowboys, they caught the cows with *la reata*. The gaucho, he rode his horse at a full gallop after a wild cow, then cut the hamstring with the blade of his lance. The quickness of the hand and the eye and the horse, all one, it is like polo, no?"

"Yes. *El señor de nada*," Luz remembered—too well perhaps. After seeing the pampas, it would seem that he was a mounted lord who ruled nothing, and therefore possessed only the arrogance of a lord.

"You have heard the stories." Hector smiled at the discovery.

"Not really. That was just something I picked up somewhere."

The ball was thrown in by Raul, and the last minutes of play were resumed. Thankfully, Rob made no more blatant errors in judgment that Luz observed, but neither did he have the consolation that someone else did during those final minutes, and so his remained the freshest. When the game ended, he separated from the other players and rode off the field by himself.

"*No se olvide*—do not forget," Hector said to Luz as she started to move away, intent on joining Rob. "We have the big feast in one hour. Then you will taste the *asado*."

"I'm looking forward to it." She was aware of all the preparations for this festive Argentine-style barbecue that had kept the household staff busy all morning. The smell of smoke from the open fires was in the air, and its gray trail was visible above the treetops surrounding the back lawn. But there were simply too many other things on her mind for Luz to take more than a passing interest in it all.

After leaving Hector, she crossed the dirt road that separated the polo field and the stables, angling to intercept Rob while allowing him time for self-castigation. When she met up with him in front of the stables, he dismounted and handed the reins of his horse to a waiting groom. He turned toward Luz, but didn't look at her as he pounded the mallet head on the ground a couple of times, his helmet and riding crop in his other hand. The disgusted expression on his face showed, as plainly as his action, his anger at himself. She didn't need to say anything.

"I thought I could do it," he muttered, keeping his voice down so that the other returning players couldn't hear him. "I knew I could make that shot. If Juan had been in a position to pick it up, we could have had an easy score."

"You were the defensive back. You have to remember the duties of your position. Your priority is to protect the goal, to stop your opponent from scoring, not to set up a score for your side. You left your man uncovered, with none of your other three teammates between him and the goal. You took a risk, and backs aren't supposed to gamble."

"Yeah." His glance flicked to the right of her, traveling upward. "I made one hell of an error, didn't I?"

Realizing he was talking to someone else, Luz turned. There had been so much activity around her, riders dismounting, grooms leading horses, and players walking by, she hadn't paid any attention when a horse and rider stopped nearby. As she met Raul's steady gaze, it was evident that he had overheard her lecture on position responsibilities. He towered beside her on horseback, tall and imposing.

"I have no quarrel with any of your mother's statements. You did leave the goal undefended. However, you committed a greater error when you hit the ball," Raul stated. "Where did you intend it to go?"

Rob hesitated, not certain what the right answer was. "Up-field."

"But to no one in particular?"

"No," he admitted.

"That is your error. A player should never indiscriminately hit the ball. Either it should be a pass to a teammate or an attempt at a goal. When you hit the ball, you must always aim it. Know where your teammates are and pass to them. Always try to get the ball to a teammate. Possession and control of the ball are the best way to defend a goal."

"You're right." Rob appeared disgusted with himself for not seeing something that now sounded so obvious.

At the same time, Luz realized that she'd been put in her place. What she'd said had been correct—as far as it went. And Raul had subtly made it clear her knowledge was limited.

"You have come here to learn, Rob," he reminded him, then touched a blunt spur to his horse's side, sending it forward.

Her gaze followed him across the stableyard. She was stinging slightly from the encounter although fully aware Raul had not belittled her in any way. Still, he made her advice sound if not wrong, then incomplete.

Then Luz saw Trisha catch the reins of his horse near the bridle and stop him. She laughingly said something to him which Luz couldn't hear. Raul dismounted and loosened the cinch of his saddle. The sight of the two of them together, no matter how aloof to Trisha Raul appeared, was more than she could stand. She turned.

"I'm going to the house," she said to Rob.

"I'll see you there later." He moved off in the direction of his fellow students, now able to face them after his enlightening talk with Raul. And Luz felt a vague resentment at the importance he was gaining in Rob's eyes.

The bonfires on the back lawn continued to blaze long after the meat was roasted, warding off the early-evening chill and throwing light at the encroaching shadows. Sitting at the long table placed outside, Luz looked at the plate in front of her, still mounded with food. It didn't appear as though she'd eaten a bite, but her stomach knew better. She shook her head ruefully. The ends of her hair, falling loose about her shoulders, brushed against the collar of her French linen jacket striped in pencil-thin lines of dusty rose and pink alternating with bands of parchment.

"I honestly can't eat any more," she declared, wiping her hands on the cloth napkin. "There is enough food on my plate for four people."

"We try to fatten you up." Hector sat across from her, his white teeth gleaming beneath his mustache. "Did you like *el asado?*"

"*Muy bueno.* Did I say that right?"

"*Sí.*" The wavering motion of his hand suggested it was

perhaps not exactly correct, but that it didn't matter. A young boy from the kitchen staff whisked her plate away, and Luz laid her napkin in its place.

"This is damned good stuff." Duke Sovine occupied the chair on her right. He sawed his knife across the roasted meat and glanced down the table at his Mexican neighbor. "Miguel, I always thought that *cabrito* you Mexicans cook was the best thing I ever tasted, but this beats it all to hell." He forked a piece into his mouth and chewed, his head moving from side to side in appreciation of its savory flavor. "I gotta find out how they do this so I can tell Angie. Angie's my wife," he explained to Luz.

The drawling, loquacious Texan was the oldest of the group at thirty-two, the son of one of the big independent oil producers in the state. There was a big gold ring on his finger designed in the shape of Texas with a two-carat diamond in the center to symbolize the Lone Star State. Polo was a hobby to him, but like most, he was hooked on it.

"That woman throws some of the biggest and best barbecues Houston has ever seen. She loves to have parties." He talked as he ate. "She wanted to come with me, but her schedule's worse than mine. She's so involved in fundraisers, the arts, and the country club, not to mention our three kids." He stopped and laid his silverware down to reach into his back hip pocket. "Gotta show ya a picture of the little ones."

Luz looked at the snapshot he removed from his wallet, wondering if he realized that in describing his wife's life, he had given an apt description of her own before the divorce. The photo showed two boys and a girl, ranging in age from three to seven, all towheads.

"They're lovely."

"Yeah, I'm kinda proud of 'em myself." Duke Sovine returned the snapshot to its plastic packet in his wallet and shoved it back in his pocket. "Lance, the oldest, has the makings of a polo player. He played in his first Little Britches game last spring. Didn't do bad."

"Rob was about that age when he started playing, too," Luz recalled.

"Ya know, Luz, I find it real hard to believe you're their mother. I figured you were an older sister. I swear, I'm just not sayin' that. You're a lovely woman," he insisted, a smile widening his square-jawed face, open and warm like the state he hailed from.

"Thank you." It was nice to hear that compliment again, although it wasn't quite as reassuring as it once had been.

"You're Jake Kincaid's daughter, aren't you?"

"That's right."

"I heard he was quite a wheeler-dealer in his day." When he leaned back from the table, nothing was left on his plate. He rubbed a hand over his stomach and glanced at the other guests sitting at the long table, their faces lighted by the candle flames burning in glass wells dotted down its length. "It's quite a group we got here."

"Very diverse." Luz avoided looking at the head of the table where Raul sat, aware that Trisha had taken a chair at that end as well.

"I don't know," Duke said, partly disagreeing. "We got Mexican oil, Argentine oil, Arab oil, and Texas oil, not to mention horsebreeders and ranchers." He rested his hands on the edge of the table, preparing to push his chair back. "'Scuse me, would you, Luz? I think I'll have a word with Hanif an' see if he can't give me a clue about OPEC's price plans for this winter."

"Go ahead." She smiled as he straightened, grabbed his beer glass, and sauntered over to the Arab's chair. Two robed figures stood like statues in the background, watching.

Behind her, Luz heard the strum of a guitar and half turned to glance over her shoulder. Three men, garbed in some native costume, stood near the outer edge of the firelight, guitars slung from their shoulders. They began softly to play a Spanish folk song.

"We have entertainment this evening," Hector said, observing her interest. "They are local musicians, but it is nice, no?"

"It is very nice," Luz agreed.

Nearly everyone at the table was finished eating, and people began to shift places, striking up conversations and getting acquainted, despite the various language barriers. Tired of sitting, Luz stood up and wandered over to Rob's chair. He was talking to Hanif about his recent visit to England and the polo matches at Windsor. She listened for a while, then spoke to the German, Gregor, about horseracing. There was a gradual gravitation away from the table toward the twin bonfires as they stood around in small clusters, talking and smoking their cigars or cigarettes.

"Luz." Trisha touched her arm, claiming her attention away from Hector and a young Argentine player. "Did you notice the clothes those men are wearing?"

"Yes." But she looked again, remembering no more than that they appeared to be wearing some sort of native costume.

"That is the traditional gaucho dress," Hector explained.

"I love it," Trisha declared. "Look at those baggy pants. They look like bloomers."

"Those are called *bombachas*." Hector paused to call to one of the musicians, in Spanish, and motioned him to join them.

The man came over, shifting his guitar to hang behind his back, and stood indifferently while Hector pointed out the details of his costume. The *chiripá*, a scarf which resembled a diaper, was strung through his legs, and the buckle of his wide belt, called a *rastra*, was made from silver coins fastened to chains. Hector asked him something, and the guitarist reached behind his back and pulled out a tarnished silver scabbard which was tucked inside his belt at the small of his back.

"This is his *facón*." Hector removed the double-edged dagger. "This was his only tool and his only weapon. He killed with it and ate with it."

"They don't still dress this way, do they?" Trisha asked doubtfully.

"Only for the tourists," Raul said dryly, wandering over to stand behind Hector. Luz could smell the pungent smoke from his small black cigar.

"The *bombachas* and the *chiripá*, they are like your cowboy boots and jeans. They still have utility, so they are worn by many of the gauchos who work on cattle *estancias*," Hector explained. "But the *hotas de potro*, they no longer wear. They were the gaucho's boots, made from the hide of a colt's hind leg. They pulled them on while the hide was still damp. When they dry, they fit tight."

"How awful." Trisha grimaced.

"And now, since wild cattle are no longer killed and slaughtered on the spot for their hides, the gaucho has no need for his lance. He uses the *boleadoras*, the thongs with balls tied at the ends, to bring down the cattle."

"I want to buy an outfit like that before I go home. I think it would look sensational," Trisha stated decisively.

"It would sure look better on you than on him," Duke Sovine said, joining them as more gathered around to see what was happening.

"You're only going to be here ten more days," Rob warned. "You'd better start looking."

"Don't remind me," she retorted.

"Won't you be remaining here with your brother?" Hanif inquired, the Oxford accent sounding foreign to his swarthy dark looks, as foreign as his ascot and blazer appeared compared to the flowing robes of his watchdogs.

"Unfortunately, no."

"Surely there is no need to leave so soon. Can't you postpone your departure and remain here at the *estancia* with us?" he suggested.

"Perhaps," Trisha replied, then tilted her head toward Raul. "But I haven't been invited."

Stealing a sideways glance, Luz watched Raul take a drag on the slim cigar he held to his mouth, squinting his eyes against the smoke. The action seemed designed to cover his silence.

"I'm sure we can change that," Hanif stated confidently.

"Ah." Hector made an approving sound and shifted on his crutches. "Everyone, we have something for you." He motioned the hovering servants forward with their trays of gourds. "It is *maté*, served the traditional way that the gaucho drank it. He brewed his tea in a gourd and sipped it through a silver straw."

As the servants passed among them, Luz took one of the gourds from the tray, then deliberately drifted to the outer fringes of the group to sip the hot herbal drink. The gaucho-clad musician rejoined his partners to lend the sound of his guitar to theirs. Trisha, instead of playing up to Raul as Luz expected, began dividing her attention among the other guests, laughing, talking, flirting, gathering them around her like hummingbirds to a bright flower. It was an obvious attempt to make Raul jealous.

Confused, Luz turned away and idly sipped the tea through the short silver tube. She wondered if they had quarreled, yet she hadn't detected any hostility between them. As a matter of fact, she couldn't recall anything loverlike in Raul's attitude toward Trisha, although knowing her disapproval, he might have concealed it when she was around.

More wood was added to the bonfires, sending up a shower of sparks. The flames crackled and blazed higher. The babble of laughter, talking voices, and the resonance of guitar music seemed to press against her. She gazed into the quiet of the gathering night and the silent shimmer of stars in a dark violet sky. She gave the tea gourd to a passing servant who was bringing drinks for some of the guests, then moved away from the fires onto the darkened lawn, slipping her hands into the slash pockets of her pink trouser-pleated pant skirt.

As she strolled aimlessly across the grass, the noise of the barbecue receded and the evening quiet settled onto her. Luz didn't try to sort through her troubled thoughts and make sense of them. She just walked. A breeze stirred in the branches of the trees that formed a windbreak around the massive house and its grounds. She wandered toward them. It was cooler away from the fires, but Luz didn't mind the nip in the air.

The shadows grew thicker along the windbreak. Luz strolled into them, idly studying the star-studded heavens above her. The ground was too flat to make her be concerned about what was in front of her. She sensed a movement, a faint rustle of sound close to the trees. Luz half expected to hear the flap of wings.

Suddenly, a man's figure loomed in front of her. She stopped abruptly, drawing back in startled alarm. "Señora." There was a low, earnest tone to the voice. *"Por favor."* When he extended his hand to her, palm up, Luz thought he was begging for money, then she caught the metal flash of a rifle barrel across his poncho.

Cold fear shot through her as she backed up a step, then turned to run. But she came up against a solid wall of flesh, and a pair of hands gripped her arms. She started to struggle blindly.

"It is all right." She recognized Raul's voice with relief, her hands relaxing to rest against his jacket. As she half turned to look over her shoulder at the dark figure, Raul said something in Spanish and the man melted into the shadows.

"I am sorry if Eduardo alarmed you."

When she turned back, Luz found Raul looking down at

her. "What was he doing there? Why was he carrying a gun?"
Her pulse still hadn't returned to its normal rate.

"I have important guests. I take precautions for their safety.
That is all," he replied smoothly. She became conscious of the
pressure of his hands on her arms and the closeness of their
bodies. She pulled her hands away from his chest and moved
away from him. Instantly, he dropped his hands from her arms.
"Perhaps we should rejoin the others," Raul suggested and
turned to escort her back to the lighted area around the bonfires.

"Precautions against what?" Luz asked.

"It has happened in previous years that people of importance
have been kidnapped. It is unlikely to occur in a rural area
such as this, but it is unwise to take risks."

Vaguely Luz remembered hearing about some kidnappings.
The victims had been executives of foreign corporations and
representatives of foreign governments. "Who does these
things?" It was more of a protest than anything else.

"Many acts of violence are committed under the guise of
politics. It is no more common here than in any other country
of the world." Raul set an unhurried pace. "These criminals
make it difficult for those who agitate honestly for change."

"And your politics?"

"I play polo." He glanced at her. "For most Argentines,
there is a feeling of indifference toward politics. They no longer
believe governments can solve all the problems. I have heard
this same thing said in your country. We have a saying: 'God
is an Argentine.' It has also been said, 'If He weren't, we'd
be worse off than we are already.' Governments come and go,
but Argentina goes on. It is like the Pampa."

"Yes." She understood what he was saying. Raul believed
in his country, not necessarily in the powers who ran it.

"I ask that you not wander off by yourself for any distance.
I don't believe you will come to any harm, but it is better not
to find out."

His request raised the specter of the dark figure that had
loomed in front of her minutes ago. Luz shuddered from a
leftover reaction to those brief seconds of fear.

"You are cold." Raul stopped. For an instant, she didn't
understand, then she saw him unhurriedly remove his jacket.

"No, I—" But he was already swinging it around her shoulders.

The material had retained his body heat. She was suffused by its warmth as her hands instinctively clutched at the overlapping folds. The smell of his cigar smoke and some tangy male cologne clung to the wool and drifted around her.

"I am accustomed to the chill," he said, as if her protest had been against depriving him of the jacket's warmth.

When Luz looked up at him, she wasn't able to speak. There was something fragile about this moment that she didn't want to break. It seemed to hold him motionless, too. She could see his eyes, their dark points enlarged by the dim light and ringed by the paler blue, and watched their slight movements as his gaze traveled over her face. Then his hands reached up and she felt the light touch of his fingers on her neck as they tunneled under her hair to lift it free of his jacket collar. A shudder of longing quaked deep inside her. Luz moved quickly before the tremblings reached the surface to betray her.

"I don't want your jacket." She opened the front and let go of one side to pull it off her shoulders, ignoring his startled frown.

"I—" He drew back when she thrust it at him.

"I said I don't want it," Luz repeated sharply and shoved it into his chest, forcing him to take it when she let go.

She walked past him toward the fire. Raul caught up with her within a few steps, his jacket on. She could sense the anger behind that long, stiff stride, and didn't care. She wasn't sure what had happened back there, or what might have happened, but she knew she couldn't stand another rejection. If there ever was another man in her life again, even briefly, she was going to be sure he wanted her, not someone else.

When they reached the firelight's circle, Luz saw that Trisha had observed their return. All those doubts and questions came flooding back to haunt her. She had to find out what was going on with them. Before she had recoiled from knowing the details. Now she wanted to know.

Crutches thumped across the ground as Hector approached. "Raul found you. I saw you—" As his glance went past her to Raul, some signal was evidently given, because the sentence remained unfinished. Instead Hector inquired, "Something to drink, Señora Luz?"

"No, thank you."

"Hey, where'd you disappear to, Luz?" Duke Sovine came up, another glass of beer in his hand.

"I just took a short stroll."

"Too noisy for you here, eh?" He grinned, then gestured to the slim mahogany-haired man with him. "You met Rusty Hanson, didn't you?"

"Yes." She smiled at the third American in the group, from Illinois.

"It's sure going to be a shame to lose the company of you two lovely ladies so soon. As a married man, I've kinda gotten used to having the company of a woman. Now these young guys"—Duke indicated the group gathered around Trisha—"they've probably got other things on their mind. They haven't quite figured out that a woman is also someone to talk to. I don't know as I'd want my daughter loose among them if she was Trisha's age, so I don't blame you for scurrying off with her."

"Actually, I won't be leaving with Trisha," Luz explained. "She has to be back to start her fall classes at college. Rob is buying some ponies while he's here, so I'll be staying a couple of weeks longer to arrange for their shipment back home."

"That's good news. Though I must say I'm surprised your husband's letting you stay gone that long."

"I'm divorced."

Duke winced. "I put my foot into that one, didn't I?"

"It doesn't matter," she assured him, and strangely it didn't.

An hour later, Luz made her excuses and went to her room. By the time she had undressed and put on her gown and robe, she heard booted feet climbing the stairs and loud male voices echoing through the halls.

After hesitating indecisively for several seconds, Luz crossed to the connecting door and went through the shared bath to her daughter's bedroom. She turned on the lamp by the bed and sat down to wait for Trisha.

The travel alarm clock, perched in its case on the bedstand beside the lamp, ticked off the time. Five minutes. Ten. Light footsteps approached the door, then the knob turned. When Trisha walked into the room, she paused briefly when she saw Luz, then shut the door.

"I should be surprised, but somehow I'm not," she said.

"We need to talk, Trisha."

"I suppose you asked Raul about me." She crossed to the window overlooking the front drive and avoided the bed. "What did he tell you?"

"I want to know what's going on," Luz insisted.

"I don't think it's any of your business."

"The other day you implied that you and Raul were, or had been, lovers. Was that true?" With an effort, she kept her voice calm while everything inside her was as taut as the ticking clock's mainspring.

"Rob may not object to the way you run his life, but I wish you'd quit messing around in mine!" Trisha turned from the window and stalked to the closet, where she dragged her night-clothes off the door hook. "Stop trying to tell me how I should behave."

Luz demanded, "I want to know how far this has gone."

"What difference does it make? What good will it do you to know?" Trisha argued, throwing her clothes in the corner chair.

"I am the one who is asking the questions, Trisha. Stop dodging them the way your father always does," she replied angrily. "Have you had sex with Raul?"

"No!" After the explosive retort, Trisha paused in the center of the room and tightly folded her arms around her middle. "But it wasn't because I wasn't willing. I did a foolish thing," she admitted more quietly. "I won't embarrass you with the details. But . . . Raul didn't take me up on my offer."

"Thank God," Luz murmured, more relieved than she had expected to be.

"After I got over the hurt, it just made me want him more. He has to care about me, otherwise he would have . . . gone ahead. I think the problem is I'm rich and he's not. I mean, look at this monstrosity of a house. You could fire a cannon through most of the rooms and not hit anything but the wall." Trisha looked around the room with critical distaste. "It's that Latin machismo. He thinks women should be seen and not heard, that wives should stay home with children. It's hard getting through that damned male pride of his."

"Listen to yourself, Trisha. Being a wife isn't what you want," Luz argued. "You told me you wanted to be a lawyer—a career woman. You wanted your life to have meaning and importance. You wanted to be more than some man's woman, raising his kids and taking care of his home. Even if you could get him, it would never work between you. He's too old to change his ways. He's too old for you."

"You're not even trying to understand, Luz," Trisha protested angrily. "I'm in love with him. When you love somebody, you can work anything out."

"No, you can't, Trisha. Your father and I loved each other, but we couldn't make our marriage work. We were too different. The only thing we had in common was you and Rob."

"It isn't the same thing."

"Isn't it? I don't think you even love him. Raul is just a challenge to you, someone you couldn't get, so now you want him."

"Oh, no," Trisha declared with a definite shake of her head. "My imagination might play tricks on me, but when he kissed me, that feeling was real."

For a minute, Luz had thought this was totally one-sided— that Trisha had nothing to base her hopes on. Obviously that wasn't true. But there was still time to stop it before it went any further.

"I'm not going to let you make the mistake I did," she stated.

"Stay out of it, Luz. I mean it," Trisha warned. "This is my life, not yours. If you want to act like a mother, then be glad that I've found someone I care about. And if my heart gets broken, be there to help me put it together again. But don't interfere."

It was wise, logical advice, Luz thought as she slowly stood up and walked to the connecting door. She paused to look back at Trisha. "You're asking me to watch you walk in front of a moving car and wait to see if it hits you. How many mothers can do that?" She stepped through the door and closed it behind her.

# CHAPTER XX

Polo classes began on Monday. After three days as a sideline observer, Luz began to have a sense of the in-depth instruction being given. Besides Raul, two other professional players, both Argentines, worked with the group. On occasion, she had gotten the impression Raul disapproved of her presence at the training sessions, regarding her as a kind of stage mother, although he had never said anything to her.

She had definitely been excluded from the rap sessions at the end of the day. They all gathered in the game room, behind closed doors. Except for Anna or some other member of the kitchen help who brought them beer or iced *maté*, no one else had been allowed into the room. Wednesday's session had lasted three hours. It wouldn't have broken up then, according to Rob, but Hector had announced dinner.

Rob said they mostly discussed position and game strategy. The green surface of the billiard table became a model of a polo field, and the balls were used to designate the players. Mistakes made during the day were gone over while they were fresh, and options were shown.

The evening routine had been something of a surprise to Luz. She had half expected a repeat of Sunday night's socializing. But all three nights, after dinner, Raul had excused himself from the group and gone into his office, where he conferred with his two other instructors for an hour, then remained to do paperwork. Trisha had gone in to see him Wednesday night, but she hadn't stayed long. Still, Luz hadn't liked the pleased look on Trisha's face when she came out.

On Thursday, the clouds that had been hanging over the

*estancia* all morning finally released their rain. It drizzled steadily. Except for occasional puddles, the ground was too flat for
the water to drain anywhere, so the six feet of topsoil on the
pampas acted as a sponge to soak up the rain.

It squished under her feet as Luz walked along the grassy
verge of the driveway toward the stables. The steady rain came
straight down, pelting the umbrella she carried. She heard the
sloshing stride of running feet coming toward her and looked
up. Duke Sovine jogged through the drizzle, his shoulders
hunched close to his neck in an attempt to let the brim of his
plastic-covered Stetson prevent the rain from running inside
his turned-up collar.

He paused when he saw her. "If you're looking for Trisha,
she's in the stable with Raul."

"Where's Rob?" After her argument with Trisha, the last
thing Luz wanted was to happen on the two of them together.
Trisha would never believe it was accidental. Up until now,
she had been encouraged by the daily routine that didn't allow
Trisha to see much of Raul. Time was running out. Next week,
Trisha would have to leave for college and they'd be half a
world apart. She hoped it would become a case of out of sight,
out of mind—eventually for herself as well.

"Rob?" He hunkered his head into the collar of his windbreaker. "At the polo pit, I think. That son of yours is real
dedicated to the sport. Practices every chance he gets."

"I know." She was proud of that. "See you later. And don't
get wet," Luz said from under the dry security of her umbrella.

"Thanks." He laughed wryly and set out for the house at
his sloshing jog.

Luz kept to the grassy edge of the driveway and skirted the
stableyard, although her gaze strayed to it. Raul and Trisha
were in one of those long, low buildings. She quickened her
stride, trying very hard not to interfere.

There were two polo pits on the *estancia*. One was located
outside and the other enclosed for use in inclement weather.
Luz headed for the small building at the end of the stable row
where the road made its circling bend.

As she entered through a side door, she heard the *thunk* of
the ball slamming into the protective netting, then the sound
of it rolling back into the pit. Raindrops tapped on the corru-

gated iron roof. She closed the umbrella and propped it against the side wall near the door.

The rectangular polo pit itself was surrounded by a wire netting stretched between four corner posts, the lower half lined with a double thickness of netting and cushioned with cloth sacking to break the force of a hard-driven ball. About halfway up the posts, the netting curved in toward the center to turn back the ball, then out again. The flooring sloped downward to a lower platform roughly eight and a half by ten. A wooden horse stood in the center, four wooden legs supporting its barrel-shaped body and a board extending from it for the head. A three-foot-wide walkway encircled the pit, providing a spectator area where the onlooker, or instructor, could watch the form of the wooden horse's rider.

Facing the netting, Luz looked into center pit, a foot and a half lower than the floor of the walkway. Rob had the mallet tucked under his arm while he stood on the floor and retied the reins to the cotton threads fastened to the end of the board "head."

"You jerked on the horse's mouth again, did you?" Luz observed.

The cotton strands broke under any strong pull or jerk on the reins, simulating an undesirable jerk on a horse's mouth while the rider hit the ball.

"Yeah," Rob grumbled as he climbed onto the saddle strapped on the wooden horse's barrel. "I can't seem to get my nearside forehand swing right."

"Are you reversing your grip?" Luz walked around to his left side so she could observe his stroking form.

"Yeah, but I keep jerking on the reins. I must have tied those bastards four times already." He tapped the ball into position for a hit on the left side, then rose in the stirrups to brace for the shot and brought his right arm over, with the mallet, arcing it behind his head.

Luz watched his swing. "The reins were too loose that time. You had no contact with the horse's mouth. And I don't think you're bringing your right arm high enough. You want your hand level with your left cheek. Your head has to move or your neck will be in the way of your swing." Rob tried it again. "That's better. Now tap the ball up the incline so you can hit it when it rolls back."

Over and over, he practiced the stroke while Luz's observations continued and she warned him against straightening his elbow too soon, swinging too late, and not bringing his hand high enough. She could see his frustration mounting when he broke the reins' strings a fifth time.

"You're getting too tense, Rob. Relax. Try some simple forehand shots, then we'll go back to it," she advised, as he dismounted to retie the reins.

"If I don't, there won't be any threads left to tie," he replied. The strands were getting shorter and shorter with each knot he tied.

With the reins secured to the "mouth" again, he stepped back into the saddle and practiced the basic strokes, sometimes hitting the ball when it rolled toward his horse and sometimes letting it go by and up the rear incline to roll back, then hitting it in a simulation of a ball being passed to him.

The overhead light was situated in the center of the peaked roof ceiling, focusing its illumination on the wooden horse and rider in the lower pit and letting the walkway receive anything left over. As a result, shadows hugged the walls. When the side door opened, the tall figure of a man was silhouetted against the gray rain. The door swung shut, and it was another second before the figure moved out of the shadows, shaking off the rain.

The thickness of two walls of netting veiled Luz's view of Raul, but she could see the wetness of his hair shining black in the overhead light and the damp patches of rain on his lightweight jacket. So far, he hadn't noticed her, and she didn't draw attention to herself when he walked to the mesh webbing around the pit. Rob drove the ball into the net with a powerful forehand swing, testing the reinforced section padded with burlap.

"I thought you were going to practice the nearside forehand." Raul frowned.

"I was. I did. I couldn't seem to put it all together, so Luz suggested that I switch to something else." The instant Rob mentioned her name, Raul's narrowed gaze sliced across the space to find her. He appeared to straighten, drawing himself up to his full six-foot height.

"Try it again," Raul ordered, and a muscle flexed along his jawline when Rob darted a quick glance at Luz.

"Sure." Rob tapped the ball to the left side of the wooden steed.

Tense, Luz watched Raul follow the walkway around the webbing, but he didn't come all the way around to where she was standing. Instead he stopped directly in front of the horse, facing Rob head-on, protected by the wall of wire netting around the pit area. Silently, he watched Rob strike at the ball.

"You are turning your body too much," he stated. "Practice the swing in slow motion. Forget the ball. Do you see where you force your bridle hand to move?"

"Yes." Rob sat back onto the saddle seat.

"Try it again, and keep the elbow bent until you have a straight line from shoulder to ball. You are trying to stiffen your arm too soon."

Three more times, he ordered Rob to practice the swing and unlearn the bad habit he'd acquired. He managed to keep from turning his body too far to the left, but he continued to straighten his arm too soon. Luz clenched her teeth together to stop herself from saying anything.

On the fourth swing, the words were forced through. "The elbow, Rob."

"Again," Raul ordered.

"I can't seem to stop it," Rob muttered angrily.

"You're trying too hard. Relax," Luz said.

"No more today," Raul stated, and retraced his path to the rear of the pit where a wood-and-mesh door opened into the pit.

"I'm not tired," Rob said.

"You can work on it tomorrow." Raul took the mallet from him, giving Rob no option.

"Come on, Rob," Luz said as she walked around the pit to the side door. "We'll go up to the house. Maybe we can talk Ramón into fixing us a cup of hot chocolate. How does that sound on this gloomy, rainy day?"

"Just the ticket." Rob smiled, but without enthusiasm, appearing to forget that when he was small, it had been his favorite.

"One moment, Mrs. Thomas," Raul said. "I would like to speak to you."

"Privately" was the unspoken word. "Go ahead, Rob." Luz

moved away from the door so he could leave. "I'll meet you at the house."

"Okay." He ducked out the door, closing it quickly behind him.

The patter of the rain on the roof sounded louder in the ensuing silence. Luz hesitated, then walked over to the pit doorway and stepped inside. Raul stood beside the wooden horse and watched her walk down the incline to the platform.

"You wanted to speak to me," she said, reminding him it was his place to begin the discussion.

"Which one of us is the polo instructor?"

"You are, of course."

"Then why are you teaching him? He cannot listen to two people at the same time. Either I am teaching him or you are. But not both of us. Do I make myself clear?" The muscles along his jaw were tautly flexed, standing out in a rigid line.

"I was only trying to help."

"Your help is not wanted." The anger that was trembling just below the surface vibrated in his voice. "You are only confusing him. Every time I say something, he looks to see if you agree. This cannot go on." His hands were tightly wrapped around the body of the stick. "I want you to stay away from the practice sessions and the training work—and from all instruction!"

Incensed by his edict, Luz crossed to the wooden horse, impelled by that inner force that demanded movement. "I am his mother! I have a right to be there. You can't forbid me to watch!" When she stopped, the wooden horse was between them.

"Do the teachers in his schools allow you to sit in their classrooms?" Raul swung around to face her, one hand letting go of the mallet to grip the neck board while the other still held the polo mallet as it rested on the curve of the saddle seat. "Are you permitted to coach him while they are giving him lessons in history or English? No! And I will not allow it here!"

"*You* will not allow?" She leaned toward him, pressing her hands against the rough board sides of the structure. "I am paying you! It is not you who dictates to me!"

Only the width of the saddle seat separated them. "Then let me do what you are paying me to do and stay away!" His eyes glittered with anger. "He does not need you to wipe his nose.

And he does not need you to tell him what is right and what is wrong. I am paid to do this." Raul drew back, the line of his mouth tight. "I have seen parents like you. You want to control everything that happens in the lives of your children. You know what is best for them, no? But what is best for them is for you to stay out!"

"Is it my son we're discussing here or my daughter?" she demanded.

"You want Rob to learn polo, do you not?" His expression became hard and cold at the mention of Trisha.

"Yes! And I want you to stay away from my daughter!"

"So you have told me. But she is the one you should be telling to stay away from me! I have no interest in her. I have been polite to the daughter of a client, and that is all. I see nothing in her worth having. Would you prefer that I treat her like the nuisance she is?" he challenged.

"Polite? Is that how you describe your actions? Just how far will you go to keep a client happy? Let's see . . . I know you've kissed Trisha and you've danced with me," Luz mocked sarcastically. "Can't you make up your mind which one of us you're supposed to please?"

His gaze narrowed on her. "Maybe I have misunderstood. Why do you wish me to stay away from your daughter?"

"Because you're too old for her. She's barely eighteen——"

"——and much too young, no?" The low tone of his voice made her wary.

"Yes, she is. I'm glad you see that." A tension that had nothing to do with her anger rippled through her as she turned and walked slowly around the rear of the wooden horse.

"And you, what of you?"

She halted, stiffening instinctively. "I don't know what you mean."

"I am old enough to be Trisha's father. And you are her mother, divorced, without a man. Lonely, I've noticed. Perhaps I did not make myself clear before you came here to Argentina. My polo skills are always for hire, but when you buy them, my services in bed are not part of the bargain."

Waves of heat seemed to engulf her. "Of all the arrogance! What makes you think I'd want you in my bed?" Hot tears burned her eyes as she angrily denied that she had ever entertained such an idea.

"That night in your hotel room in Paris, you were not inviting me to your bedroom?" he taunted.

"No! And if you remember that night very well, you'd recall that I told you to get out." Luz trembled violently from a mixture of shame and anger.

"You are not the first wealthy woman who has attempted to . . . proposition me," Raul countered.

She could feel the tears gathering on her lashes and turned to leave the pit. "There is no point in continuing this conversation," she declared thickly as she moved toward the door cut into the netting.

"You will stay away from the polo lessons in the future," he stated as she ducked through the opening.

The shadows by the wall reached out to enfold her in their concealing darkness. Luz paused by the side door. "I will do as I damned well please. And if you don't like it, Mr. Buchanan, then you can tell me to get out!"

Tears ran down her cheeks, and she bolted out the door while she still had the last word. The heavy drizzle had turned into a downpour that drenched her the instant she stepped outside. Too late, Luz remembered the umbrella propped against the wall of the polo pit. But it would take more than a soaking to make her go back in there. At the moment, she wanted to get as far away from Raul, and everything associated with him, as she could.

As she started to run across the road toward the house, a car pulled up and the driver hopped out, one of the stablehands. He dashed through the rain, slowing when he saw Luz. "*El señor?*" He gestured toward the polo pit, supplementing his question with sign language to ask whether Raul was inside. He said more, but the only word that sounded familiar to her was *teléfono*.

She nodded, her face too wet from the falling rain for him to notice the salty tears mingling with the moisture. As he continued to the polo pit, she glanced at the old car, its fenders dented and its sides splattered with mud. The motor idled, sending a blue-gray trail of vapor fumes from the exhaust. Luz ran to it and climbed quickly behind the wheel.

There wasn't any solid thought in her head except to get away. Her vision was still blurred with tears as she scanned the unfamiliar instrument panel and tried to locate where things were. The second knob she turned sent the wipers slapping across the windshield. She shifted the car into drive and stepped on the gas. As the vehicle shot forward, she heard someone shout and pushed the pedal to the floor.

Despite the driving rain and her blurring eyes, she managed to follow the muddy road that circled behind the stables and the gray stone house. She didn't want to go back there, not yet. Another road branched off from the machine sheds, taking off toward some distant point across country where the flat land and the clouds met. The open stretch pulled her, urging her to race across it—to run and run and never look back. She swung the car onto the narrow track and tromped on the accelerator again, spraying muddy water from the wheels.

The wiper blades swished frantically at the rain coating the windshield, but it didn't matter to Luz that she couldn't see. Sniffling, she wiped at the tears on her cheeks. The rain hammering on the car roof seemed to mock her flight, taunting her that she couldn't run far enough. Raul had guessed her interest in him, and she doubted that he believed her denial. It had been a mistake ever to come here.

She felt so vulnerable now, so open to more hurt, yet she didn't see how she could leave. If she changed her plans, it could be construed as an admission that he had been right all along. It *would* be an admission. She gritted her teeth to hold back the frustrated sobs rising in her throat.

The steering wheel was nearly jerked out of her hands as the front tires hit another of the many holes in the rutted track. Luz managed to hold on to it and keep the car heading straight down the muddy road. She had no sense of how far she'd come nor how long she'd been bouncing and sloshing over the track. Gray rain surrounded her, the *estancia* buildings long out of sight. She felt the pull of the mud dragging at the car and realized she didn't dare slow down.

The road had run straight across the level ground for so long that Luz had become lulled by it. When it made a bend to the right, she wasn't prepared for it. With the combination of speed and obscuring rain, she was on the curve almost before she saw it coming. She couldn't hold the car on the mud-slick track. It skidded off the road into sodden grass. Instinctively, she let up on the accelerator and turned the car in a swinging arc to get back on the muddy trail. But when the wheels hit the thick muck at the car's reduced speed, they lost traction. Without the car's momentum to compensate for the sucking drag, they started spinning. Luz tried to control the wild fish-tailing and keep the car plowing forward, but the speedometer needle kept dipping lower and lower.

Finally, the tires spun uselessly. No matter how much she gunned the motor, the car wasn't going anywhere. It was hope-lessly stuck. Luz slumped back in the driver's seat and auto-matically shifted it into park. The subdued rumble of the idling engine was drowned by the sound of the beating rain and the rhythmic slap-slap of the windshield wipers.

"Damn." She clenched the steering wheel, shaking the im-movable object in frustration while more tears scorched her eyes. "Stupid. Stupid." She cursed the imprudent decision that had taken her down this road.

Blinking to clear the hot tears from her eyes, she looked through the rain veil at the sweep of land in front and to the sides of the car. It was a desolate stretch, completely empty except for a strange-looking tree not far from the road. There was a small adobe dwelling of some sort beneath its branches, and a faint trail leading to it. It was nearly as crude as that shanty section of Buenos Aires they'd driven through. Maybe one of the *estancia* workers lived there, although Luz couldn't think why anyone would live so far from the headquarters.

The building represented an outside chance for help to get the car unstuck. The alternatives were either to wait for some-one to come looking for her or to walk back in this downpour—however far it was—to the *estancia*. Neither of those appealed to her. She'd gotten herself into this, and she'd rather get out of it on her own.

Luz switched off the motor and took hold of the door handle. After an instant's hesitation, she opened it and plunged into the sheeting rain. Her feet sank into the mire almost to the tops of her shoes. With her head down to protect her eyes from the pelting raindrops, she slogged through the mud to the side of the road and looked up once to get her bearings on the crude dwelling half hidden by the broad tree trunk. When she reached the narrow, overgrown footpath, she ran as fast as the slippery footing allowed.

The large oval leaves of the tree broke some of the rain's force once she ducked under its branches to hurry to the door.

The humid air reeked with some strong, offensive odor. Luz unconsciously held her breath as she passed the swollen base of the towering tree.

"Hello!" When she pounded on the makeshift wooden door, it bounced freely in its rotting frame. It wasn't latched. Luz hesitated only a second, then stepped quickly inside and out of the rain that had soaked her to the skin. "Hello." Her voice faded.

The leaking metal roof, the broken window panes and tumble-down benches informed her the place had been long abandoned. The door swung shut with a bang behind her and Luz jumped at the sound. Shaking the rain off her hand and arms, she moved cautiously into the middle of the one-room shack. As her eyes became accustomed to the gloom, she noticed a prim-itive-looking cot in a dark corner, covered with a lumpy straw mattress that seemed a bed more suitable for rodents than for people. A scurrying sound came from a pile of debris on the opposite side of the room, confirming her suspicions. She crossed to the window that faced the road, avoiding the pieces of glass on the tamped-earth floor. The mired car was a forlorn mud-coated lump against the iron-gray clouds.

The rain splattered loudly on the metal roof, a combination of raindrops and runoff from the crowning tree branches over-head. A steady plop-plop punctuated the heavy patter, the drips of a leaky roof. Luz lifted aside the wet hair plastered to the sides of her face and neck and pushed it back, conscious of her sopped clothes and the wet patch she was making on the dirt floor. She shivered with the damp chill invading her skin and turned, nearly stumbling over a broken chair. Its back was broken and one leg was canted at an odd angle, but its seat and three legs were intact.

It was relatively dry inside the abandoned building, and she had a place to sit. Instead of slogging back to the car in that downpour, she decided to wait in the adobe hut, at least until the rain let up. Cautiously, Luz sat down on the chair, testing its solidness. Satisfied that it would hold her weight, she hud-dled in the chair and rubbed her arms to stir her circulation.

She thought she heard a noise, and paused to listen, but it was difficult to hear anything but the incessant rattle of the rain on the corrugated metal roof. She huddled into a tight ball again. A second later, Luz was certain she heard someone shouting her name. Frowning, she stood up and moved to the window facing the road. A truck was parked behind her car.

As she turned, the door burst open. "Luz!" Raul stopped abruptly inside the door, his head coming up like an animal unexpectedly finding its quarry.

"How did you know I'd be here?" Of all the people who could have found her why did it have to be him?

"These dirt roads often become impassable in a hard rain." He stepped farther into the shack and ran a hand over his face, scraping off the rainwater. "When Carlos told me you took this road instead of driving to the highway, I knew you would have trouble. Would you prefer that I had left you stranded here alone?"

"No." Luz swung back to stare out the window and protectively hugged her arms around her middle. "It was stupid of me to drive off like that," she admitted tightly before he could say it.

"It was."

"You didn't have to agree!" She glared at him.

"If I agree, I am wrong. If I disagree, I am wrong, too. No matter which I said, I would be wrong," Raul muttered in exasperation.

"That's true, so you should have said nothing," Luz snapped, then turned aside again, aware of how bedraggled she looked with her wet hair and wet clothes. She wiped at the undersides of her eyes, afraid her mascara had run. "Since you've come to take me back to the *estancia*, let's go."

"We will wait until the rain lets up. It won't be long."

She was not as confident as he was that the rain would soon diminish. "All I want to do is get out of here. I'm wet, cold, and uncomfortable."

"And you have the disposition of a wet cat," he retorted and turned away from her.

Luz silently acknowledged that she was guilty of hissing at him like some foul-tempered feline. She struggled to control those self-protective instincts that prompted her to lash out and keep him at a distance. She watched him rummage through the pile of trash on the floor. His shirt and jacket clung to his shoulders and back like a second skin, outlining the curve of his long spine and moving with the ripple of his muscles.

"What are you doing?" she asked.

"Looking for things to burn so we can build a fire." Crouching, he pivoted on one foot to stack an assortment of rags, broken pieces of furniture, and rotting planks to one side.

"Where? There isn't a fireplace." Luz glanced around the four walls again to see if she had missed something he had seen.

"I will make the fire here." Using the rags and jagged splinters of wood for kindling, he arranged them in the center of the earth floor. "The smoke has many ways out through the holes in the roof and the windows."

The chilling dampness of her clothes raised the flesh beneath. Luz welcomed the prospect of a fire and dragged the broken-legged chair closer to the middle. As she sat down, Raul tore a long strip from a rag and used the lighter from his shirt pocket to set it on fire, then laid it atop the kindling and added large splinters and chips of rotten wood crosswise on top of that. Water dripped from the wet tendrils of his dark hair when he bent to blow on the spreading red embers. Luz resisted the impulse to reach out and smooth those wet-black strands off his forehead. She concentrated her attention instead on the tiny flame darting around the wood.

"I thought somebody lived here," she said. "I thought he might help me get the car out of the mud."

"When you were not in the car, or walking on the road, I guessed you must have come here." Raul straightened, sitting back on one heel, and let the small fire get a good start before he added more fuel. "Although I could not be sure you were not walking in the opposite direction."

"I was angry." Luz offered no apology for it either. Her pride was still smarting from their argument in the polo pit.

"I noticed," he commented dryly.

She didn't want that subject introduced again, not even by inference. "What is this place?" she demanded instead. "An old gaucho's hut, I suppose."

"You would not have a chair to sit on if that were so." His mouth slanted in a line that held little warmth and even less humor. "The gauchos used ox skulls for their chairs. This place long ago belonged to a farmer. It has been empty for years. Carlos Rafferty tells me a family named Ortega lived here before I came, but they left more than ten years ago to go to Buenos Aires to find work."

Raul snapped two thin boards across his knee, then added them to the small blaze. When he looked up, it was to glance slowly around the room, his expression thoughtful and distant. His gaze encountered her curious stare, and he turned his attention once again to the fire.

"When I was a small boy, I lived in a place like this one . . . maybe bigger. Or maybe I was small and it looked bigger."

She leaned closer to the growing fire and held her hands over the small flames, then rubbed them briskly together to spread the warmth. "When I was little, Hopeworth Manor always seemed so big and grand to me," Luz remembered with a vague smile. "It is big, but the staircase doesn't seem quite as tall anymore and the rooms don't seem quite as huge. A child's perspective of size is always larger than reality."

"Yes."

The rain continued its ceaseless hammering on the roof while its whispering fall outside the adobe walls drifted past the jagged panes of the broken windows. The faint crackle of the fire was a warm sound; Luz suppressed a shiver and inched closer to it. Its meager heat almost made her feel colder. Her glance strayed to Raul. His wet skin glistened in the firelight, the black of his brow and his thick, stubby lashes standing out darkly against the shiny tan. She tried to imagine him as a small boy playing in a room like this, but an image wouldn't come. Something in the relentless blue of his eyes told her he hadn't known much softness or laughter in his life.

"Did you ever dream when you moved to Buenos Aires with your mother that you'd become a well-known polo player someday?" she mused.

"No." He stacked more wood on the fire, propping them against each other like teepee poles. "We have not settled this situation with your son."

# CHAPTER XXI

Luz was on her feet in an instant, her abruptness knocking over the wobbly chair. "I don't want to talk about it." Every muscle in her body felt rigid as she walked away from the fire and Raul to stand at the window, fighting the tremors that were part anger and part chill.

"We must resolve this if he is to learn," Raul insisted firmly.

"And your interpretation of 'resolve' is for me to stay away from the training," she stated, then remembered her parting ultimatum. "Or do you want me to leave completely?" She challenged him with it again, angling her body toward him.

He didn't move from his crouched position by the fire, balanced on one foot with one leg drawn under him, allowing him to rest on his heel. "I want to teach your son polo. I have told you that it is impossible with your presence distracting him. I think the choice now becomes yours."

"What choice? Am I supposed to quietly accept being banned from watching my own son practice?"

"Why did you allow him to attend this school?" he questioned.

"So he could improve his polo game." Her answer was quick and definite. "I thought you understood that in Paris."

"Then why are you making it difficult for him now?"

"I'm not!"

"You are." He breathed in deeply, turning his head away as if to control an answering surge of anger. "Come back to the fire, Señora Thomas, before those wet clothes chill you to the bone," Raul instructed in a perfectly reasonable tone.

But the formal use of her name made her pause. When he'd

burst into the cabin a few minutes ago, he had called her Luz. She walked slowly back while he reached over and righted her chair. She wished she hadn't remembered that. She wished it didn't matter to her.

Raul waited until she had sat down. "Your knowledge of polo is adequate," he began. "It is considerably better than most, which I am sure is to the credit of Jake Kincaid. However, it is not on a professional level."

"I never claimed it was," Luz said stiffly.

"In the past, you have probably been very helpful to Rob. I also recall our conversation in Paris. You told me you only wanted the best for your son. Did you mean that?" he challenged.

"Yes."

"Then you must turn his instruction over to me. You cannot coach him in the things I can teach him. If you try, you will slow his progress," Raul stated firmly. "Is this what you want?"

"Of course it isn't." She tightly interlocked her fingers. Her elbows rested on her knees as she bent close to the fire, keeping her head down.

"Two people cannot tell him how to do the same thing. There must be one authority. When a child goes to a school, he is removed from his parents so that the instructor can have authority over him. If the child were taught in the home, there would be conflict. The parent could say this is right or this is wrong, and the child might believe that until the teacher could show him differently. Time is lost. It is the same here when you sit on the sidelines."

"I'm not trying to make it harder for him. I only want to help," Luz insisted, yet she saw the truth in what he said.

"Then help him by staying away. What I am asking is not unreasonable." He stirred the fire with a stick, pushing the half-burned wood into the glowing center. "I am not saying you cannot talk to him about what he has learned or how a session went, only that you do not attend."

"I understand what you're saying, but I know Rob better than you do."

"And you make allowances that a teacher would not, no?"

"Yes." She knew how Rob would push himself, sometimes trying too hard, like today.

"Is that good or bad?"

"I don't know." The drumming rain on the metal roof seemed to echo the confused pounding in her head. "My children are very important to me. You're not a mother, so I doubt if you can understand that."

"When your husband left, you made them your life, no?" It was a challenging statement, and Luz caught the rough edge in his voice. There was a tightness to his mouth. "A mother's love can also smother."

"They're all I have," she answered defensively while wondering if he was speaking from personal experience.

"You have yourself." A hard, steady quality was in his gaze, which Luz found impossible to hold. Her eyes skittered away from him.

The fire crackled and popped. Its radiating heat touched more of her body now. She unzipped her jacket and peeled the wet sleeves down her arms, removing the barrier so more of the warmth could reach her skin. She hung the jacket on her knees so that the fire could dry it and stared into the dancing flames.

There was no use explaining to a man who was obviously so self-sufficient how incomplete she felt having only herself. There were so many needs that went unfulfilled. The absence of physical contact was an agony—not sex as much as a caring touch, or a pair of arms around her, a someone just to hold her. She needed to be loved. Rob and Trisha were all she had to fulfill that need.

Aware of the lengthening silence between them, she breathed in deeply, inhaling the smell of woodsmoke. Its wispy trail drifted to the broken window near the door. Her gaze followed its path until it disappeared in the falling rain. The fat, gnarled trunk of the tree outside the adobe hut was visible through the downpour.

"What's that smell outside?" She remembered the vile odor she'd noticed when she'd first reached the cabin and asked about it, avoiding sensitive subjects.

"*El ombu.* I think you call it an umbra tree." Raul shifted to add more wood to the fire. "When the Spanish first came to the Pampa, the *ombu* was the only tree that grew here. The ones you see around the *estancias* were all brought from Europe. They are not native to the Pampa, only the *ombu.* In Spanish, it is known as *belasombra,* which means 'beautiful shade.' In the heat of summer, crossing this flat grassland, it must have seemed like that."

"And it gives off that odor?" She frowned.

"*Sí.* The sap, if you rub it on your skin, will keep away the insects." He straightened and walked over to a work table along the wall, then dragged it close to the fire.

Luz thought he intended to break it into firewood. Instead he removed his jacket and hung it on a corner to dry. When he turned, he held out his hand, offering to take hers. She gave it to him. Something in the way he looked at her made Luz conscious again of her appearance. She bent her head to avoid his gaze and ran her fingers through the stringy wetness of her hair.

"I'm a mess." She picked at the clinging front of her blouse, pulling it away from her skin, then again pushed at her hair. "I wish I had a comb."

She saw his muddy boot an instant before a black comb was thrust almost under her nose. "Thank you." She took it from his hand without looking up.

Raul moved away, crossing to the pile of debris to search for more firewood. She listened to the rummaging sounds he made while she raked the comb's teeth through the wet tangle of her hair, slicking it back and away from her face. When she had finished, she self-consciously fiddled with the comb until Raul came back to the fire and added a few more pieces to the dwindling supply of fuel.

She passed him the comb, doubting that her disheveled appearance had been greatly improved.

As she lowered her glance, she saw him slide the comb into his hip pocket. Luz couldn't help noticing the way his wet breeches clung to his lean flank and muscled thigh, showing the outline of his jockey shorts. She looked quickly away when he crouched down to assume his former position beside the small fire.

"You have not said whether you intend to comply with my request." Raul poked at the fire, sending up sparks, not leaving it alone any more than he let her alone.

The chair wobbled under her when she shifted positions to grip the sides of the seat. She smiled wanly at the thought that she was literally and figuratively on shaky ground, then sighed.

"I'll stay away." It occurred to her that they wouldn't be

sitting by this fire if he had explained his request earlier instead of attempting to make it an order. But he'd lost his temper, and so had she, and here they were. "Polo is important to Rob." Luz explained her change of mind. "It's the most important thing in his life right now. I don't know if you can understand how determined he is to prove himself. He wants to be at the top. I want to help him do that, in whatever way I can, even if that includes staying away from the workouts."

"I think you will not regret it," Raul said. "And I have noticed the way he drives himself. Polo is not simply a sport to him. For the moment at least, it is his life. We will see if that will last."

"I believe it will." She hesitated thinking of Drew's plans for Rob to attend college. "Although I'm not sure that's good."

"Does it bother you that he may wish to make a career of polo?"

"Not really. I know it's a dangerous sport, and players have been killed or crippled by falls, but that's part of it." Luz paused, the corners of her mouth pulled down in grim resignation. "It's his father who won't be pleased by the decision." Leaning forward, she let go of the chair seat and crossed her forearms, resting them atop her legs. Her gaze turned thoughtfully to Raul, studying his impassive features. "Did your mother object to your playing polo?" she asked.

"By the time I took up the game, she had died," he replied without emotion. Something in his sharp glance rejected any polite mouthings of sympathy from her.

"What do you think of Rob's ability? I know you haven't worked with him long, but does he have the potential?"

"Possibly. He wants it badly enough." Raul broke off a large splinter of wood from his fire-stirring stick and tossed it into the flames and watched it catch fire. "Sometimes I see some of myself in him."

"What do you mean?" Other than their mutual interest in polo, she saw no similarities.

"I suppose it is the determination you mentioned, the demand you make on yourself for perfection and never being satisfied with less."

"How did you learn to play polo? I mean, I know you worked for a man who played, but did anyone teach you about the game?"

"Here and there, this one would show me that. But I was a groom playing with my employers' guests. Not much notice was paid to me unless I did something wrong. Hector taught me many things about horses. But the game itself, I learned by trial and error—mostly error."

"You've known Hector a very long time then." Hector had implied as much. "How old were you when you played your first game?"

"Fifteen. When I played in my first club match, I was seventeen. Before that, the others had been friendly games on the *estancia's* polo field, but this one—it was an official game with umpires, scoreboards, timekeepers, spectators." A sardonic humor seemed to twist his mouth. "Señor Boone, my employer, provided me with my polo equipment and colored shirt. Hector loaned me his spurs. My white breeches were an old pair Señor Boone's son had outgrown. I remember they smelled of mothballs. And I spent every bit of money I had on a pair of shiny new boots." As he paused, he looked at her. "No one told me that you shouldn't wear black boots because the blacking comes off when you rub against another player's white breeches. I was very unpopular that day."

Luz could well imagine the derisive comments he'd drawn, and the ridicule, either to his face or behind his back, but Raul would have known. She knew how humiliated her son would have felt if it had happened to him at seventeen. "I imagine that was the last time you wore them."

"They were all I had. I tried to polish them brown, but it was not very successful. It took me six months to save up enough money to buy another pair."

"*Why* did you go back on the field?" She marveled at his ability to swallow his pride and continue to play—in his brown-polished black boots, knowing he'd be subjected to more ridicule. Considering how many times his pride must have been crushed, it was no wonder he had acquired such a thick skin. Perhaps he was entitled to some arrogance now.

"I knew I was good at polo. I was determined to prove I could be the best, not because they scorned my black boots, but because I knew I could do it. There were other things I could not do, but at this I could be the best."

His expression became strained with the intensity of his feelings. The glitter in his eyes and the aggressive angle of his

jaw were hardened by the passionate determination that drove
him. Nothing was going to stand in his way of achieving this
end, Luz realized. Nothing else mattered to him. She frowned
as her bewilderment deepened.

"For more than twenty years, I have practiced and played,
practiced and played. I have studied every facet of the game,
gone over every play, every mistake, and worked to do a little
bit better. It is impossible to be at one hundred percent for
every game, not when you play nearly every month of the year.
But I try for seventy-five percent, eighty, ninety, to raise my
game standard. Still they rate me at nine goals. I wonder what
it is I have to do—what I have missed that keeps me from the
ten." Frustration brought his teeth close together, forcing the
words through them. "In my gut, I know it can be."

"You sound like Rob." Tears welled in her eyes.

"Then you know how it is," he said tightly.

"No. I don't." She shook her head numbly from side to
side. "I don't understand at all. I've never wanted anything so
much that I hurt inside. I don't know what you're talking
about."

As she listened to Raul, remembering similar thoughts expressed by Rob and recalling Trisha's need for a purpose, all
of it came crashing in on her. There was nothing like that in
her life. There wasn't any goal she was striving to attain. She
had nothing in particular she wanted to accomplish. If she'd
had any dreams of anything beyond a husband and family, she
didn't remember them. She'd gone on from day to day, certain
there was nothing she lacked. She was Luz Kincaid; she had
everything.

"What is it?" Raul frowned.

"Nothing." But her wavering voice betrayed her.

In one continuous motion, Luz stood up and turned her back
to him. She shut her eyes for a moment to stem the flow of
tears and breathed in deeply through her nose to steady her
shaken senses. Then she felt his presence very close to her.
When she opened her eyes to look, she found him beside her,
frowning intently at her.

"What is wrong?" he questioned again. When she tried to
turn away, his hand checked her movement and gently drew
her back to face him. "Why are you crying?"

"Because . . ." Luz stared at the row of buttons down his

damp shirtfront. "Because I've never felt that way about anything in my life. I don't know what you're saying. Isn't that crazy? Everybody I know has his heart set on something except me. With Rob, it's polo. Trisha wants to be a lawyer. Audra wants to keep the family together. For God's sake, even Drew is waiting for the day he can try a case before the Supreme Court. I'm forty-two years old. And I don't know why I'm on this earth!"

His frown deepened. Almost tentatively his hand touched the combed-slick side of her hair, then lightly stroked it. "Luz . . ." But he didn't seem to know the words that would reassure her.

She turned her face against his arm, resting her cheek against the damp sleeve. "I don't want to write a book. I don't want to sing songs. I don't want to make a million dollars. I don't want to be the best at anything. My God." She choked on a sob. "What's wrong with me?"

*"No se,"* he murmured.

The sobs broke from her, and she started crying and couldn't stop. She wasn't even conscious of his arms going around her. His shoulder offered a solid pillow for her head, and she cried softly against it. There was no measure of time, only the steady patter of the rain on the roof and the soft crackle of the small fire.

Long after the tears stopped falling, Luz remained enfolded in his arms, too drained to move or feel. There was comfort in the slow, gentle rock of his body and the soothing stroke of his hand on her head. Finally, she wiped at the tears on her cheeks, then felt the downward turn of his head.

"You are better now?" he asked.

"Yes." Self-consciously, Luz moved to disentangle herself from his comforting embrace. "You must think I'm a blubbering fool."

"I think nothing."

But she didn't believe him. She moved to the fire and held her hands out to its rising warmth. The smell of him clung damply to her. It stirred up longings that she'd struggled too hard to bury. In her side vision, she caught his movement as Raul crossed to the fire. Crouching beside it, he added more fuel to the hot center. The flames leaped greedily around it, their light flaring through the room. Raul straightened and met her gaze. The adobe hut suddenly seemed much too small and confining.

"I think the rain's let up," she said, even though the rapid tempo of the raindrops pelting the corrugated iron seemed unchanged. "Why don't we make a dash for the truck?"

"Your clothes are almost dry," he observed. "We will wait another quarter of an hour. There is no need to get them wet again."

"You can stay if you like." Luz moved toward the door, thinking to force him into acceding to her wishes. "But I'm leaving."

The rain showered her face the minute she opened the door. She had one foot over the threshold when Raul caught her and dragged her back inside. *"Idiota!"* The momentum carried her against him. She clutched at his shirt to keep from falling while his hands gripped her shoulders to steady both of them.

When Luz tipped her head to look at him, her gaze traveled no farther than the line of his mouth. It was so close. A stillness claimed her as her pulse took an erratic course, skipping beats all over the place. Before when he'd held her, she hadn't been conscious of the flatly muscled contours of his body. She was too lost in her own pain. Now she was aware of the wide shoulders and narrow hips and the hard wall of his stomach.

He raked a hand into her hair and cupped the back of her neck. The pressure of it drew her more fully against him and tilted her head farther back, forcing her gaze upward. His gaze skimmed over her face, finally stopped on her lips. Luz didn't want to breathe.

"This was inevitable, I think," he murmured thickly.

Her lashes drifted down as his face came toward her. He rocked into them with loving force. The remembered sensation of a man's kiss was not equal to the real thing. Luz had forgotten the other things that went with it——the tightening circle of his arms, the caressing fan of his breath on her skin, and the taste of him on her tongue.

The needs in her were strong, and she responded with long-unsatisfied hunger. Delicious little shudders danced along her skin when his mouth grazed across her cheek to find the sensitive hollow below her ear. She slid her fingers into his hair, its damp, fine texture so silken to her touch. Turning, she searched for his mouth, her lips trailing across the hint of bristles on his shaved cheek. She found the deep groove that flanked the corner of his mouth, then Raul was turning to end her search.

This time there was no leading contact as he immediately plunged deeply inside, filling her up until she thought she would burst. But it only made her hungry for more. There never was enough. No matter how much he gave and how much she took, she always wanted more. She'd been so empty for so long. It would take a lot of filling up before she was full.

Through the dampness of his shirt, she could feel the warmth of his body and the solidness of his flesh. While she continued to feed on his kiss, she brought her hands down and began unbuttoning his shirt, loosening every one of them down to the waistband of his tan trousers. She felt the sharp intake of his breath when her hands slid onto the smooth skin covering his ribcage.

A moment later, she could no longer feel the roaming pressure of his hands on her back and waist, but there was movement behind her. When he lifted his head, drawing slightly back, she saw that he'd unbuttoned the cuffs of his shirt. She watched the naked expanse of his chest come into view as he shrugged out of his shirt. Her hands ran over the curves and indentations of the muscles across his chest and shoulders.

His fingers took hold of the top button on her blouse, and she looked up at his heavy-lidded eyes. Until that moment Luz hadn't really thought about his wanting her. It had all seemed so one-sided, something she had to grab for herself while she had the chance, a chance that might never come again. Suddenly it was much more important that Raul wanted her.

She watched his face uncertainly, conscious of the manipulations of his fingers and the draft against her skin when the front of her blouse separated. Slowly he parted the material and pushed it off her shoulders onto her arms as if unveiling a statue. Luz tugged it the rest of the way off, then he took it and tossed it on the bench with his shirt.

His hands came back to her, their roughened texture sliding onto her back. When she felt his fingers on her bra hook, her lashes fluttered down and her hands dug into the flexed biceps to steady her suddenly shaky knees. The minute the fasteners were released, the loose straps slid off her shoulders, of their own accord, it seemed. Swallowing convulsively, she let go of his arms and took it the rest of the way off.

Covertly she watched him look at her. This wasn't Drew gazing at the rise and fall of her breasts as she breathed—not Drew, who knew every inch of their mature contours. There was no sameness to this moment. It was new, and in its newness, there was uncertainty. With a husband of twenty-odd years, what did she care how she compared to other women? Maybe she should have, but she hadn't. Now she wondered.

His hand slid up her ribs and cupped the underside of a breast, taking the weight of it in his palm. The stroking caress of his thumb across its point started a curling sensation in her stomach. Slowly, Raul pulled her toward him again until her bare skin was against the heated wall of his chest and stomach. A little groan of pleasure broke from her throat as his mouth descended onto hers again. She strained into it, giving, giving, giving, yet always finding more pleasure being returned.

He framed her face in his hands, kissing her nose, cheek, and lips while he studied every inch of her face. She couldn't seem to breathe. His blue eyes looked so dark that she felt absorbed by them. Her heart pounded while she waited for some signal, but none came. She couldn't stand the suspense.

"Raul, do you want me?"

His thumb rubbed the center of her lips and slowly stroked over their outline, then his lips came down to brush back and forth across their softness. "*Sí,*" he murmured against them. "I want you." And the pressure that had been so light became firm in possession.

The tension that had held her desire in check melted under his assertive kiss. Luz returned the kiss with driving need, while she wrapped her arms tightly around him, a hand pressing down on the back of his head to deepen the kiss. She was flooded by a renewed sense of worth and value, so many of her doubts about her own desirability fading as his arms enfolded her.

But the hands gliding down her shoulders and spine didn't stop. One arm tightly circled her waist while the other continued down over her rounded buttocks. With a dipping movement of his body, Raul curved his arm behind her thighs and scooped her up, nestling her sideways on his hip. She felt weightless in his strong arms. In more than one way, her feet weren't touching the ground as he carried her across the room.

When he set her down, it was on the edge of the corner cot. In a wonderful daze, she watched him crouch down, one knee resting on the earthen floor, and pick up her foot. As he pulled off its mud-caked boot, Luz gazed at the strong bone structure of his face, handsome in a way that Drew had never been. Without being conscious of directing her actions, she unfastened the waistband of her slacks. When her boots and socks were removed, Luz stood up, the fine-grained dirt under her bare feet oddly stimulating her sensitive soles. As she stepped out of her slacks, Raul took her place on the cot and pulled off his boots.

Taking her time so that she could watch him undress, she pushed her silk panties down and stepped out of the clinging, wet undergarment. The rather hesitant curiosity that sent her glance traveling up the muscled length of his leg to the hollowed cheeks of his lean flanks, then skittering away from his erection, almost made her smile at such schoolgirl silliness. He was hardly her first man, but he was the first in what seemed like a long time.

After laying the silk and lace panties aside, she turned to him slowly. Her figure was slim and firm, maturely curved, and she wanted him to see her. She wanted him to like what he saw. Motionless she stood before him, conscious of the slow downward travel of his gaze. When it made its return journey, she was trembling inside. The space between them suddenly seemed so wide. Raul moved toward her.

His hands touched the rounded points of her shoulders, then glided around them to draw her into his arms. The kiss was long and slow, a reconfirmation of all that had gone before. Then the weight of his body pressed her backward onto the cot while he followed her down, stretching out beside her, the long length of his body angled to lean over her.

While his nibbling, nuzzling mouth kissed her throat, the hollow near her collarbone, and the corded ridge of her shoulder, his caressing hand wandered over her breasts and the flatness of her stomach. It paused at her navel, then moved downward to her hips and the silken nest of her pubic hairs, and glided with arousing interest along her inner thigh. Luz shifted under its tantalizing touch, the straw-stuffed mattress rustling beneath her.

As his hand traveled back to hold her breast for his mouth to explore, Raul slid a hair-roughened thigh between her legs to let her ride it and assuage the pressure building within. Her hands were splayed across his back, pressing to pull him closer while she arched against the exciting suction consuming her breast. The sensations she felt were contradictory, a melting weakness counterposing a soaring strength and aching need conflicting with glorious fulfillment.

More of his weight shifted on top of her as he came back to her lips. His husky voice vibrated against her skin, but the caressing words were in Spanish. Luz moved her head in protest to the unintelligible sounds.

"I don't know what you're saying." And she wanted to know.

He lifted his face inches from hers, looked at her face, then downward at the rest of her that his body covered. "Your skin is like fire. It burns me." He let his lips form the words against the corner of her mouth. "You look so cool, but you feel so warm."

She tasted the fine beads of perspiration on his upper lip. "You are hot, too."

"For you." His mouth closed on her lips as he mounted her.

The mating instinct guided her action, her hips automatically shifting into position to receive him, her hand showing the head of his bone-stiff organ to her opening. The fitting of two parts designed to unite was the same, but the movement—the rhythm together once linked—was markedly different. There was no pattern to follow, no routine of tempo, no knowledge of the other's pleasure points.

Reveling in the slow, grinding thrust of his hips, Luz pushed to meet it while her mouth grazed over his shoulder and arm, tasting the rainwater freshness of his skin and the tang of wood-smoke. Her fingers followed the ridged notches of his spine all the way to its base, his muscled flesh so warm and solid to her touch. She had no thoughts except the absent conviction it had never been like this before as her mind gave itself over to the sensations of the flesh.

When he levered the upper half of his body away from her, bracing on his arms, her passion-heavy eyes watched the play of his chest and shoulder muscles, flexing and straining with each stroke. With each deep plunge, she tightened to hold him inside, the pressure building, the sensations rippling. She didn't want it to stop. Then it was all peaking in an eruption of glorious satisfaction that was too mind-sweeping for Luz to notice the shuddering twitch of his muscles.

Slowly, unwillingly, Luz came back from the magical place which seemed far away, yet located deep inside. As her breathing became regular, her awareness of Raul increased. The cot was barely wide enough for the two of them. He lay sideways along the length of her, their legs still partially intertwined, an arm masking his face.

She wanted to touch him and reestablish the satisfying contact, then to lie in his arms as they came back to earth together. She wanted to tell him how much she enjoyed his lovemaking, but she couldn't initiate either action, not until she knew how he felt. She couldn't make herself that vulnerable.

The old insecurities that Drew's leaving had evoked in her resurfaced. Luz didn't know if she had pleased Raul, whether it had been as good for him as it had for her. She waited for him to say something, to make the first move, but there was nothing. She closed her eyes, hating Drew at that moment for her doubts about her sexual attractiveness and prowess. She wasn't sure whether she was any good in bed.

The silence became painful. Her body became rigid with the tension building inside, a chill spreading over her naked flesh. Luz stared at the dark metal undersides of the roof and listened to the hollow splat of water dripping from the tree outside.

Unable to stand it any longer, she sat up and swung her legs free of his, setting her feet on the earth floor. A stirring movement rustled the lumpy straw mattress, but as far as she was concerned, it came too late. She picked up her clothes.

She hesitated a mere instant, then stepped into her slacks and pulled them up. "It's stopped raining. We can leave now." She heard the clipped sound of her voice. "It seems you were right when you said it wouldn't last long."

Propped on his elbow, Raul watched her sit down on the edge of the cot and tug her boots on, observing the stiffness in her body. He resisted the urge to pull her back onto the mattress with him and try to discover again what it was about her that disturbed him so. She had touched something inside him, appealed to some need that he didn't understand. He couldn't entirely convince himself that it was only desire he felt.

When she left the cot and walked over to the bench for the rest of her clothes, Raul got up and pulled on his own breeches and boots. The firelight played across the smooth skin of her back, briefly highlighting the curve of a breast when she slipped on the lacy brassiere. Her slender body was unquestionably beautiful, warm and firm-feeling in his remembrances. But it was the woman inside it that got to him. Frowning, Raul crossed the room to retrieve his shirt from the same bench. As Luz tucked the tails of her blouse inside her slacks, she paused to hand the shirt to him.

"Why the scowl? Was it that bad?" she mocked, but he looked beyond the proud lift of her head and the coolly defiant expression on her face to the questioning hurt in her dark eyes.

"No." He smoothed out the frown and shrugged into his shirt. "I broke a rule of mine never to get involved with the people who hire me."

"It's a little late to be remembering that," she said stiffly and looked down to finish tucking in her blouse. "You should have thought of it earlier."

"I did." And it hadn't mattered to him then either. Raul ignored her startled look as he reached for his jacket. "Are you ready?" He moved toward the door.

"What about the fire?"

Pausing, he glanced back at the dying flames on the dirt floor. "It will burn itself out." And it would be the same for whatever heat she had ignited in him, he told himself.

Her clothes were still damp, but despite their rumpled appearance and faint smudges, they retained their expensive look. The pale, sand-colored hair was smoothed away from her face, accenting her patrician fineness. She was a wealthy divorcée who wanted an affair. She'd picked a polo player for a lover. The situation was not uncommon. Yet Raul knew he felt more than detached interest. It made him wary of her.

# CHAPTER XXII

When Luz saw her reflection in the bathroom mirror, her spirits sank. No wonder everyone downstairs had acted so concerned about her. It hadn't been just her damp, mud-spattered clothes. She looked positively washed out. Not a trace of makeup remained except for the mascara smudges under her lower lashes. The soft rainwater had left her hair silken, but limp. Her hands moved over her cheeks as she stared at her reflection, remembering how Raul had held her face in his hands.

Resolutely she swung away from the mirror, determined to make some drastic changes in her appearance. She turned the shower faucets on, and the water pipes rattled and groaned before they sent forth a spray from the shower head.

An hour later, Luz had showered, shampooed, dotted on layers of moisture cream to soften the lines at her eye corners, blow-dried her hair, and applied her makeup. Selecting an outfit had been difficult. No one dressed for dinner at the house, although the men usually changed out of their riding clothes. She hadn't brought that many afternoon dresses. Out of the three that she regarded as particularly eye-catching or flattering, she picked a flowery jacquard chemise of raspberry crepe.

The oval wall mirror in the bedroom couldn't show her a long view of how she looked, and neither could the square mirror on the medicine cabinet above the bathroom sink. Luz tried to be satisfied with what little she could see and plucked at the stand-up mandarin collar that slashed into a v neckline.

"Hello?" Trisha poked her head around the door standing open to the bathroom.

"Come in," Luz said absently as she first held the matching

sash, then a silver-corded belt to her waist. Deciding on the belt, she tossed the sash onto the bed with the other dress choice she'd laid out.

"Quite a transformation," Trisha declared.

With the belt fastened, Luz turned to her daughter for an opinion. "What do you think? Does it look all right?" She fluffed the billowy sleeves, buttoned at the wrists, and adjusted the pads under the shoulders.

"It looks wonderful," Trisha replied.

Without a decent mirror to dispute it, Luz had to take her word for it. She walked over to the jewelry case atop the chest of drawers and picked through the bracelets. "Should I wear this chunky silver rope chain or these silver bands with this dress?"

"The little jingly ones."

"They're too noisy." Luz put them back and draped the heavy silver one around the wrist to fasten the latch.

"Why did you ask me?" Trisha shook her head in annoyance.

"I don't know." Her fingers fumbled with the hook, too unsteady to fasten it. "Will you do this for me, Trisha?" she said in exasperation and held out her arm.

Trisha took hold of her wrist to fasten the bracelet's latch, then glanced at her in surprise. "Luz, you're shaking. Are you feeling all right?"

"Yes, I . . ." She met that concerned look and realized she couldn't possibly explain why she was so nervous. "I've been hurrying to get dressed. I know Hector likes to have dinner served promptly at seven-thirty."

"Is that all? I thought maybe you had gotten chilled from that soaking you took. It's twenty minutes until dinner; you've got plenty of time." She snapped the safety fastener closed. "What ever possessed you to go driving when it was raining so hard?"

Luz walked back to the dresser, wondering how to answer that question without mentioning the argument she'd had with Raul. She picked up the perfume bottle and tipped it upside down to moisten the stopper.

"It was raining and I didn't want to get wet walking back to the house, so I took the car that was parked outside the pit. Unfortunately I missed the turn to the house and I had to keep going until I found a place to turn around." Luz dabbed the perfume-wet tip of the stopper to the hollow below her neck while keeping her back to Trisha. "The car got stuck in the mud before I could find a place."

"It certainly took Raul a long time to find you."

"Yes." She looked at the perfume bottle in her hand as the tension built inside. What was she to say to her—"The man you wanted made love to me this afternoon"? There was nothing beyond that to tell. She hadn't intended it to happen. Not once had she even thought about the possible repercussions for her daughter.

Raul had said he wasn't interested in Trisha. Maybe it was best just to let things die their own death without killing Trisha's trust in her. She had been so caught up in her own jealousy of Trisha that it had never occurred to her that Trisha would ever have reason to be jealous of her.

"I wish I'd gone with him to look for you, but he'd already gone by the time I found out about it," Trisha said. "Maybe we wouldn't have found you any sooner, but think of how much time I could have spent with him."

"Is that all you ever think about, Trisha?" She felt trapped. "You'll be starting college in a week. Aren't you excited about getting ready for that? You're supposed to be so determined to get a law degree. Or was that just a passing fad, influenced by Claudia?"

"Luz, where have you been for the last ten years?" Trisha retorted sharply. "A woman can be interested in a career and a man, too. If she has one, it doesn't mean she can't have the other. And I had made up my mind to study law long before I ever met Claudia."

"I know you did." Luz sighed. "I shouldn't have said that." She glanced down at her dress, remembering the schoolgirl pains she'd taken to look especially attractive for Raul and wondered if she wasn't more foolish than Trisha. Trisha at least could blame her actions on her youth. She set the perfume bottle on top of the dresser and turned, smiling brightly. "Shall we go downstairs?"

"Sure."

The others were already gathered in the informal living room when Luz walked in with Trisha. She saw Raul standing by the fireplace, staring at the drink in his hand, taking no part in the discussion. Hector was the first to notice their arrival.

"*Buenas tardes.*" He swung toward them on his crutches, drawing the room's attention to them. "You look lovely, señora."

"*Gracias,* Hector." She smiled while fully conscious of Raul's stare. She derived some satisfaction from it, but a guilty satisfaction since Trisha was at her side.

"Well, would you look at this?" Duke Sovine declared as he politely stood up, acknowledging the presence of ladies in the room. "You look radiant, Luz. I wouldn't have given a plug nickel for you when you walked in the door this afternoon."

"It's a pity no one had a camera to take a picture of me then. You could have blackmailed me with it." She smoothly returned his banter as she crossed the room. One of the Argentine instructors offered her the leather armchair he had previously occupied, and Luz sat down.

As Trisha took a seat, the others shuffled around to find a place to sit, their arrival causing a game of musical chairs. Raul moved into Luz's side vision, walking over to set his empty glass on the drink tray. It was difficult to look at him without images and sensations flashing in her mind, so she tried to ignore him.

"That was quite a rain we had today," Duke Sovine commented. "Back in Texas, we'd call that a gully-washer. How long before the field will be dry enough to play on, Raul?"

"If the wind is strong, perhaps as quickly as tomorrow afternoon," he replied.

"Don't you men ever get tired of riding around all day hitting polo balls?" Trisha criticized playfully. "To hear you talk, a person would think the only things that interest you are making money and playing polo."

"Probably because it takes money to play polo," Duke Sovine suggested, then laughed with the others. "The only thing I know that might be more expensive is a pretty woman."

"Is that what you think, Raul?" she said, flirting with him. "Do you consider women expensive?"

"Some, perhaps."

The tall clock in the entry hall chimed the half hour. It was followed by the sound of Hector's crutches thumping off the area rug on the hardwood floor. "We will go in to dinner now," he announced.

As Luz stood up and started around her chair toward the hall, she encountered Raul. His gaze held hers for an intimate second, then fell away. She saw a nerve twitch along his jaw. She remembered his rule not to become involved with his polo clients, and had the impression that he had reconsidered his action and intended to observe it. Although it hurt, under the circumstances it was probably best. But there were times when emotions would not listen to the mind's logic, and this was one of them.

She stepped quickly forward and walked alongside Hector, no longer uncomfortable with his dragging gait. Behind her, she was aware that Trisha had latched onto Raul's arm.

Dinner was an ordeal. Seated on Raul's right at the table, Luz constantly felt the strain of his company and suspected from his straight-lipped expression that it was mutual. She barely tasted the food on her plate. All her senses seemed to be tuned to his presence. The steady stream of banter Trisha directed to Raul only made everything worse.

At last the coffee was served. Luz declined. "I think I'd prefer to take a brandy in the living room. If you'll excuse me." As she pushed back her chair to leave, there was an accompanying scrape of other chair legs on the hardwood floor, the men including Raul, respectfully standing.

"Shall we all take our coffee into the other room?" he suggested.

"A brandy with it sounds good to me," Duke Sovine seconded the proposal.

Luz had hoped for a respite from this brittle tension, but it wasn't to be as they followed her en masse into the formal living room. She didn't want company, especially Raul's. Carrying a snifter of brandy, she moved to the fireplace, where a new log had been thrown on the blaze. It crackled noisily, like her nerves. She tried not to listen to the hum of voices around her, not wanting to be drawn into conversation. Rolling the rounded sides of the brandy glass between her palms, she wished Raul would retire to his office the way he always did. It was quite obvious to her that he regarded this afternoon as a mistake. She knew it was, yet . . .

"Are you feeling well?"

Luz started visibly at Raul's sudden appearance beside her,

then lifted her chin to coolly meet his gaze. "Of course. What could possibly be wrong?"

"You barely touched the food on your plate this evening."

"I wasn't hungry." She looked past him to Trisha, who had overheard the exchange.

"My, but you're certainly receiving the attention today, Luz," Trisha remarked while looking at Raul. "You never did explain why it took you so long to find her."

"Does it matter?"

"No," Trisha admitted with a small shrug. Luz turned away to stare at the fire, refusing to watch her daughter's seductive efforts. The pain of rejection stung her anew, and she quickly gulped down a swallow of brandy to deaden it. "Maybe I should become lost, then you could come rescue me the way you did Luz," Trisha suggested to him. Her innocent choice of words was almost more than Luz could stand.

"Surely you can come up with something more original than that, Trisha," Luz said tersely, then got up and crossed the room to put distance between them.

Stopping by the drink tray, she glanced at the decanter of brandy. Her nerves felt jangled, and the glass in her hand was almost empty. She downed the last of it and felt the delayed burning of her throat.

"Is something wrong, Señora Luz?" Hector peered at her with concern.

"I am fine. Why is everyone so worried about me all of a sudden?" she flared in irritation, and instantly regretted her sharpness. A heavy sigh broke from her. "It's been a long day. I think I'm more tired than I realized." She set her empty glass on the tray. "Good night, Hector."

"Good night."

Not bothering to take her leave from the others in the room, Luz made a quiet exit and climbed the heavy staircase to her room. There had simply been too much emotional turmoil today. She couldn't cope with any more of it.

She began undressing as she crossed the room, removing the bracelet and earrings and kicking off her shoes, stripping off everything that she had earlier selected with such care. She grabbed a robe from the closet and slipped it on. Tying the sash, she jerked the knot tight. The pile of discarded clothes lay on the floor in front of her. Luz started to step around them and leave them for the maid, then changed her mind and impatiently gathered them up. She was in no mood to hang up her own clothes.

At the knock on her door, she dropped them on the bed. "Come in," she called, briefly grateful that Hector had thought to send Anna up to her room. She didn't want to deal with any of this.

But when the door opened, Raul walked in. Her heart seemed to stop a second, then it raced off crazily. He paused a moment as he saw she had changed into her night attire, then he shut the door behind him. But there was nothing in his expression to encourage her. Luz turned and picked up the dress, shaking it out.

"What is it you want, Mr. Buchanan?" She was deliberately formal and cold. "Or are you here to assure yourself that I suffered no ill effects from my afternoon outing in the rain?"

"What exactly did you tell Trisha?"

Her hands faltered an instant as she held the dress by its shoulders. Luz knew precisely what he meant. "Nothing." She reached for a wire hanger. "She wouldn't have anything to do with either one of us if I had. Why would you even ask such a thing?" she demanded angrily, and jammed the hangered dress into the closet.

Raul stood by the bed. "Some mothers and daughters find it amusing to share things, including men."

Incensed by his disgusting insinuation, Luz lashed out, slapping him as hard as she could. "How decadent do you think we are?" She was angry and trembling, her hand and arm aching from the jarring impact with his jaw.

He spun her back around, hauling her against his chest and crushing her lips against her teeth with his mouth all in one violent motion. Luz had no time to react. An instant later, the bruising pressure changed to one of driving softness as his mouth rolled about her lips, sensually tasting and persuading. She couldn't make that rapid switch from anger to passion, but neither could she fight the sensation.

At her passive response, Raul pulled abruptly away and released her to walk stiffly to the window. Trembling with hurt confusion and anger, Luz watched him light a small black cigar and impatiently exhale the smoke.

"What was that kiss supposed to represent, Raul? An insult

or an apology?" she demanded tautly. "Sometimes I think you despise me and other—" She left it unsaid.

"You are not as confused as I," he retorted sharply. "First I think it is an affair you want. You left the cot the way a whore leaves a bed. When you want a man, any man will do. That is what you indicated in Paris, no. So now I wonder what it is you expect from me."

"I expect to be treated as more than a piece of ass!" Luz was too indignant to care how rude or vulgar she sounded. At the same time, she was hurt by his base opinion of her. Hugging her arms tightly around her, she half turned to avoid his piercing blue eyes. "I haven't gone to bed with any man other than my husband for over twenty years—until today with you. And I don't give a damn whether you believe that or not! So if I behaved like a whore it was simply because I didn't know what I was supposed to do afterward except to get dressed. And you certainly weren't indicating that you expected anything else from me!"

"I thought it was all I wanted." He stabbed the freshly lit cigar in the ashtray on the dresser, grinding it out in a gesture of irritation, then moved almost reluctantly toward her. "It seemed enough for you. And I could not know of these other things you have just told me." When Raul stopped in front of her, she sensed his indecision, his uncertainty. "Later I found it was not all I wanted. There was something more. Now I think it is the same for you."

As he reached to take hold of her, Luz knocked his arms away. "Don't touch me," she ordered with leftover anger.

"Tonight I kept remembering the way it felt to hold you. And I remembered how it was to look at the sidelines where you always stand to watch the workouts and see you there. Maybe you are more distracting to me than to Rob," Raul suggested without humor.

This time when he lifted his hand to touch her face, she didn't slap it away. The intent expression on his own carved features was compelling. Luz couldn't look away.

"Do you remember that first time we met, when you touched me, feeling all over my face?" he recalled absently. "You troubled me then and you trouble me now. When I look at your face, I see something I want."

"Then take it," Luz urged softly.

His hesitation lasted no more than a second before she felt the moist heat of his mouth closing on her lips and the satisfying feel of his arms circling tightly around her. The long drugging kiss seemed to melt her bones. She leaned against him, shaping herself to his frame. When he dragged his mouth away from her lips to bury it in her hair, she felt the tremor that shook him and heard the raggedness of his breathing. Her insecurity regarding her ability to arouse and please vanished as she recognized that his disturbance was as great as her own.

"Luz, I—"

A knock interrupted him. Raul lifted his head, an impatient frown creasing his forehead. Smiling, Luz ran a caressing hand over his flexed muscles in his jaw, sharing his frustration while enjoying seeing it in him.

"Hector probably sent up Anna," she murmured.

The knock was repeated. "Luz? Are you in there?" The muffled sound of Trisha's voice shattered her blissful mood. She flashed a stricken glance at Raul, then broke free of his arms.

"She mustn't know," she whispered to Raul. Despite a displeased look, he nodded his agreement. Reassured that he wouldn't give anything away, Luz glanced nervously at the door. "Yes, I'm here," she answered finally.

Trisha walked in, then stopped abruptly. "Raul. What are you doing here?" She glanced quickly from one to the other.

"I came to assure myself that your mother is well, despite her drenching this afternoon," he said, then included Luz in saying, "Good night." He walked by Trisha and out the door.

"Is that really what he was doing here?" Trisha looked skeptical.

"Is it so surprising that he would be concerned about the welfare of a guest in his house?" Luz folded the silk slip into a neat square, wondering if her face was as flushed as it felt. "Did you want something?"

"Yes, I—" It didn't seem nearly as important to her now as she answered somewhat distractedly. "I came to tell you that I think I might have talked Hanif into letting me fly to Buenos Aires next week in his private jet."

# CHAPTER XXIII

When it came time for Trisha to leave that midweek, Hanif did volunteer the use of his private jet to fly her to Buenos Aires to catch her scheduled flight to the States. After driving Trisha to the airstrip and seeing her off, Luz returned to the *estancia*. She left the car parked in front and went inside, feeling guilty because she was glad her daughter was gone. She and Raul had not had a moment alone, and the frustration had become almost intolerable.

Her footsteps had a hollow sound as Luz wandered into the big, high-ceilinged living room. She glanced at the closed double doors to Raul's office, then unconsciously moved toward the room where he spent so much of his time. Curiosity and a need to be near him impelled her. She opened the doors wide and looked into the room.

A desk and chair, two worn and bulky armchairs, an old wooden filing cabinet, and a woven rug in front of the fireplace were the room's furnishings. The walls were bare except for the one lined with bookshelves, and those were mainly empty. There was no resemblance to the comfortably cluttered library office at Hopeworth Manor.

Nothing showed the stamp of his personality, Luz thought as she entered. Or maybe it did. Maybe Raul was as empty as this, showing no warmth and comfort because he had known none. It was a curious thought. Her mind turned back to the things he had told her in the adobe hut about his early pursuit of polo—the scorn and ridicule, the brown boots he hadn't been able to afford to buy. Polo was an expensive sport, she knew, and it must have been more of a struggle for him than she had previously realized.

She wandered over to his desk and glanced at the neat stacks of papers on top of it. Much of it appeared to be correspondence, with some advertisements as well. Luz saw the penciled notes on the pad of yellow paper and recognized Raul's small, tight handwriting, the letters laboriously scrawled, like a child's writing.

Her gaze was drawn to the bookshelves on the wall behind the desk. She turned to scan the titles of the few books sitting on two of the shelves. Most were in Spanish, but polo was spelled the same as in English. All the books appeared to be related either to the sport or to horses, and they all appeared to be well used, some of the backs cracked and thready.

One looked particularly worn. She leaned closer to read the partly obscured title. A surprised smile broke apart her lips when she realized it was the polo book written by the late Lord Mountbatten. Luz removed it from the shelf, noticing the edges were completely worn, exposing the stiff cardboard. When she opened the book, she saw that the pages were not simply well thumbed. They were tattered, the edges in shreds from being turned so much. Some had broken completely loose from the binding. It was like a Bible that had been read and re-read. He had learned polo the hard way, he'd said—by trial and error, teaching himself. Frowning, Luz stared thoughtfully at the book, only now guessing what that meant.

"Ah, Señora Luz." At the sound of Hector's voice, she turned with a faint start to face the double doors. She had grown so accustomed to hearing the thump and drag of his walk around the house that it had become part of the background noise. He altered his course past the double doors to enter the office instead. "I heard the car outside, but when I did not see you in the living room, I thought perhaps you had gone to the polo field."

"No. I've been told I'm a distraction," Luz replied easily, aware that Hector was the first to mention it. Not even Rob had commented on her absence.

"I think I know who it is that says this." The knowing gleam in his eyes teased her.

Luz doubted if very much escaped Hector's notice, but she didn't comment on his remark. "I was looking through the books and happened on this one. I'm afraid it's almost falling apart."

"Many, many times I have seen Raul with that one. He was always reading it . . . asking about this word or that."

"That was long ago . . . when he was just learning the game, wasn't it?"

"*Sí*. It was very difficult for him. He worked very hard to learn."

"It must have been." Luz closed the book and absently held it to her breast, rubbing a hand over the worn cover.

"Is there anything you wished? Tea, perhaps?"

"No. *Gracias*, Hector."

His crutches thumped the floor as he turned. "I must go see to lunch."

After Hector left the room, Luz sat down on a corner of the desk and tipped the book away from her to look at the worn and tattered cover. She suspected that polo was Raul's religion—his god and his mistress. Nothing had ever stood between them. He had let nothing else into his life. She wondered if he would let her in.

And if he would, did she want it? She hadn't wanted to get involved with another man, and look at her—mooning over some old book of his. She sensed it was too soon. She hadn't had time to get her feet squarely on the ground after the divorce. But if she was on the rebound, what better place to land than in Raul's arms? He made her feel like a woman again, gave her back some of her old confidence. That was a lot.

A door slammed, followed by the tramp of boots on the hardwood floor and weary male voices. Luz straightened from the desk and turned toward the door as Raul appeared in its wide frame. He hesitated in midstride when he saw her, then walked in and swung both doors closed.

"How did it go this morning?" Something in the hardened set of his jaw gave her pause. "I hope you don't mind me being here. After I saw Trisha off, I—"

He roughly took the book from her hand and jammed it back into its place on the shelf, then walked behind his desk and began leafing through the papers on top of it.

"That book is special to you, isn't it?" Luz hadn't considered how special it might be to him. "Hector told me you used to read—"

"Hector talks too much," Raul muttered.

"You're not being fair," she protested in Hector's behalf.

*"Pues bien,* so he told you that this was how I learned to read with this book." He braced his hands on the desk top, his head turned to the side. "I did not have the privilege to have a formal education. I had to work in order to eat, but this is something I am sure you cannot comprehend." Straightening, he picked up a stack of papers and began shifting through them. Luz recognized that his fierce expression was one of pride, not anger.

"Truthfully, Raul," she said quietly, "I thought that book was how you learned to play polo. I didn't know that you used it to learn how to read. Hector never said that." Swearing under his breath in Spanish, he dropped the papers on the desk.. "I know you may not believe this, coming from me, but I don't think it matters where or how you learned to read. Jake always told Drew that he never gave a damn where a man went to college. He only cared whether the man knew his business."

"Do you find it amusing the way I learned to read?" he challenged making it apparent that others had.

"No, although I'm surprised you didn't go to school. From what I've seen, Argentina is a very literate country."

"I went for three years when we lived on the pampas. That's where I learned my letters and numbers."

"How did you learn English?"

"My employer, Señor Boone, was descended from English settlers who came here to build the railroad. He was educated in England and spoke very bad Spanish. His friends who came to play polo were mostly English, too. This was part of polo, I thought. They became my models. I copied the way they talked and the way they dressed, and when I was a good enough polo player to be invited to their homes, I copied the way they ate and drank."

Yet none of it meant anything to him, she realized—not the clothes, the fine foods and wines, the plush homes, and the haughty airs. That was the world in which polo was played, and he had adapted to it without embracing it.

"You went through all that just to play polo," Luz murmured.

"Just to play polo," he repeated. "Polo gave me freedom. No one tells me what to do. You do not order me to teach your son. It is my choice. I answer to no man."

"And to no woman."

"No, and to no woman." Raul turned and sat down on the edge of the desk, catching hold of her hand and pulling her over to stand between his legs. His hands then curved to her hips while her own settled on his shoulders. "Trisha has gone, no?"

"Yes, she should be landing in Buenos Aires now." Sensual shudders quivered over her skin as he nuzzled the curve of her neck.

She tunneled her fingers into his dark hair, forcing his head up, but he needed little coercion to find her lips. The hunger of a long wait deepened the kiss to a full-blown mating, and Luz drank in the taste of him, the nicotine flavor of his tongue and the salty tang of his lips. She leaned into him, letting him take her weight while she strained for more.

The warning click of the doorlatch did not alert them quickly enough to break apart. "Raul, lunch . . . is ready," Hector faltered over the announcement, but a wide grin sent his upper lip disappearing beneath the heavy mustache. Raul turned from the waist to glare at him, an arm circling her hips to keep Luz from moving away from him.

"It is best if you remember to knock from now on, Hector," Raul suggested curtly.

"*Sí*, and maybe we should fix the locks, too." He pulled the door shut. The pounding of his crutches sounded extraordinarily loud, as though he wanted them to be sure they heard him leave.

Studying the sheen of his dark hair, Luz combed her fingers through it, smoothing down the areas she had previously ruffled. When he tilted his head to look at her, she was filled with a toasty warm feeling. His hold shifted, his hands spreading to cover the rounded cheeks of her bottom and applying pressure to arch the lower half of her body more fully into the open cradle of his hips.

"I had forgotten how very soft you feel to me," he murmured against her cheek, his accent thickening. "It has been too long."

"I know."

"Tonight . . ." Raul pulled slightly back, letting their noses touch and their breaths mingle. "Shall I come to your room or will you come to mine?"

"I don't know where you sleep."

"At the far end of the upper hall. It is better that I come to you. No one will think anything if they see me in the hall." He kissed her again, long and hard.

"Lunch is ready," she unwillingly reminded him.

"That is not all." The comment needed no explanation; Luz was fully aware of the bulge in his breeches. But he loosened his hold, setting her away from him so that he could stand up. When she started to move away from the desk, he repeated, "Tonight."

"Yes."

Long after the last bedroom door had closed, Luz waited in her room, straining to catch the smallest sound in the hallway. All she could hear was the creakings of the house. For the third time, she paced to the window and stared out the dark pane that reflected her image in the lamplight. She glanced at the nightgown draped over the corner chair, debating whether to give up and go to bed. It was late and getting later. The soft makeup, the perfume discreetly dabbed in indiscreet places, the sexy silk peignor—all seemed destined to seduce only her own pillow.

Two light taps sounded on her door, and Luz nearly ran across the room, slowing herself at the last minute. As she opened it, Raul slipped quickly inside, clad only in a terrycloth robe. After the door was shut, there was an instant when they merely looked at each other, posed like a stag and a doe before the mating ritual begins.

Luz wasn't sure which of them moved first, and it didn't matter. She was in his arms, feeling the heat of his kiss. Her hands slid inside his robe and spread over his chest, discovering the hardness of his nipples. The bedcovers were turned invitingly down, and they gravitated to them, stopping to shed their robes, then gliding onto the sheeted mattress. The bedsprings groaned under their combined weight.

"I should have warned you about the squeaky springs," Luz murmured as she leaned over him, the tips of her breasts brushing across his smooth chest.

"The house is blessed with thick walls," he assured her as he pulled her head down to devour her lips.

Her hands caressed him, traveling over the hard planes of his body while she dragged free of his mouth to rub her lips over his clean-shaven jaw and down the tanned column of his throat. There was none of the hesitancy of the first time, none of the uncertainty and waiting to see what he wanted her to do. Luz did what she wanted, and that was to explore and enjoy this man of muscle and bone and hard flesh.

She was conscious of the stimulating caress of his hands, kneading and stroking her body with building urgency. They aroused her, as he was aroused. Traveling from the hollowed cheek of his flank, her fingers spread into the silken hairs covering his thigh, her arm brushing the head of his erection. She felt his involuntary flinch when she cupped his male sacs in her hand. A low groan broke from his throat as she stroked his engorged flesh, rediscovering the power a woman held equally over a man.

Shifting, Raul lifted her easily and rolled them both over to assume the position of dominance. She saw the desire in his heavy-lidded eyes. It excited her own. Now it was his hands that began the stimulating play while his lips, tongue, and teeth created their own havoc with her senses. Before they were through, she swore he had discovered every perfume-dotted place. When his hand glided between her thighs and his fingers located the swelling bud of her sex, it was she who writhed convulsively under their teasing manipulation, the soft, involuntary cries torn from her throat, as she had done to him.

The satisfying weight of his body at last moved onto her as he sheathed himself in her. Passion moved them together, gloriously out of control. Neither of them heard the rhythmic creak of the bed springs, or the increase of its tempo.

When his seed was spilled and it was over, they lay for a long while lightly cradled in each other's arms, absently kissing and touching, murmuring things that were not as important as the sound of the voice.

Finally, Raul got out of bed and donned his robe. Luz sat up and plumped a pair of pillows behind her, then leaned against them, pulling the sheet and tucking the hemmed facing under her arms. He paused beside the bed.

"I must go. You will sleep well, no?" There was a lazy quality to his look as if all the hard-driving energies had been drained from him. That was what she had done for him, Luz knew.

"Very well," she assured him, still feeling like thick, rich cream inside.

He pulled the knot of his sash tight. "Tomorrow."

"*Sí.*" The corners of her mouth deepened in a tiny pleased smile. "*Mañana.*" She saw the amused glint in his eyes at her use of Spanish.

Then Raul moved away from the bed, and she watched him leave as silently as he had come. For a little longer, she lay reclined against the pillows, then she reached over and switched off the lamp and snuggled under the covers. The scent of him clung to the sheets. Luz closed her eyes, breathing it in. Sleep came easily to her totally relaxed body.

A pattern was set that night. The days went as they had before, with Raul instructing at the practice field, holding the rap sessions in the game room, and working evenings in his office. Luz saw little of him except at meals in the company of the others. However, Hector had taken it upon himself to change the seating arrangements at the dining table, insisting that Luz sit at the table and act as hostess. With Trisha gone, the change appeared to be a natural one, a courtesy to the only lady present. While Luz liked looking down that long table and seeing Raul sitting at the head of it, the distance limited communication to smiling glances. But they made up for that separation late at night, after everyone else had gone to bed.

September brought sunnier skies and warmer temperatures—and a change in the week's routine. The Argentine polo season was in full swing, which meant weekend competitions at the various polo clubs in the Buenos Aires suburbs. All week they practiced and refined their skills, and on weekends they played polo in earnest. The level of competition, high-goal or low, dictated the makeup of the various teams.

Sometimes Raul and his other professionals made up three of the four. When it was high-goal play, Luis, Carlos, and Raul played with a fourth professional, the Mexican ten-goaler Juan Echevarria. As Raul had explained to Luz, this foursome would compete for the Argentine Open Championship in November, and these preliminary competitions gave them an opportunity to become used to playing together as a unit.

At the Hurlingham Club, Luz stood at the picket line with Rob and watched the four professionals on the field. It was an aggressively played match marred by frequent fouls that continually halted the flow of action for penalty shots, so no momentum was established by either team. But when the final bell rang, Raul's team, Los Pamperos—the Spanish word for the wild wind on the pampas—rode off the field the victors.

Luz walked forward to meet the four returning riders, applauding their skills. "Congratulations! *Magnífico!*" Raul reined his horse to a halt beside her and swung down, elation tempered by fatigue. "Great game." With onlookers around, Luz was careful to keep her attitude casually friendly. When Raul rested an arm about her shoulders, she lightly hooked his waist and glanced at Carlos Rafferty. "That was some goal you made, Carlos," she said as he swung a leg over the front of the saddle and jumped to the ground. "You had hardly any window at all to the posts." Raul's hand tightened on her shoulder, instinctively fitting her closer to his side and making her conscious of his hard-breathing rhythm, a mark of the physical exertion the game required.

"*Sí*, it was something." Carlos grinned. "I did not think I would make it."

As they turned in unison to lead the horses to the picket line, Luz noticed the way Rob was looking at her. She became self-conscious about the arm she had around Raul's waist and let it slide away, angling away from him so that it appeared his hand dropped naturally from her shoulders.

"Are we going to have drinks at the club before driving back?" She moved away from Raul, toward Rob.

"Yes." His glance briefly questioned her action, then darted to her son.

"Rob and I will meet you there." Linking arms with Rob, she turned him in the direction of the clubhouse. "That was a hard-fought game, wasn't it?"

"I guess." He shrugged unresponsively and lifted his arm free of hers, shunning the contact. Frowning, Luz studied the tired, brooding look on his face.

"Is your shoulder hurting? That was a nasty spill you took in the fourth chukkar." Rob had played in an earlier game on another of the club's fields, a game his team had unfortunately lost.

"No. It's all right," he mumbled.

"What's wrong then?"

"Nothing's wrong. Why does something have to be wrong? Can't a guy just not feel like talking?" he retorted sharply in anger, displaying the foul temper she had sensed. She walked, saying nothing, knowing it would blow over as quickly as it had blown up. "Are you planning to fly home on Friday or Saturday?"

"Neither. I thought I'd stay awhile longer." She smiled quickly at him, falsely casual. "After all, there's no real rush to get back."

"What about the horses? I'm not buying more than the nine we've purchased. Aren't you going to ship them back to the States?" Rob challenged.

"Yes, but I decided to send them via Hopeworth Farm. Stan Marshall has imported horses before, so he's familiar with all the paperwork and quarantine procedures. He'll be on hand to accept delivery, so it isn't necessary that I be there." At this time of year in Virginia, the first hint of autumn colors would be showing, but here the green of spring was all around. Here new life was beginning, and Luz felt it was true for her. "Besides, what would I do in Palm Beach by myself? It would be the same old thing—luncheons, benefits, charity socials, committee meetings. I'd rather stay here with you and make sure you learn something." The attempt at lightness was deliberate as she tried to imply there was no special significance to her decision.

"Yeah. I know how interested you are in what I do."

She didn't like his tone. "What's that supposed to mean?"

"You haven't been on the sidelines watching me since before Trisha left, and that's been three weeks ago already," Rob accused. "You're real interested in how well I'm doing."

"I am, Rob. It's just that I've been busy getting all the papers transferred and the bills of sale finalized for the horses you bought." Seven were from Raul and the other two from individual breeders in the area. "Besides . . ." Luz realized she had to tell him the truth about her absence from his workouts. "Raul felt I was distracting you."

"I'll just bet that's what Raul felt," he mocked bitterly, then stopped, causing Luz to halt. "Is it true what the guys are saying about you two?"

The challenge took her completely by surprise. She had thought he was upset over her absence from the practice field.

No words came out. She just stood there looking at him. How did a mother admit to a grown son that she was having an affair?

"It is true, isn't it?" Rob accused in disgust. "He's screwing you, isn't he?"

"Rob, stop it." She clenched her fingers into her hands, holding them rigidly at her side to keep from slapping him.

"You were really all broken up over the divorce, weren't you. It really tore you up, didn't it?" he taunted. "Five months! That's all it's been and already you're hopping into bed with another man. It really hurt you, didn't it? You needed me. That's what you said."

"And I meant it. Rob, you're my son," Luz insisted angrily. "Whatever is between Raul and me has nothing to do with you."

"Hasn't it? Do you think he's going to want me around? Look at the way he's already persuaded you to stay away from the practice sessions. If you can't see what he's doing, you're blind!"

"That isn't true. That came about before I . . . we . . . ever became involved. Raul is no threat to you. You're being childish." She realized immediately that it was the wrong thing to say, however accurate it might be. She was the one guilty of encouraging Rob's closeness and dependency on her. She couldn't blame him for being possessive of her now. "I'll speak to Raul about observing the training sessions again. I'm sure he'll reconsider."

"Be sure to ask him while his cock is stiff. A man will agree to anything then."

She slapped his face. "Don't ever speak to me like that again!"

He went white, his features drawn and pinched with rage. He glared at her for a long second, then turned on his heel and stalked away. Her outrage died almost instantly, leaving a heavy anxiety and confusion in its place.

After four weeks of playing, eating, and relaxing with the other players, Rob was familiar with their backgrounds, habits, and vices. He knew exactly which one to seek out and headed straight to a young Argentine, Tony Lamberti. More than once he'd caught him slipping outside in the evenings to smoke a joint; he had shared one with him a couple times.

"Tony, come here. I gotta talk to you." Rob dragged him away from the trio of giggling girls.

"*Che!* I will let you have one." The handsome dark-haired, dark-eyed man of twenty-two considered himself the consummate lover. Rob had even seen him turning on the charm with Anna.

"You can have all three," Rob muttered indifferently. "Just tell me how I can get my hands on some coke." At the initial frowning stare he received, he added more explicitly, "You know, cocaine."

"*Che! El loco pibe!*"

"English, dammit. And I'm not crazy." Rob struggled to control the seething rage that pushed at him.

Everything had gone sour for him lately. Admittedly he was learning a lot, but somebody was always riding him, criticizing him and finding fault—usually Raul. Now his own mother was going against him. He needed the lift coke could give him. Everybody was trying to drag him down, but he'd show them. Hell, he wasn't hooked on the stuff. It had been four weeks since he'd had any—and he'd been free-basing. That proved he wasn't addicted to it. But he needed its boost right now. Luz could go screw herself silly. He didn't need her.

"Listen, Tony," he lowered his voice. "I want a couple bags of cocaine. I got the money to pay for it. Don't worry. And you know where I can get it. What do you say, *compadre?* You've got your car here." Still hesitant, Tony eyed him warily and Rob's impatience grew. "Don't try to tell me you can't get it. The damned stuff grows here."

"*Sí.* The coca plant is a crop that is grown here. It used to be sold to your Coca-Cola Company. But your government made them take the coke out of the cola, no? Now the workers in the mountains, they are smarter. They chew the leaves so they won't feel so tired or cold or hungry. This has been so for hundreds of years. The coca was considered a divine plant by the Incas. Did you know this?"

"I'm not interested in a damned dissertation on the history of cocaine. Are you going to put me in touch with your dealer or not? All I want is yes or no," Rob demanded.

For a long, slow minute, there was silence as Tony made

up his mind. "He will not sell to you. I will make the buy for you."

A smile spread across Rob's face as he relaxed. "I knew I could count on you, Tony."

"I will make a phone call. We will see."

"Sure, Tony. Sure."

The late return from the polo matches necessitated a late dinner at the *estancia*. After changing clothes, Luz went downstairs to join the others. But her mind wasn't on food. She was just going through the motions for the sake of maintaining the routine so that she didn't draw attention to herself and arouse questions she didn't want to answer. This matter was strictly between herself and Rob, and no one else's business.

The softly flaring skirt of parchment linen brushed her calves as she entered the large living room where the group had assembled. She paused an instant, scanning the faces, then walked in. "Where's Rob? Hasn't he come down yet?"

"I don't think he's back," Duke Sovine replied. "He and Tony left the club together, and they haven't showed up here so far."

"I see," she murmured while her fingers worried with a button on her cream-colored cardigan vest.

"They probably stopped somewhere and ran into some girls. You know how Tony is," the Texan reminded her.

"Yes, of course." It was a logical explanation, and probably accurate. Knowing Rob, he was probably staying out just to make her worry about him. And it was working, she realized with vague irritation. Fixing a smile in place, Luz glanced at Hector and avoided any contact with Raul, the source for Rob's bitter confrontation with her. "I hope you were not planning to wait dinner for them, Hector. They could be quite late."

"*Sí*, we will eat now, but I will make certain there is food waiting for them in the kitchen when they return," Hector promised.

It was late when Rob and Tony returned to the *estancia*. Luz sat tensely in front of the small television set in a corner of the living room, indifferent to the Spanish program being broadcast. When she heard the front door open and boisterous, laughing voices in the entry hall, she made herself remain in the chair. She waited until the approaching footsteps entered the living room, then rose and turned to meet her son. His laughing smile never faded when he saw her, but the defiant glitter in his dark eyes mocked her for waiting up for him.

"Where is everyone?" Tony Lamberti stared at the half-dozen occupants lounging in the living room.

"They've retired to their rooms for the night," Luz replied, aware Raul was among those who had gone upstairs in the last half hour. "It is late," she reminded Rob pointedly and advanced toward the wide doors to the hall. "I believe there is food in the kitchen for you. I'll let Hector know you've returned."

"Don't bother," Rob said. "I'm not hungry."

"Me neither, señora," Tony echoed. "We have already had something. Is that not so, Rob?"

Rob grinned at his companion. "We sure did."

"In that case . . ." Luz paused, turning slightly to face him. "I'd like a private word with you, Rob."

Tony mockingly clicked his tongue at Rob. "Your *madre* is upset with you. You are a bad boy for staying out so late, no?" He gave Rob a shove, pushing him toward Luz. "You must tell her how sorry you are. You do not want her to be angry with you." He walked away laughing, mocking Rob for being a mama's boy.

Reluctantly and defiantly, Rob walked over to her. She had the distinct feeling he'd been drinking, although she could smell no alcohol on his breath. "Where do you want to have this 'private word'?"

"In here." She walked stiffly to the game room, waited until Rob followed her in, then closed the doors. He wandered over to the pool table and began rolling the billiard balls across the felt-covered slate.

"What is it you want? As if I didn't know."

"We need to clear up this business about Raul." Luz caught the ball he was rolling, obtaining Rob's attention. "I was under the impression that you thought a lot of him."

"Yeah, as a polo player." Rob straightened from his bent position. "But if you couldn't stand not having a man, I don't see why you had to pick him."

"I like him, Rob." At the moment, that was as far as it went. Their relationship was more physical than emotional. They enjoyed a sexual intimacy, but they weren't together for long enough periods for it to have advanced very far beyond that. Luz cared for him, but she wasn't sure how much. It hadn't been important to find out yet. "But you are my son. I love you. Nothing—no man—will ever change that."

"Yeah." He picked up another ball and rolled it between his hands.

"That is the truth."

"So you're going to keep sleeping with him, is that it?" A sideways fling of his hand sent the ball careening wildly around the table. "Go ahead. In the meantime, I'm going to pick his brains clean. I'm going to be a better polo player than he ever dreamed of being. I can do it, you know." He tilted his head, a smug confidence in his look. "You'll see. I'm going to be the best."

"And I'll always be there, Rob." She wanted to reassert his importance to her.

"Yeah." He thrust his hands inside his jacket pockets. "If that's all you wanted to talk to me about, I'll go to my room now."

"That's all, I guess." Containing a sigh, Luz decided this grudging acceptance of the situation was the most she could expect from Rob for the time being. Later maybe he'd understand, and there wouldn't be this wedge between them.

After Rob had left the game room, she lingered for a while longer, wondering what else she could have said. Finally she went upstairs to her own room, but the conversation continued to dominate her thoughts. She stood at the window, leaning a shoulder against the heavy wood frame, and stared into the black night. She and Rob had always been so close. Now there was this distance between them.

The divorce was partly to blame for his attitude, Luz realized. She had always known that Rob felt Drew had abandoned him, too. But it had never occurred to Luz that he would regard her relationship with another man as a kind of abandonment as well. In his thinking, Drew had left him for Claudia, and maybe now she was leaving him for Raul. She hadn't thought he'd look at it that way. Somewhere she'd gotten it into her head that only young children went through the trauma of their parents' divorce. Rob was supposedly old enough to understand that it wasn't a rejection of him. But age had nothing to do with some feelings, she realized.

The light rap on her door failed to penetrate her thoughts.

She wasn't conscious of any sound until she heard the click of the latch turning. She glanced toward the door, her start fading when she saw Raul step inside. A frown flickered across his expression as he paused, his gaze taking note of her fully dressed state.

"Is it that late?" She straightened from the window and turned into the room, attempting a welcoming smile.

"It does not matter." Raul crossed to her side and lightly took her shoulders, bending to kiss her upturned face. Her response to the warm pressure of his mouth was not what it could be, she knew. So did Raul. He lifted his head to study her expression. "What is it?"

"Rob knows about us." Luz felt Raul should be aware of it. But this was her problem, not his.

"It upsets you that he knows?"

"Yes . . . no." It was difficult to explain. "I'm not ashamed of being with you. But Rob sees it as some sort of defection. He's angry and hurt. And I am upset that he feels that way. I expected problems with Trisha, but not Rob. I knew he liked you, but I never suspected he would become jealous."

"He will get over it."

"In time, I suppose." She stared at the rough terry cloth of his robe, then put her arms around him and rested her head on his shoulder. His hands moved onto her back, his arms crossing to hold her. He bent his head, rubbing his cheek and jaw against her hair while she absently listened to the steady beat of his heart. Luz closed her eyes, satisfied just to be held. "I'm afraid Rob has gotten the idea that you'll take me away from him. He thinks you're deliberately trying to keep us apart, and my staying away from practice is proof, as far as he's concerned." She tilted her head back to look at him. "Raul, I have to watch the sessions again."

"Even though it will not help him?"

"My not being there has turned into more of a distraction, I'm afraid. It's made him wonder why, and he's come up with the wrong reason. Under the circumstances, I'll never convince him differently. I'll have to be on the sidelines to prove he's wrong."

"And if I say no?"

"Don't, Raul. Don't make me choose," Luz warned. "Because I'll have to choose my son."

"This is your decision, then. My opinion is of no importance even though I am his instructor," he challenged.

"Of course it's important. But don't you see, Rob already resents you. How long do you think it will be before that manifests itself in the workouts? I'm doing this as much for you as for me. Even though Rob is jealous of you, he still respects you. I don't want that to change." She absently studied the narrow line of his lips, so firm and unyielding. A rueful smile slanted her own. "I'm selfish, I guess. I want you both."

"And you always get what you want, no?"

"Yes." Luz smiled before she realized he wasn't making a small joke. She felt his arms loosen their hold. "Raul, is it wrong to try to keep what I have? Isn't there some compromise we can reach? I've already told Rob that he has no say in whom I see. He didn't like it, but he accepted it. Why won't you agree to let me attend practice?"

"It is a compromise you seek. Very well. Then you can watch occasionally, but not every day. Does that suit you?"

"Yes." Raising on her toes, she pressed her lips against his mouth to seal the bargain. She wasn't prepared for the angry way he kissed her back, driving her lips into her teeth.

When she tried to pull away, his hand gripped the back of her head and she was caught between the vise of his mouth and his hand. It was a long moment before the fierce pressure eased and the touch of his lips became almost apologetic in its gentleness. Their lips moistly clung an instant as he slowly broke the contact, then pressed her head against his shoulder.

"I think neither of us is in the proper mood tonight." His voice rumbled huskily from his chest. "It is best if I go, Luz."

"Yes," she agreed, relieved that he saw she wasn't in the mood for lovemaking, although she believed he could change that if he tried. Luz was also aware that he didn't understand her problem and made no pretense that he did. "I'm afraid my mind is elsewhere."

"I noticed." When he released her, she walked with him to the door. He paused there, studying her. "Rob sees tomorrow better than you do, Luz. The day will come when you will leave him, or he will leave you. It always happens."

"I don't believe that." She shook her head in a definite rejection.

"As you wish." Raul shrugged, not arguing the point. Yet

the certainty in his expression vaguely frightened her. She held the door open as he stepped into the hallway.

"Good night." Impulsively she moved to kiss him, seeking some kind of reassurance that nothing had really changed.

Before the contact was made, someone coughed delicately to warn them of his presence. Luz jerked her gaze toward the sound, instantly locating the source as Duke Sovine sauntered down the hallway.

"I left my cigarettes downstairs." He held out the pack to show them, then stopped outside a room two doors away from hers. His knowing glance shifted to Raul. "You know, you're slowly wearin' a path on this carpet," he drawled, then disappeared inside his room.

Luz realized that Rob was right. The others knew about Raul's late-night visits to her room.

"Did you think we were fooling them?" Raul asked, and she saw it was no surprise to him.

"Not really," she supposed. "In the beginning, I guess I wanted to keep it private. Now . . . maybe it's better that it's in the open."

# CHAPTER XXIV

As the buildings of the *estancia* came into sight, Luz slowed her horse and waited for the slower-traveling Hector to catch up with her. The shoulder-high stalks of the pampas grass swished noisily as his palomino moved up alongside her liver-colored mount. The accompanying outrider, one of the modern gauchos who tended the *estancia's* cattle and horse herds, rode with them, maintaining a discreet distance.

"It's so beautiful out here I almost hate to go back." Luz gazed at the sea of green grass that surrounded them, rippling in the wind like ocean waves. In the last two weeks, spring had exploded across the pampas as September had given way to October. Everything was a vibrant green, bursting with new life.

The palomino whickered, nodding its head. Hector laughed. "Rubio agrees with you."

"Rubio, is that his name?" She glanced at the well-trained gelding, so palely golden in color with a flaxen mane and tail.

"His full name is El Rubio Rey, the blond king. You see how proudly he walks, never paying any attention to the fluttering of wings or the crash of a cow through the grass. He expects them to move out of his way, no?"

"He does." Smiling widely, she agreed with the description. It was also this unblinking steadiness that made the palomino a reliable mount for the crippled man.

The outrider spurred his horse to ride ahead and open the pasture gate for them. After they passed through the opening in the fence, they crossed the dirt road and trotted their horses into the stableyard.

The area was astir with activity. The morning session on the polo field was over, and the yard was crowded with ponies and grooms while the riders drifted toward the house. Luz looked first for Rob, finding him, as expected, with Tony. Lately it seemed that he spent almost all of his free time with the young Argentine. Rob had always been such a loner that it was good to see him making friends. Still, she sensed that part of it was a means of getting back at her, showing her that he preferred someone else's company to hers as he believed she had done with Raul. Rob nursed his hurts for a long time, and was very slow to forgive an injury. He was deliberately going to make it tough on her.

It was a spoiled and selfish attitude. Luz could see that, but she didn't know what to do about it, other than to play his game. She had resumed watching his practices on an irregular basis, catching a morning or afternoon session almost every other day, sometimes staying for all of it.

Now that her affair with Raul was common knowledge, she no longer watched how she acted around him in front of everyone. She wasn't openly demonstrative with her affection, but neither was she shy about touching him or taking his arm, smiling at him warmly or simply gazing at him while he talked to someone else. Gradually, Raul had become less circumspect in his actions, too, sometimes putting his arm around her as they sat together in the evenings. Several times she had looked at him and seen the smile in his eyes. Two nights he had even walked upstairs with her.

Rob's reaction had thus far been a determined effort to ignore them, sometimes to the point of leaving the room. Luz was certain he'd get used to seeing them together in time. She liked this new dimension in her relationship with Raul. It was no longer a strictly sexual companionship, although the passion between them remained as strong as before. It was talking and having him listen to her, whether they were discussing the weather, horses, or training methods—and vice versa. Sometimes she believed she was falling in love with him, but she always backtracked from that thought. It was too soon. She couldn't open herself to that potential hurt yet.

Still her heart gave a very definite leap when she saw him walking to meet them. A small part of her, still sensitive from Drew's rejection, doubted that a man as handsome as Raul could be seriously interested in her. He caught at the reins of her dark red chestnut and halted it beside him.

"Did you enjoy your ride?" His hand was at her waist, steadying her when she jumped to the ground. It stayed, maintaining the contact, while he gazed at her.

"It was wonderful." But it was equally wonderful having him waiting here. She knew her expression indicated as much.

"It must have been to put such a sparkle in your eyes," Raul observed.

"Are you on your way to the house for lunch?" Luz asked as Hector unbuckled the leg straps that held him in the saddle. Two stablehands waited to help him down.

"No. El Gato injured a tendon this morning. I will be there after I have looked at him," he said, referring to one of the ponies on his playing string.

"Good. That will give me time to freshen up."

"Leave the sparkle." Raul smiled.

Filled with a warm, heady feeling, Luz watched him walk toward the near stable, then turned to check Hector's progress. As the two men lifted him from the saddle, she fetched the crutches lying nearby and gave them to him one at a time. It was difficult to remember how conscious of his handicap she had been less than two months ago. She rarely thought about it anymore.

"Ready?" she asked after he had adjusted his leg braces.

*"Sí."* With a swing of his crutches and a drag of his legs, he started for the house, moving briskly and forcing Luz to do the same. "You are good for Raul," he stated. "Many times I have wished he would take himself a woman."

"You'll never convince me, Hector, that he hasn't had a woman before," she said dryly.

"He has had many women in his bed, Luz, but none in his home," he informed her, his expression very serious. "He has not known this warmth a woman can give to his life."

"It can't be for the lack of willing females," she mused, then glanced curiously at Hector. "Surely there's been some he loved. You have been his friend for years. You must know."

"Once or twice. But the leopard cannot change its spots and a man cannot change what he is. I think they did not like being alone so much while he was away playing polo. But that is what he is: So, he goes alone. With you, it is different. You do not begrudge him the time he spends on the polo field, no?"

"No."

"Then you are good for him."

But was she? Luz found herself wondering. She had not considered before what she could give him. There wasn't much more she could offer him, but herself. Money, of course, but its importance to him was linked to polo rather than a desire for a personal accumulation of wealth. A home, yes, but a family—children of his own—at her age? It was doubtful that she would be able to conceive, and if she could, did she want to raise another family as Drew was about to do? She didn't think so. The realization sobered her. Raul was younger. He deserved those things.

When they reached the house, she automatically waited for Hector to open the front door for her as he always did. "I have said something wrong, no?" He leaned on his crutches and tipped his grizzled head to the side, to study her.

"No. I was thinking of something else," she lied. Eyeing her skeptically, Hector turned the doorknob, then pushed the heavy door open with the end of his crutch. Luz walked past him into the house, then paused a moment while he followed her inside and pushed the door shut with his crutch. "I'm going up to my room and get cleaned up. I enjoyed the ride, Hector. Thanks for coming with me."

"It is I who thank you. I do not often have the pleasure of a beautiful lady's company."

"You are dangerous, Hector." She laughed in her throat. "You make a woman want to believe your lies."

But he had succeeded in pushing aside her pensive mood. A faint smile curved her mouth as she ran lightly up the stairs in her riding boots. Nearing the top of the steps, Luz heard a loud commotion in the upper hallway, a pair of voices raised in anger. One of them sounded like Rob's. She hurried the last few steps and rounded the newel post on the second-floor landing as a door banged open and the muffled voices became distinct.

"Get out of here! Get out, you gruesome old hag!" Rob emerged from his room, shouting at a confused and shrinking Anna. "If I ever catch you in here again, I'll—" He advanced on her threateningly, his face livid with rage.

"Rob!" Luz ran forward to intervene, stunned by his fury. Instinctively she put her arms around the stout woman, both to comfort her and to shield her from Rob's wrath. "What's going on here?"

"I walked in and caught her stealing!"

"No, señora, no. *Por favor.*" Anna shook her head wildly in denial, and a spate of Spanish followed. Luz had picked up a little of the language since they'd been here, but not enough to understand the maid's frantic, rapid flow. Yet it was obviously a protestation of innocence and it sounded very genuine to Luz.

"*Momento. Momento, por favor.*" She interrupted the incomprehensible flood of Spanish from Anna and turned to Rob. "Are you sure, Rob? What did she take?"

"Nothing, but only because I caught her in the act! That fat old bitch was going through my drawers when I came in! My watch, my billfold, my money, my credit cards—everything's in there. She was going to make a damned good haul," he accused viciously.

"No. No, señora." Again, a torrent of Spanish began.

"Anna, *más despacio, por favor.*" Luz asked her to say it again more slowly. The maid tried speaking more slowly, all the while throwing Rob wild-eyed glances. A great deal Luz couldn't follow, but she caught the word *lavado*. "*El lavado?* Laundry?" she asked to make sure she had understood.

"*Sí, sí.*" Between the Spanish that followed and the pantomime from the maid, Luz finally understood.

"Rob, I think you jumped to the wrong conclusion. Anna was only putting your clean laundry away." She glanced through the open door to his room. "Look. Some of it is still sitting on top of your dresser."

"She just used that as an excuse to protect her ass," he jeered.

"Rob, I don't appreciate your language." She could overlook the things he'd said in the heat of anger, but this continued vulgar abuse she found offensive.

A second later, she heard the rapid clump of Hector's crutches on the carpet runner in the hall. She turned to meet him, as did Anna, who immediately launched into vociferous Spanish. When she was finished, Luz explained Rob's side of the incident.

"Señor Rob, I am sorry, but Anna was only putting your laundry away as she always does," Hector assured him. "She would take nothing. She is an honest woman."

Displeased with the verdict, Rob pressed his lips tightly together, thinning out their line. "I know what I saw," he muttered.

"Rob," Luz murmured in exasperation, wishing he would simply admit he was wrong.

"I don't want her going through my drawers anymore—ever! From now on, she can leave the laundry on the bed and I'll put my own clothes away."

Hector exchanged glances with Luz, then acceded to the demand. "If that is what you wish, I will tell her. I would be most happy to lock your valuables in our—"

"No. I'll keep them where I know they're safe." Rob angrily waved a hand in Anna's direction. "Just make sure she stays out of my things. I don't want her snooping around."

"*Sí*—"

But Rob never gave him a chance to finish as he swung around and stormed into his room, slamming the door. He went straight to the open dresser drawer and pulled out the pair of socks at the bottom of the pile, the pair he'd caught Anna transferring to the top. His stash of cocaine was still inside. He closed his eyes, relief sagging through him.

There was a knock on his door, and his hand tightened instinctively on the sock. When he heard the door open, he turned, quickly thrusting his hand behind his back to hide it from his mother. "I think you're supposed to wait until you're invited in," he said curtly.

"If there is going to be any lecture on manners, you are the one who needs it. You were worse than rude out there, Rob. Even when your suspicions were proved wrong, you didn't have the grace to apologize. What has gotten into you, Rob?" she demanded.

"All right, so maybe I made a mistake. You'd be upset too if it happened to you," he retorted. "If it will make you feel any better, I'll apologize the next time I see her. Will that satisfy you?"

"It's better than nothing." Luz moved her head in a confused shake, sensing the chip on his shoulder. He'd always been a little withdrawn, but never this distant. "Rob, what's wrong? It isn't like you to be so churlish."

"I found somebody going through my drawers and I'm upset. That's what's wrong. Why don't you go back to your Latin lover's arms and leave me alone? Nobody asked you to interfere."

She stiffened at his sarcastic rejoinder. "Are you still upset about Raul?" She had hoped he'd gotten over his initial resentment of their relationship, but it seemed he still intended to punish her for deserting him. "Rob, you are of my flesh and blood. No man on earth can change that."

But he refused to listen to her. "Forget it. Look, I've said I was sorry. What more do you want? A guy can be wrong once in a while, can't he?"

"Yes. And you were wrong about Anna—just as you're wrong about Raul." Nothing she said seemed to reach him. This wasn't the Rob she knew, and she wondered at the change in him, telling herself he'd been under considerable stress lately, weighted by his driven determination to excel at polo. Maybe that was why he was reacting so strongly against Raul. A little more time and a little more patience on her part seemed to be in order. She opened the door, then paused, finally saying, "I'll see you downstairs."

The minute the door shut behind her and he heard her footsteps moving down the hall, he hid the socks in his drawer, then tore off a strip of note paper from his writing tablet on top of the chest and wedged it between the edge of the drawer and its frame so he'd know if anyone snooped in his drawers again.

Shivering, Luz hugged the beach robe more tightly around her as she hurried into the house. The mid-October sun had been warm, but the water in the swimming pool had been decidedly cool. She headed directly to the stairs, rubbing the towel over her wet hair. As she passed the lonely side table in the foyer, she noticed the stack of mail on top of it and paused. Obviously someone had just brought it in, since Hector hadn't sorted it yet. She hesitated, then riffled through it to see if anything had come for her.

There was a skinny letter from Trisha, which she set aside, and one from Emma, no doubt containing the monthly household report and a tactfully worded inquiry as to the date of Luz's expected return. Luz grimaced slightly when she saw the thick envelope bearing her mother's handwriting. She didn't have to read it to know what was inside. If it ran true to the previous ones, there would be three pages of not so subtle demands to know when Luz was coming back and why a trip of three or possibly four weeks had turned into more than two months. After that, there would be three pages of family news.

The bottom third of the stack of letters were all addressed to Raul. She started to lay them aside, then her eye was caught by the familiar handwriting on one of the envelopes. It was from Trisha. She chewed at the inside of her lower lip, absently tasting the chlorine, and tapped the envelope against her hand.

Was this the first time Trisha had written him, or had there been others? Not once in all the letters Luz had received from her daughter had she mentioned Raul beyond asking that she say hello for her. Lately, that hadn't even been tacked on to the end. She had hoped the newness of college surroundings had put Raul out of Trisha's mind. Obviously, it hadn't.

Luz debated a minute longer, then added Trisha's letter to Raul to her stack. When she heard Hector approaching from the living room, she turned, smiling. "I've already gotten my mail. When Raul comes in, will you tell him I want to see him? It's important."

"Sí, I will tell him."

"I'll be in my room." With the letters clutched in her hand, she moved to the steps and hurried up the stairs to her room.

Once inside, she tore open the letter from Trisha addressed to her and scanned the contents. It was filled with references to the courses she was taking, the sorority she had pledged, and classmates and professors. She asked how Rob was doing, obviously accepting that Luz was staying in Argentina because of her brother. But not one word about Raul. Luz glanced at his envelope, then laid them all aside and went into the bathroom to take a hot shower and get dressed for dinner.

An hour later, she heard muffled voices and the heavy tread of booted feet along the upper hallway. The afternoon session was over, which meant time for a quick shower and change before they all congregated in the game room. Raul should be coming any moment. She paced absently, waiting, her gaze continually straying to the unopened envelope addressed to him, lying on her nightstand.

Time dragged and her tension mounted, but still he didn't come. A half-dozen times, Luz went to the door and paused with her hand on the knob, debating whether she should seek him out. Maybe Hector hadn't given him her message. Instinctively she knew better, and she never turned the knob. Her irritation grew with each passing minute.

When he finally knocked at the door, she jerked it open and barely gave him time to step inside the room before she verbally assailed him. "Where have you been? Practice broke up more than an hour and a half ago. I have been waiting all this time to talk to you. I told Hector I wanted to see you as soon as you came in. Didn't you get my message?"

"Yes, he told me you wanted to see me. I was busy. I came as soon as I could." The assertion was confirmed by the smudged and sweaty riding clothes he still wore, but Luz was too annoyed to notice.

"As soon as you could." She hurled his words back at him. "Didn't Hector tell you I said it was important? Do you realize how long I've been waiting here for you?"

"I was busy," Raul snapped. "Do you think because you snap your fingers, I must come running? I am not some gigolo who answers to your beck and call!"

"I never implied you were!"

"No? I come the moment I am free, and it is not good enough for you. I kept you waiting, no? What do you call this?" he demanded angrily. "What is it you expect from me? What is it you want?"

Luz drew back from his challenge, her anger receding to a protective wariness. "Nothing. I wanted to talk to you about something."

"Talk." He moved toward her, and Luz stood her ground. When he stopped in front of her, he seemed to loom around her, enveloping her in his presence while not touching her at all. His narrowed gaze bored into her, delving deep, too deep for comfort. "Is that all you want from me? Do you want me to touch you, to hold you, to kiss you? Do you want me to make love to you? You have never said any of this. Do you want me, Luz?"

A protest clamored inside at the open admission he was

demanding from her. "It isn't fair to ask that. If I answer yes, I sound like some weak female who can't exist without a man," she argued. "I am allowed some pride."

"I say these things to you," Raul reminded her tautly. "Does that make me sound like a female? I am a man. Where is my pride? Always I come to you. You never come to me. Where is the fairness in that? Must I always be the one? Will you never lie in my bed, only yours? You asked me once whether I wanted you. Now it is my turn. Do you want me?"

"Sometimes—sometimes I want you so much, Raul, that it frightens me." Perhaps never more than now had she wanted him so much, nor been so frightened by the force of it. Until now, the affair had been conducted on her terms, and she'd felt safe, always making him seek her out, never exposing herself to possible rejection.

But there was no rejection as his hands pulled at her waist to draw her into his embrace. Her half-known fears seemed very foolish under the warm, demanding pressure of his kiss. She didn't have to hold back anymore, nor was she driven by a vague desperation to take and hold on to the glorious sensations of the moment in case they never came again.

"I do want you, Raul, I do," she murmured over and over again, all the restraints finally gone. When she finally pulled away, it was to say, "Let me make love to you."

She saw the desire glazing his blue eyes as he nodded slowly. Her fingers pulled at the bottom of his snug-fitting polo shirt where it was tucked inside his breeches. When it was free of them, she hiked it over his ribs and across the breadth of his chest. Raul flinched visibly.

"*Cuidado!*" Pain edged his cautioning mutter.

"What is it?" Frowning, Luz scanned his face, not raising the shirt any higher.

"My left shoulder. I have bruised it." Raul took over the task of removing his shirt, pulling his right arm free of the sleeve, then dragging the shirt over his head and easing the left sleeve off his injured shoulder.

Nearly all of the skin on his upper arm and back shoulder was mottled black and blue. Luz hesitantly touched the bruised area with her fingertips, guessing how very sore it must be. "You fell." Vaguely she remembered that he'd barely used that arm at all when he'd embraced her moments ago. It had been his right hand and arm that had pressed and urged closer contact.

"*Sí*. Lamberti's horse went down in front of mine. He broke his wrist and arm in the fall. I had to take him to the small hospital in the village. That is where I have been the last three hours," he said. "Or I probably would have come when you snapped your fingers."

Luz backed a step away from him and turned to cover her mouth, realizing how petty and self-centered she had been. "You should have slapped me . . . walked out . . . or something." She swung back to him. "Is he all right?"

"*Sí*. He will be in a plaster cast for a few weeks, but the breaks were clean," he assured her. "Hector should have told you the reason I was delayed, but I think he was busy. I am glad I did not hit you or walk out. I have waited a long time to hear you say that you want me as I want you." His fingers traced the curve of her throat and lingered on the pulsing vein. Raul brought his hand down and stood facing her. "I have only one good arm, so you will have to make love to me."

"It will be my pleasure," Luz said and meant it literally.

Much later, she lay utterly contented, nestled against his right side, her arm curved on his chest. The sensations she felt with Raul were so different from anything she'd known with Drew. It was funny, but she could think about Drew without rancor now, remembering the happier times instead of the bad.

Maybe she owed that to Raul along with so many other things, like her renewed self-esteem and confidence. She wouldn't put a name to the feelings she had for him, but she admitted to herself that she didn't want the affair to end. Before she hadn't wanted to look beyond today. Now she wanted to make plans for tomorrow.

"How is Rob doing? Are you getting along with him?" Luz hadn't mentioned the unfortunate incident between her son and the maid. If Hector had told him, Raul hadn't said anything to her. Ever since, she had wondered if the rage Rob had exhibited had been the release of pent-up resentment toward Raul. From the stick-and-ball sessions she'd observed, she hadn't sensed any hostility between them, but she hadn't been close enough to catch the nuances of voice or expression.

Raul rolled onto his right side, levering himself up on his elbow to look down at her. "After we make love, you want to question me about your son?" he challenged while his hand stroked the bare flesh of her hip and stomach.

Involuntarily she moved in response to his caress while she tried not to be distracted by it. "Lately he seems different, and I wondered if you had noticed it."

"He has been on edge, moody on occasions." His hand continued to make its lazy, stroking circles over her flesh. "Why do you ask?"

"Sometimes I have the feeling he still resents our being together, and I wondered how he acted toward you when I'm not around."

"He respects me. He does not necessarily like me," he replied, and Luz wondered if she was making a bigger problem out of this than it was. Perhaps she was being too sensitive. It was natural for Rob to respond negatively to her involvement with another man, to feel a little threatened.

Bending, Raul kissed a quiescent nipple and teased it erect with a curling lick of his tongue. She felt the involuntary tightening in her loins. "Are we through talking about him?"

"Actually . . ." Her hand glided along his arm, avoiding the bruised area at the top. "It was a way of leading up to my next question—whether you've made any playing commitments for the winter season in Florida yet."

"I have been approached by some team sponsors, but nothing has been confirmed. Why?" But he seemed more interested in toying with her breasts.

"Because . . ." She paused, liking the way he was distracting her. "I'm going to sponsor a team for Rob. I want him to play with the best, and that's you. I also thought you might continue to coach him if you two were getting along. Does the idea appeal to you?"

"You appeal to me."

"Raul," Luz protested his avoidance of her question, but not too vigorously.

Much to her regret, he lifted his head to gaze lazily at her. "I have never played for a woman before."

"You've only played *with* them, is that it?" she murmured, stroking the outline of his mouth.

He chuckled in his throat. "It is more fun, no?" he countered and kissed her teasing finger.

"And maybe it would be more fun to do both?" Luz suggested. "I have a big house, stables on the grounds, a practice field, and a huge king-sized bed. Where will you ever get that kind of an offer? Just think of the fringe benefits. What's your answer? Will you play *with* and *for* me?"

"It will be my pleasure." He leaned down, kissing her lips slowly and thoroughly, then nuzzled their corners. "Is this the important thing you were so anxious to talk to me about?"

She went still beneath him. "No." When he raised his head to investigate the peculiar flatness in her voice, Luz shifted on the rumpled quilt and reached for the envelope on the nightstand. "This came for you today." She gave it to him and watched his expression. When he turned the envelope over to glance at the back flap, she said, "I didn't open it." Not that she hadn't been tempted. "I wasn't aware she was writing to you."

"Only twice before." Raul absently studied the envelope but made no move to open it.

"What does she write you about?"

"Do you want to read this?" He offered it to her.

"No." She turned her head on the pillow in a negative movement. It was better if she didn't know the private things Trisha wrote him.

"Nor do I." He tossed it back onto the nightstand.

"I haven't gotten around to telling her about us."

"Why?"

"I wasn't sure how long it would last." Luz studied the faint white line of an old scar on his chest where a horse had kicked him. "I wasn't even sure if I wanted it to."

"Now?" There was a measuring quality in his look.

"And now, I want you to play on my team," she answered lightly.

"What if this is not what Rob wants? Or your daughter?" Raul questioned the depth of her commitment.

She had thought through the first part of his question. "Rob wants to play polo and he wants to improve his game. Regardless of how he may feel about you personally, I think he still believes you can help him to do that. Trisha is another matter," she admitted heavily. "I guess I can't put off writing her about us any longer. Maybe she'll have time to get over the worst of it before we see her. I'll know more in November.

Trisha always surprises me. She never does what I expect her to do."

"November. It is so close." He rubbed the soft point of her shoulder.

"You'll come before the end of the month, won't you? We'll have the holidays together before you and Rob have to start selecting the other players on your team in December."

"I think I can arrange that."

She smoothed her hand over his chest. "Do you suppose dinner is ready yet?"

"Perhaps we can enjoy an appetizer, first," he suggested as his hand slid lower on her stomach.

"What about your shoulder?"

His kiss proved to be a very satisfactory answer.

Late that evening, Luz wrote the long-postponed letter to Trisha. It was the most difficult letter she had ever written; she tried to word everything carefully to soften the blow, implying an affair without baldly stating it. She had even more misgivings the next day when she gave the envelope to Hector to mail. But it was done, and she was, at least, freed from the guilt of hiding it.

# CHAPTER XXV

Shortly after breakfast on Friday, Luz walked out the front doorway and paused to wait for Hector to join her. The dark sable coat was draped over her arm, the white linen jacket providing sufficient cover for the spring temperature of the pampas. Her glance strayed to the car parked in front of the mammoth gray stone house as Raul stowed the last of their luggage in the trunk. Although she and Rob weren't scheduled to leave for the States until Monday, the polo matches being held this weekend in Buenos Aires made it practical for them to spend their last days in the city.

She heard the door shut and swung her attention back to the gray-haired man with her. He made his awkward-looking turn away from the door and started immediately for the car, as if conscious of the wait she'd already had while he'd maneuvered out of the door and closed it.

"There is still time to change your mind and come to the polo matches with us, Hector." Luz made a last attempt to persuade him as they walked to the car.

"The *estancia* could not function without me for three days," he insisted, then showed her a mustached smile. "It is the truth."

"I believe you." But she regretted parting from him so soon, and swung around to face him when they reached the car. "I will miss you, Hector—our talks and our rides."

"We will all miss you, Señora Luz. You have filled the house with your 'light.'" His dark eyes seemed more brilliant, fond in their gaze.

Raul joined him, but his attention was centered on the two

men digging close to the front foundation of the house. "What are those workers doing?" He frowned.

Smiling, Hector looked at Luz. "They are planting vines. I remember what you said. The next time you come, Señora Luz, those gray stones will have a shawl of green and the house will not look so cold."

The next time you come. The phrase echoed in her mind. She wanted to come back—to Argentina, to the pampas, to the *estancia*. Hector wanted her to come back. She hoped Raul would, although she tried not to think too far ahead. There was no comment from Raul, regarding either the planting of the vines or Hector's reference to her return. The frown was gone from his face, leaving his features void of expression.

Turning, he opened the passenger door. "We should leave."

"Goodbye, Hector." She clasped his hand and kissed him on both cheeks.

"In Argentina, we say *chau*. Too many Italians," Hector said to explain the marked similarity to *ciao*, thus covering his emotions while he gently squeezed her hand.

"*Chau.*" Luz smiled, then turned to the car, sensing Raul's impatience.

Moving past him, she slid onto the seat and concentrated on arranging the fur coat on her lap while Raul closed the door. Briefly she wished Rob had chosen to ride with them instead of traveling with the other players, although the three of them confined together in a car for nearly four hours might have been a considerable strain. It was natural, she told herself, that Rob would prefer to ride with his friends and fellow players. Sometimes she felt she was being overly sensitive, reading things into his normal moodiness that weren't there.

As Raul climbed into the driver's side, Luz turned and waved to Hector. When they pulled away, her glance took in the austere manor house, the roofs of the stone barns, and the green of the polo fields for the last time. The broad leaves of the eucalyptus trees formed a canopy over the long driveway, casting shadows on the car. The next time you come . . . the words came back, and she wondered when that would be.

"Have the horse vans left yet?"

"Nearly an hour ago," Raul replied.

"Rob will probably meet us at the hotel." She glanced at

Raul's unsmiling face and noted its brooding look. "Is something wrong?"

"No." His response seemed unusually abrupt. Reaching down, he flipped on the radio and tuned in some music to fill the silence. Frequently, Raul became quiet and introspective prior to a polo match. It was his way of concentrating on game strategy, he had once told her. Luz didn't intrude on his thoughts and soon became lost in her own.

Spring in Buenos Aires fulfilled the promise Luz had seen on her arrival in the country. The jacaranda and *paraiso*— paradise—trees lining the city streets lavishly adorned the vistas with purple and yellow blossoms. At almost every street corner, there was a flower stall, a vibrant splash of colors as vivid and varied as an artist's palette.

It was infinitely better to gaze out the side windows of the car than to look where they were going, Luz had discovered. She was fairly certain only licensed daredevils drove in the downtown traffic, although Raul seemed unperturbed by the mad changing of lanes by the cars in front or beside him.

Luz recognized the facade of the hotel as Raul drove up to the entrance. After the car rolled to a sensible halt, the uniformed doorman stepped up to open her door, bowing slightly and extending a hand to help her out of the car. She waited on the front steps while the luggage was unloaded from the trunk. Raul said something in Spanish to the doorman, then joined her, his hand gripping her elbow to guide her into the lobby. His expression remained preoccupied, almost grimly so, Luz noticed.

After registering at the desk, they were escorted to the bedroom suite. When Luz glanced into the second bedroom, she noticed Rob's polo shirt and breeches hanging in the closet. "I guess Rob's been here and gone." Raul stood at the window overlooking the city and the Rio de la Plata, giving no indication he'd heard her. Luz hesitated, then went into the bathroom to freshen up. When she came out a few minutes later, Raul was still standing at the window, his position unchanged.

Hesitating, she studied him, then walked over to the window and smoothed the frown from her face with a smile. "What are you thinking about?" She tried to inject a lightness into her voice.

For a moment, he stared at her as though she were a stranger to him. Luz was suddenly and unexplicably uneasy. "Come." Moving, he curved an arm around her shoulders and turned her from the window. "There is something I want you to see." He propelled her toward the door.

"Where are we going?" she asked, but he didn't answer her.

The *estancia* car was still parked in front of the entrance when they emerged from the hotel. Raul guided her to it. As soon as she was settled in the passenger seat, he slammed the door and walked around to the driver's side. Luz watched him slide behind the wheel and start the motor. The muscles stood out along his jaw, betraying the tension that charged the air. He seemed almost angry, which thoroughly confused her.

While Raul battled through the downtown traffic, Luz sat silently, trying to figure out what was wrong, and half worried it had something to do with Rob. She didn't understand why Raul was keeping their destination a secret. If they were going to the polo grounds, why didn't he say so? It didn't make sense.

Caught up in her thoughts, she paid little attention to the areas they traveled through until Raul slowed the car and turned onto a narrow street. Luz stiffened when it finally registered where they were. On both sides of the car, squalid huts of tin, wood, and cardboard littered the blocks. *Las villas miseria.* Why would Raul bring her here? She stared out the window at the clutter of shabby dwellings, a television antenna poking incongruously from the tin roof of one of them. He turned onto a side street, narrower than the last. It took them deeper into the shanty district, and her apprehensions increased.

"Raul, where are we going?"

At last her voice made an impression on him, and he glanced at her, his eyes appearing cold with challenge. "I want to show you the place where I once lived." He faced the front again, his gaze sweeping the miserable shacks all crowded together. Her mind went blank at his stunning announcement. She was completely at a loss for words, unsure whether she was shocked, dismayed, or repelled by this revelation of his past. "Would you like to see it?"

Her mouth worked for an instant before anything came out. "Yes. I would."

She stared out the window at the makeshift hovels, oblivious to the turns he made that failed to change the scenery. She remembered what he'd told them when they had driven past this area on the way to the *estancia*—about the shortage of housing and the constant immigration of people from rural areas into the city, more than could be accommodated.

Raul stopped the car on one of the back streets, switched off the motor, and stepped out. Luz waited an instant, then realized he wasn't going to come around and open her door. He was standing at the collection of shacks across the road. She hesitated, then climbed out of the car by herself. Conscious of the eyes staring from behind rickety fences and crude doorways, Luz walked cautiously forward. In her white linen suit and white open-toed heels, she felt decidedly out of place. There was little sound except for the distant laughter of playing children, as if their presence had hushed everyone in the immediate vicinity. She tucked her purse more securely under her arm and continued to Raul's side.

She saw the cold, remote look on his face. Although he appeared to take no notice of her, he waited until she was beside him, then started across the street. Luz followed a step behind and stopped when he did.

"It was there, where that brush grows." He indicated a spot half enclosed by a rickety fence. Luz stared at it, unable to visualize what he saw in his mind. "I made a shelter out of cardboard boxes, big enough for me to sleep in. Sometimes I would build a little fire outside, but only a little one. I did not want my house to burn. It was not always easy to get more cardboard boxes. And a stableboy does not make much money. I was always hungry." Raul spoke as if she weren't there. "Many times, I stole from the vegetable gardens of the others who lived here. Sometimes I would fill my pockets with the grain from the stables and make a mush that I heated in a can over my little fire."

Silently she studied him, unable to find anything to say. She wanted to touch him, to link her arm with his, but she couldn't do that either. They stood side by side, but separately.

"I wanted to be a horse—like one of the fast, powerful animals I cared for—only I would let no man ride me. I would run free with the wind." For a long minute, he simply stared at the patch of ground by the scraggly bush, green leaves sprouting where its twiglike branches weren't broken. "I had

a small sack in which I put my few belongings. I took it with
me wherever I went. I was like one of your bag ladies in New
York, no?"

"Yes," she murmured.

The sound of her voice seemed to break the spell of the past
that had ensnared him. His head lifted as he turned to look at
her, again his action giving the impression he had forgotten
she was there. "You have seen enough?" he demanded.

"Yes."

They walked back to the car, and Raul escorted her to the
passenger side. Luz was unwilling to break the long silence
during the drive back to the hotel. A thousand questions tangled
in her mind. There were so many holes in her knowledge of
him, missing pieces that kept the picture incomplete. And there
was nothing she could say about what she'd seen, no comment
she could make that wouldn't sound inanely trite.

When they reached the hotel, Raul left the car for the attendant to park and silently accompanied Luz to their room.
Once inside the suite, she walked to a side table and laid her
purse on it, then turned to face Raul. He lit a thin black cheroot
and blew out the smoke he'd inhaled, looking at her through
its trailing cloud.

"I see the questions in your eyes. You want to know it all,
no?" he observed tersely.

Briefly she dropped her gaze, then brought it back to him.
"I wish I could say—only if you want to tell me. But, yes, I
do want to know. I'd be lying if I said I don't."

He took another drag on the narrow cigar as if stalling for
a moment while he debated whether to tell her, then he turned
and walked away from her to the window, giving her only a
side view of him. "Before I came to Buenos Aires, I lived in
the Pampa." Again he spoke in the singular, as he had done
at the *villas miseria*. In previous conversations, he had indicated
he had come with his mother, which meant it should be plural—
*we* came, *we* lived. Luz was confused by this apparent contradiction. "You have not seen the western pampas."

"No," she admitted.

"The land is much drier, more desolate than where the *estancia* is located. Always there was dust." He stared out the
window, idly taking a puff on the black cigar. "My father was
a farmer. He had a small piece of land. My mother told me

our life was good then. There was always plenty of food on our table. Then one day he left when I was three years old. I never knew why. I only remember *mia madre* crying . . . crying all the time. We had to move off the farm. It was not ours anymore. I think my father sold it and took the money with him." His accent became more pronounced as his voice dropped to a husky level. "My mother went to work at a big *estancia* not far from where our farm had been, and we were allowed to live in a worker's hut on the land. It was made of adobe, one big room with a metal roof, much like the one by the *ombu* tree where we took shelter from the rain."

"I remember." And she also remembered how he had compared it to the home he had known.

"I earned my first money when I was six years old carrying water for the horses on the *estancia*. The year I was eight, my mother became sick. All the money we had saved to go to Buenos Aires went to the doctor. That is when I quit school and went to work as a stableboy at the *estancia*. My mother did not get well. The following year, the priest from the village came to see me. He told me my mother was dying. I think I already knew that she was never going to get better." He rolled the cigar between his thumb and fingers and studied the ravel of smoke. "That night I took the few pesos we had, some food and clothes, and left."

"You left your mother?" Luz was stunned.

"*Sí.*" Raul gave her an emotionless look. "She was dying. There was nothing I could do for her. Soon she would be gone. If I did not go to Buenos Aires then, when would I go? I suppose this is what I thought. She was dying and there was no more reason for me to stay."

"So you left her, the way your father did," she accused, then a second thought occurred to her. "Or did you leave her before she could leave you?"

"I no longer know what was in my head then. It has been too long. I heard later that she died shortly after I ran away. The rest of my story you know. It is well you know. A man cannot change what he is."

"That's what Hector said about you," she recalled. "Yet you have changed, Raul. Look at where you've been and where you are." But had he changed? Was he still the little boy wanting to be a horse? He had learned to ride as one with a horse—

like the legendary gaucho, half man and half horse—and his life-style was one of a roamer, running free, always leaving something or someone behind. "The women you loved, Raul, I wonder if you left them because of polo or because you wanted to avoid finding out if they would leave you. Leaving is your specialty, isn't it? You always leave before somebody gets too close to you."

"You have forgotten Hector," Raul said, dismissing her amateur analysis. "He has been my friend for years. I depend on him."

For an instant, Luz believed she was wrong, then she remembered, "But Hector is safe, Raul. He's a cripple. How can he leave you?"

"You have seen too many psychiatrists. Perhaps I am only realistic. My life is polo. Women do not want a husband who is gone all the time, not the ones I have known. So, yes, I leave before I care too much or they do." He crushed the cigar in the ashtray.

"What about me, Raul?" Unconsciously she moved toward him. "When are you going to leave me?"

Straightening, Raul looked at her for a long, motionless moment, then lifted his hands to frame her face in them. There was so much gentleness in his touch that Luz almost wanted to cry. His gaze made a minute search of every detail of her features, from the curl of her lashes to the pores of her skin.

"When I look at your face, I see something. It has haunted me from the beginning," he murmured. "But now I know what it is. I look at you and see the need to be loved. It pulls me because I have this same need, too. I have no wish to leave you, *querida.*"

He lowered his mouth onto hers, and the gentleness gave way to the need they shared. It was a fevered heat that swept them and sent them straining against the physical limits of the flesh. In mating, they glimpsed the glory a man and woman could know together, but never hold.

Later, lying tangled in the sheets in blissful exhaustion, Luz glanced at the scattered piles of hastily discarded clothes, then turned on her side to face Raul and walked her fingers over his ribs. He caught them, stopping their ticklish journey, and lifted them to his mouth, kissing them, then brought them back to lie on his chest, enclosed in his hand.

Someone knocked at the outer door to their suite. "It must be the maid coming to turn down the bedsheets." She started to throw back the covers and get up, but Raul wouldn't let go of her hand.

"When we are in them? That will be interesting to see." He smiled lazily and pulled her on top of him while she laughed in protest. Another knock came, more strident than the last.

"Let me up, Raul," she insisted in a low murmur, conscious of the hand on her back pressing her down and flattening her breasts against his chest. "She has a key. She could walk in any moment."

"It would be most compromising, no?" His hand slid under the covers to cup a bottom cheek.

"Yes." Both heard the rattle of a key in the lock. "Raul, will you let me get some clothes on?" There was a trace of franticness in her laughing voice. Raul didn't attempt to hold her as she rolled away from him and scampered from beneath the covers.

None of her bedclothes were lying out. The only garment Luz could find that would sufficiently cover her was Raul's shirt. Hurriedly, she pulled it on, shaking back the long sleeves to free her hands to fasten the buttons. The outer door opened, and she heard footsteps in the small sitting room that divided the two bedrooms. The connecting door stood open. She glanced at Raul as he stepped into his pants and pulled them up around his hips.

"That is my shirt," he accused lightly. "What am I to wear?"

"I'd rather the maid ogled your chest than mine," Luz retorted, then heard the footsteps approaching the bedroom. *"Uno momento!"* she called, quickly rolling back the sleeves to expose her hands. She darted another glance at Raul as he zipped up his fly, then turned to face the door.

Shock froze her expression when she saw Rob standing at the room's entrance. The livid redness in his neck crept into his face as his accusing stare went from her to Raul to the tousled bedcovers, then the full brunt of it came back to Luz.

"I didn't expect you back this afternoon," she murmured.

"That's rather obvious." His lips curled over the words while a violent trembling of rage and hurt quivered through him. "Did you enjoy your roll in the sack, Mother dear?"

His sarcasm hurt as much as the anguish she felt over his

look of wounded outrage. Luz suspected it was one thing to know about her affair with Raul, and another entirely to be confronted by the evidence of it.

"Rob, please try—"

"Try what, Luz?" he hurled bitterly. "Try to understand that my mother is a tramp who shacks up in hotel rooms with some polo-playing gigolo?! You're no different from some slut off the street!"

"That is enough!" Raul came around the bed, anger flashing in his eyes as he advanced toward Rob. Luz moved quickly to step between them and to check Raul's forward movement with her hands.

"No, Raul." She didn't want him involved in any confrontation with her son. She didn't want to risk the consequences. "Let me handle this." Raul hesitated, his muscles flexed and taut beneath her hands.

She turned to look back at Rob, but he was striding through the door. She ran after him, refusing to let him walk out like this. "Rob, wait." She caught up with him in the sitting room and tried to grab his arm before he reached the hall door, but he jerked it away, then swung around to face her.

"You're disgusting, do you know that?" Luz recoiled from the contempt and loathing she saw in his face, stunned that it was coming from her own son. "Nothing means anything to you, but what you want. You don't give a damn how I feel."

"That isn't true. I care very much," she insisted.

"You have a helluva way of showing it. Do you have any idea what it's like to have your own mother screwing your coach, the man who's going to captain your polo team? My God, you're older than he is. Don't you see how cheap and sordid that is?"

"No, I don't!" Luz refused to listen to any more of his insults. "You don't own me, Rob. I may be your mother, but I don't have to live my life to suit you."

"Then to hell with you!" he raged and stormed out of the hotel room before she could stop him, the door slamming in her face.

Shaken by the exchange, she covered her mouth, wondering what she'd done, her anger fading under an onslaught of fear that she might have driven Rob farther away from her—the very last thing she'd wanted to happen. She doubled her hand into a fist and pressed it tightly to her mouth.

A pair of hands touched her shoulders, and she started in surprise, but it was Raul. Gently, he gathered her into his arms, and she let her head rest on the comforting solidness of his chest.

"Why did I argue with him?" she asked herself. "That isn't the way to reach him. Rob is too sensitive."

"He will get over his anger."

There was little solace in that. "I'm worried about him." Her clenched fingers lay on his muscled chest near her mouth, muffling her voice. "He was so angry when he left. What do you think he'll do? He doesn't know this city. He can't even speak the language," Luz said, and pushed out of Raul's arms to start toward the bedroom. "I've got to find him."

Raul caught her wrist. "Where will you look?"

"I don't know. But he must have gone somewhere. I've got to look for him," she insisted. "You saw the state he was in. I can't let him go wandering through the streets of a strange city."

"And I am not going to let you wander the streets looking for him," Raul stated. "It is possible he has gone to the polo grounds."

"Yes." It was a logical place.

"You stay here in case he comes back and I will see if he is there."

Unable to argue with his sensible suggestion, Luz gave in reluctantly. "You will call me if you find him?"

"Yes," Raul promised.

But the waiting was hell as the minutes dragged into hours. Raul called once to report that Rob hadn't been seen on the grounds and that he was going to check another polo club. Luz was half out of her mind with worry, wondering if he'd had an accident or gotten into a fight, visualizing him walking the streets alone or drinking away his hurt in some bar. A thousand times she wished she hadn't answered him so sharply, that she'd waited until he'd gotten rid of all that hurt and resentment built up inside him, then reasoned with him. Every time she heard the elevator stop on their floor and footsteps in the hall, she thought it might be Rob, but each time it was another hotel door that was opened.

Outside, twilight tinted the city's haze with its purpling pink shade. A sprinkle of lights dotted the concrete buildings, while below the glitter of streetlamps lined the broad avenues, all anticipating the imminent darkness. Luz stood at the window, watching their brightness grow along with the increasing number of headlight beams in the string of traffic.

Her ears strained for some sound, but the crushing silence of the room was all she heard until a key rattled in the lock. Luz swung around to face the door, hope leaping yet half afraid it was Raul. When the door opened, Rob walked in, moving with a jaunty stride. An intense relief flooded through her as she broke from the window.

"Rob. Where have you been? I've been so worried about you. Are you all right?" Anxiously she inspected him for bruises or injuries of some kind.

"I'm fine, really," he assured her with a laughing smile. His whole demeanor had changed. The anger and bitterness were gone. Instead of returning in a sullen mood as Luz had expected, Rob seemed cheerful.

"You've been drinking, haven't you?"

"I've had one beer." But he must have noticed her skepticism. "What would you like me to do—recite Peter Piper picked a peck of pickled peppers or stand on one leg and touch my finger to my nose?" His speech was unslurred and his coordination was obviously unimpaired.

"Where have you been all this time? What have you been doing?" Luz demanded in confusion.

"I caught a cab and went to see Tony. I had to autograph the cast on his arm. He's coming to the polo matches tomorrow, so you can see my signature on it for yourself," he offered as further proof, then moved past her to stroll into the middle of the room. "I did a lot of thinking after I left." He paused and shot her a bright glance. "It's amazing how clear it all is to me now. I can't understand why I didn't see it before. The same as you have no right to tell me what I should or shouldn't do or who I can see, I shouldn't tell you either. It's none of your business what I do in private, so I guess that what you do is none of mine."

His complete turnabout threw her. "Rob, do you mean that?"

"Hey, I was way out of line. I admit it. I had no right to

blow up the way I did." He sounded so sincere it was impossible to doubt him, yet Luz was nagged by a vague feeling that something else had prompted this about-face. Mentally, she shrugged it away, telling herself it didn't matter what had caused his change in his attitude.

"I'm glad you feel that way. I—" She was interrupted by the rattle of another key turning in the lock. A second later, Raul walked in, his expression grim. He checked his stride when he noticed Rob standing with her. "He came back a few minutes ago," Luz explained.

"Your mother has been worried about you," Raul stated, his tone faintly accusing.

"She told me."

Although she watched Rob closely, she noticed little difference in his expression with Raul present. His attitude remained brightly confident. There wasn't a hint of resentment or dislike. If anything Rob acted as if he were an equal to the man who was his mentor as well as her lover.

"Rob went to see Tony," she explained to Raul, then hesitated. Coming to a decision, she moved to Raul's side and slipped a hand under his arm. "I think you should know, Rob, that when Raul comes to Florida next week, he'll be staying at our house." She had intended to inform him of the arrangements during their flight home, but it seemed best to have it in the open now.

Something flickered across Rob's face, then he looked at Raul. "I guess that means you'll be staying in Dad's old room."

"Actually, he's going to share my room," Luz stated.

"As I said, Luz"—Rob shrugged indifferently—"you have no right to tell me how to run my life and I have no right to tell you how to run yours." He stuffed his hands in the pocket of his windbreaker. "I think I'll go get cleaned up for dinner."

She watched him enter his room and shut the door. She turned to Raul, her hand tightening on his arm. He stared after Rob. "It's amazing, isn't it?" she declared, marveling at her son's rapid change in attitude.

"*Sí*, very amazing."

"I always knew he would ultimately accept it, but it's such

a relief that he finally has." Luz wasn't sure what she would have done if she'd encountered opposition from both her children. As it was, she had yet to hear from Trisha since she'd written that letter. That was something she still had to face after she flew back to Florida. At least Rob was on her side now.

# Part IV

# CHAPTER XXVI

A letter from Trisha awaited Luz's return from Argentina. She hurriedly scanned the short, stilted message, then read it again, slowly. Its tone, more than its wording, was sharply critical and disapproving. Luz tried to tell herself that Trisha's reaction was exactly as she had expected, but that didn't make her feel any better about it. The letter closed with the cold blunt statement: "I intend to come home this weekend." Luz stared at the last sentence, aware that Raul was arriving on Friday. Sighing, she returned the letter to its envelope and began concentrating on all the things that had to be done between now and then.

Trisha wasn't the only one to be faced. Luz telephoned Audra on her return and managed to postpone confronting her until the end of the week, pleading travel fatigue and a backlog of correspondence and work that required her attention.

When Luz had informed Emma Sanderson that Raul would be staying in the house, in the master suite with her, Emma hadn't so much as flickered an eye. Luz hadn't detected either disapproval or approval. Of course, she had never asked Emma's opinion, and it wasn't likely to be volunteered. Yet Emma had been so faithful to her ex-husband that Luz couldn't help thinking the woman didn't approve of her actions. However, she doubted that her mother would be quite so reticent.

"You are a Kincaid! I should think you would have more sense of propriety than to engage in such a tawdry liaison," Audra Kincaid declared in shocked disapproval after Luz had finally dropped her little bombshell on her mother. "It is one thing to engage in a discreet affair with this polo player. But it is entirely another matter to have him living under your roof—sleeping in your bed. A Kincaid, living with a man without the sanctity of marriage! I never!"

"No, Audra, I'm sure you haven't," Luz agreed dryly. She had precisely anticipated her mother's reaction. It wasn't that Audra's attitudes were outmoded. She could be very liberal in her thinking, except when it concerned the standard of conduct for a Kincaid.

Standing off to one side, Mary applauded her comeback. "I think it's wonderful! The old bold and brassy Luz is back. I can hardly wait to meet him."

"You'll see him soon. I'll be leaving shortly to pick him up at the airport." Which was why she hadn't postponed telling Audra again, realizing there never would be a "right" moment. "But don't come barging over tonight, Mary."

"How can you encourage her, Mary?" Audra demanded indignantly.

"It's her life. She has to live it the way she sees fit, not the way you do, Audra." It was Mary who sounded like the gentle but firm parent.

"You mark my words—she'll regret it!" The emphatic statement was punctuated by Audra's sharp turn from them. She simultaneously had her say and washed her hands of the matter.

Mary looked at Luz and shrugged a what-else-could-you-expect, then both smiled. But Luz was remembering what Mary had said earlier, "the old bold and brassy Luz" was back. Bold and brassy? Maybe she had acted that way, but this was the first time—at forty-two—that she had ever truly defied her mother.

No mention was made of the subject again. Half an hour later, Luz left her mother's oceanside residence and drove to the airport. At the air freight terminal, she learned that the plane had landed, and she waited outside the customs section for Raul. It had been a week since she'd last seen him, but it had gone by so fast. There had been so much to do and to organize that the time had flown. Now the minutes were dragging. Mixed in with her eagerness to see him was a vague unease. Maybe she was going too far too fast. Maybe she was acting too quickly. Maybe she was jumping from a marriage into an affair without enough time in between to know what she really wanted. She had never really learned to live with herself.

All her doubts faded when Raul walked through the door, so tall and attractive with those black-lashed blue eyes looking only at her. Luz went into his arms with no hesitation and felt the quick hard pressure of his mouth on her lips. A warm and heady feeling was running through her veins when he finally lifted his head.

"How was the flight? What about the horses? Did they fare all right?"

"Good. We had some turbulence, but nothing serious," he assured her.

Reluctantly she moved out of his arms. "My car is parked outside if you're ready."

With all his tack and polo equipment and luggage, it took a while to load the car. Luz was glad she'd driven the station wagon instead of the convertible or there wouldn't have been enough room for everything.

There was an easy run of conversation between them during the drive to the house. They talked about everything from polo, the *estancia*, and Hector to the weather, the flight, and the things Luz had been doing since she came back.

"I had a letter from Trisha. She mentioned she would be coming home this weekend. She'll probably catch the late flight tonight or the first one in the morning," Luz told him almost as a warning that everything wasn't likely to run smoothly.

"You have not spoken to her since you returned?"

"No." She flexed her fingers, loosening their tight grip on the steering wheel, and kept her eyes on the steady stream of traffic. "I'm sure this has upset her, but she'll come around in time . . . the way Rob has. It's bound to be awkward for both of them in the beginning, though. And for you, as well." She glanced quickly at him, then back to the road.

"Does it worry you that there may be problems?"

"I expect some." She was trying to be realistic. "I just don't want the children to resent you if it can be avoided. Disagreements are going to occur from time to time between me and Rob or Trisha. I'd rather you didn't become involved with them."

"They are your children," Raul said. "I will not interfere."

Luz smiled, relieved that he agreed with her. "I think that will spare us a lot of misunderstandings in the future."

"I agree."

Reaching across the seat, she clasped his hand and held it tightly for an instant. "I'm glad you're here, Raul."

"So am I."

When they reached the house, Luz took the road that branched off the front circular driveway and curved behind the large Spanish-style abode to the rear garages and the stables. Rob was on the stick-and-ball field, working one of the ponies they'd purchased from Raul. She slowed the car as they neared the turn into the garage area.

"Do you want to unload your things at the stable first?" In truth, she wanted to keep him to herself a little longer. Going to the stables would entail introducing him to their handler, Jimmy Ray Turnbull, and talking to Rob.

"Later there will be time," Raul said.

"That's what I thought." She was conscious of the smile spreading across her face as she swung the car toward the garage.

After she had parked the station wagon, Raul unloaded his suitcases from the back and followed her to the house. Luz took the shortcut across the pool area and entered the living room through the double French doors. After the brilliant sunlight outdoors, the interior seemed dim. Luz was halfway into the room before she noticed Trisha sitting on the couch.

"Trisha." A smile broke across her face. It had been too long since she'd seen her daughter for her initial reaction to be anything other than gladness. "I thought you'd fly in on tonight's plane. How long have you been here?"

"Long enough." Trisha stood up, her expression icy-cold as her glance went past Luz to Raul and his luggage. "Long enough to talk to Rob and find out just what's going on here." Despite that surface air of brittle calm, Luz sensed the violent trembling of hurt and anger inside. "I didn't believe him, so I waited to see for myself whether it's true he's moving in here with you." She looked again at the luggage he'd set on the floor. "I guess I have, haven't I?"

"Trisha, I'd like to explain." The words sounded so inadequate to Luz. "I know it's difficult for you to accept."

"Do you? Do you really?" she challenged. "It's one thing to lose a man to another woman, but to your own mother!"

"I was never yours to lose, Trisha," Raul inserted quietly.

"You're right. I know you're right." She rubbed her fingers over the point of her forehead. "But it doesn't make it any easier."

"Raul, would you mind if I spoke to Trisha alone?" If there was to be any arguing, she didn't want him included.

"I will be at the stables."

She waited until he'd left by the French doors, then walked over to the sofa. "Let's sit down, Trish, and talk about this." Grudgingly, Trisha sat back down on the cushion, and Luz curled a leg under her to sit sideways on the sofa facing her daughter. She studied the taut features, so proud and so beautiful. "Trisha, what can I say that I didn't write you in that letter? It just happened. The attraction was there and we had so much in common that . . . it just grew." Luz resolved this time to remain calm and not erupt in anger the way she had with Rob.

"And as you pointed out, we had nothing in common." Trisha shook her head ruefully. "He was too old for me, but he obviously wasn't too young for you."

"He isn't that much younger, only five years. You're supposed to be the liberated member of this family," she reminded her. "What's wrong with an older woman and a younger man?"

"Nothing. I—I just can't believe the two of you . . ." She stopped and picked at the pleat in her skirt. "Yet when I saw you two walking across the patio, laughing and smiling at each other, it looked right. Maybe that's what hurts."

Luz had not expected such an admission. It brought a lump to her throat. "I was so afraid you might hate me for this, Trisha."

"When I got your letter, I think I could have murdered you," Trisha said. "But I had a lot of time to think about it. Maybe I didn't love him. Maybe I just loved the idea of loving him. When something's one-sided, it isn't really love, is it?"

"I think I know why I never worried about you as much as Rob. You have your head on straight almost all the time."

Trisha came to her feet in a stir of agitation and took a few steps away from the sofa as if to pace the room. "I want to be angry. I keep telling myself I'd feel better if I stormed and raged, started throwing things and calling you names. That's what I was going to do. That's *one* of the things I was going to do," she amended sardonically, pausing with her back to Luz. "I had played out several alternatives in my head. All of them, I assure you"—she made a sweeping turn to face her—"were marvelously melodramatic. I was going to be sophisticated, outraged, scornful. In all of them, I think I walked out swearing you had seen the last of me."

"I'm glad you haven't done that yet." Luz smiled more in sympathy for her daughter than from any sense of relief for herself.

"But I can't figure out why I'm not doing any of them. It's like a rug has been pulled out from under me and I'm sitting on the floor trying to decide where I hurt. My pride, I know, but what else?" She moved restlessly. "My head hasn't been on straight for a while. I turned it when I met Raul. I was eighteen, or almost, and a full-fledged woman. And here was a man—handsome, older, glamorous, foreign—everything exciting. This was going to be *la grande passion*. There were so many obstacles to overcome—age, culture, careers—so we fought these feelings we had. But everything was going to work out because we were really so wildly in love with each other." She was mockingly extravagant in her description of the pretend affair, then she stopped and sighed, looking at the floor. "It all sounds so stupid, doesn't it?"

"No." It was simply one of the many impossible fantasies of the very young. "When I was sixteen, there was a young groom working at Hopeworth Farm. I mooned over him all summer, fully aware that Jake and Audra would go through the roof—they'd disown me—if I married a common stablehand. But that agony was wonderful. Mind you, he never knew any of this. I was just the big boss's daughter. But I imagined all sorts of things when he'd saddle my horse for me or help me onto its back." She didn't tell Trisha how she'd seen him in a parked car necking with some girl from town. It had been a cruel blow, and she'd hated him violently and vigorously afterward. "I know it wasn't quite like that for you, because you are older than I was, but the experiences are similar."

"I wish you had remembered that before. Not that I would have listened." Trisha released a bitter, laughing breath of self-scorn. "One of my housemates, Mika, suggested that maybe it was like falling for somebody famous—a rock star or a football player. More glory worship than anything else. In my head, I can reason out these feelings for Raul. But I can't make myself accept that *you* got him!"

"I wish there were something I could say, Trish, that would make it easier, but there isn't." She looked down at her hands.

"I can't be a good sport about this and say I'm glad for you. The best man . . . woman . . . won and all that rot. That isn't the way I feel."

"I didn't expect you to."

Trisha walked back to the sofa and sat down, a heaviness in her action, then leaned forward to rest her elbows on her knees. "I guess part of it is knowing that you and Dad will never get together again. Now that you've gotten involved with someone else, he won't want to come back. If you had waited for him, maybe—"

"Do you realize what you're saying?" Luz frowned. "If he wanted to come back, I'd be expected to forgive and forget that he left me to marry another woman. But now because I'm with another man, he won't. Where is all your modern thinking against the double standard?"

"It isn't me. It's Drew who has the old-fashioned view. I know that's the way he'd feel," she insisted, then paused grimly. "It doesn't matter anyway. Dad isn't going to leave Claudia, not now that the baby's here."

"The baby," she murmured.

"Yes." Trisha looked up. "I guess you didn't know. I have a new baby brother, Tremayne Allen Thomas. He was born last night. Dad was in the delivery room. You should have heard the way he sounded when he called me this morning. It was like he'd had the baby instead of Claudia."

Luz couldn't help remembering that Drew had never stayed with her when Rob and Trisha were born. He had changed considerably, she realized. "I'm glad for him. That's the way it should be."

"Actually that's part of the reason I came early, so I could see my new brother. I came by here to pick up my car." She hesitated and glanced at the luggage Raul had left sitting inside the door. "I think it would be best if this weekend I stayed with Dad."

"I'm sure he'd like that." Although she regretted that Trisha felt that way, she understood that her daughter needed more time to adjust. "Give Drew my congratulations when you see him."

Shortly after Trisha left, Emma Sanderson paused in the archway to the dining room.

"Hello, Emma. Have there been any calls while I was gone?" Luz inquired, wondering how much her housekeeper had heard.

"A few."

"Anything important?"

"The usual." Which meant a few more people had learned she was back in town and called to extend invitations or chit-chat—gossip, actually.

At the click of the French doors, Luz turned and watched Raul reenter the house. She saw the questioning look in his expression and drew his attention to her housekeeper. "Raul, you remember meeting Emma in Paris, don't you? She's my secretary and majordomo—my Hector, I guess."

"I do. How are you, Mrs. Sanderson?" He nodded to her.

"Fine, thank you. Welcome to Florida, Mr. Buchanan," Emma responded with a polite smile.

"I'll check my messages later, Emma," Luz said in dismissal and waited until she had gone, then squared around to face Raul. "You'll have to bear with her, I'm afraid. She isn't as open-minded as Hector, so she'll probably seem distant with you for a while."

*"No importa.* I saw Trisha leave in her car."

"Yes, she's staying with her father this weekend. It's all going to work out, though. We parted on relatively good terms," she added quickly to assure him she wasn't concerned. Suddenly she was anxious for him to like everything about the place where he would be living. Nervously she pressed her palms together, lightly rubbing them. "Now, what would you like? A drink? Or shall I show you the house so you can get settled in?"

"The house." He picked up the suitcases by his feet.

"The dining room is there, and the kitchen off it." She gestured toward the room where the gleaming wood table and chairs were partially visible, then moved quickly toward the door to the study. "This is the study." She opened the door for him to look inside. Without all of Drew's law books and various other possessions, it looked slightly bare. "I thought you might like to use it as an office where you can work."

Without waiting for him to comment on her suggestion, Luz moved away from the door and went to the foyer. There was a childlike eagerness about her desire to show him her home, part pride and part a need for him to like it. She didn't want him to say anything until he'd seen it all.

"You can leave your suitcases by the stairs and pick them up later," she instructed and waited until he'd set them down by the carved newel post, then took his hand to lead him into the galleried hall. She paused outside the door to the morning room, glancing briefly at the gray-haired woman seated at the desk alcove. "We call this the morning room, which is where you usually find me. Emma and I use it as an office. Her quarters are at the end of the hall." Still holding his hand, she retraced their steps back to the foyer arch. "Trisha and Rob have their bedrooms down the other gallery. The guest bedrooms are there, as well."

Back at the oak staircase, she released her grip on his fingers so that he could reclaim his luggage. She glided up the steps ahead of him and opened the door to the master suite. Pausing inside, she held it open while he maneuvered his bags through the opening.

"This, of course, is the master suite." Luz walked directly into her room, ignoring the adjoining bedroom that had been Drew's. "I've cleaned out the closets, so you'll have room for your clothes. And two of the dresser drawers are empty. If you need more, I'll have the chest of drawers from the other bedroom moved in here." She was talking a mile a minute, she realized, and stopped abruptly. Turning, she saw Raul glancing around the room. Slowly, he lowered his suitcase to the floor. When he looked at the bed, Luz had her first moment's unease. "I never thought . . . does it bother you, Raul? Do you consider this another man's house?"

The possibility had never crossed her mind until now. Men were such proud, territorial creatures. Maybe he'd object to sleeping in a bed where she'd lain with someone else.

Unhurried, Raul walked over to her and cupped her shoulders with his hands. "If I did, then I would have to consider you another man's woman, no?"

"I suppose so, and I'm not." She relaxed into him, her hands gliding onto his waist as she tipped her head back. "I've missed you, Raul."

"I have missed you." While his arms gathered her in, his mouth set about the pleasurable task of telling her how much. Luz found his method very stimulating as well as satisfying.

After they drew apart, she remained in his arms, arched against him, and traced the sensual outline of his lips with a fingertip. "Do you like the house?"

"It is very comfortable, but I knew it would be."

"Dinner will be at eight. Would you like anything before then?" She meant it seriously; only afterward did she think of herself as an alternative to food or drink. A chuckle came from deep in his chest.

"It is tempting, but first I would like to shower and change after flying all that distance in the cargo hold with the horses."

She sniffed at the open collar of his shirt, breathing in his distinct smell, separating it from the rest of the odors. "You do have a horsy scent," she admitted, then lifted her head to gaze at the creases near his eyes. "You must be tired after the flight. We'll just have to go to bed early tonight."

"An excellent idea." Raul smiled in knowing agreement.

Those two nights at the Buenos Aires hotel had given Luz a taste of sleeping with a man. After a week of waking up with his arm draped over her, or curled up against him, or his leg hooked across her, she definitely preferred it to the many mornings she'd opened her eyes to look at an empty pillow. Her fitful slumber didn't appear to bother Raul as it had Drew. A couple of times her tossing had disturbed him. In each case, he had pulled her against him, spoon-fashion, and growled sleepily in her ear, "Lie still." And on both occasions, she had found she didn't want to move.

There were adjustments to be made during that first week—getting used to each other's daily habits, and learning how to share bathrooms, closets, and dressers. Gradually they worked out compatible routines. It was an intimacy that Luz hadn't enjoyed with a man since her early years of marriage to Drew.

And that was too long ago for her to remember if it had been different or better than what she had now.

Socially, Luz kept a low profile, centering most of her activities on the house and the stables. She would have kept it that way completely, but Thanksgiving was approaching. She wasn't surprised when Trisha called to say she was flying to Aspen with some of her new college friends to go skiing. Despite the good grace Trisha had ultimately shown in accepting the situation, she still found it awkward being around them. But she seemed to harbor no bitterness, which gave Luz hope that in time the awkwardness would fade.

When Audra telephoned to confirm the time of the holiday meal, Luz had almost expected her to exclude Raul from the family gathering, since she so thoroughly disapproved of the affair. But she had forgotten her mother's ability to overlook indiscretions.

"Will you be bringing your friend?" she had inquired.

From that moment on, Luz knew that's how Audra would refer to Raul. She would never acknowledge that he was her live-in lover. She was going to pretend not to know, just as she had pretended not to know about Jake's mistresses. Luz found it sad, but at least she was assured Raul would be treated as a friend.

An early winter storm hit the New England area and prevented her brothers and their families from coming to Palm Beach for the holiday. Therefore only Mary and the five of her family still at home and Luz, Rob, and Raul would be attending the Thanksgiving meal at the Kincaid winter estate. Luz was just as glad. The gathering of the whole Kincaid family could be overwhelming to an outsider.

When Thanksgiving Day arrived, Luz discovered she was the nervous one. Raul's calm bordered on indifference. At first she was hurt by his attitude, then she realized family had never played a major role in his life. He hadn't grown up needing their approval, support, or permission. Nor did he seek that from hers, now. He felt none of the pressure that she did.

Precisely at two o'clock they all sat down to an elaborate Thanksgiving meal. Luz knew it was Audra's habit to separate couples when she arranged the seating placements, so she expected her namecard to be at one end of the table and Raul's at the other. She was pleasantly surprised to find him occupying a chair diagonally opposite hers.

After the soup course, the young maid carried in the large platter with the plump golden-brown turkey. Audra signaled her to place it before Ross Carpenter, Mary's husband. Now that Jake was no longer with them, on this second Thanksgiving since his death, and with none of her sons present, the duty of carving the turkey was given to her son-in-law.

"You don't celebrate Thanksgiving in your country, do you, Mr. Buchanan? It's a uniquely American tradition. But I think any occasion that brings a family together is a good one. My family is very important to me, but I am certain that is something you understand, being Spanish yourself." Audra looked every inch the matriarch presiding over the dinner from her chair at the head of the table.

"I am Argentine," Raul politely corrected her. "And I have no family, so perhaps my feelings are not as strong as yours."

"How unfortunate that you have no one but yourself," Audra said sincerely.

"In my profession, I have found it to be an advantage. I have to travel a great deal playing polo, which means I am away for long periods of time. This would be hard on a family."

"But I understand you own a ranch in Argentina."

"I do, but I am there only three or four months a year. I have a man who runs it for me. It is where I raise and train polo ponies, and conduct courses in polo, such as the one Rob took. It is a sideline of my work. That is all, Mrs. Kincaid."

"I understood it was your home." She frowned slightly.

"It is the place where I go," Raul replied, and Luz considered that an accurate description. Although it was the closest he had to a home, she didn't think he had any real attachment to it.

"How sad. My home and my family have always been very important to me. My children know that my doors are always open to them. They always have a place to come. This is their home, too." Audra expounded on her favorite theme while the maid brought the various dishes that accompanied the roast turkey to the table.

"That is what makes a family strong. Over the years others

have become a part of us." Audra smiled benignly at the pudgy Ross, then looked rather pointedly at Raul. "But nothing comes between us."

"Well said, Grandmother Kincaid," Rob remarked. It was the first time since Raul's arrival that Rob had even hinted he still felt Raul could alienate Luz's love for him. Audra's message had been more subtle—Raul might join them, but she would not allow him to separate her daughter from the family, specifically herself.

Later, after dinner was over, the adults retired to the living room. Luz noticed Rob and Mary's teenagers heading for the enclosed stairs to the oceanfront cabana where they could play their music without being hassled about the volume. She moved to intercept him before he reached the stairwell.

"Rob," she said to stop him.

A resentful look flashed across his expression. "I'll be right there," he told the others. When the clatter of footsteps had receded along with the loud sibling banter, Rob turned to her. "I knew you were going to say something to me as soon as I made that remark."

"Then why did you? I thought you understood—"

"I understand. I just wanted to make sure *he* did," he retorted. "What is it? Do I have to watch everything I say around him or what?"

"Of course you don't."

"Then what are you climbing on me for? I make one innocent remark and you turn it into a federal case," Rob protested.

"I just want the two of you to get along. I thought you were—"

"We are! We're real bosom buddies—polo pals, okay? Satisfied?" It was an angry and impatient challenge.

"Okay, Rob." It wasn't true at all, but Luz knew she would gain nothing from harping on the subject. At least he accepted the situation. She wasn't the only one who had to get used to having a man around the house. She just had to give them more time. "The others are waiting in the cabana for you. You'd better go or you'll miss refereeing their latest squabble."

"How long are we going to have to stay? I'd just as soon get back to the stables."

"Audra will expect us to stay another hour, minimum. We'll

go as soon as we can." She straightened his shirt collar with affectionate care, wishing there was something she could say to this lean, raw-boned son of hers that would ease his mind.

"Okay." He turned and headed for the stairwell.

Luz watched him run out of sight down the steps, and she sighed, vaguely discouraged. Rob was so touchy lately, not just with her but with everyone. Yet the other day, she'd seen him at the stables, happy as a lark. She had hoped these mood swings were an adolescent phase he'd outgrow. So far, it didn't appear that he had. If anything, they were getting worse.

"Something wrong?" Mary asked.

Turning, Luz shook her head. "No. It's just Rob." And that said it all. She deliberately changed the subject. "Aren't you going to tell me what you think of Raul?" she asked dryly.

"I like him, actually better than I thought I would. He stood up to Audra rather well. I remember poor Ross the first time I brought him home. He was more intimidated by Audra than by Jake."

"Weren't we all," Luz murmured.

"I left Audra alone in the living room. I'd better be getting back before she thinks the entire family has deserted. Are you coming?" Mary paused by the door.

"Where's Raul?"

"Out on the sun deck smoking a cigar. Maybe we should take up smoking, Luz. I've never tried that excuse." A grin stretched across her handsome features.

"And be lectured on the perils of getting cancer? Spare me," Luz declared mockingly. "Tell Audra I'll be there shortly. I'm just going to check on Raul."

As Mary headed back to the living room, Luz walked to the glass doors that led to the sun deck. Raul stood at the railing gazing absently at the waves rolling in from the ocean. A sea breeze swirled away the smoke curling from his cigar. The sound of her footsteps on the planked deck reached him, and he turned his head toward her. She walked over to stand beside him and leaned her hands on the rail.

"It was a good dinner," he said.

"The food was excellent." She still wasn't sure about the dinner. "The Kincaids can be overpowering at times," Luz ventured to elicit his reaction.

"So that is your secret." The grooves deepened near his mouth.

She laughed, suddenly reassured. "You've finally learned it's the Kincaid in me you find so irresistible."

He removed his hand from his pocket and hooked it around her waist, pulling her against him. "Among many other things."

She kissed him lightly, then pulled away to stroke the point of his chin with her finger. "We won't have to stay much longer."

"You want to go?"

"I think you've been exposed long enough to Audra."

"Hector would call her a formidable woman." Raul smiled. "As he also once described you as a tiger cat protecting her kittens."

"Hector?"

"You are like your mother in that respect," he said.

"I'm going to have to think about that awhile before I make up my mind whether it's a compliment or not," Luz accused.

"It is the truth, and truth can be neither flattery nor insult." He kissed the corner of her lips to bring back their softness. "We should go back inside so your mother will not think me rude—or that I am stealing her daughter."

"I suppose we must." She sighed.

"Why do you come if you dislike it?" Raul frowned.

The question surprised her, forcing her to think about her answer. "I guess the truth is I do like coming. Outwardly all of us protest Audra's possessive demands, but we still come. We are all very close, and she's kept it that way. Maybe we don't see each other as often anymore, except Mary and myself, but when we need help, we always go to each other, never strangers. We Kincaids are a tight clique. I know Drew sometimes felt left out at the family gatherings. A lot of the spouses do. It isn't intentional. I guess that's what I came out here to say."

"Perhaps we should go back inside then."

"We should," she agreed reluctantly.

With the holiday weekend over and December just around the corner, Raul spent the following week holding what Luz could only describe as tryouts for the two remaining positions on the polo team he was putting together for Rob, and for himself of course. Many players of the caliber he sought were already committed to other teams. Most of his choices he had contacted while he was still in Argentina. This week he had narrowed that number to six.

"What do you think?" Luz asked as they left the stables to walk back to the house for lunch. Raul's arm was a heavy weight on her shoulders, indicative of the weariness she saw in his face.

"I think I am like a tired horse who needs a warm bath and a good rubdown after a hard morning's work." Even his crooked smile showed the strain of effort.

"I meant about the players, as if you didn't know. I thought Brubaker did well when you put him in the defensive slot." She had watched most of the morning's workouts, during which Raul had played riders at various positions, sometimes switching them after a chukkar of play and changing sides occasionally.

"He is steady. He may make a good anchor." But Raul wasn't prepared to commit himself. "I liked Masterson at the Number One position. He has a lot of flash. He could spark the team. However, Rob is against him. He claims Masterson wants to hog all the glory to himself. I admit he does have a tendency to show off."

"Lawless has a good string of polo ponies," Luz remarked.

"The decision is not an easy one." The creases around his eyes crinkled in amusement when he saw her trying to weigh the various contributions each player might make. "Many factors must be considered—the player's skill, his style of play, whether it is compatible, his ponies or whether we must supplement his string so he is better mounted. But most of all, is he *simpatico?*" As they approached the French doors, he took his arm away from her shoulders so Luz could precede him. "After that we must consider how much we will have to pay him."

"Then it comes down to the business of polo. And I wanted to sponsor a team." Luz realized how much more was entailed than she had thought. "Do you want to work this afternoon on selecting which tournaments to enter, so we can come up with a tentative travel schedule and estimate expenses?"

"Yes, and we need to make sure we allow time for the ponies to rest if we have to trailer them any great distance." Upon entering the house, they walked straight through the living room to the foyer.

"That's what bothers me about going from Texas to New York. We might be wiser to catch the Oak Brook Tournaments. I—"

"Excuse me, Luz," Emma Sanderson interrupted, coming into the entry foyer from the galleried hall. "I heard you come in, and I have Connie Davenport on the telephone. She is calling to find out why you haven't RSVPed her party invitation. She's concerned whether you've received it. What should I tell her?"

Luz paused and glanced at Raul. "It's her annual million-calorie pre-Christmas party," she explained while studying him with a considering look. "I suppose I can't keep you to myself forever, can I?" she said, half in jest, then responded to Emma. "Tell her we'll come."

"Very well. I'll put it on your calendar for Saturday," she said and retreated into the hallway.

"I hope you don't mind going." Luz slipped her hand in his as they started up the great oak staircase. "I know you aren't much for parties."

Strangely, she hadn't missed the social whirl. Once her world had revolved completely around it. If she hadn't been planning an event herself, she'd been going to this one or that. Now her time was occupied with so many other things, most of it involving the business of polo, whether it was horses or players or the logistics of transporting ponies and equipment from one city to the next.

"Some parties are not as bad as others. It depends on the company." Raul gave her one of his warm, lazy looks that always seemed like a caress.

"I know exactly what they're going to say when they see you with me. 'That lucky Luz Thomas. You might know she'd find somebody like him. She's a Kincaid,'" she mocked. "Oh, the tongues will wag."

Suddenly she was looking forward to the party. The revenge was going to be sweet after all the pitying looks she'd had to endure when Drew left her. She could hardly wait to see their faces when they saw Raul. This was one party she was going to enjoy thoroughly. No more was she "poor Luz."

Upon entering the bedroom they shared, she directed Raul toward the bath. "Take that hot shower. Afterward, we'll see about that rubdown."

# CHAPTER XXVII

Cars were stacked along the driveway, and the grand house blazed with lights. Garlands of green spiraled down the white columns of the front portico, and a huge wreath of ribbon-tied pine boughs hung on the door. Luz elected to stay in the car with Raul while he found a place to park instead of being dropped off at the entrance. There wasn't any way she was going to walk into the party without him.

Muffled sounds of the party in progress filtered through as Raul rang the doorbell. Luz ran an admiring glance over the flattering cut of his dark suit. She faced the door, feeling proud and confident.

One of the catering staff admitted them into the house. As Luz surrendered her long cloak to him, she was conscious of the flash of sequins that striped the red silk georgette of her tunic-style dress, the yoke beaded with linked squares. The eye-catching choice had been deliberate.

"Luz! It's been ages since I've seen you!" The gushing greeting came from the plump, rounded Connie Davenport, approaching to welcome them to her house. "You look stunning in that dress—all Christmas and glittery. And who is this?" she asked without drawing a breath, then murmured conspiratorially. "Is this *him?*"

Luz's lips twitched with the smile she tried to contain. "Connie, this is Raul Buchanan. Our hostess, Connie Davenport."

"I swear I'm going to start attending the polo matches at the club. I feel like I'm the only one who didn't know who you were." She hung on to his hands with her pudgy fingers.

"Oh, Luz, no wonder you kept him hidden away all this time. He's *won*-derful!"

"You are very kind, Mrs. Davenport." Raul gently pulled away his hand.

"My God, that voice." Connie shivered in exaggerated reaction. "It makes me feel like the creamy center of a bonbon." The doorbell rang, announcing the latest arrivals. "I'm sure you know everyone here, Luz. I invited Drew, but he called and begged off at the last minute. He couldn't find a sitter. Isn't that hysterical? At his age!" She backed toward the door. "Remember the rules of the party. If you're on a diet or restricted foods, you must leave immediately. Everything here is full of calories and cholesterol. The eggnog, I promise, is made with pure cream. Enjoy!"

"She means it," Luz warned in an undertone as she linked her arm with Raul's and started toward the main room. "Everything here is probably a thousand calories a bite . . . or swallow. Food is her passion—the richer the better. She's the only woman I know who comes to a party and wants to take the leftovers home."

Christmas decorations adorned the large room, dominated by a huge tree with gingerbread men and candy canes hanging from its silver-garlanded branches. Candy dishes of every shape and size, mounded with a multitudinous assortment of confectioneries, sat on every flat surface in the room except the floor. Guests crowded the room, sitting or standing in clusters, the sweet temptations around them.

As Luz and Raul entered the room, a tall, thin woman in a beaded green dress that appeared to weigh more than she did immediately stopped them. "Luz, darling. Should I dare ask where you've been keeping yourself?" Her throaty greeting was accompanied by a slyly knowing look.

"Hello, Veronica. I'm surprised Connie allowed you to come."

"I explained that the doctor said I had to gain weight, and she loved the idea of fattening me up."

"I don't believe you've met Raul," Luz began.

"Actually I have, although I don't know if he remembers me." She placed her long, bone-thin fingers in his hand. "It was last year at Chet Martin's party when he won the Kincaid Cup. I'm Veronica Hampton."

"Of course." Raul bowed slightly over her hand, his expression polite, but showing no recognition.

"It was prophetic, wasn't it?" she said to Luz. "When you decided to stay so long in Argentina, I guessed the reason. Who wouldn't if you had a chance of bringing home something like him? I won't ask if you enjoyed yourself."

Luz chatted for a few minutes more with Veronica, then made an excuse to move on. "Raul and I haven't been to the bar yet for our cup of Christmas spirit. We'll talk again later."

"Better keep an eye on him," Veronica warned.

As they moved away, Luz leaned close to Raul and murmured, "I hope she does listen to her doctor and gain some weight. Otherwise she is going to prove that *die* is part of *diet*."

She was aware of the heads turning to look at them. Inwardly she was pleased at the stir she was creating with Raul at her side. She knew she was smiling like a contented cat. Which was just the way she felt. When they neared a small group of guests standing by the buffet table, Luz recognized the flaming red hair of one of them.

"There's someone I want you to meet." She gave a little pull on Raul's arm to alter his direction. "Billi Rae, how are you?"

The woman excused herself from the group to come hug Luz. "You look wonderful, Luz."

"You look . . ." Laughing, she shook her head as she stared at the bold red satin dress that made such an arty clash with her hair. "I don't know how you do it. The combination is terrible and you look stunning in it."

"It's called guts—and a little theatrics," she admitted huskily, the heavy mask of her makeup disguising the fact she was fifty if she was a day. Billi Rae's green eyes darted to Raul, then back to Luz. "He's the one, isn't he?"

"Yes. Billie Rae, meet Raul Buchanan. This is Billi Rae Townsend. She owns an art gallery on Worth Avenue."

"It's a pleasure to meet you," Raul said.

"It's all mine," she assured. "The gallery is a hobby. You see, I love beautiful things. I understand you play polo."

"That is true."

"It's a physically demanding sport. You must be in superb condition." Billi Rae looked him over, then glanced at Luz. "Now, if I had a nude of him in my shop, it would sell."

Luz laughed at the remark. "I've been meaning to stop by your gallery. While I was in Buenos Aires, I saw some wonderful work done by local artists. I have business cards from two of the places. I thought you might want to look into it."

"I will. Come by the shop soon," Billi Rae urged.

"I promise."

They were waylaid before they reached the bar, then again after they had gotten their drinks. Luz's smile widened as more envious looks were cast her way, if not envious comments. It took nearly two hours to make the rounds and see all the guests. Luz got so much satisfaction from watching their faces when they met Raul. With the circuit made, they looked up their hosts and took their leave of the party.

Outside the house, Luz was consumed by a sweet, heady feeling. It was like being drunk, and she was walking on air. She'd gotten her retribution, and it was glorious. She hugged Raul's arm tightly and stifled the impulse to laugh out loud.

"I'm so glad we came." She kissed him when he opened the car door for her, then slid inside.

Vaguely impatient, she waited for him to climb behind the wheel. She moved over to sit close to him, turning slightly sideways so she could look at him, too. The rumble of the engine matched the purring sensation she felt inside, all because of him.

Shifting, she tucked a silk-clad leg beneath her while Raul maneuvered the car out of the parking space and onto the street. Leaning toward him, she bent her head and nibbled at the sinewy cord in his neck, following it down to his shoulder, then working her way back up to his ear. His clean, warm skin tasted good to her.

"Luz, I am trying to drive." The sternness of his voice didn't deter her, although she drew back.

She slid her hand inside his jacket and tried to unbutton his shirt so that she could feel the hard muscled flesh of his chest. His hand firmly gripped her wrist and pushed her hand back to her side.

"We're almost there."

"Home. We're almost home," she corrected him, then rested her chin atop his shoulder and drew an imaginary line around the opening of his ear with the tip of her fingernail. Raul turned his head away from the feathery touch.

When the car turned into the driveway, Luz swung away from him, straightening in her seat and leaning against its back. She ran her fingers through her hair, her smile still in place. "It was a wonderful party," she mused aloud.

Raul parked the car in front of the garage, then came around to open the door for her. She climbed out and waited while he shut the door. He turned and headed in the opposite direction from the house. Startled, Luz watched him take a step away.

"Where are you going?"

"I noticed a light was on at the stable." Raul paused. "Someone may have left it on."

"There's no need for you to go." She moved toward him. "We can call Jimmy Ray from the house and have him check." She slipped her arms around his neck and linked her hands behind it while she arched against him. "I had a glorious time tonight. Thank you." Luz started to force his head down so she could kiss him.

His neck muscles stiffened, resisting the pressure as his hands came up and pulled her arms from around his neck, then pushed her away from him. She was stunned by his rejection and the coldness she now saw in his face.

"What's wrong?" She frowned.

"Tonight you paraded me around your friends as if I were some new stud you'd bought. You do not own me, Luz." His low voice vibrated with anger.

Stung by his reaction, her temper flared in defense. "Is that the way it looked to you? Well, maybe I was guilty of showing you off to my friends, but it so happens I was proud to be seen with you! I thought you would see that! And I am not interested in owning you! Thanks for spoiling what had been a glorious evening!" She started to walk away, then hesitated a second. "I've changed my mind. I think it's an excellent idea for you to go check that light in the stables."

Raul's anger was expelled in a heavy breath as he watched the sequins flash on the skirt of her dress when the cloak billowed from her rapid pace. Her strident denial made him doubt that his accusation was just, but his irritability remained. The way the guests had regarded him at the party left a bad taste in his mouth. Perhaps Luz wasn't to blame for it, but at the moment, it was a grudging concession.

Raul struck out for the stable, where the tack-room light

gleamed in the night, intent on walking off his annoyance. The breeze was cool against his face, the smell of horses and hay mixing with its tangy fresh ocean scent.

Arriving at the stable, he opened the main door and stepped inside. A crack of light showed beneath the door to the tack room. He flipped on the switch to light the corridor and runway. A horse shifted in its stall, the straw rustling. Somewhere along the row, another one whickered softly, curiously.

As Raul approached the tack-room door, he caught the smell of something burning. He tried the door, but it was locked. He reached atop the doorsill, where he kept the key Luz had given him for the tack room. He heard a sound from inside as he turned the key in the lock. Pushing the door inward, he took a quick, long step into the room and stopped to face an equally startled Rob, whirling around and halting with his back to the workbench.

"Hey, man." Rob laughed uncertainly. "You could scare a guy out of a year's growth barging in like that. What's the idea, anyway? You're supposed to be at a party."

"We just came back. I saw the light and thought someone had forgotten to shut it off." That strange burning odor was fainter, but Raul could still smell it. Frowning, he looked around the tack room, expecting to find something smoldering.

"Nobody forgot. It's just me. I was messin' around down here. You can go on back to the house now. I'll turn it off when I leave." The quickly offered reassurance had a nervous edge to it, as Rob shifted and leaned back against the work counter.

"I smell something burning." Raul eyed him suspiciously.

"I don't smell anything." Rob shrugged, the offhand smile not matching the anxiously averted glance that darted all around Raul. "I know what it might be. I smoked a joint in the john earlier. Maybe you can still smell that."

Raul slowly realized that Rob hadn't budged from the counter. "What are you working on?" He stepped forward, and Rob shifted to block his view.

"I don't think it's any of your business." That nervous smile remained, but it was edged with defiance.

"What are you hiding?" When Raul took another step forward, Rob attempted to push him away. The movement permitted Raul to see the drug paraphernalia on the workbench. Angrily he shoved Rob backward. "What is that? Cocaine?"

"What if it is? So maybe I decided to do a little celebrating of my own, have a little fun. It's got nothing to do with you. It doesn't affect the way I play polo, and that's your only concern," Rob answered belligerently. "You may be shacking up with my mother, but that doesn't give you any right to tell me what I should or shouldn't do!"

Raul grabbed his shirtfront and pushed him backward, arching over the counter edge. "You will never speak of Luz like that again," he ordered harshly and released his hold on the shirt to step away, disgust and anger trembling violently through him.

"She's my mother," Rob declared. "And you had better not forget that."

"Does she know about this?" Raul jerked his head toward the counter.

"Go ahead and tell her," he challenged. "I'll deny it. I'll blame it all on Jimmy Ray. Who do you think she's going to believe? Me, that's who. So you'd just better keep your mouth shut. You go trying to make trouble and you're the one who's going to be in it."

Raul recognized the truth in what Rob was saying. Where her son was concerned, Luz had a blind spot. She'd warned him before that she'd side with her son. And he knew she'd never thank him for telling her Rob was using cocaine. It wasn't his place. His involvement with Rob was strictly limited to the polo field. He had stayed out of the family disagreements in the past, and he'd stay out of this problem, too.

"This stays separate from polo, Rob. If you ever combine the two, you will have to answer to me," Raul warned. "What you do in private is your concern. And what I do in private is none of yours. That includes your mother."

"I knew you'd back down." Rob grinned. "You don't dare open your mouth. I almost wish you would. I'd give anything to watch Luz show you the door."

"If she is hurt by this, you will be the one who does it." Raul turned and walked out of the room.

He shut the door behind him and put the key back in its place. Leaving the stable, he walked slowly toward the house, wishing he didn't share Rob's secret. Cocaine was an expensive habit. Rob had the resources to support it, but sooner or later, Luz was going to find out. Raul dreaded that day, then was faintly surprised by the discovery that he expected to be there when it happened.

Returning to the house, Raul left the foyer light on for Rob and climbed the stairs to the master suite. He passed through the sitting room and entered the empty bedroom. The red sequined dress lay neatly over a chair back, but there was no sign of Luz. Frowning, he looked around the room.

"Luz?" he called, and started back into the sitting room.

The reply, when it came, had a distant, flat ring to it. "I'm on the terrace."

The French doors in the sitting room stood open onto the private sun deck. Raul walked over to them and paused in the opening when he saw the red-robed figure standing at the rail, her back to him. Her shoulders were curved downward, her arms folded in front. Her head was tipped up as if she was contemplating the confusion of stars in the night sky. Raul walked onto the deck, but she didn't turn at his approach. Her position remained unchanged until he stopped behind her, then she bowed her head.

Looking at her subdued pose, he remembered her apprehensions over Trisha's reaction to their relationship and over Rob's jealousy of him. Inadvertently he had already caused Luz problems with her children—problems that were not yet fully resolved. They were her children, and her problems. She had not sought his advice, and he was in no position to offer it even if he knew a solution. He realized how fragile the bond between them was. It could not take much testing of its strength. He wouldn't test it to see if it could withstand the weight of the new knowledge he had about Rob's drug use.

As the silence lengthened, he placed his hands on her shoulders and felt her tension. He absently kneaded the taut cords while he stared at her slightly bowed head. Her hair was pale golden in the starlight, its delicate fragrant scent drifting to him.

"Tonight I used you as an instrument of revenge," she said quietly.

Until that moment, Raul had forgotten about the quarrel they'd had earlier. It seemed very unimportant now. He started to tell her so, but she began talking again, so he let her continue.

"Not out of hatred or a desire to hurt anyone," Luz added. "It was more to restore my own worth in the eyes of others. When Drew left me, all I saw in their eyes was pity, and not necessarily the gentle kind. They were always whispering behind my back. 'Her husband dumped her for a younger woman. At her age, she'll never find anyone else, unless it's her money he's after.'" Behind that mocking hauteur, he heard the bitterness and the hurt it had caused. "I had to show them that I found somebody who wanted me for myself, and I wanted to see the envy in their eyes when they met you. So I did parade you around to them to wipe the pitying smirks off their faces. I never intended it to be an insult to you."

Her explanation was the closest she could come to an apology. Raul understood that. In the time he'd known her, he couldn't recall Luz ever saying she was sorry. She would admit to being wrong about something and explain her reasoning, but she was too proud to actually apologize. Yet her pride was one of the things he admired in her.

*"No importa,"* he assured her. Raul bent to nuzzle the curve of her neck, nibbling at its sensitive cord just as she had done to him in the car. He felt the involuntary quiver of her response, and slid his hands down her crossed arms, overlapping them and drawing her back against him.

Luz closed her eyes, savoring the sensations his teeth and tongue evoked. The warmth of his embrace assuaged the hurt that had followed their quarrel. Always his arms made her forget everything but the pleasure he gave her.

At midweek, Luz finished the initial estimate of the travel expenses the polo team and its entourage of horses and grooms were likely to incur. She brought it into the study for Raul to review and laid it on the desk in front of him.

"Would you check this over and see if I've over- or underestimated the stabling fees, lodging, or meal costs? I think I might be off on the gasoline expense for the trucks hauling the horse trailers. It's on the second page." She walked around the desk and stood beside his chair to point it out to him.

"It appears low." Raul skimmed the other itemized figures. "This is very thorough."

"You sound surprised," Luz said, chiding him for doubting her money management knowledge. "Don't forget, we Kincaids came from a banking background. We were taught the worth of a dollar despite being reared in the lap of luxury, so to speak. And I've managed the household budget for years and been on countless fund-raising committees. And when you're trying to raise money, the idea is to take in more than you spend. I'm not exactly frugal with money, but I don't squander it either."

Smiling, Raul held up his hands in mock surrender. "I retract the comment."

"Excuse me." Emma Sanderson paused in the study doorway. "The mail is here, Luz."

She came around the desk and took the stack of letters from her secretary. "Thank you, Emma," Luz murmured and sat down on the leather couch to go through them while Raul went over the estimated expense list she had prepared.

The mail was mostly household bills and charge-account invoices along with the usual junk advertisements addressed to "Occupant."

"A letter from Trisha." It was the first she'd heard from her since Thanksgiving when she had called to let her know she was back safely from the ski trip. Luz tore open the flap with suppressed eagerness and quickly scanned the first paragraph of the letter, bracing herself for the possibility Trisha might be writing to say she was making other plans for the Christmas holidays. "Raul, she's coming home . . . this weekend." She couldn't believe it and read on hurriedly. "She'll be flying in Friday night. The baby's being christened on Sunday." Luz didn't care what reason was bringing her as long as she came. "Emma!" Leaving the couch, she hurried to the doorway, the letter clutched in her hand. "Emma?"

The plump, gray-haired woman was halfway across the living room when she stopped and turned back in answer to the summons. "Yes?"

"Trisha's coming home this weekend. Be sure and have her room ready for her."

"I'll see to it right away, Luz."

"Good." She started to turn back into the study, then checked the movement. "Oh, and Emma, get all the Christmas things out. We'll be decorating the house on Saturday. You know how Trisha has always insisted that she be here when we do it."

"I remember." Emma smiled.

Luz swung back into the room and walked slowly to the desk while she read the rest of the letter. The rest of it mostly had to do with her activities at college. Luz paused beside Raul's chair, unconsciously resting her hand on his shoulder.

"Isn't it wonderful?" she murmured as she reread the first part of the letter.

"Yes, it is," Raul agreed. She was too wrapped up in the contents of Trisha's letter to notice the quiet way he studied her face.

Balancing on the stepladder from the handyman's toolshed, Luz held the end of a red velvet ribbon against the top curve of the dining-room arch. A mistletoe-covered ball swung from the ribbon. She arched backward, trying to gauge the distance on either side of it.

"Emma? Trisha! Anybody? Does this look like the center?" she called as she held the decoration in the place she'd selected and tried to eyeball it from her ladder perch.

"Will I do?"

Luz glanced over her shoulder at Raul, her expression mockingly dubious. "I don't know. I really need an expert at this. From what I saw at your house, you aren't much of a hand at decorating."

"Ah, but the pictures I do have were hanging in the center of the wall," he reminded her.

"You have me there." She laughed. "So what do you think of this?"

"An inch to the right," he instructed. Luz moved the ribbon over. "That is the center."

While she held the end of the ribbon in place, she took a thumbtack from the small box atop the stepladder and pushed it through the material into the wood. Holding it there, she picked up the hammer and tapped the thumbtack firmly into position. When she finished, Raul held the ladder steady while she climbed down with her hammer and tacks. She stepped back to look at the ball of mistletoe hanging in the archway.

"You're right. It is the center."

"Of course."

"Are you familiar with the custom of kissing under the mistletoe?" Luz didn't even try to understand this mood she was in, half flirty and half simply high spirits. Having Trisha home, the Christmas things out, and Raul here, everything seemed gloriously perfect.

"Perhaps you could freshen my memory," Raul suggested.

"I would be delighted to." She hooked her hands around his neck and raised onto her tiptoes, but Raul drew back when she started to kiss him.

"I thought we were supposed to stand under the mistletoe." He arched a thick brow in question.

"A minor detail, my love. A minor detail," Luz murmured, and brought her mouth against his lips, pushing into them with building interest. His arms went around her, his hands tangling in the loose folds of her oversize sweater while he pressed her to him and returned the lazy passion of her kiss.

"Is that how it is done?" Raul questioned when she drew away and let her heels touch the floor again.

"That's just the first lesson."

His peripheral vision noted a movement in the foyer. He glanced over the top of Luz's head and saw Trisha standing in the opening, a papier-mâché piñata shaped like a horse in her hands. She had seen them kissing, he realized. When she saw him looking at her, she ducked quickly back into the foyer out of sight.

"Luz?" Emma bustled into the dining room. "I have your candy canes for the centerpieces and new bulbs to replace the burned-out ones in the tree lights."

"Back to work," Luz murmured to him and moved reluctantly away to take the items from her secretary. "Trisha!" she called. "We've got the lights, so we're back in business." When there was no response she glanced at him. "I think she's finishing up in the foyer. Do you want to tell her on your way upstairs?"

"Of course." Raul crossed through the living room into the large foyer. Pine boughs twined around the carved railing of the staircase, adorned with red velvet bows at intervals along the way. Trisha knelt beside the newel post, positioning the red-and-green piñata horse near its base. Raul paused, aware that she was aware of his presence even though she didn't look up. "Luz asked me to tell you the bulbs for the tree lights are here."

"Thanks. I'll be right there." She straightened as he moved toward the steps. "The piñata looks pretty ratty, doesn't it? Dad brought that for me when I was eight or nine. He'd flown out to Los Angeles on business and picked it up for me at the airport on his way back. We've dragged it out every Christmas and set it here, just where I found it. Of course, this year Dad won't be here to see it." She lifted her head, thrusting her chin a little higher than normal. "But that's the way it's going to be from now on, so I might as well get used to it."

Raul had the feeling she was referring both to her father's absence and his presence. "I am glad you came home this weekend, Trisha."

"Why?" she challenged.

"Because you have made your mother very happy."

Trisha tipped her head to the side, narrowing her gaze as she frowned at him. "You're really crazy about her, aren't you?" He looked slightly taken aback by the remark. "I didn't mean to pry." She looked away. "I guess that's between you and her."

"Not entirely," he replied, then admitted, "I care about her very much."

She looked at him for a long second, then smiled. "I'd better go help Luz with the tree."

# CHAPTER XXVIII

"The house always seems so quiet after Trisha leaves," Luz remarked as she sat down in the chair Raul held for her. "She's been gone two days. Still I expect her to come sailing in, talking a mile a minute."

"Excuse me, Luz." Emma Sanderson paused in the dining-room arch, beneath the mistletoe, Raul noticed. "Mr. Carstairs from the bank is on the phone. He'd like to speak with you. Shall I have him call back after lunch, or would you like to take the call now?"

"I'll talk to him. We're waiting for Rob anyway." She got up from the table and followed Emma into the living room.

Sitting alone at the table, Raul unfolded his napkin and laid it across his lap. A pitcher of tea sat on the table. He picked it up and poured some into his glass. Hearing footsteps, he glanced up as Rob entered the dining room. Absently, Raul watched him walk around to the chair he always occupied.

"Where's Luz?" Rob paused beside it.

"On the telephone." Raul noticed that Rob's face looked leaner, and he recalled the number of times he'd skipped a meal or eaten only sparingly. He'd known others who used cocaine regularly. They, too, had lost weight and slept little, the stimulating effect of the drug numbing them against hunger and fatigue.

"What are you staring at?" Rob demanded after he had sat down.

"Nothing." Raul picked up his glass and took a drink of the tea.

"What is that supposed to mean?"

"It means nothing," he replied smoothly, aware of the tension that was always between them off the polo field.

"Well, quit staring at people. Didn't your mama ever teach you it was rude to stare?" With a snap of his wrist, Rob shook out his napkin and laid it across his lap.

"I must have forgotten."

"I know what you're wondering, and I haven't. I keep my pleasure separate from my work," Rob informed him curtly. "That was our deal, remember?"

"*I* remember," Raul said with faint emphasis.

Rob's glance darted past him, and he closed his mouth on whatever retort he'd been about to make. A second later, Raul heard Luz reenter the dining room. As she walked around to her chair, he noticed the faintly troubled look on her face.

"That was Mr. Carstairs on the telephone, the vice-president of the bank." She studied Rob's face. "Rob, he called because he was concerned about the large withdrawal you made from your account yesterday."

"So?" Rob challenged. "It's no concern of his whether I take out a lot or a little. And he had no business calling you. It's my money. I can do what I want with it."

"Of course you can. It's just that . . . as Mr. Carstairs said, ten thousand dollars is a lot of cash to be carrying around. Rob, what are you doing with that much money?"

"Hey," he protested, "what is this? How come you're checking up on me?"

"I'm not. I just don't understand why you need ten thousand dollars in cash."

Agitated, Rob pushed away from the table and flung his napkin onto his plate. "In case you've forgotten, the season is Christmas. It never once occurred to you that I might be buying presents, did it?"

"With cash?" Luz persisted. "For heaven's sake, Rob, you have charge accounts and credit cards of your own. You could write a check for whatever you want to buy. It's foolish to carry around that much cash."

"It's my damned money! And if I want it in cash, then that's my business! I don't tell you how to spend your money; don't you tell me how to spend mine! I'm not a kid anymore. I don't have to come running to you every time I want to do something.

If I want your advice, I'll ask for it. In the meantime, butt out."

"I think you have had your say, Rob," Raul inserted smoothly. "Sit down so we can have lunch."

"And you!" He jabbed a finger at Raul. "You stay out of this, if you know what's good for you."

"Rob—" Luz protested, then paused when he stalked away from the table. "Rob, where are you going? You haven't had your lunch."

"I'm not hungry."

Dismayed, Luz sank back in her chair and stared after him. "I don't understand him anymore. He's changed so much since . . ." She glanced at Raul and didn't finish the sentence. Yet it seemed that Rob had begun to display this irrational anger only after she and Raul had first gotten together in Argentina. "I suppose I was just as independent at his age, wanting to do things my way whether they were wise or not."

"He is headstrong."

"He was always moody, even as a child, but he never lashed out in anger like this. I think he's been pushing himself too hard lately. He spends nearly every waking minute at the stables either practicing or playing. Have you noticed?"

"Yes."

"It's become too much of a strain on him, I think. We all crack under too much pressure." She was troubled by his actions and tried to find excuses for it. "He really needs to slow down."

As Emma joined them at the table, the cook brought out the fresh seafood salad. "Rob has decided he isn't hungry, so he won't be having lunch with us, Katie. You can take away his place setting," Luz instructed.

"Our new team is playing a friendly game tomorrow afternoon against the Black Oak team. Are you going to come and cheer for us?" Raul asked.

"Of course." She forced a lightness into her voice and pretended that nothing was wrong.

The next day, nothing seemed to be. Exuberant over the trouncing they gave the Black Oak team that had stolen the Kincaid Cup last year, Rob was laughing and slapping his teammates on the back. Luz even saw him locking a forearm with Raul and giving him much of the credit for captaining the team to a win.

When Rob suggested celebrating their first victory at the clubhouse lounge, Raul declined and waved him off with his other two teammates. He joined Luz, and together they walked to the parking lot, where she'd left the car.

"How come you didn't want to go with them?" she asked.

"They will enjoy themselves much more if I am not there to listen to their bragging." He smiled at her, fatigue around his mouth, then curved an arm around her shoulders to bring her closer until they walked hip to hip.

"Rob played very well, didn't he?"

"Better than he has in the past."

"I wish I could have been a fly at the picket line between the second and third chukkars." Luz laughed to herself. "Chet Martin must have been livid. If there's one thing he hates more than losing, it's losing to a Kincaid."

"He was not happy," Raul agreed.

As they passed the tennis courts, Luz noticed two players walking out of the webbed enclosure, rackets in hand and towels slung around their necks. She recognized Drew instantly, his trim tan body in tennis shorts. She felt a little tug of nostalgia, a touch of poignant regret. It surprised her. She saw him glance her way, and noticed the slight hesitation in his stride as their paths converged.

"Hello, Drew."

"Luz. How are you?" He paused and mopped at the perspiration sheening his face with one end of the towel.

"Just fine, thank you." She saw the look he darted to Raul, catching the disapproval—or was it jealousy? She wondered if even though he didn't want her, he didn't want anyone else to have her either. "I don't think you've met Raul Buchanan. Raul, this is my—my ex-husband, Drew Thomas."

"I have heard a great deal about you, Mr. Buchanan." Drew shook hands with him, very brusque in his manner. "My daughter tells me you're coaching Rob in his polo game."

"I am."

"Rob has improved tremendously," Luz inserted. "I wish I had known you were here, Drew. They just played a 'friendly' game with Chet Martin's team and beat them soundly. You could have seen for yourself how well he is playing now."

"Where is Rob?"

"He's at the lounge, celebrating."

Drew glanced in the general direction of the building. "Maybe I'll stop by and say hello to him." But he sounded doubtful, aware that Rob didn't want to see him.

"He'll come around in time, Drew. I'm sure of it." Luz wished there were something she could say or do to end this estrangement between father and son, but Rob tended to become very stubborn if he felt he was being pushed into something. Time healed, she herself had found out. "How is the baby? Tremayne, is it?"

Drew nodded, a smile slowly spreading across his face. "Happy, healthy. He's a good baby."

"I'm glad. A person can't ask for more." She smiled at him with an odd tenderness that sprang from regret for all the things they'd had and lost. "You must be eager to go home to him. It was good seeing you again, Drew."

"You, too, Luz." He held her hand for an instant, clasping it warmly between his own. It was as if they were sealing a bargain to put the bitter acrimony of the divorce behind them. "Take care." He glanced at Raul. "It was a pleasure meeting you. Be good to her. She's a fine woman."

As Drew moved away, her gaze lingered on him. After a moment, she became conscious of Raul at her side and turned her head to look at him. "Despite all I've said about him to the contrary, Drew isn't a bad man. It just couldn't work for us, that's all." Slipping an arm around his waist, she lightly hugged against him. The air she breathed smelled fresher and cleaner. She let her head touch his shoulder. "Let's go home, Raul."

A cloud drifted across the face of a three-quarter moon as Rob whipped his car into the driveway, the radio blaring. His hand tapped the steering wheel to the beat of the loud music, his head and shoulders moving to the rhythmic tempo. He wheeled the car onto the side drive and headed for the garage in the rear.

A garage door gaped open, showing its empty car stall to Rob's headlights. He aimed the car into the slot and braked to a stop less than three inches from the back wall. He felt like a racecar driver. Rob bet he could do that, too. It required timing, coordination, the ability to judge speed and distance. Hell, he had all that. He switched off the motor, automatically silencing the radio, and hopped out of the car.

The music continued to play in his head as he walked out of the garage, jingling the car keys on the ring hooked around his finger. Few lights were on when he looked at the house. It seemed silent and dead to him. Rob halted. The thought of going to his room and just sitting there made him pause. It would be a total letdown after the thrill of the game, the heady satisfaction of trouncing Martin's ass, and the victory revel at the club. He was feeling good, and he wanted to hold on to it.

Grinning, Rob tossed the car keys in the air and made a one-hand grab of them, then stuffed them in the pocket of his windbreaker. He turned away from the house and swung jauntily toward the stable. There was enough pure stuff in his stash that he wouldn't have to come down for a week if he didn't want to. But one toke, that's all he was going to have, and save the rest. It would be suicidal to burn up ten thousand dollars' worth in one night. He wasn't going to be stupid enough to get into a marathon smoking session, not when Raul expected him at the practice field in the morning.

Later, when Rob began to lose the euphoric feeling that charged his senses, his energy level remained high—too high to think of bed and sleep. He wondered if he should have taken that bottle of sleeping pills Jimmy Ray had offered him, then decided he'd been right to refuse it. He wasn't about to get hooked on sleeping pills the way Jimmy Ray was. Of course, the handler was old and needed his rest, while he could get by with a couple of hours of sleep if necessary.

Sometimes, he felt as if he didn't need sleep at all—like now. He glanced at the stash of cocaine he'd left on the counter. Hell, he had plenty, and what would it matter if he stayed up another hour or so? Humming merrily to himself, he walked to the counter and began mixing the magic potion of cocaine and ether.

Suddenly fire flashed in the air. In that fraction of a second of reaction, his horrified glance darted to the canister containing the highly volatile ether. And in the next, he saw flames leaping over his jacket sleeves. Petrified, he stared at them in shock as they crawled up his arms.

The heat searing his flesh seemed to break the grip of terror. Backing blindly away from the workbench, he slapped at the fire, his hands flailing wildly. But it greedily licked over the material, spreading rapidly to consume it all. The fire was everywhere. He could feel it crawling up his back, and he tried to take the jacket off, but the flames burned his fingers. Raw, animal sounds of panic roared around him, coming from his throat.

Terror-stricken, he ran to the door. "Jimmy Ray!" he screamed as he fought with the lock, finally getting it turned. He burst out of the burning tack room and staggered into the wide walkway between the rows of stalls. "Help!" he screamed hoarsely, holding his flaming arms away from his body, horrified by the stench of scorched flesh and aware it was his own. "Jimmy Ray! Help me!"

He lunged toward the side door at the end of the corridor. Outside, he turned to the stairs leading to the groom's quarters above the stable. The fiery heat was consuming him. His hair. His hair was on fire, he realized, and the bloodcurdling screams were his. Suddenly, he knew he'd never make it to the door.

Roll. That's what he was supposed to do. Roll and smother the flames. He threw himself onto the floor, screaming his agony and mindless of the frightened whinnies of the horses. He tried to roll, but he bumped into something. Fire danced all around his eyes, eating up the scattered straw. The hay bales. He had one last conscious thought as the flames ignited the bales stacked along the wall.

Something disturbed her. Turning, Luz drowsily opened her eyes. The other side of the bed was empty. She heard a noise in the room and looked toward the sound. She could barely make out Raul's shape in the darkness. He appeared to be dressing. Leaning over, she flipped on the bedside lamp, then squinted against the glaring light.

"What's the matter? Where are you going?" She frowned as she watched him fasten the waistband of his pants. He seemed in a hurry.

"Something has frightened the horses." Quickly, he pulled on his boots and grabbed his shirt. "Hear them?"

The instant he said that Luz realized it wasn't the muted night cries of a bird she was hearing, but the muffled, shrill neighs of the horses. She flung back the covers and reached for her robe at the foot of the bed. When Raul left the room, she followed him, pulling on the robe and tying the sash as she went.

The trees and shrubs around the pool and the garage roof blocked the stable from view as Luz hurried out of the house after Raul. She smelled smoke, but it wasn't until they had rounded the garage that she saw the flames leaping from the tack-room window. Cursing in Spanish, Raul grabbed her and shoved her back toward the house.

"Call the fire trucks. *De prisa!*" He waited while she backed away from the sight to make certain she obeyed. When he saw her turn and run back toward the house, he headed for the burning stable.

The panicked screams of the trapped horses rent the night, but his first thought was for the groom who lived above. There was no sign of the thin man outside the building. Raul raced to the side door and pulled it open, thinking Turnbull might be inside trying to get the horses out. Flames mushroomed with a crackling roar, their intense heat driving him back.

Shielding his face with an upraised arm, he tried to see inside, but he had only vague impressions of wooden stall partitions burning and a blazing ball of flame in the corridor where the hay bales had been stacked. Ignoring the wild drumming of hooves and wrenching screams of the horses, Raul turned away from the fire-blocked door and raced up the outside stairs, taking the steps two at a time.

"Turnbull!" He pounded on the door at the top. When he tried the knob, the metal burned his hand. Using the tail of his shirt for protection, he tried it again. The door was locked. Bracing himself against the stair rail, he kicked at it. On the fourth try, the door gave with a splintering rip of wood and metal.

At the sudden inrush of air, flames exploded, and he reeled from their blasting heat, retreating down the stairs. When he reached the bottom, Raul backed away from the building. Fire engulfed it, silencing the screams of the horses. Sweat poured from him as he sucked in air, breathing with difficulty, half suffocated by the oxygen-stealing flames. He stared helplessly at the burning building, hearing the wail of approaching sirens and knowing the trucks would arrive too late to save anything.

"Raul!"

Turning, he saw Luz running toward him and moved to stop her before she got too close to the fire. "There is nothing we can do." He held her firmly, seeing the horror in her face as she stared at the building all in flame.

"Where is Rob?" She turned her beseeching frightened gaze on him. "His car is here, but I couldn't find him in the house. Raul, you don't think . . ." She looked back at the fire, and he couldn't tell her what he was thinking.

Two fire trucks with lights flashing and sirens howling came barreling up the driveway and rolled quickly into position near the blazing stable. Almost before the trucks came to a stop, the firemen were on the ground, stringing out the hoses. The fire marshal's yellow car was right behind them.

"My God, the horses . . . Mr. Turnbull!" The exclamation came from Emma Sanderson. Raul turned to see the ashen-faced woman standing behind them, swaddled in a long robe, with a silk bandana tied around her gray hair.

"Stay with Emma." He forced Luz over beside her, and added, "Keep her here." He headed for the marshal's car as a section of the roof caved in with a loud, crashing roar of sparks and flames.

A middle-aged man climbed out of the car and shoved his helmet on his head, adjusting the strap under his chin. "How did it start? Do you know?"

"No. We discovered the fire only moments before we called you. By then it was too late. The flames had already spread through the whole structure."

"The horses?"

Raul shook his head. "The groom lived above the stable. I tried to get in, but the fire blocked the door."

"Anyone else in there?" In the background, the two-way radio chattered.

"Mrs. Thomas . . . her son is missing. His car is here, so we know he was home. He could have been in there."

"Let's hope you're wrong," he said gravely and moved off to join his men as high-pressure hoses sprayed water from the pumper onto the flaming structure.

There was a leaden feeling inside Raul as he walked back to Luz, and the tortured look on her face only made it worse.

There was nothing he could say, no hope he could give. He wanted to be wrong, but he didn't think he was.

"Where is Rob?" she demanded, but Raul just shook his head. "He could have seen the fire and gotten some of the horses out. Maybe he's taken them into the big paddock." She strained to see into the darkness beyond the outreaching light of the fire. "He could have," she insisted desperately.

"I will look." But he knew it was useless. "Go back to the house with Emma. There is nothing you can do here."

"No! I'm not going anywhere until I find out where my son is!"

In the predawn hours, the firemen searched through the smoldering rubble amid a rising, acrid stench of burned hides and roasted horseflesh. They recovered two badly burned bodies. With one of them, they found the charred remains of a belt and a metal buckle bearing the initials RKT, identifying one of the victims as Rob Kincaid Thomas. The coroner's ambulance took their bodies from the scene. A second search continued for the cause of the fire, while Raul led a shocked and grief-torn Luz to the house.

"It's a mistake. I know it is! Rob can't be dead! He can't!" Wildly she fought against it, not wanting to accept it, not wanting to believe her only son was gone. "It isn't true. It isn't true." Hugging her arms tightly around her, Luz rocked back and forth on the living-room couch, mindless of her surroundings. Something was held in front of her and lifted to her lips, but she turned away.

"Drink this," Raul's voice urged gently.

"I don't want it. I don't want anything," she protested. "I only want Rob. I want my son back."

"Sssh, now, girl." Emma sat down beside her. "It hurts deep, I know. Drink this hot, sweet tea I made you."

Luz took the cup, but simply held it between her cold, cold hands. "Emma, I've got to call Drew. I've got to tell him."

"It's all right, dear. I've already phoned him. He'll be here soon."

"Audra? Mary?" And Emma nodded that she had contacted them as well. Luz stared at the tea. "How am I going to tell Trisha? I don't know what I should say to her . . . how I should tell her." She covered her eyes with her hand, feeling the wetness of her own tears. "I don't believe it. He was so happy after winning that game. How did it happen? Why? Why did he have to die?"

"Don't torture yourself with the why of it," Emma comforted her. "It isn't for you to know. It isn't for any of us to know why our loved ones are taken from us."

"He was so young! It isn't fair!" she protested. "He had his whole life ahead of him." The teacup was taken from her hand as she began sobbing uncontrollably. A pair of arms went around her and cradled her. A distant part of her mind knew it was Raul, but mostly she was aware only of her own pain.

Half an hour later, Audra and Mary arrived at the same time. Audra swept into the living room, taking charge. "Emma, I want you to call the police at once. There are reporters outside. This is private property and I want them removed from the premises immediately. I will not have my daughter harassed by their tactless questions at a time like this."

Mary came to the couch, her eyes red from crying, and embraced her, hugging Luz tightly. "I'm so sorry, Luz." They cried together. Then Raul shifted, leaving the couch to make room for Audra.

"My baby," she said, taking Luz into her arms and pressing her cheek against her forehead. "I prayed that none of you would ever know the pain of losing a child. But you have your family, remember that. Frank and Michael are flying in this afternoon. Don't you worry about anything. We'll take care of all the necessary arrangements."

The doorbell rang. When Luz saw Drew walk into the living room, the numb shock of grief in his expression, she went to meet him, going into his arms. "Our son. Our baby boy. Drew, they say he's dead."

"But what happened?"

"The fire . . . we think he went in to get the horses out and . . . got trapped." She was haunted by images of Rob trying to get out of the burning building and flames leaping up to block his escape. It made it worse to know the horrible way he must have died.

"My God." Drew buried his face in her hair, holding her tightly.

Emma carried a tray laden with a complete coffee set into the living room and placed it on the low coffee table. "I have tea brewed in the kitchen if anyone would care for it instead of coffee," she said. Mary poured a cup for herself and one for Audra, but Raul refused any.

"We have to call Trisha, Drew," Luz said, her chin quivering with the effort to hold back her tears while he cried for both of them. "I don't want her finding out about Rob from the newspaper."

"No. No," he agreed in a choking voice, and cleared his throat loudly as he straightened and attempted to stand erect.

The doorbell rang, and this time Raul excused himself from the group to answer it. When he opened the door, the sooty fire marshal hesitantly stepped inside and removed his hat, tucking it under his arm.

"We . . . think we've determined the cause of the fire, Mr. Buchanan." He shifted uncomfortably. "I . . . uh . . . don't want to disturb Mrs. Thomas, but I feel I should talk to her if she's up to seeing me."

Raul knew by the look in the man's eyes what he was going to say, and he wanted to tell him that Luz wouldn't see him. He wanted to spare her this, but he knew he couldn't. "One moment, please." He left the marshal in the foyer and stepped into the living room. "The fire marshal is here, Luz. He would like to speak to you."

"Tell him to come in," Audra instructed.

Raul turned back to the foyer. "The family will see you," he told the man and preceded him into the room.

The marshal hesitated inside the doorway, appearing slightly discomfited by the group confronting him. "As I mentioned to Mr. Buchanan, we believe we've determined the cause of the fire." He paused, but no one prompted him with a question. "We've found evidence that suggests someone was . . . uh . . . free-basing cocaine in the tack room."

"Cocaine!" The word was shocked from Drew as he turned to look at Luz, who looked as confused and incredulous as he did.

"We found what was left of the pipe they smoke it in, and the canister of ether. It's a highly volatile substance. The slightest spark can set it off. We think that's what happened. Someone was smoking cocaine and there was a . . . kind of explosion."

"You think, but you can't be sure," Luz protested. "If you're saying our son—"

"Mrs. Thomas, I'm sorry. The fire started in the tack room. We found your son's body not far from the door. More than likely his clothing caught on fire and he ran. We recovered your groom's body in the rubble of the collapsed second story. All the evidence indicates that it was your son in the tack room. I know it's hard to hear something like that about your own child. It would be for me if it was mine. But it doesn't change the facts."

"No." She turned away from him.

"Who knows about this?" Audra demanded.

"At the moment, myself and one of my officers. I haven't talked to any of the press outside—didn't want to until I'd seen Mrs. Thomas."

"You indicated that you suspect my grandson was *smoking* cocaine, is that correct?" Audra asked.

"Yes, ma'am."

"Then would it not be accurate to say that *smoking* was the cause of the fire?" she challenged. "It has been known to cause many stable fires, has it not?"

"Yes, ma'am, it has."

"You do understand that I'm not suggesting you lie about the fire. But the family would greatly appreciate being spared any sordid press coverage of my grandson's death. I believe the tragic consequences of his actions are punishment enough, don't you?"

"I will do everything I can." He removed his hat from under his arm. "Again, my sympathies . . . to all of you."

After he'd left, Luz sank into a chair. "I can't believe it," she murmured, slowly shaking her head. "Rob was using cocaine. I never . . . suspected. The money," she remembered and looked up at Raul. "Oh, no, was that why he took that ten thousand dollars from the bank? To buy cocaine?"

"Yes."

"Yes! What do you mean—yes?" Drew demanded. "Did you know about this?"

Raul looked at Luz for a long second, then slowly nodded. "Yes. I knew."

"You knew?" Luz pushed out of her chair with an effort and walked to him in a daze. "You knew and didn't tell me?"

"How could I tell you?" he reasoned. "Would you have believed me?"

"I don't know. How can I know now?" she asked brokenly. "Maybe I wouldn't have, but you never gave me the chance! I'm his mother. I had a right to know! If you had told me, I could have done something! I could have stopped him!"

It was a rage that filled her—a rage that Rob hadn't had to die. If she had known, she could have done something to help him. She began to shake with sobs, silent ones at first, then loud tearing sounds in which she repeated Rob's name over and over.

Raul's arms gathered in her shaking body and held her against his own, absorbing her weeping shudders. Dimly she knew it was Raul. "Why? Why didn't you tell me?" she sobbed.

"I am sorry, *querida*," he murmured against her hair. "I thought it was not my place to interfere. I could not know this would happen. Now I see I was wrong."

"Rob." She wept for her son.

The morning passed in a blur of pain and tears. At some point, Audra insisted that Mary take Luz upstairs so that she could dress before people began calling at the house to extend their sympathy. It was arranged for her brother, Frank, to fly to Boston, and inform Trisha of Rob's death and accompany her home. But for Luz, it was a grief that knew no end, that dominated her every conscious minute.


After the funeral, Luz retreated to the privacy of her sitting room, leaving her family downstairs to cope with the mourners. Hating the sun for shining, she closed the drapes across the French doors, then crossed to the drink cart and filled a squat glass with straight whiskey. The image of Rob's closed casket haunted her, and she couldn't stop those agonizing screams of the trapped horses from echoing in her mind.

When she started to take a drink, her black face-covering veil got in the way. Impatiently, she pulled it back over the pillbox hat, then swallowed half the whiskey in the glass. It hardly burned at all. She was too numb, the desolation too strong. She topped the glass and walked over to the sofa. As she sank onto it, all the torment and pain of his needless death closed over her. She couldn't live with it. Tipping the glass back, she poured more whiskey down her throat. Something had to dull this pain.

She had no idea how long she sat there. Every minute was

agony. The sound of the door opening and the invasion of voices from the gathering downstairs stirred her awareness. She looked up as Raul came in and shut the door. Luz had known that sooner or later someone would come up to check on her. Her family rarely left her alone for long, making sure someone stayed with her, although Raul wasn't exactly a member of the family. He belonged without belonging.

"If you would prefer to be alone, I will go into the next room," he offered.

"No." Moving, she walked back to the drink cart and refilled her glass. She took a long swallow and felt the heat in her throat. Lowering the glass, she breathed in deeply to sigh, but even the air in the house seemed permeated by the lingering smell of burned wood and flesh. Her hands tightened on the glass. "I can't stand that smell. I want that charred rubble cleared as soon as possible."

"It has been arranged for the bulldozers to come in the morning." Raul lit a thin cigar and let its aromatic smoke scent the air.

Unconsciously she moved her head from side to side. "I can't believe he's dead. It doesn't seem real." She squeezed her eyes tightly shut. "I keep thinking he's just out on the practice field. Why? Why did he have to die? What did I do wrong?"

The cigar was left to burn in an ashtray as Raul moved to her side and gripped her shoulder. "You must not blame yourself, Luz. You are not responsible for his actions. Rob caused the fire, not you."

She shrugged free of his hands and turned away. "You don't understand." Nobody did. Nobody could. She took another drink of the whiskey, then walked back to the sofa and sat woodenly on its cushions. When Trisha walked in, Luz absently studied her pale face and tear-swollen eyes. She could only guess how ravaged by grief her own face was. Hesitantly, Trisha came over to sit beside her and rub a hand on her shoulder.

"It's dark in here. Don't you think you should turn on a light?" she suggested.

"No."

"I know how it must hurt, Luz. Rob was always your favorite." Trisha's voice cracked under the weight of her sorrow.

"It hurts me, too. I keep wondering if there was something I could have done."

A part of her recognized that Trisha was seeking comfort. Luz knew she should pull herself together for her daughter's sake, but she couldn't make the effort. She had lost her son, admittedly her favorite. Trisha couldn't fill the void it left in her life.

"Rob always needed me more than you did. He needed me, and this time I wasn't there." The agony of it washed through her. "If only I had known he was using drugs," she moaned, then remembered a fragment of Trisha's words and wondered, "Did you know, Trisha?"

Avoiding her gaze, Trisha moved uneasily and knotted her fingers together in her lap. "This last summer, I caught Rob smoking in the tack room. He claimed he'd been smoking marijuana. It's the same thing he told Raul." She glanced in the direction of the drink cart where he stood. "Only Raul didn't leave it at that the way I did."

"But why . . . why did he use cocaine?" Luz doubled her hand to an impotent fist. "That's what I don't understand. He had everything he possibly could want. What was he trying to escape?"

Agitated, Trisha rose to her feet and moved stiffly away from the sofa, where she had found no consolation. "I don't know. They claim one of the appeals of cocaine is the supreme feeling of confidence it gives—the belief you can accomplish anything." She hugged her arms about her middle, her chin tautly quivering. "Rob was always trying to live up to everybody else's expectations of what a Kincaid should be. That's all he ever heard. That's all we both heard, 'You're a Kincaid,'" she accused, mocking the phrase bitterly. "Poor Rob never thought he was good enough. Probably the only time he did was when he used cocaine." Angry tears filled her eyes as she looked at Luz. "I hate being a Kincaid!" A second later, she bolted from the room in tears.

Stunned and shaken, Luz stared at the door. It couldn't be. Her mind reeled from the things Trisha had said. She drained the glass, trying to drown them out, then moved stiffly to the drink cart and picked up the whiskey decanter. There were too many tears in her eyes. They blinded her as she tried to fill the glass, spilling half the liquor on the cart top.

"This will not help you." Raul took the decanter from her shaking hands and set it down, then took her in his arms and held her close.

"It's my fault," she murmured and began sobbing uncontrollably.

Her grief seemed inconsolable. He was sobered by how deeply a mother could love a son and how devastating the loss of a child could be. Nothing seemed to penetrate that wall of pain that imprisoned her, not even his love.

# CHAPTER XXIX

In the week after the funeral, Raul watched a pattern form. Each morning, Luz poured whiskey in her coffee so that she could face the reality of Rob's death and get through another day. There was always a drink in her hand, although she never actually became drunk. She seemed to consume just enough to dull the pain that hollowed her eyes. In that alcoholic haze, she wandered the house or sat for hours in Rob's bedroom.

She ventured outside once that week. After the bulldozers had finished removing all evidence of the burned stable, including the foundations, Luz went to inspect the site and ordered sod to be laid. After that, Raul wasn't able to persuade her to leave the house again.

When Trisha left to return to college, Luz managed to be on hand to tell her goodbye. Raul hoped Trisha's departure would rouse Luz from her grief-stricken stupor and remind her that she had another child, but she seemed not to care whether Trisha stayed or left.

At night, she turned away from his caresses, and recently had begun to reject even the physical comfort of his arms. Every day he watched her sink deeper into mourning. Nothing he said or did seemed to make any difference. He was frustrated, wanting to help and knowing she wouldn't let him in.

For her, everything had come to a standstill since the night of the fire, but Raul couldn't remain in limbo with her. The fire had destroyed more than Rob's life. All Raul's polo equipment and gear had gone up in those flames. Although more than half his ponies had been stabled at the club, a third of his polo string had been killed in the fire. All of it had to be replacéd. Polo was still his profession. He had to practice and he had to play.

Still dressed in his boots and breeches, Raul entered the house through the French doors and halted abruptly at the confusion that greeted him. Boxes and tissue paper were scattered about the room. The yardman and his helper stood on stepladders, taking down the Christmas garlands and mistletoe that decked the archways, while Emma removed the brightly colored balls from the tree and wrapped them in paper to be put away in the boxes.

"What is this?" Raul demanded.

With lips pursed in disapproval, Emma replied, "Luz has decided she isn't having Christmas this year. I am to mail everyone's gift, including Trisha's. Yours are upstairs."

"Where is she?"

"In the sitting room."

Raul went up the steps two at a time and burst into the sitting room, but his impatience died at the sight of Luz curled in a chair wearing her rumpled red kimono and nursing a drink . . . and looking tortured. He closed the door quietly and crossed the room to the veranda doors. Reaching behind the drapes, he pulled the cord to open them and flooded the room with light. She shielded her eyes from the glare, then shifted to turn her back to it. Raul dragged a chair over and sat down in front of her, demanding her attention.

"Luz, there is something we must discuss."

"Not now." She took a drink of whiskey, trying to shut him out.

"Yes, now," Raul insisted. "This cannot be postponed."

"What is it, then?" She sighed.

"What do you intend to do about the polo team?"

"The polo team." Luz frowned at him.

"It is entered in next week's tournament at the club. Are you going to continue your sponsorship of Rob's team?" He remembered how involved she had been in it, how much time she had devoted to organizing it with him, and hoped that it would be the key to bring her out of this stupor. "He would have wanted you to, Luz."

She looked at him for a long minute. It seemed he had reached her at last. Then she shook her head. "No."

She wasn't certain anymore that she had sponsored the team

solely for Rob's benefit. It might have been a vague idea before she met Raul, but it was afterward that the plan took shape. The team had been a way of justifying Raul's presence, a way to keep him with her while she pretended it was for Rob. How many times had she used Rob as an excuse to be near Raul? Meeting him in Paris, flying to Argentina, staying at his *estancia*, creating the team—all those things she had done in Rob's name when it had really been because of her own desire to be with Raul. She refused to continue the charade. She owed at least that to Rob.

"What about the players?" Raul argued. "You have made commitments to them."

"I'll compensate them for the time they've lost. They're good players. I'm sure they'll find positions on other teams." Uncoiling her legs, she stood up and walked to the drink cart.

Hanging his head, Raul breathed in deeply in defeat. Although she hadn't said it, she had meant that for him as well. It was true he would have little difficulty joining another team, and there were plenty of tournaments between Palm Beach and Boca Raton to keep him here through the winter season. Maybe by spring, she would be over the shock of Rob's death and come to terms with her grief, and her guilt.

Luz walked behind the counter bar in the living room and splashed more whiskey in her glass. "Are you sure I can't fix you something, Mary?" She glanced in her sister's direction, at the moment welcoming any diversion that would lead the conversation away from her failure to attend Christmas dinner at Audra's this year.

"No, thanks."

Christmas meant children. Children meant Rob. The holiday had been agony to her without him. Luz sipped at the whiskey, needing the depressant to ease the awful ache. She took the bottle with her when she walked out from behind the bar and crossed the room to sit in a chair opposite Mary.

"Where's Raul this afternoon?"

"Playing in a tournament at the polo club."

"You should have gone with him, Luz. You need to get out more. You can't stay cooped up in this house forever. You're turning into a recluse, and I don't like it."

"I couldn't have sat in those stands, Mary, without remembering all the times I watched Rob play." Tears filled her eyes while her throat became choked with pain. "Why did I have to find out after he was dead that Rob was using drugs?"

"Parents are usually the last to find out, Luz. Maybe we don't want to see it because we don't want to believe it can happen to our children. God knows, we're all afraid it will."

"The signs were there," Luz went on as if she hadn't even heard Mary's response. "The personality change, the paranoia, the secretiveness. I see them all now."

"Luz, you must stop blaming yourself. It wasn't your fault," Mary protested.

"But it was," she said flatly. "Don't you see, Mary? I've failed at everything. I wasn't a good wife to Drew. And I wasn't a good mother to Rob."

"That isn't true."

"Yes, it is. Those outbursts of anger from Rob, they were cries for help, but I wasn't listening. I didn't want to hear because it was too inconvenient. Rob accused me of being selfish, and he was right. I was happy and I didn't want anything unpleasant intruding on that, so I pretended it would all go away if I ignored it long enough. He needed me and I wasn't there," she declared bitterly.

"Stop torturing yourself with guilt like this, Luz." Mary leaned forward and gripped the hands that clutched the whiskey glass so tightly. "Chances are there wasn't anything you could have done even if you had known."

She stared at her sister. "You don't understand, do you? As long as I had Raul, nothing mattered unless it affected my relationship with him. Rob's behavior upset me because I thought it might cause problems for us. I pretended my children's opinions mattered, but I had already forsaken them emotionally. All I cared about was what *I* needed . . . and I needed Raul."

Rising to her feet, Luz brushed aside Mary's hands and walked swiftly from the room, breaking into a sobbing run when she reached the stairs. The tears didn't help, and the whiskey couldn't dull the wretched pain. She simply couldn't forgive herself for the way she had failed Rob.

She sent away the supper tray Emma brought up to her, but a few minutes later, Raul entered the room carrying it. "You have to eat, Luz." He was still dressed in his polo attire of brown riding boots, white breeches, and blue knit shirt.

"I'm not hungry. Take it away." She wouldn't let herself look too closely at him as she reached for the whiskey bottle on the nightstand beside the bed.

"No more." He took it away from her and slammed it down on the stand. "There is nothing in there but misery."

"Without it, there is more misery." But she didn't reach for the bottle. Instead, she cradled the empty glass in her hands and stared at it. "I want you to leave, Raul," she said tightly.

He sighed heavily. "I will leave the tray—"

"No, I mean I want you to leave this house." Luz finally looked up and saw his stunned, disbelieving look. "Can't you see it's no good for us?" she protested angrily.

"Why?" he asked quietly.

"Because it happened too fast. The ink had barely dried on my divorce papers when I met you. I was frightened and alone, and I rushed into this without thinking. Emotionally it was too soon. It was a mistake, and I'm paying for it."

"And I have nothing to say in this."

"I need to be alone so I can think without having you around to influence me," Luz insisted and raked her fingers through her hair in agitation. "Just go away! Go away and leave me alone! I don't need you anymore. I don't want you here! What else do I have to say to make you leave?"

"Nothing." He broke his rigid stance to move toward the closets. "It will not take me long to pack."

Taking the whiskey bottle, Luz went into the sitting room and tried very hard to drink herself into oblivion, but she was still conscious when Raul walked out the door with suitcases in hand. She wept long and bitterly, crying for the past and all the pain it had caused.

In the following weeks, her tortured grief failed to lessen. The whiskey became her sole companion and confidant, greeting her in the morning, sharing her agony in the day, and lulling her to sleep at night. Luz rarely left the house and refused all calls. Half the time she didn't bother to get dressed or to brush her hair. She simply sat and thought and remembered.

There were so many incidents that took on new significance when she looked at them in retrospect. She remembered that afternoon when Rob had walked into the hotel room in Buenos Aires and found her and Raul together. She recalled how abusive he'd been before he'd stormed out, then how ebullient he'd been when he returned, blithely accepting the affair he'd earlier condemned. He must have been high on cocaine then, but she hadn't questioned the radical change of mood. No, she had been relieved because it meant he wasn't going to make things awkward for her and Raul.

And those hours he'd been gone, claiming he was with Tony. She recalled that he had spent a lot of time with Tony away from the polo field. There had been evenings at the *estancia* when Rob and Tony had acted like a pair of schoolboys out on a lark. Luz suspected now that they might have been sniffing cocaine. Tony could even have been the one who supplied it. At the time, she hadn't paid too much attention to their antics, because she was thinking about later in the evening when she would meet Raul in her room.

All the spare time Rob spent at the stable after they returned from Argentina—she realized he must have gone there to use the drug. It was where he had stashed his paraphernalia. He had rarely been at the house in the evenings, but she had never bothered to check on him because it meant she had Raul to herself, just the two of them together.

Always, always the thought of Raul, of being with him, and it had blinded her to the things she should have noticed. So she drank, never getting drunk but drinking just enough to deaden some of the pain. She had failed Rob.

There were odd moments when Luz knew she should get herself together for Trisha's sake, but she couldn't make the effort. She had lost her son. And Trisha didn't need her. She never really had. She was back at college, too far away to matter greatly.

Moving with stiff care, Luz descended the staircase to the foyer, her hand constantly gripping the railing for balance. When she saw the suitcases sitting by the front door, she frowned in hazy confusion.

"Emma?" she called and heard brisk footsteps in the galleria. Turning, she saw the plump woman as she entered the foyer. Her frown deepened when she noticed the light suit and hat Emma wore. She glanced back at the luggage and rubbed her fingers against her left temple, trying to clear her head. "Is it your vacation time already?"

"No." The expression on the woman's face was what Luz

had always called her no-nonsense look. "I have quit. I gave you my notice two weeks ago. I doubted at the time that you were sober enough to understand. So I took the liberty of notifying Mrs. Kincaid of my resignation. I believe she is arranging for someone else to come in and stay with you."

"You're leaving? But you can't," Luz protested, the shock sobering her.

"I was not hired to be a nurse and bartender. For three months, I have waited for you to come to terms with your grief, but it appears that you prefer to wallow in self-pity. You are not the only woman who has ever lost a loved one. Life goes on. And I intend to get on with mine. I am a social secretary and house manager. I am not going to allow those skills to go to waste. I need the stimulation of challenging work."

"You can't go. What will I do without you?" Emma had always been there, it seemed, making sure everything ran smoothly. Luz couldn't imagine the house functioning without her.

"I suggest you go to work," Emma retorted.

"What?"

"I'm well aware of the fact you're a Kincaid, so my advice hardly applies to you," she replied with some irritation that she had even mentioned it. "But work, a stimulating occupation, is what a person needs when she has lost someone she cared about very much. I'm not saying that it makes the pain or the grief any better. But it stops you from being so absorbed in yourself, and eventually you can deal with your loss. Yes, it would be best if you had to get a job."

"A job? Can you imagine Luz Kincaid Thomas looking for a job?" The idea was ridiculous, she couldn't help mocking it. "My God, that's rich."

"I am sure you find it very amusing," Emma said stiffly.

"Be honest, Emma." She tasted the bitterness of remembering how Trisha had once described her life as doing nothing all the time. "What am I qualified to do? Hire out as a social secretary?"

"If that's what interests you. It has to be something you enjoy, whether it's cooking, gardening, or whatever." The woman stopped abruptly and sighed. "I'm wasting my breath. You probably aren't sober enough to remember this conversation. Goodbye, Luz. I did enjoy our past association. Mrs.

Kincaid has kindly agreed to provide a reference, so you needn't concern yourself about it."

Motionless, Luz watched Emma pick up her suitcases and set them outside the front door, one by one. When she carried out the last one, a taxi pulled up the driveway. As the driver began loading the luggage in the trunk, Luz went to the door.

"You're really leaving, aren't you?" she murmured.

"Yes. I'm sorry," Emma said, then walked to the cab.

As the taxi drove away, Luz slowly shut the door and turned to face the empty house. Everyone had left her—Jake, Drew, Rob, Trisha, Emma, Raul. Or had she driven them away? Had she rejected them? Or was it a combination? She couldn't think. Her head pounded.

She moved away from the door, her steps slowing as she neared the living room. She looked down at the robe she was wearing, the drink stains on the red material. Her hand went to the straggly tangle of her unbrushed hair. It was early afternoon and she hadn't even attempted to dress.

Work. She laughed shrilly at Emma's parting advice. Who would ever hire her to mop floors looking like this? "Something you enjoy." What had she ever enjoyed doing? What had there ever been in her life beside home, family, and social functions? There were so few activities she had ever truly enjoyed— helping Rob with his polo ponies, fox-hunting in Virginia, working with Jake at Hopeworth Farm.

Hopeworth Farm. Her eyes filled with tears as she remembered those early carefree days at her childhood home. She looked around the beautifully decorated room, so empty of life and love. She wanted to go home.

Nothing was keeping her here, she realized. Not anymore. With quickening steps, she walked to the study and headed straight for the telephone directory atop the desk. She opened the yellow pages to the airline listings and picked up the phone, dialing the number.

"Reservations? Yes, I'd like to know what flights you have going to Virginia. Richmond."

Ten days later, Luz rang the doorbell at her mother's ocean-side estate. The maid answered its summons and showed her into the sunroom. Audra looked up from the stack of correspondence she was answering and lowered her glasses, as if they were deceiving her.

"Hello, Audra." She smiled sunnily, her heels striking a quick tattoo on the tiled floor.

"Luz." She rose to greet her. "I thought you were in Virginia."

"I was." After a warm peck on the cheek and a brief hug, Luz moved away, setting her purse on the table and clasping her elbows with her hands, trying to contain the eagerness she felt. "As a matter of fact, I've just come from the airport."

"The trip certainly seems to have done you some good," her mother remarked. "You're almost glowing with health."

"I'm feeling better," she admitted, although the grief was still with her, still haunting her waking hours. "Audra, I want to lease Hopeworth Manor from you."

"What?"

"And I want to train some of the colts that I feel would be good polo prospects. You can have Stan Marshall—or whoever you like—establish a fair market value for them as they are. After I have trained them, we can sell them and we'll split the profits."

"What?"

"Hector once told me that you don't have to be an expert at polo to train a polo pony. And I believe him. I am good with horses, Audra. I can give them everything but game experience. Later on, I might be able to work out something with one of the polo instructors at the university. But this is something I want to try."

"Who told you?" Audra frowned. "Luz, are you all right?"

She laughed shortly, suddenly realizing how carried away she had gotten about her project. "I haven't been drinking, if that's what you're wondering. I am very serious about this, Audra. I'm not claiming that I'm going to become the world's greatest horse trainer, but I need something more demanding than parties, committees, and fund-raisers to occupy my time. And I love horses . . . and I love Hopeworth Farm."

"But what about your home here?"

"I'll sell it." She had already decided that. Ideally, she'd move to Hopeworth Manor, if Audra agreed to her proposal. If not, then somewhere. "It's just a house now . . . a house with memories. I can't live in the past. Well, Audra?"

"I can't say that I approve."

"I'm not asking you to approve of what I'm doing. I'm asking if you'll lease the manor house to me."

After a long, considering look, Audra smiled softly, her eyes shining moistly. "I never could stand to see anything go to waste."

# Epilogue

It was a sticky, humid Texas afternoon in May, and only a reluctant breeze stirred the heavy air. Standing alone on the grass sidelines away from the grandstand, Luz watched the white ball rolling parallel to the line toward her and the rider chasing it, his mount straining for every ounce of speed. With eyes hungry for detail, she studied the man in the saddle. Everything was so familiar about him; even if she hadn't known Raul was playing in this exhibition match, she would have recognized him. But she had known.

The polo club had touted the ten-goal players who would be participating in the match being held in conjunction with the annual polo pony sale, and Raul was one of them. That's why she had come to the game. Maybe it wasn't fair to want to see him again after more than a year apart, but lately she'd been wondering if there was anything left between them. She had to find out. With four of her polo ponies consigned to tomorrow's auction, she had the perfect opportunity.

She watched Raul guide his mount into position for a shot. His head came up, and she saw him take his eyes off the ball and, for a split second, look directly at her. The discovery splintered through her in little shock waves, but it was so brief that an instant later she thought she had imagined it. Then she saw him swing at the ball and miss an easy shot.

"Buchanan missed the ball. That's something you aren't going to see very often, ladies and gentlemen," the announcer's voice boomed over the loudspeakers. "But I guess it proves even ten-goal players can make mistakes."

Raul had seen her, Luz realized. She had distracted him for an instant and thrown off the timing of his swing. A little hope sprang that maybe he'd want to see her. He reined in his horse and looked back at her. There was no one else around her, so she had to be the object of his gaze.

The play continued on the field with less than three minutes left in the game. After hesitating a split second longer, Raul wheeled his pony to pursue the play of the ball. Luz didn't wait for the finish of the game. She started walking toward the end of the field, where a small pavilion stood, offering shelter to the players between chukkars.

When the final bell sounded, Luz stood beneath the shade of the awning and fingered the belt buckled around the waist of her slim four-pocket safari dress. She didn't realize how nervous she was until she saw Raul riding off the field toward the pavilion. Dismounting at the picket line, he turned his horse over to the groom and shed his helmet, mallet, and knee guards, then picked up a towel to wipe the sweat from his face and neck. It was still in his hand when he walked toward her.

She was conscious of her heart-lift. He had changed so little, still a stirring sight in his white breeches and snug-fitting polo jersey, more tanned maybe, a few more lines, but his hair was just as dark and his eyes as blue as she remembered. She felt a little awkward being here like this, remembering the way she'd asked him to leave.

"Hello, Raul."

"You are looking well, Luz."

"Thank you." She searched for words, trying to think of something else to say.

The other players rode by to their individual picket lines and called to Raul, some congratulating him for a well-played game and others chiding him for missing an easy shot. He acknowledged most of them with a curt nod, then reached to take Luz by the arm.

"Shall we walk?" he suggested.

"Yes."

The pressure of his fingers on her arm was a pleasant sensation as he guided her away from the milling crowd of grooms, riders, horses, and bystanders. They walked toward the shade of the trees, where the initial preparations were underway for the traditional barbecue and dance to be held that evening under the club's famous oak tree. Their steps slowed automatically when they reached the coolness of the shade. Luz was conscious of the silence that lay between them.

Raul broke it. "When did you leave Palm Beach? I heard this last winter that you had moved."

"A little over a year ago. I live in Virginia now, at Hopeworth Farm. I've begun training polo ponies. That's why I'm here." One of the reasons, anyway. "I have consigned four ponies to tomorrow's auction. So far I have two interested buyers who want to take some trial rides. I'm supposed to meet them at the barns in an hour."

"You were always good at handling young horses."

"It's a pity I was never as good at handling other things," Luz murmured ruefully, then glanced upward into the spreading branches of the big oak. "I almost wish they still held the auction here under this ancient oak instead of at the new sales pavilion. I always thought it was unique."

"Hector said I should tell you the house is wearing its shawl of ivy. He hopes someday you will come and see how good it looks."

"How is he?" She smiled, and inwardly wondered how much of that invitation Raul seconded.

"He is fine."

"When I learned you were going to be here in Houston, I hoped I'd have the chance to see you. I wanted to congratulate you on obtaining your ten-goal rating. I know how much it meant to you." She offered to shake hands with him, but he held her hand and studied it.

"It was not a fair trade, Luz. Losing you and receiving the ten," he stated.

A tightness gripped her chest. "I wasn't sure you'd want to see me again, Raul."

"You were the one who asked me to go."

"I needed time alone to think. I went from my ex-husband to you with hardly any time in between to solve the riddle of who or what I was, or what I wanted." She studied his proud, rugged face, finding it so achingly familiar. "You see, I was raised to believe I was worth something only if I had a man. I've been totally on my own for a year now, and I've learned to like it. Now I know I'm a person in my own right. I have a value."

"I could have told you that."

"But I had to find out for myself," she said, just as she ultimately had to accept that she couldn't shoulder the blame for Rob's death. It was unlikely she could have prevented it even if she had known.

"Now that you have, what will you do?" He continued to hold her hand.

"I'm not sure. Sometimes it's difficult to pick up where you left off." Unconsciously she held her breath.

"Not for me," Raul told her. "I have not seen you for almost a year and a half, but my feelings for you are stronger than before. I love you, Luz."

Slowly she smiled as tears misted her eyes. "We never did get around to saying that to each other, did we?" There was a faint shake of her head, almost disbelieving it could turn out this way. "Raul, you deserve someone who can give you a home and a family. You're young enough. You still have time to raise children. I'm forty-four years old. I can't give you sons and daughters."

"Children are not what I want. You are."

She didn't bother to wait to hear any more as she went into his arms, at last needing him because she loved him.

# A MESSAGE
# FROM JANET DAILEY

Dear Readers,
At the back of *The Pride of Hannah Wade*, I told you all
about my new novel, *The Great Alone*. I'm so excited about
this novel I can hardly wait 'til Poseidon Press publishes it
this June! So I thought I'd share yet another chapter of it
with you. This one is from the early part of the novel, when
the Russians first come to Alaska. Tasha, the girl in this
chapter, is one of my very favorite characters and plays a
major role throughout the novel.

As I told you before, I've worked longer and harder on
*The Great Alone* than on any other novel—but for me it
was worth it; I'm in love with Alaska and proud of *The
Great Alone*. I hope you'll love the book as much as I do.
Be sure to look for it this June, coming from Poseidon Press.

Sincerely,

Janet
Dailey

# CHAPTER X

Overhead, mewling seabirds wheeled, their ivory wings flashing white against a backdrop of gray clouds. Leaping and diving, a porpoise swam alongside the vessel's bow as though escorting it out of the bay. A steady wind bellied the sails. Tasha turned her face into the wind and gazed at the wide stretch of sand, the bidarkas lined up on the shore. From this distance, the outline of her village was barely discernible and then only because she knew where to look.

Her heart ached to be leaving all that was familiar to her—the island, her home, and family—her mother and old Weaver Woman most of all. But her regret wasn't equal to the excitement she felt. Hunters frequently traveled to other islands to trade or visit, but women seldom went unless the whole family, sometimes the whole village, made the journey. Tasha hadn't been off the island since she was a little girl. Then it had been a trip to nearby Agattu to visit her mother's family. Now, she was on her way to some unknown destination. Andrei Tolstykh, her new husband, had indicated to Many Whiskers that it might be as many as two summers before he returned to Attu.

Turning, she asked her brother. "Where will we go?"

"I have told the Cossack about Adak and the small islands clustered around it where the sea otter live in large numbers." The reluctance with which he had imparted the information was evident in the flat tone of his voice. Walks Straight did not share Tasha's enthusiasm for this adventure.

"The hunting will be good there."

"If the villages give him permission to hunt in their territory," added Walks Straight.

"They will. He will give them gifts in exchange, and we will tell them that he seeks to trade with them and live in peace." She saw the skepticism in his look. "You know this is true. He is not like the others."

"No," he conceded grudgingly. "But he is a Cossack. Don't trust him too much."

Lately when he looked at his sister, vague memories stirred of another time when the Scar-Eyed One had made his mother cry. Now Tolstykh was her husband. He didn't want his sister hurt, yet he felt powerless to prevent it. And he hated the Cossacks for making him feel this way. He had agreed to accompany the smooth-faced commander partly to honor the wishes of Many Whiskers and his mother, but mainly he hoped that by leading the Cossacks to new hunting grounds, they would all eventually leave his home island.

Walks Straight could tell by the look in Tasha's big dark eyes that she paid little heed to his warning. She never looked beyond the sky color of the Cossack's eyes to see the selfish greed. Before the Cossacks came, the Aleuts never killed just to take an animal's skin. Now they killed the otter, took its fur, and threw its body to the sharks. It was not their way, and the Cossacks were to blame.

But his sister was a woman. She couldn't understand that the life of a hunter was tied to that of his prey. Still he tried. "To the Cossack, an Aleut is like the sea otter. When they have taken what they want from him, they will throw the rest away."

The waves crested to six feet in the heavy-running sea. When the vessel breasted the first of them and it broke across the bow, Tasha felt a rush of exhilaration. The journey had begun. She stood at the rail watching the roll of the sea and listening to the straining groans of the boat's timbers as it slammed into another wave.

Within an hour, her head was pounding dully. The constant pitching of the vessel made the horizon go up and down with sickening regularity. The undulating motion made her stomach churn. She started feeling hot, and perspiration coated her skin. Moving closer to the bow, she let the sea spray cool her face, but it didn't ease the rising pressure in her stomach. Her knees felt strangely week.

It slowly came to her that she was getting seasick. The symptoms she had were the ones Weaver Woman had described when she told about two Aleut hunters on Attu who suffered from this malady. Tasha struggled to control her growing queasiness and tried to fix her gaze on some object that didn't move, but her senses constantly told her of the heaving motion of the deck. They didn't alert her, however, to the sound of approaching footsteps.

Once they were clear of the offshore reefs and well out to sea, Andrei ordered his mate to set an easterly course and relaxed his vigilance. He knew the dangers of this ocean, the quick onset of its fogs, high winds, and storms; and he took his time of ease whenever it came. As he left the mate at the helm, Andrei noticed Tasha standing at the bow, poised like a figurehead, her face lifted to the spray. The sight awakened fires in him that had long lain dormant. He walked to the bow.

"The winds favor us." At the sound of his voice, she swung around. Andrei had a brief glimpse of the pallor of her face and the hugeness of her eyes.

A second later, she turned back and reached for the rail, to lean over the side. Thinking that she intended to throw herself overboard, Andrei grabbed for her. As his hands caught her shoulders, he felt the convulsive heave of her body and heard the retching sound she made. The vomiting spasms came one after the other until she finally sagged against the rail, too weak to support herself.

His hands continued to steady her against the pitching and rolling of the vessel. Reaching inside his heavy coat, he took out his kerchief and wiped the spittle from the corners of her mouth and chin. She was drenched with sweat, but her skin felt clammy to the touch. She murmured some sound of gratitude, the words unintelligible.

A pair of callus-toughened feet entered his side vision, sticking out from the length of an inverted bird-skin parka, the red-ocher-dyed skin to the outside. Andrei looked up at Walks Straight and met the accusing glare of his eyes.

"She is seasick," he announced.

The Aleut's glance swept Tasha's pale face as if to confirm it, then he grunted something and walked off, apparently indifferent to her illness. But her weakened state aroused Andrei's protective male instincts.

He motioned to one of the promyshleniki on deck to come help him, then said to Tasha, "We will take you below where you can lie down." Her head moved, but he wasn't sure it was an acknowledgment.

The continuous rise and fall of the vessel made it difficult to keep their balance as Andrei and the promyshlenik lifted Tasha to her feet. She made a feeble attempt to help them, but the effort was almost more of a hindrance. She moaned softly as they worked their way across the lurching deck to the hatchway, her slack body leaning into Andrei.

The hatchway wasn't wide enough for three. Andrei nodded a dismissal to the Russian hunter. "I will take her from here." He half scooped her limp body into his arms and carried her down the steps.

Pausing outside his cabin, he kicked the door open and maneuvered them inside his quarters. Her head lolled against his jaw, the texture of her hair silken against his skin. He glanced down at her as she moaned again, then carried her to his bunk and set her down.

Andrei knew that he'd been wanting her in his bed, but this wasn't the circumstance he'd had in mind. Sweat beaded on her forehead and above her lips as she sat on the side of the bunk barely able to hold herself upright. Andrei glanced at the long fur parka she wore, remarkably unstained by vomit.

"Let's take this off," he muttered, mainly to himself, since he doubted she was in any condition to understand him.

After some difficulty, he managed to get it over her hips. After that it was easy to pull it over her head. Briefly he was treated to the sight of her nude body, the young upward thrust of her breasts. She swayed without his support, and he reached out to steady her, feeling the firmness of her flesh, a sensation he hadn't enjoyed in some time. His wife's body had long been flaccid, and there were few whores in Siberia who were not fat or infected or starving bags of bones. Siberia was a place where young women quickly became old. A rich man like himself had his choice, but the pickings were slim.

A groan came from Tasha's throat. She looked at him, her eyes appearing as round as saucers. Suddenly she clamped her hand over her mouth. Reacting swiftly, Andrei grabbed the chamber pot and lifted its lid in time to catch the spewed vomit.

When she had finished, he laid her down on the bunk and reluctantly covered her naked body with a blanket. He moved away to moisten a cloth with water from the container in his cabin, then came back to the bunk to wipe her damp face. She lay motionless with her eyes closed, the fringe of black lashes making long shadows on her pale skin. Andrei noticed she was lying on the knot of her hair and gently reached beneath her head to loosen the confining bun. He fanned it away from her face, letting the smooth strands slide through his fingers.

"I feel so sick," she murmured weakly.

"I know you do." Andrei folded the damp cloth and laid it across her brow.

Rising, he looked at her for a moment, then walked over to the table where his charts of the island chain were spread out. He studied them again, searching to see if there was another cluster of islands besides the one he'd found that matched the description Walks Straight had given him.

Several more times she threw up, until there was nothing left in her stomach except bile. Eventually exhaustion claimed her and she fell asleep. Andrei remained in the cabin a while longer, then went topside to check on their course. He stayed on deck only a short time, drawn back to his quarters by the thought of Tasha lying in his bunk.

Come evening, she was racked by dry heaves. Andrei had some broth prepared for her and fed her a spoonful every few minutes. Some of it eventually came up. It wasn't compassion or pity that kept him in the cabin. Andrei guessed it was the opportunity to indulge in his growing fascination for this Creole—to stare for as long as he liked at the curve of her cheekbone or the nipple of an exposed breast, and to imagine whatever he chose.

A knock sounded on his cabin door. "Yes, what is it?" Andrei demanded.

"It's fog, sir, thick as curdled cream."

"I'll be right there."

Andrei waited for the footsteps to retreat, then walked over to the bunk and tucked the blanket around Tasha once more. She moaned softly in her sleep. He stroked her cheek with his finger, her skin so smooth and cool to his touch. She stirred. Reluctantly he turned and left the cabin.

On the deck, a dense fog swathed the vessel, obscuring the outline of the bow and hiding the top of the masts. Visibility was reduced to a few yards. An eerie stillness heightened every sound. The clump of his boots rang hollowly on the slick deck as Andrei moved to the helm. Wisps of mist swirled around him, disturbed by his passing, while water dripped from the sails. Only the motion of the deck and the slap of the waves against the wooden hull confirmed they were still at sea and not drifting on some ghostly cloud.

The compass indicated the vessel was maintaining its easterly heading, but it was impossible to see what was ahead of them. According to his charts, all islands were supposed to be to the south of their present course, but the map details were sketchy at best. Andrei did not need to warn any of the men to be alert for the crash of breakers or the presence of kelp beds that would mean they were near land. The blinding fog made them all vigilant.

It was well into the early hours of the morning before Andrei returned to his cabin, satisfied his vessel was in no immediate danger. Tasha lay draped along the side of the bunk, uncovered from the waist up. The sight of her body aroused a surge of energy that overcame his tiredness. But however great the temptation to crawl into the bunk with her, the smell of vomit was a sufficient deterrent.

Finding her nudity too much of a temptation to resist, Andrei took one of his cotton shirts from his sea chest and slipped it on her. Her lashes fluttered open once when he lifted her and pushed an arm through a sleeve. After fastening some of the buttons, he let his hand cup the jutting roundness of a breast, feeling the way it filled his palm. She moaned, turning her head to the side. Grimly he recognized that the low sound came from her sickness, not from pleasure.

He pushed to his feet and gathered up the extra blanket on the bunk, then walked to the lamp swaying from a cross beam. He turned down the wick, allowing only a small flame to throw off a dim glow. The lurking shadows immediately closed in. Wrapped in the blanket, he sprawled in the chair, letting the dipping swing of the boat rock him. Sleep was a long time coming as he stared at the female in his bunk—his native bride.

For an entire week, Andrei spent the bulk of his time in the cabin, where Tasha alternated between bouts of violent seasickness and a nauseated stupor. She had lucid times when she objected to being spoon-fed the broth or gruel he'd had prepared for her and tried to do it herself, but she hadn't the strength.

Twice he bathed her, the motion of his hand invariably becoming a caress.

Several times her Aleut half brother entered the cabin unannounced to see how she was. Andrei always detected an element of distrust in the young man's eyes, but the Aleut never said anything, simply lingered a few minutes and then left. There was no doubt in Andrei's mind that Walks Straight didn't like Russians. Even without the chief's saying so, he would have known it. The native hunter had held himself aloof from the whole company during the voyage thus far. Sometimes Andrei wondered how much he could trust him, but it was plain that the Aleut thought a great deal of his half sister. As long as Andrei had her, he had a hold over him.

While the water heated in the brass samovar, Andrei added the loose leaves of China tea to the small pot. Holding the teapot under the spigot at the urn's base, he turned the handle. Nearly boiling water plunged over the tea leaves in the bottom of the pot, releasing their piquant aroma. It was a welcome smell in a cabin that reeked of sickness. Andrei let the tea steep for a few minutes, then poured it into two glasses in metal holders. He carried one to the bunk where Tasha sat propped against the bulkhead and gave it to her. The cuffs of his cotton shirt were rolled back to free her hands. They slipped further down her forearms as she lifted the glass to her lips with both hands. She took a small sip, then weakly lowered the glass to rest it on her lap.

"I think I'm feeling better," she said, but her voice lacked strength.

He smiled absently, aware that she had been keeping down more fluids these last two days. "Would you like to go up on deck after you finish your tea and get some fresh air?"

"Yes, I would."

He carried her topside, swaddled in a blanket, and settled her on a keg in a sheltered corner of the deck where the wind couldn't reach her. His attitude toward her was neither gentle nor solicitous; rather it was possessive, leaving the men in little doubt that their commander had claimed her for himself alone.

Breathing in deeply, Tasha filled her lungs with the sweet, fresh air. The motion of the shitik didn't seem to bother her nearly as much. She hoped fervently that she had finally become accustomed to it. She never wanted to be that sick again.

It shamed her to think how much trouble she had been to Andrei, yet she was warmed, too, by the memory of the countless times she'd opened her eyes and found him there watching over her.

Her eyes sought him out among the hunters on deck. She decided she liked his craggy profile as much as she liked his eyes. There was strength and determination in it, along with a canny intelligence. Beneath the blanket, she touched the shirt of his she wore. She had gotten used to the feel of its material against her skin and the protection it offered from the scratchy blanket. He had been good to her. Even Walks Straight had to acknowledge that. She saw her brother standing alone at the rail, scanning the sea. She realized he would never make friends with the Cossacks, not even with her new husband.

The outing quickly tired her. The least effort seemed to exhaust her. It frightened her to realize how weak she had become, when she'd always been so strong. She sagged against the hatchway's bulkhead and shut her eyes to rest a moment. A hand touched her shoulder. Tasha looked up to find Andrei bending over her.

"Do you feel all right?"

"I am tired," she admitted.

He said no more and picked her up, carrying her back to his cabin below deck and laying her on the bunk. Tasha rolled onto her side and fell asleep almost as soon as the door swung shut behind him.

The following afternoon, Tasha lay in the bunk. Her stomach felt comfortably full from the small bowl of soup she'd eaten. Andrei had assured her that food and rest were what she needed to get her strength back. Yet now that she was feeling better, the idleness made her restless.

She heard a sudden commotion on deck—muffled shouts and the clumping of boots. She strained to catch the cause of the excitement but she could only understand snatches of words. The cabin door swung open and her brother stepped soundlessly into the room.

"What is happening? Have they seen a whale?" Nothing else in her village would have created such a stir.

"They have sighted the islands. The tall, pronged peak of Adak stands clear of the clouds. The boat heads for it now."

"Then we have arrived," Tasha said.

"Soon they will see how good the hunting is here and they will know I did not lie."

She looked at her brother. "Did they think you had?"

"I heard some of them wonder if I was guiding them into the middle of the sea. One of them cut a hole in my bidarka so I could not escape in it," he answered bitterly.

"Is it a big hole?" Without his bidarka, a hunter was powerless.

"It crosses almost two skins."

"I will patch it for you," Tasha promised, then asked, "Does Andrei know of this?"

"It would do no good. The Cossacks claim something fell on it, but I know the way a hide looks when a knife cuts it." His resentment went deep, and this incident was like sea water on an open wound. Tasha understood, too, that Walks Straight was saying this to warn her. "You are feeling better?" he asked at last.

"Yes." She nodded.

"Good." His gaze lingered on her another minute, then he turned and walked out of the cabin.

Alone again, Tasha listened to the waning flurry of activity on the deck overhead. With the island in sight, Andrei would soon have need of her to speak to the villagers for him. She swung her legs over the side of the bunk and stood up to test her strength. She wobbled uncertainly for an instant, but they held her. Walking slowly, Tasha crossed the cabin to the table and stopped there to lean against it, fighting the light-headed feeling. She heard footsteps approaching the cabin and recognized them as Andrei's. The door swung open as she turned toward it, keeping a hand braced on the table for balance.

"Tasha—" The sight of the empty bunk stopped him in midstride. With a jerk of his head, he looked around and saw her standing by the table. The lines of his forehead gathered into a frown. "Tasha, what are you doing up?"

"I had to see if I could walk by myself. I wouldn't be much help to you lying down."

The tails of his shirt hung down to her thighs, leaving a long expanse of bare leg exposed to his view. Andrei noticed the barely perceptible buckling of her knees and realized she was less steady than she appeared. He moved quickly to her and girdled her waist with his hands, catching up the loose material of his shirt. Her hands immediately grasped for the support of his upper arms as she swayed into him.

"From now on, Tasha, let me decide how best you can help me." Until this minute, Andrei hadn't realized how tall she was. She stood eye-level to his chin. When he tipped his head down, it brought her face closer still. He was conscious of the bareness of her skin beneath his shirt and the firm feel of her flesh.

Too many times these last days he'd held her naked limp body and wished for her to be alive in his arms. Too many times his hands had caressed her and received no response. Now her hands were clutching him, never mind that it was out of weakness. His gaze shifted to the full curve of her lips, parted slightly.

The burning look in his eyes was one Tasha had seen before when a man desired to lie with a woman. It heated her skin and made her feel warm all over. The band of his arm circled her back and pulled her against him. She was instantly conscious of his thighs and torso.

She knew about this touching of the mouths the Cossacks called kissing. Curiosity held her motionless when he lowered his head and covered her lips with his mouth. At first she found the pressure unpleasant, then she discovered that if she didn't hold her mouth so still, the sensation wasn't so bad. She was just beginning to enjoy it a little when he abruptly pulled away, holding her at arm's length. The sudden movement made her head swim dizzily.

"I'll be damned if I am going to make love to a woman who is too weak to do anything more than lie there," he muttered thickly and ushered her over to the bunk. "Stay there until you are stronger."

"Moving makes you stronger, not lying down," Tasha said, but she was conscious of the shakiness of her limbs.

"You have done enough moving for a while," he ordered, then paused. "Why are you looking at me that way?"

Tasha could only blame her recent illness for making her think so slowly, but it finally registered that he had desired to lie with her. Many Whiskers had given her to him, but Andrei wanted her. She looked at him now with new interest, regarding him as a potential lover. Despite his many summers of life, he looked vigorous and healthy.

"You do not regret that Many Whiskers gave me to you. You wanted me," she said.

"That is a small way of putting it, Tasha." She heard him sigh.

"I have heard that Cossacks are rough with women."

He studied her long and hard before he answered. "Sometimes a man's needs are great and he forgets his own strength. Stay in that bed and rest before I forget mine." He swung around and left the cabin. Tasha smiled, secretly pleased by her discovery.

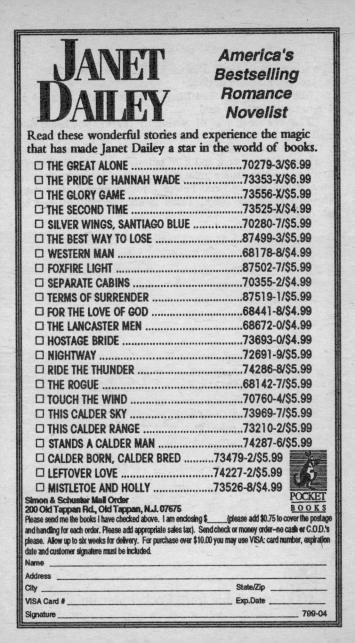

# JULIE GARWOOD

Julie Garwood's gloriously romantic, breathtakingly passionate novels have made her one of America's most beloved romance authors. *USA Today* says that it is her "timely subjects set against a timeless background that attract so many modern readers."

Now she brings us her most compelling novel yet, the story of an indomitable Saxon lady determined to fight for her freedom in a world ruled by men...a woman whose life would be transformed by the rare, unexpected gift of love.

# SAVING GRACE

**"THE GLORY GAME** is set against a glamorous, fast-moving international backdrop... Dailey is at her best when she focuses on the love relationship between Luz and Raul... The most interesting character in the novel is Raul, because Dailey has managed to create in him both an aloofness and an intensely magnetic appeal that makes him seem the quintessential Latin lover."
—*Chicago Sun-Times*

"International polo... country clubs and glittering parties are the backdrop for what is sure to be another hit for Janet Dailey, one of the most widely read authors in the country."
—*Richmond Times-Dispatch*

"Romance readers familiar with Dailey's many bestselling novels will not be disappointed with her latest work... exotic locales and... suspenseful plot twists. An entertaining potboiler."
—*ALA Booklist*

"Dailey carves another notch of success with this enveloping drama."
—*Publishers Weekly*

"The Dailey magic is evident... THE GLORY GAME can't help but touch the reader's heart."
—*Los Angeles Herald Examiner*

Published by POCKET BOOKS